About th

Amber Page has been writin_ _ _ _ _
She's also an avid reader and l_ _ _ _ _ _ _ _ _ _ _ _ _ romances
since she first discovered them in the dusty shelves of
her library as a young teen. Writing for Mills & Boon is
a dream come true. Amber lives with the love of her life,
their daughter, and a menagerie of animals in the heart of
Indiana. When not penning happily-ever-afters, she works as
a copywriter. Learn more about her at amberpagebooks.com

Award-winning author **Louisa George** has been an avid
reader her whole life. In between chapters she managed
to train as a nurse, marry her doctor hero, and have two
sons. Now she writes chapters of her own in the medical
romance, contemporary romance, and women's fiction
genres. Louisa's books have variously been nominated for
the coveted *RITA*® Award, and the NZ Koru Award and
have been translated into twelve languages. She lives in
Auckland, New Zealand.

Andrea Laurence is an award-winning contemporary
author who has been a lover of books and writing stories
since she learned to read. A dedicated West Coast girl
transplanted into the Deep South, she's constantly trying
to develop a taste for sweet tea and grits while caring for
her husband and two spoiled golden retrievers. You can
contact Andrea at her website: andrealaurence.com

A Christmas Craving

AMBER PAGE

LOUISA GEORGE

ANDREA LAURENCE

MILLS & BOON

First Published in Great Britain 2023
By Mills & Boon, an imprint of HarperCollins*Publishers* Ltd,
1 London Bridge Street, London, SE1 9GF

www.harpercollins.co.uk

HarperCollins*Publishers*
Macken House, 39/40 Mayor Street Upper,
Dublin 1, D01 C9W8, Ireland

Special thanks and acknowledgement are given to Louisa George for her contribution to *The Flat in Notting Hill* series.

ISBN: 978-0-263-32119-7

MIX
Paper | Supporting
responsible forestry
FSC™ C007454

This book is produced from independently certified FSC™ paper to ensure responsible forest management.

For more information visit: www.harpercollins.co.uk/green

Printed and Bound in the UK using 100% Renewable Electricity at CPI Group (UK) Ltd, Croydon, CR0 4YY

ALL'S FAIR IN LUST & WAR

AMBER PAGE

To my husband, my biggest cheerleader and occasional butt-kicker. Thank you for refusing to let me give up.

To Allison, Amanda, Christina, Meagan, Rhonda and Tanya, whose speed-reading skills and smart critiques helped make this book what it is.

And to everyone else who cheered me along the way (you know who you are).

PROLOGUE

MARK AWOKE SLOWLY, his mouth fuzzy and his limbs strangely heavy. He rolled over, expecting to see…who? Certainly not the empty pillow that greeted him.

Head spinning slightly, he lifted himself up on his elbow to look around the room. He was in his hotel room, right? Seeing his laptop on the desk, he decided it was probably safe to assume he was still in Vegas and hadn't hopped on a plane to Bangladesh or something.

He kept his gaze moving, noting two wine glasses, a knocked-over bottle of red wine—damn, he hoped they didn't charge him for that stain on the carpet—and there, by the heavy hotel room door, a pair of cheetah-print stilettos.

Suddenly memory came rushing back.

Walking down to the AdWorld closing party. Seeing the pretty blonde in the tight red dress giggling into her phone. Feeling compelled to talk to her. And then—*wham!* Being hit in the gut by a lightning bolt of lust when she turned to grin up at him with her sparkling green eyes.

He would have done anything to get closer to her. To get to know her.

Which was probably why he'd found himself doing something totally out of character.

"I'm Mark," he'd said, taking her hand in his and grazing her knuckles with his lips. "May I have the honor of escorting you this evening, my lady?"

She'd swallowed loudly, and he'd seen the desire sparking in her eyes.

Nonetheless, she'd been as cool as ice when she'd answered him. "I'd love that. Shall we?"

He'd held out his arm for her to take and together they stepped through the ballroom doors into the strobe-lit party beyond.

That had been followed by copious drinking, he was sure. His mind showed him an image of her gazing at him uncertainly before raising a tequila glass.

"Let's toast," she'd said. "To one wild night."

"To one wild, scandalous night," he'd answered.

And there'd been dancing. He remembered how she'd laughed as she spun away, then melted when he drew her close again. And how sweet her lips had tasted when he'd pulled her in for a kiss…

The first of many kisses.

Eventually she'd clung to him and said, "Mark, I can't believe I'm saying this, but I *need* you. Take me back to your room?"

What had followed had been one of the most…no, *the* hottest night of his life.

She'd been so hot, so willing to do anything… And when they'd finished she'd rolled over and said, "Wanna do it again?"

His answer had been, "Hell, yes."

But what was her name again?

Just then the bathroom door opened and she stepped out, engulfed in the hotel-issue robe, her long blond hair dripping down her back. She looked at him and smiled, green eyes sparkling.

The lightning bolt hit home again.

"Becky," he said. Her name was Becky.

"Hey, gorgeous," she said.

"Hey, yourself. What are you doing up so early?"

"Oh," she said, a momentary frown crossing her small face. "My flight leaves in a few hours, and I've got some work to do this morning. I figured I should probably get a move on."

"Ah," he said, overcome with an inexplicable sense of disappointment. "I thought maybe we could go get some breakfast. Or, you know, have breakfast in bed." Which, honestly, had been the last thing on his mind until she'd emerged from the bathroom. But once he'd seen her he'd been able to think of nothing he'd rather do other than peel that giant robe off her tiny frame.

She gave him a pained smile and perched on the edge of the bed.

"I'd love to, but you know how it goes. Duty calls."

Reading her tense body language, Mark realized it was no use. He also knew he wasn't ready to let her go yet. "All right. I understand," he said slowly, seeking a conversational gambit that would keep her talking. "You know, we never even talked about our jobs. What do you do?"

"I'm a copywriter. For an agency in New York—SBD," she said slowly.

"Really? What a coincidence. I'm starting a new gig—"

Gently, she placed her hand over his mouth. "You know what? Don't tell me about you. Last night was—well, it was magical, but I'm not looking to start a relationship. Even a casual one. If you don't mind, I'd just like to think of you as Mark the Magic Man from Las Vegas…not a real person I might run into at the supermarket."

Wow. That was a first. Usually it was *him* trying to duck out while a girl tried to pry information out of him. He wasn't so sure he liked being on this end of things. But his pride wouldn't allow him to admit that to her.

"Hmm," he said. "I kind of like being a Magic Man. Maybe I should go into business."

She threw her head back and laughed, and suddenly the tension eased. Then she leaned forward and kissed him. Hard.

"Thank you for last night. Believe me when I tell you it's one I'll never forget."

He smiled. "Me neither," he said. And he meant it.

Moments later Becky finished getting dressed and, holding her heels in one hand, she blew him a kiss.

"Bye, Magic Man."

"Bye, Gorgeous Girl."

And then she was gone.

"Until tomorrow, then," he said to himself.

Reaching for his iPad, he loaded up the search engine. It was time to look up his gorgeous new coworker.

CHAPTER ONE

BECKY WAS ENGROSSED in the dreary task of sorting through her inbox, attempting to make sense of the three hundred and fifty-seven emails that had accumulated while she was in Vegas, when a cardboard coffee cup was slammed down on her desk.

"One venti dark roast with a splash of vanilla soy milk," Jessie said. "Just the way you like it."

Becky looked up and grinned at her redheaded friend.

"Aw, thanks, Jessie. You didn't have to do that."

Jessie shrugged her coat off, threw it on the visitor's chair, then collapsed at her desk.

"It's bribery. Now, *spill*."

"Spill? You want me to spill this delicious coffee?"

Jessie threw her rainbow-colored scarf at her. "Don't be an idiot. You know what I want to know. What happened after you texted me Saturday night? Were you able to prove to yourself that your libido isn't dead?"

Becky blushed. "It's alive and kicking," she said. "And very insistent."

"Woo-hoo! My girl scored! I knew you could do it!" Jessie said, grinning. "Now, tell me the juicy bits."

Becky shook her head. "A lady never kisses and tells," she said, laughing.

"Give me a break," Jessie said, rolling her eyes. "I've known you for ten years, and in all that time you've never kept a secret from me. Give it up, sister."

Becky shook her head again. While it was true that she

and Jessie had always told each other everything, this felt different. Special.

"I'm sorry, Jessie. It just doesn't feel appropriate to talk about it here. Besides, you know what they say. What happens in Vegas…"

Just then her boss's voice rumbled from the vicinity of her open office door. "Is supposed to stay in Vegas, right?"

Becky whirled, readying a snappy comeback. But what she saw stopped her in her tracks.

Her boss, David, was standing there, smiling. And with him was…Mark.

Mark? How could Mark be standing in her office? Becky stared at him, mouth open. It was not possible. Completely impossible, in fact.

Mark belonged in Vegas, not in New York City.

Heat flared in her belly as she remembered the last time they'd met. She'd been texting Jessie, trying to find the courage to walk into the closing night party by herself.

Just picture them standing in their underwear…then stalk the guy that makes you drool, Jessie had texted.

"Right. Underwear," she'd said to herself. "Must picture delicious-looking men in underwear."

And that was when she'd heard Mark's rumbling voice for the first time.

"Well, if you're looking for volunteers, I happen to be available."

"What?" she'd yelped, whirling to face the interloper. Then her heart had stopped. The man smiling at her was the living, breathing definition of delicious, from the tips of his artfully rumpled black hair to the toes of his polished leather shoes.

Brilliant white teeth flashed as he grinned down at her. "If you need help. Picturing what a man looks like in his underwear, I mean. I'm happy to serve as a model."

Becky's face flamed. "Oh, I…uh…no one was supposed

to hear that. I just…I was having trouble walking into the party by myself. My friend suggested I picture everyone in their underwear. As, you know, a motivator."

Mr. Gorgeous tilted his head back and laughed, and as he did Becky felt it. The zing. The tingle. If she'd been alone she would have done a happy dance. He'd just proved she wasn't dead inside!

Now that he was standing in her office, she kind of wished she had been.

Becky shook her head to clear it. She needed to pay attention to the conversation that was happening now if she wanted to make sense of the situation.

"Yeah, you're supposed to leave all the juicy details at the airport," Jessie said. "But I was trying to convince Becky to give me some of the gory details anyway."

"Any luck?" asked Mark, giving Becky a sidelong glance.

"None." Jessie pouted.

"Well, I was there," he said. "You didn't miss much. Although the closing night party was unexpectedly awesome."

Becky's head snapped up. Was he teasing her? And, if he was, how dared he? Mark just looked at her with a half smile on his face, his dark eyes glinting mischievously.

"That's what Becky said. Did you two meet?" Jessie asked.

"No!" Becky practically shouted.

"Yeah, you could say that," Mark said at the same time.

Becky stared at him. He said nothing, just quirked one damnably expressive eyebrow at her and leaned back against the doorframe, letting her take the lead.

"Well, what I meant was we didn't really spend much time together," she said.

Just twelve mind-blowing hours and fifty-three bone-melting minutes. Not that she'd been counting or anything.

Her traitorous mind flashed back to their first kiss. The

way he'd claimed every part of her mouth and set her whole body aflame. Within seconds she'd known she wanted more from him than a few kisses.

But it was only supposed to be for one night. If she'd known he'd turn up here she would have never...

"Mark, here, is an amazingly talented art director," her boss said, reaching up to clap him on the back. "I've brought him in on a freelance basis to work on a special project. And I want you to work with him, Becky."

"Me?" she squeaked. "But I'm busy with... I mean, I've got..."

"Whatever you currently have on your plate will be given to someone else," her boss replied. "I need you on this. Be in my office at eleven. We'll talk."

Becky snapped her mouth shut, knowing further protest was useless and foolhardy. When David told you to do something, you did it. At least you did if you wanted to keep your job.

Which she did. Unfortunately.

"Okay," she said. "I'll see you then."

"Good," he answered. "Then I won't keep you any longer. Come on, Mark."

After they were gone Becky put her head down on her desk, banging it lightly against the keyboard.

"Why, universe, *why?* Why would you do this to me?"

"Becky? What's wrong?" Jessie asked.

Becky shook her head mutely.

"Oh, come on, you can tell me. You have to."

Becky knew she was right. If she didn't, her soon-to-be-bizarre behavior wouldn't make much sense. And if there was one person she didn't want to alienate it was Jessie.

Besides, Jessie was the only one who knew what had happened...*before.* And what she had been trying to prove to herself that night in Vegas.

Becky got up to close the door before turning to face

her friend. Blowing her hair off her forehead, she said, "It was him."

"Him? Who? I'm not following," Jessie said.

"Mark. Mark was the man I met in Las Vegas. And things went a little bit further than I had planned."

"What do you mean?"

"I spent the night with him…" Becky groaned.

"Are you kidding me?" Jessie asked, falling back into her chair.

Becky shook her head.

Jessie tilted her head back and howled with laughter. "Oh, my God. Only you… This is…it's unbelievable."

Becky glared at her. "I really don't think this is funny."

"Of course you don't. But, girl, you gotta believe me when I tell you it is."

Easy for her to say. She wasn't the one living in a nightmare.

Finally Jessie sobered.

"All right, so Mr. One-Night Stand has become Mr. Works Down the Hall. What are you going to do about it?"

"Nothing," Becky said flatly.

"Why? Was it…bad?"

Pictures from their night together flashed through Becky's brain. His lips kissing her mouth. His tongue on her breast. His hands…everywhere.

"It was amazing."

"Did you hit the big O?"

Becky blushed. "Oh, yeah. More than once."

Jessie looked thoughtful. "Then why not see if this could go somewhere? You know—like, casual relationshippy. Fate seems to be telling you it should."

Becky stood up, restless. "You know better than anyone why not. After everything that happened with Pence I'll never have a relationship with someone I work with again."

Jessie came up behind her and hugged her shoulders.

"I understand. But, Becky, that was a long time ago. You were a different person. And he was your boss, not a coworker. Besides, you can't let him ruin your whole life. If you do, he wins."

Sneaking a look at the clock on the wall, she groaned.

"We'll have to talk about this more later, Jessie. I gotta go to the Hall of Doom."

"All right, girl. Knock 'em dead."

Mark wasn't sure how much more of this small talk he could take.

He'd been sitting in David's office for what felt like hours, talking about everything except the reason he was here. He now knew where the bald man's favorite golf course was—South Carolina—what he preferred to drink—bourbon, straight up—and even how he had gotten his name—his mom had named him after Michelangelo's *David*.

But he still didn't know what his first assignment was going to be or why it had to be secret. When David had called him to see if he might be interested he'd said only that he needed help winning a giant piece of new business—one that had the potential to change the future of the agency.

That was interesting enough, but it was what David had said next that had sold him on the job.

"Mark, I've been searching everywhere for someone who can help me bring this home. When your name came up I knew you were the man for the job. I need you on this."

"How did you get my name?" Mark had asked, afraid that it was another one of his stepfather's pieces of charity.

"Mark, you've taken home gold from almost every major advertising competition there is. Your name is everywhere."

Which meant this was a job he'd gotten on his own merits—not through his damned stepfather's connections.

Even better, David had all but promised him a permanent spot in the creative leadership team once they landed the account.

It was the opportunity he'd spent the past ten years working toward. He couldn't wait to get started.

He just wished he knew what Becky had to do with it.

When he'd looked her up, he'd been amazed at how talented she seemed to be. In the five short years she'd been working as a copywriter she'd earned herself numerous awards. The whole reason she'd been in Vegas was because she was being honored with another award—this one for a social-media campaign she'd masterminded that had gone viral.

In short, she was as amazing in the boardroom as she was in the bedroom.

And what he wouldn't give to experience that again!

He remembered how hot she'd looked, standing in his room clad only in her red lace bra and panties. And how much better she'd looked out of them...

Unfortunately the look on her face when she'd found him standing in her office had been completely and utterly horrified—and, if he wasn't mistaken, more than a little bit furious. He didn't think she was having the same kinds of thoughts he was having right now.

Just then there was a soft knock on the door.

"Come in," David said.

The door opened and Becky quietly entered the room.

He wasn't sure how it was possible, but she looked even sexier in her blazer and jeans than she had wearing a cocktail dress.

She flashed a quick look at him, and flushed when he caught her eye. Man, how he'd love to see how far down that flush went.

"Thank you for coming, Becky, my girl," David boomed. Although he couldn't have been much more than forty, the man mimicked the vocal mannerisms of a *Mad Men*–style ad man. "Sit, sit, sit. We have a lot to talk about."

She glided across the thick red carpet and sat primly in the oversize club chair next to Mark.

"I trust you had a good time in Vegas, my dear?" David asked.

Becky seemed to force out a smile. "It was amazing, David. Thank you so much for letting me go."

"Of course—you deserved it. Besides, I knew you were one woman I could trust not to get too carried away in Vegas. I would have never sent that partner of yours. She's trouble with a capital *T*."

Becky's laugh sounded even more forced than her smile had been. "Yeah, you know me. Married to my job and all that."

"Oh, not to worry, Becky. Sooner or later a fine-looking girl like you is bound to get snapped up. Then you'll be too busy having babies to write brilliant campaigns for me anymore. That's how it always goes. Right, Mark?"

Mark was floored. People still talked like *that?* In an *office?* It was a miracle this guy hadn't been slapped with a multimillion-dollar lawsuit yet. Or, judging from the fury flashing in Becky's eyes, murdered.

"I don't know about that, David. I know plenty of working mothers who—"

David cut him off. "Right, right. I know. Girls can do anything men can—blah, blah, blah. None of that matters right now, because my brilliant little sparrow is as single as they come…and I'm going to be keeping you both too busy for her to change matters any."

Becky sucked in a breath and seemed about to say something, but she never got the chance.

"All right. Enough of this chitchat. Let's get down to business, shall we? You two are among the most talented creatives this business has to offer," David said. "And I'm going to need every bit of juice you've got. We've been asked to take part in the agency search for Eden. You both know what that is?"

Becky nodded. "The yogurt company?"

"You got it," David said. "They're coming out with a new line of low-fat, all-natural Greek yogurt flavors designed to get all those pretty hipster ladies hot and bothered. Our job is to figure out how to do that. And, since their advertising budget is a quarter of a billion dollars, we damn well better nail it."

Becky practically bounced up and down in her chair. "Oh, I'd love to get my hands on that one," she said.

"Oh, those pretty little hands are going to be all over it. So are yours, Mark. Just...er...hopefully not on the same spot at the same time!" he said.

Mark laughed uncomfortably. "No chance of that happening, sir." At least not that David needed to know about.

"Good. Now, the Eden people tell me they don't want any 'suits' working on their account. They want something young and fresh...something none of our existing creative directors are. That means you two have the opportunity of a lifetime."

David got up from his chair and started to pace.

"So here's what we're going to do. We're going to break the agency into two creative teams. Becky, you're going to head up one. Mark, you'll be in charge of the other. Whichever one of you comes up with the winning concept and sells it to the client will win a fifty-thousand-dollar bonus—and become the youngest creative director this agency has ever had."

Mark blinked slowly, trying to wrap his head around this new twist. David had never said anything about a competition.

"You're making me compete for the creative director position?" asked Becky, her eyes sparking angrily in an otherwise pale face. "But you told me that when I came back from AdWorld the job was as good as mine!"

"It is," David said. "All you have to do is win the Eden account."

Mark watched as Becky sprang up from her chair. There was no doubt that murder was on her mind.

"I will," she said from between clenched teeth. Then she turned to glare at Mark. "And don't you dare think for a second that you've got a shot!"

With that, she strode from the room, controlled fury in every movement. Good thing he had no problem with beating a sexy woman at her own game, because there was no way he was losing *this* job.

Turning to David, he said, "This competition's going to be quite a challenge."

"I'm counting on you to win," David said. "Don't let me down."

"I won't."

Becky slammed her office door so hard the wall shook.

"Wow. What's up *your* butt?" Jessie asked.

"David," Becky said.

"Ewww, that sounds uncomfortable!" Jessie giggled.

Becky glared at her. "It's not funny," she said. "That stupid blowhard is trying to give away my promotion again."

"The one he swore would be yours after you got back from Vegas?"

"The one and the same." Becky sighed, her heels tapping a staccato tune across the cement floor as she paced.

Jessie grabbed Becky's coat. "All right, you're going to tell me what's happened. But not here. A discussion like this calls for hot-fudge sundaes."

* * *

"You don't have to win this by yourself! You've got your whole team behind you," Jessie said between bites of hot fudge.

"I don't know who's on my team yet," Becky said, picking up her spoon, watching as the melting ice cream dripped back into her bowl. "I could get stuck with anyone."

"Did David lay out any rules when he said the creative department was going to be split in half?"

Becky shook her head.

"Then I vote we make the rules for him," Jessie said, grabbing a pen and paper out of her green velvet purse. "All right. No thinking allowed. Tell me who would be on your dream team."

"You," Becky said slowly.

"Yeah, well, obviously. Who else?"

Becky fell silent and looked out of the window at the busy street outside. Three girls walked arm in arm, laughing and talking as they went. Just then one lone man broke through their line, forcing their arms apart. They let him through, but shot up their middle fingers at him after he passed.

"I know what we need," she said, excitement zinging through her pores. "Jessie, we need girl power. Let's make this a battle of the sexes."

"Wait—what?"

"David thinks women creatives don't have it in them to be as good as men. Let's prove him wrong. Let's gather all the women in the department on our team and let Mark have the men."

"But there are more guys than girls in our department. It won't be an even match," Jessie said.

"Numbers aren't everything," Becky said. "Especially since the product in question is aimed squarely at women our age.'"

Jessie put down her spoon. "You, my dear, are brilliant."

"Well, yeah," Becky said. "Haven't you seen my awards shelf?"

"I have." Jessie snorted. "You think it's bigger than Mark's?"

"Hmm, I don't know," Becky said, her mind showing her wicked images of Mark's thick penis twitching in her palm as she kissed his muscled chest. "I honestly don't know much about him at all. Other than the fact that he's magic…"

"Magic?"

Becky started, reluctantly letting her daydream disappear.

"That's what I told him he was. Magic Man from Vegas."

Jessie stared at her, her blue eyes almost green with jealousy. "Man, that must have been one good night."

"The best," Becky said. Seeing the question in Jessie's eyes, she put her hand up in a "stop" gesture. "But it was just one night. I don't want or need a man in my life right now. What I need," she said, grinning, "is a team of Magic Women. Let's go put it together."

"I *knew* my girl was in there somewhere. And—" Jessie grinned, handing Becky the check "—since you're about to be fifty thousand dollars richer, I'll let you get this."

Becky rolled her eyes. "Fine," she said. "But only because you're about to work your ass off for me."

Mark was staring out through the window of his office at the crowds teeming past on Madison Avenue, wondering what on earth he had gotten himself into.

Usually he was brought in to save the day. Agencies never called him until they were facing a problem they couldn't solve—a challenge they couldn't meet. He got to play the part of vagabond hero. He came in, slayed the dragon, claimed a few hot nights with the delicious advertising damsels he had rescued, then left.

He didn't get to know the other players in the story. Never bothered to worry about whose toes he was stomping on, or what effect his actions had on those left behind when he rode off into the sunset.

His life, both professional and personal, was very much a case study in the "Wham, Bam, Thank You, Ma'am," approach to life. And that was the way he liked it.

After all, the one and only time he'd allowed himself to fall in love he'd found out the hard way that it had been his stepfather's name—or, more aptly, his money—that had gotten him the girl. And when she'd found out that Mark would never inherit the family fortune Sandra had turned to someone who *did* have top billing on a rich man's will.

The day he'd found Sandra in bed with his stepbrother hadn't been the first time he'd cursed his stepfamily, but it had been the last time he'd admitted to being part of it.

These days he didn't need anybody or anything. Well, nothing except for a killer job and a place among advertising's greats—a place he'd earned on his own.

So why did a certain blonde keep interrupting his thoughts?

Just then Becky strode in, fire in her eyes.

"Wow, hey—thanks for knocking," he said, trying to ignore the way his pulse quickened when she entered the room.

She stalked forward until she was standing directly in front of him. She took a long, slow look around the room and he knew she must be taking in the overly plush carpet, richly upholstered furnishings, the floor-to-ceiling windows and comparing it with her own small if brightly colored closet.

"Nice setup," she said. "What'd you do? Sleep with David to get it?"

He snorted. "I think you know that's not the way my tastes run, babe."

Her face flushed, and he would have given anything to know what she was thinking. She looked up at him and he could see the heat veiled behind her professional fury.

"Let's get one thing clear," she said. "What happened was supposed to stay in Vegas, just like David said. It will *never* happen again."

"Never, huh? That's a long time."

She looked away quickly, but not before he saw the desire flashing in her eyes.

"I'm *serious*," she said, folding her arms across her chest. "I've worked too hard to get where I am to let some man screw up my life again."

The disdain in her voice struck deep. So she thought she could just dismiss the maddening attraction that raced between them, huh? It was time to prove her wrong.

He pulled her into his arms and tilted her face up to his, giving in to the urge he'd been fighting since she'd walked into the room.

"I think you know I'm not just 'some man,'" he said, as he brushed his lips across hers. "I'm magic."

With that, he deepened the kiss. For a second she stiffened, but then something in her seemed to give. With a soft moan, she relaxed against him and opened her mouth.

He lost himself in the chocolate-flavored cavern as hunger roared to life. Their tongues darted and danced and he pulled her closer, wanting more.

He was reaching for the buttons on her blouse when the sharp whistle that signaled the arrival of a text message on his phone blared.

Becky jumped back, staring at him with undisguised horror.

"I'm not sure if you're magic," she whispered. "But I am beginning to think you might be the devil."

Mark took a breath, shaken by how fast he had lost control. Obviously the heat that had sparked between them in Vegas had been no fluke.

"I've been called worse by my competition," he said. "But usually not until after I beat them."

She briefly closed her eyes, and when she opened them again her stare was fiercely competitive.

"Right. The competition. I came to tell you that I've chosen my team. I'll take the women—you take the men."

"A battle of the sexes, huh? All right, if that's the way you want to play it," he said, still trying to get himself under control.

"No, that's the way I plan to *win* it," she said. "I never lose."

"Neither do I, Gorgeous Girl," Mark said, getting angry. "But guess what? One of us is going to. And it won't be me."

She took a deep breath and straightened her spine.

"Yes. It will. This job is mine and there's no way I'm going to let you steal it," she growled, then strode from the room.

"I'm not going to steal it. I'm going to earn it," he said to her departing back.

And he would. He just hoped he didn't have to crush her in the process.

CHAPTER TWO

BECKY LOOKED AT the team gathered around the tempered glass conference table. All eight women in the SBD creative department were looking at her expectantly.

"Raise your hand if David has ever belittled your abilities," she said.

Eight hands shot into the air.

"That's what I thought. Now, raise your hand if you'd like a chance to prove that chauvinist pig wrong."

Again hands shot into the air, this time accompanied by hoots and hollers.

Becky smiled. "Good. Today's your lucky day, ladies. We're going to win a two-hundred-and-fifty-million-dollar piece of business—and we're going to do it without the help of a single man."

Her crew burst into spontaneous applause.

"Now, let's get down to business. Cheri. What do you think of when I say delicious low-fat Greek yogurt?"

"Um…breakfast?" the brunette answered.

Becky turned to the whiteboard and wrote "BREAKFAST" in caps.

"Good. What else? Tanya?"

"Healthy."

Becky wrote it down.

"What else? Anyone?"

"A shortcut to skinny," Jessie said.

"Oh, I like that," Becky said, writing it down and underlining it. "Let's explore that."

"Not just skinny. Strong," someone else said. "Because it's got lots of protein in it."

"Popeye!" Tanya said.

Becky laughed. And then inspiration struck.

"Forget Popeye. This yogurt is for Olive Oyl. It's Olive's secret weapon for kicking Popeye's ass!" she said.

The women around the table laughed.

"Now we're on to something," Jessie said. "Here—give me the marker."

Becky handed it over and Jessie drew a ripped Olive Oyl, flexing her guns, one foot resting on top of a prone Popeye.

"Eden Yogurt. For the super-heroine in you," Jessie wrote.

Becky stepped back with a grin on her face, feeling the giddy high that always struck during a good brainstorming session.

"Ladies, we *are* on to something here. Really on to something. Something no guy would think of. So let's make sure they can't steal it. Tanya, do you know where there's any black paper?"

She nodded.

"Great. Go get it. We're going to make ourselves a good old-fashioned, women-only fort!"

A short while later all the conference windows were blocked off with thick black paper.

Jessie handed Becky the sign she'd made. It read, "Women at Work. No Boys Allowed" in pink glitter.

Becky skipped over to the door, tape in hand. She was just about to stick it up when she saw Mark approach. Opening the door, she waggled her sign at him.

"We've already come up with an idea that's going to kick the ass of anything you can come up with," she said, and grinned.

"Oh, really? Then why all the secrecy?" he asked with a raised eyebrow.

"Well, you're already in the boys' club. We thought it only fair that we create a girls' club with an equally exclusionary policy."

"I'll have you know I don't take part in any boys-only activities. I far prefer the company of women."

"Well, right now the women of this agency do not want your company. So go play with the boys. We'll let you back in after we beat you and all your testosterone-addled buddies."

He sighed. "Becky, Becky, Becky. How many times do I have to tell you? You can't beat me. I'm magic."

She sighed in return. "Mark, Mark, Mark. How many times do I have to tell you? You can't beat us. Talent beats magic every time."

"You go ahead and believe that," he said. "But soon you'll be kissing up to your new boss."

"Nope," she said. "Soon you'll be kissing this." And she slapped her denim-clad rear.

"You'd like that," he said.

"I would. Especially if you did it while I was booting your butt out of the office," she said, slamming the door.

He didn't need to know how very much she would love to kiss every inch of his magnificent body—and to have him kiss hers in return. Again.

She would beat him and then he'd be gone, taking his career-endangering sexual magnetism with him.

She had to. If she didn't she'd be lost forever.

Mark sat behind his heavy oak desk, the eerie white light of his monitor providing the only break in the darkness.

He was trying to polish an ad layout, but every time he turned his attention to the screen Becky's mocking face filled it.

Accusing him of being in the boys' club was pretty rich. Truth was, he didn't have a single close friend—in fact, he didn't have *any* male friends. Not real ones, anyway. The last time he'd had a best friend he'd been in sixth grade. His mom had still been single and they'd still been coexisting fairly peacefully, even if she'd never stopped moaning about how tough it was to be a single parent.

Then Bill had entered their lives, and everything had gone down the toilet.

Mark called up Facebook and scanned his friends list, searching for the familiar name. It didn't take long. He clicked onto Tom's profile, telling himself he was just curious. Not lonely.

Tom's page was filled with pictures of his goofy grinning kids and the short, plump brunette who had married him. He wasn't rich. Or particularly successful. But he did seem happy.

Mark leaned back in his chair and sighed. If things had been different—if he'd stayed in the working-class neighborhood where he'd been born instead of being forced to move into the frigidly upper-class world his mom had married into, where nothing mattered more than money— would he have a life like Tom's?

Would he have a wife? Kids?

Unbidden, an image of Becky holding a baby popped into his head. Feeling a sharp pang of panic, he shook his head to clear it. He didn't want a wife or kids. All he had to do was picture Sandra on the day she'd married his stepbrother to remind himself that the only kind of marriage that worked was one based on money. And he was hardly sugar daddy material.

All he needed was a distraction. Pulling out his phone, he scanned his contacts for one of his favorite sex buddies. A little sexting would straighten him right out.

* * *

Becky stood in front of the big laser printer in the central creative area, hands on hips. All her senses were on high alert. She was printing out her team's latest concepts and she didn't want anyone from the opposing side to get a glimpse.

Fortunately it was quiet in the agency. Most of the office doors were closed, and those stuck in the wall-less cube maze were plugged into their headphones. The only sounds were the click-clacking of keyboards and the occasional muffled curse word.

Finally the printer started to hum. Becky took another quick look around, but saw no movement.

She relaxed her guard, pulling out her phone to take a quick peek at her Twitter feed. She'd lost all track of what was going on outside the advertising bubble she lived in.

Suddenly she heard paper shuffling behind her. She whirled just in time to see Mark snatching her ads off the printer.

"Hey, give those back!" she snapped, reaching for the papers in his hand.

"In a minute," he said, turning his back on her. "But not before I see what you're working on."

"That's none of your business," she said, making another grab for them.

"That's what you think," he said, then strode off down the hall with her printouts.

Swearing silently to herself, she hurried after him, hoping with every fiber of her being that no one was watching them. She didn't need her team to see how easily the other side had managed to outwit her.

Once he reached his office he sat down on the front of his desk, still staring thoughtfully at her designs. She slammed the door, then launched herself at him.

"Give. Them. Back," she said, trying to snatch them from him.

He easily deflected her attack, then surprised her by pulling her against him. She went still as she registered his closeness, the heat emanating from his body putting her nerves on high alert.

Damn, he smelled good. Like grass and clean air with a hint of musk.

"Just chill out," he said, from somewhere over her left ear. "I'm not going to steal your ideas. I've got plenty of my own. I just wanted to sneak a peek."

Forcing herself out of the hormone-induced fog his presence induced, Becky pulled away. How was it possible to be so attracted to someone so infuriating?

"Fine," she said, holding her hand out. "You've had your peek. Hand 'em over."

He did, looking at her with a strangely intense expression.

"Don't you want to know what I think?"

Of course she did. "No."

"Well, I'll tell you anyway. I think they're pretty awesome."

"Oh." That wasn't what she had expected him to say. "Really?"

He nodded. "It's a really original idea. One I never would have come up with. The only thing is…"

Instantly anger sparked in her brain. Of course he couldn't let the compliment ride. Men never could. "The only thing is *what?*"

"Hey, don't get mad. I was just going to say that you might try to push the design. The copy carries it, but I think your art directors could give you more."

She looked down at the ads in her hands. He was right. She'd been thinking the same thing.

"Thank you for the advice. But I think we're doing just fine. Jessie is killing herself for me."

"Suit yourself." He shrugged.

She nodded and turned to leave.

"Don't you want to see what we've got going on?"

She stopped. "You're willing to show me?"

"Sure. Fair's fair. But you'll have to look at them on screen. I haven't printed them out yet."

Wow. A man playing fair. That was a first.

She padded across to his computer, prepared to hate whatever she saw. But when she saw what he was working on she couldn't help but smile. This guy sure seemed to know women.

"This is good," she said. "Funny. But…"

"But what?"

"It's just the headline. It's a little too much. Too smug. Tell your copywriter to dial it back a little."

He nodded. "I was thinking the same thing. Thanks."

She headed back to the door, but stopped before she turned the knob. No need to leave on too much of a friendly note.

"I'm still going to beat you," she said.

"Keep dreaming," he retorted.

"Oh, I will." She smiled. "But no matter how good my dreams are, the reality will be even better."

Becky sat staring at her blank computer screen, exhaustion beating at the backs of her eyelids with every blink of the cursor. It was eleven-thirty p.m. on Thursday, and although her team was giving her their all she still worried that it wouldn't be enough.

Three days just wasn't enough time. Not when there was a quarter of a billion dollars on the line.

As tired as she was, she couldn't keep the memories from invading. Couldn't keep from hearing the sneering voice telling her she'd never get anywhere without him. That she was a hack, and always would be. That the only way she'd ever attain any success would be if she kept warming his bed…

A gentle hand clasped her shoulder.

"Hey, space cadet? Did you hear a word I just said?" Jessie asked.

Becky blinked, shaking her head to clear it.

"No, I…"

"You were listening to the mini-Pence in your head again, weren't you?" she said, sympathy plain in her bright blue eyes.

Becky forced a halfhearted smile. "What? Of course not. How could I when I'm surrounded by such a fantastic group of talented women?"

Jessie snorted. "Liar. When was the last time you slept?"

Becky thought for a second. She honestly couldn't remember.

"I can tell by your silence that it's been too long. Go home. Rest. You need to bring your A game tomorrow. It's D-day, you know."

As if she could forget.

"I know. I'll go soon, I promise."

Jessie gave her a long look. Becky could tell she wanted to say something else.

"Really. I will. Don't worry about me."

"All right," Jessie said. "Well, I'm heading out. And I'm taking mini-Pence with me. You don't need *him* being a backseat driver."

This time Becky smiled for real.

"You're right. I don't. Get him out of here, and good riddance."

After Jessie had left Becky headed for the kitchen, and the free coffee that awaited her there. As she waited for her mug to fill with the magic brew she laid her head on the cool metal of the stainless steel countertop and closed her eyes. Just for a second…

Next thing she knew a big hand was shaking her awake. She bolted upright, trying to get her bearings.

"I'm on it, Pence. Don't worry. I just…" she blurted, her mind still in dreamland.

"Hey, it's all right. There's no Pence here. It looks like you just drifted off for a second," a familiar voice said.

Becky blinked. Sure enough, Mark was standing there, smiling gently at her. And in his hand was the cup of coffee she'd been waiting for.

"Here. It's still hot," he said, handing it to her.

She took it silently, waiting for him to comment on what he'd heard her say. He didn't disappoint her.

"Who's Pence?"

She looked at him, expecting to see ridicule in his eyes. But there was only compassion.

"He's the reason I don't do workplace relationships. Or relationships at all, for that matter."

"Ah. Why?"

Without knowing why, Becky found herself wanting to confide in him.

"He was creative director at the agency where I interned during grad school. He was my mentor, and then he became…more. Much more."

That was the understatement of the year. But Mark didn't need to know how bad things had gotten—or how far she'd run to get away from him.

She shrugged her shoulders. "The whole thing left a bad taste in my mouth. So I decided to focus on my career instead. And now here we are. Competing for the promotion that should be mine."

Mark smiled ruefully and lifted his coffee mug. "Indeed we are. Although I have to admit I'd rather be competing to see how fast we can make each other come."

Becky raised an eyebrow. "You don't want this job?"

"Of course I do," he said with a heated smile. "And I'm going to get it. But I'd also like to hear you screaming my name again. Creating killer ads makes me hot."

Becky couldn't stop the laugh that bubbled up. "Well, that's nice to know. But I'm afraid I can't help you. I've got an equally hot campaign to finish."

Mark slowly got out of his chair and walked over to where she stood. "Okay, but just so you know, I'll be thinking about you," he said, dropping a kiss on her neck.

Her blood sizzled at his touch, and she found herself hoping he'd keep going.

Instead he turned and walked away. "Sweet dreams," he called.

Grabbing her still-warm coffee cup from the counter, Becky started the trek back to her office. Sleep would have to wait. She had a campaign to perfect—and a devil of a man to vanquish.

Mark took a deep breath, straightened his black sport coat, and walked into the crowded conference room. He had timed his entrance carefully, so that he was almost late but not quite. He needed every tool in his arsenal to keep Becky off balance.

"Nice of you to show up!" David boomed.

"I was just putting the finishing touches on our concept," Mark answered. "Nothing less than perfection will do, after all."

"That's what I like to hear," David said. "Now, since you're so sure of yourself, how about you go first?"

Mark took a deep breath, then snuck a look at Becky. She was sitting quietly at one end of the giant conference table, her emerald-green dress the only bright spot in the overly industrial room.

She looked at him mockingly. "Yes, Mark, why don't you go first? We're dying to hear what you've come up with."

Mark looked at her, then looked at David.

David nodded encouragingly.

He took a deep breath as he strode to the head of the table. *This is it,* he told himself. *Time to knock their socks off.*

"I've spent a fair bit of time around women," he said. "I like to think I know what makes them tick. In fact," he said, turning to write on the whiteboard behind him, "the way I see it, women want three things… First, they want to look good. Which, for most women, means being skinny. Second, they want other women to be jealous of them. And third," he said, writing the number three with a flourish, "they want a man. Not only that, they want a man of their choosing. And they want him to drool over them. Which, if we're honest, brings us back to number one. But there are plenty of yogurts promising to make women skinny. To stand out, we need to say something different."

He turned the first board over, so the whole room could see a woman in a cocktail dress being admired by a host of attractive men. Once he was sure they'd seen it, he read them the headline.

"'Eden. The yogurt for the woman who knows what she wants.' That's our tagline. We'll use it in connection with women in all kinds of situations. At the beach," he said, flipping over boards sequentially, "in the dressing room, hailing a cab. In every scene men will be staring, open-mouthed, at the female."

When he'd finished a momentary silence filled the room. He glanced from one face to another but couldn't read what anyone was thinking. This crew would be awesome at poker.

Finally he looked at Becky and cocked an eyebrow at

her. The concept had come a long way since the last time she'd seen it.

She cleared her throat.

"So your message is pretty much: 'Eat this, be skinny, get men to lust over you'?" she asked.

He shrugged his shoulders. "In a nutshell. It's taking the bikini-clad woman in a beer commercial and turning it on its head. *Men* get to be the hangers-on."

"Huh… But what about women who aren't interested in men?"

Mark turned to look at her, expecting to see spite in her eyes. But instead he saw genuine interest. "That's a good point," he said. "But I think this idea has legs. It could cover different topics."

She walked around the room, grabbed the marker out of his hand and began to write down ideas. "Like instead of men it could be openmouthed business associates admiring her. Or cyclists left in her dust."

"Oh, I see where you're going," he said. "That could be cool."

She grinned at him, and for the first time since they'd returned to New York he got a glimpse of the happy, gorgeous girl he'd shared a night with in Vegas.

He grinned back. "So, what if—?"

David cleared his throat.

"I like where this is going—but, Becky, didn't you have a concept to present, as well? This *is* a competition," he said.

Becky blinked, and the laughter in her eyes disappeared.

"Right. Of course. Mark, can you clear your stuff out of the way? I'll grab my boards."

A few moments later Becky took center stage. And when she did she was magnetic.

"So, on my team we got to thinking about what women really want. And we think it goes deeper than just being skinny or attracting the right man. That's what our mothers wanted. But we want more. We want to be recognized as the strong, independent beings we are. We want the superhuman feats we accomplish every day to be recognized. After all, today's woman works like a dog at her corporate job, putting in twice as much effort for half the pay, then heads to the gym to ensure she stays model-thin, then goes home to run a household. Today's women are incredible. We think it's time for a marketer to sit up and acknowledge that."

Then she flipped a board over.

It showed a business-suited woman standing in a superhero pose on top of a conference table as her colleagues clapped.

"'You save your world every day before lunch. Choose the only yogurt high-powered enough to keep up with you,'" she said.

She flipped more boards. One of a soccer mom pulling a dirt-covered boy from a vat of quicksand. One of a runner flying ahead of the pack, cape billowing out behind her. And another of a lab-coated woman punching an oversize germ in the mouth so her patients could get away.

After she presented the last board she looked up and smiled. "Every woman deserves to feel like a superhero. Because she *is* one."

Her team applauded.

Mark had to stop himself from joining in.

David looked at Mark, seeming to be waiting for something. Oh. Right. He was supposed to be shooting holes in her concept.

"What about all those young hipsters who don't feel like they're accomplishing anything yet?" he asked.

"Well, we could have smaller situations. A woman stopping a cab before it can get away," she said.

"Or wowing a crowded club with her dance moves?" he suggested.

"Or saving a cat from a snarling dog?" she chimed in.

"Or what about—?"

"I hate to break this up, but we're not in a brainstorming session," David broke in. "We're supposed to be making a decision about which concept to present to the client."

Mark snapped his mouth shut. *Damn it*. He'd gone from shooting her down to making her case for her.

Thinking fast, he smirked in David's direction. "I think the choice is clear," he said. "Superheroes are great—if you're seven. I think most women would rather fantasize about a good-looking man than dress up in a Spandex suit."

The look Becky shot him was murderous. But before she could open her mouth David held up his hand.

"You have a point, Mark," he said. "But there's something in Becky's idea, too. Let me think for a minute. Everybody be quiet."

Instantly the conference room was deathly quiet.

David moved to the front of the room. "Mark, put your boards back up."

"Sure," he said, reaching for them.

"Just do it. Don't talk about it," David snapped.

Mark blinked, then did as he was told. This man could give any dictator a run for his money.

David paced back and forth, picking up boards, shuffling the order, then shuffling them again. After what seemed like an eternity, he finally spoke.

"All right. Here's what we're going to do. I want you to merge these campaigns. They both have their good points, but together they'd be stronger. So," he said, smiling broadly at Mark and Becky, "I want the two of you to work together."

Shocked, Mark stared at Becky.

She stared back, panic in her eyes.

"Together?" she blurted. "But we were competing."

"Not to worry," David said, patting her on the shoulder. "You still are. We'll just have to think of a different way to evaluate you. From now on consider yourselves partners as well as competitors."

CHAPTER THREE

DAVID'S WORDS ECHOED in the now silent room.

"Partners?" Becky squeaked.

David looked at her, a frown working its way between his piercing blue eyes. "That's what I said."

The whole idea was insane. How could they possibly get anything done when they were both focused on winning the competition? Plus, it meant spending a lot of time alone together. Too much time.

"This is a lot of work," she said. "How are Mark and I supposed to get it done without the help of our teams?"

"Well, Becky," David said, looking at her with more than a little disdain, "if you want to be a creative director at this agency you're going to have to learn to be resourceful. Figure it out."

Mark cleared his throat.

"I don't see any reason why the teams can't help us blow the campaign out after we've finalized the concept," he said.

David clapped him on the back. "Now, *that's* the way a creative director thinks. Becky, pay attention to this guy. You could learn a thing or two from him."

As Becky seethed, David gave his full attention to Mark. "You two have the weekend to get this nailed down. I expect you in my office at nine a.m. sharp on Monday morning to present it to me. Any questions?"

Mark looked over the top of the bald man's head at Becky. "You?"

She had plenty of questions. Like, why was David such

a Neanderthal? What did he see in Mark? Why the hell had she decided to be a copywriter, anyway? Surely there were better ways to make a living. Picking up the city's garbage, for example.

But neither of the men in the room could provide the answers, so instead she just shook her head.

"All right. I'll leave you to it," David said. "Jessie, would you come with me to my office, please?"

The redhead nodded and followed him from the room. Everyone else followed her lead, and soon they were alone.

Becky collapsed in one of the deliberately uncomfortable metal chairs. "Now what?"

"Now you let me take you to dinner," Mark said.

Good Lord. The man never let up.

"Dinner? No. We might be partners, but we don't have to be friends."

"Who said anything about being friends? This is just dinner. You gotta eat, right?"

He looked at her with that damn eyebrow quirked and she felt her resolve melting. She *was* hungry. And they had a lot of work ahead of them. It made sense to fuel up before they got started.

"All right. Dinner. But I'll pay. And I'll choose the place."

"You've got a deal," he said, smiling triumphantly.

"Good. Meet me downstairs in fifteen minutes," she said.

That gave her time to come up with a game plan for winning the promotion…and keeping her clothes on this weekend.

Mark paced in front of the glass doors that marked the entrance to SBD, dodging tourists with every turn.

He'd arrived at the designated spot on time. Unfortunately Becky was nowhere in sight. Just like a woman, he found himself thinking. Probably trying to figure out how big his bank account was. Then he caught himself. Where had *that* come from?

Surely David couldn't be rubbing off on him already?

Just then Becky burst through the doors. The killer green dress was gone. In its place was a pair of worn-looking jeans and a baggy rust-colored sweater. And *damn* if she didn't look just as good.

"There you are," he said. "Where are we off to, chief?"

She looked up at him and he noticed her face was scrubbed free of makeup. Without it, she looked all of nineteen.

"That's for me to know and you to find out," she said. "Come on."

He followed her as she wound her way through the congested city streets, ignoring the pressing crowds as only a seasoned New Yorker could.

"So, are you from here?" he asked.

She seemed to hesitate before answering. "No. But I like to pretend that I am."

He wasn't sure what to make of that statement, so he ignored it. "Then where *are* you from?"

"Detroit," she said shortly.

"Ah. Where the weak get killed and eaten, huh?"

"Or pushed to the end of the unemployment line," she said. Then, seeming to realize that she was being rude, she smiled up at him. "How 'bout you? Where's your magic come from?"

"Oh, here and there," he said. "I moved around a lot." From boarding school to summer camp to anywhere else his mother had been able to think of sending him that kept him far from home.

Looking around, he realized they were standing at the corner of Fifty-Third and Sixth. Tourist central.

"Hungry for some overpriced deli sandwiches?" he asked.

"Nope. Just spicy deliciousness," she said, pointing to a food cart.

"Really?"

"Don't look so surprised. It's the best halal cart in town. And it's cheap."

A few minutes later, when they were seated on a bench with their plastic containers on their laps, he had to admit that she knew what she was talking about.

"This is good," he said between bites of lamb and rice. "I wouldn't have pegged you for a street food kind of girl."

"Really? What do I seem like? A steak and champagne enthusiast?" she said with a sarcastic grin.

"No, more like a vegan foodie."

She snorted. "We don't have vegan foodies in the Midwest. Just a bunch of overweight carnivores."

"So what brought you here? To New York?"

Her expression closed. "The bright lights and big agencies, of course. Just like everybody else."

She took a big bite of lamb and rice, then abruptly steered the conversation back to him.

"So. In all your moving around you never made it to the Midwest?"

"Nope. I have an aversion to corn fields."

"Where did you live, then?"

"Well, I lived in New Jersey until I was ten," he said, hoping that would be enough to satisfy her.

"And then…?"

Man, was she persistent. He sighed.

"And then my mom married a rich man and moved to Connecticut."

"Didn't you go with her?"

He laughed bitterly.

"Well, I had a room in her house. But I wasn't really wel-

come there. She was too busy with her new family. I spent
most of my teen years seeing how many boarding schools
I could get thrown out of."

Her eyes went round. "Why?"

Thanks to the years of therapy his mom had forced him
to do, he knew it was because acting out had been the only
thing that got his mother's attention. But he wasn't going
to tell Becky that.

Instead, he shrugged. "Why does a teenage boy do anything? But I saw a lot of the East Coast. Massachusetts,
New Hampshire, Maine…everywhere fancy pants rich
people live."

Becky snorted. "I would have hated you when I was a
teenager—you know that?"

He looked at her, genuinely surprised. "Why do you
say that?"

"I was the kid doing extra credit projects and sucking
up to teachers, hoping they'd help me when it was time
to apply for college. I thought kids like you were idiots."

"And what kind of kid was that?"

She looked at him, her eyes flashing with remembered
anger.

"Kids who spent all their time screwing around, knowing they could buy their way into college even if their
grades sucked. You would have been one of the people
making my life miserable because I couldn't afford to waste
my time partying with you."

He sat silently for a long minute, unsure of what to say.
She was probably right. After his mom had married Bill
money had lost all real value. No matter how much he'd
charged to his stepfather's accounts, or how outrageous the
purchase, no one had blinked an eye. Except…

"Not me. I went to all-boys schools. Girls were rare and
always appreciated, no matter how geeky. Besides," he said,
brushing her hair back from her face, "even if you were a

nerd, I'm sure you were a gorgeous nerd. I would have been just as desperate to get in your pants then as I am now."

She rolled her eyes, looking pleased nevertheless.

"Whatever," she said, looking down at her phone screen. "Whoa. It's almost seven already. What do you say we go back and get our war room set up? That way we can start fresh in the morning."

"That's a good plan. You're just going to move your stuff into my office, right?"

Becky froze. "I...uh...thought we should set up shop someplace public. With more space, I mean. Like, you know, the conference room."

"Why? Are you afraid to be alone with me?" Mark asked, half hoping that she was. He'd love to know he had that kind of power over her.

"What? No. Of course not. I just thought we might need the whiteboards or something," she said, pointedly not looking at him.

"I've got plenty of whiteboards in my office," he said. "I don't know about you, but I like a little privacy when I'm working hard. And everybody can see into the conference room."

She picked at her fingernails. "I don't know..."

He couldn't resist the urge to tease her.

"I promise to be on my best behavior. I won't show you my underwear even if you ask me to."

Becky laughed at his reference to the first time they'd met.

"Okay. Deal. I won't show you mine if you don't show me yours," she said. "But you'll have to help me move my stuff."

By the time they'd finished moving her desk, laptop dock and giant monitors, dark had fallen and the lights from the skyscrapers that surrounded them twinkled like stars.

Becky gazed out of the window and sighed.

"I could get used to a view like this," she said.

Mark came to stand beside her. "It is pretty sweet. Definitely beats the view I had at my last office."

"Oh? Where was that?"

"Los Angeles," he said.

"Oh. Yeah… I can see how you'd get tired of looking at palm trees and bikini-clad babes," Becky teased.

"I was a contract worker. Which meant I was one small step away from sitting in the basement with a red stapler. The only thing I had to look at was fuzzy cubicle walls."

"Ah. At least I'll always have Ryan Gosling to keep me company," she said, motioning to the poster she'd tacked to the wall by her desk.

"If you get tired of looking at him I'm happy to pose for pictures," Mark said.

Becky stepped back. "Now you want to be my eye candy, huh?"

"Nope. I just want you to want me to take my shirt off."

If he only knew… But she wouldn't. She wouldn't even kiss him—at least not again. That morning in his office had been an aberration.

"Dream on, buddy. I don't sleep with the competition."

"I know, I know," he said. "But you can't blame a guy for trying. You know, if you slept with me I might not try so hard to win."

"Yeah, right. I'm pretty sure you don't give up that easily," she said, giving him a sideways smile.

Then she turned away. It was either that or give in to the temptation to rub her hands over the hard planes of his chest.

"I'm going to check my email and then head out for the night," she said. "You?"

"I think I'm just going to head out," he answered. "I

need to hit the hay so I'm ready to rock tomorrow. See ya in the morning."

Becky waved vaguely in his direction as he left and fired up her laptop. She didn't really need to check her email—that was what smartphones were for. But she did need some time to get used to her new surroundings and wrap her head around the situation.

Truth really was stranger than fiction. If she'd set out to write a book she'd never have come up with anything as screwy as this. It was almost reality-show-worthy.

She could see it now: *Flung: Where One-Night Flings Compete.*

Giggling, she peeked at her inbox. She was surprised to see it was flooded with messages of support from the whole creative team. The guy in charge of the agency might be a sleaze, but he sure did hire good people.

She was just about to close it up when she saw a name that froze her heart.

Pence.

What did *he* want?

She considered deleting the email without reading the message, but knew that was the coward's way out. Taking a deep breath, she clicked on his name, willing herself to stay calm.

Hey Babe
Saw you at AdWorld, but I knew you wouldn't want to talk to me so I didn't say hello. Couldn't stop thinking about you, though. You look good. Done good, too. I'd like to say I'm surprised, but you learned from the best—me.
Did you know my agency is pitching to Eden, too? I'd say may the best man win, but we both know who that is—me. I'm sorry I'm going to have to crush you. But, hey, there'll always be a job waiting for you here! Oh, and Chelsea hit the road, so there's a room for you, too.
Pence

Becky read it twice, unable to believe what she was seeing. Unfortunately the message only got more infuriating the second time around.

Could the man be any more repulsive? Was he really inviting her to take his wife's…er…his *ex*-wife's place over email?

Unable to contain her rage, Becky screamed. Her shriek echoed in the mostly empty office, carrying her pain right back to her ears.

She slammed her laptop shut and got up to pace.

There was no reason this should affect her so much. She'd outgrown him. Outstripped him. She was twice as good as that scum-sucker had ever been on his best day.

Seeking confirmation, she grabbed one of her awards off her desk, stroking the golden statue. She was good. *Damn* good. And nothing that man could say would convince her otherwise.

But still she heard the echoes in her brain. "No-good hack," they spat. "Bed-hopping social climber," they hissed. "As terrible on paper as you are in bed," they screamed.

Unable to help herself, Becky chucked the award across the room. It landed with a dull thud, the thick red carpet seeming to reach up to protect it from damage.

Becky caught the sob before it could escape from her throat. It was time to go home.

Becky turned the key in the faded red door that marked the entrance to her third-floor walk-up and trudged up the stairs.

This morning she had felt so confident. So alive. She'd been sure that the world was hers to conquer.

Now? Now all she wanted was a giant glass of wine and the oblivion that came with sleep.

Without bothering to flip on the light switch, Becky stepped into the kitchen and opened the tiny fridge. Wincing at the glaring light, she pulled the Pinot Grigio from the top shelf and took a swig straight from the bottle.

A cockroach scuttled across the bloodred countertop directly opposite her. Without thinking, she slammed the bottle down, reveling in the sickening crunch that sounded as it met its demise.

"There's one pest that's out of my life forever," she said, grabbing a paper towel to wipe its remains from her salvation.

She grabbed a plastic tumbler and filled it to the top before collapsing in the purple velvet chaise that was her prized possession.

Gazing out at the gently waving branches of the oak tree that graced her front window, she tried to relax.

It was no good. As soon as she let her guard down memories started to invade. And they weren't all bad. For a long while Pence had been everything she'd needed.

She remembered how patient he'd been when critiquing her first efforts at advertising copy. He'd never laughed or shown disdain, no matter how awkward the headline or script construction.

And how he'd loved to surprise her. A midweek picnic aboard a chartered sailboat here. Front row seats to the summer's hottest concert there. A private dinner prepared by the city's top chef whenever anything was seriously amiss.

All wrapped in miles and miles of seemingly sincere promises. He'd painted beautiful pictures of the life they would create together—working opposite each other all day, then playing together all night, making sweet love whenever the mood struck them. He'd even included children in their mythical future: a girl with her hair and his height, and a boy with her eyes and his strength.

She'd thought she'd been transported from her dreary hand-to-mouth existence straight into a fairytale. Unfortunately her happily-ever-after had never put in an appearance.

At least not with Pence. And not in Detroit.

But she'd spent the last five years here in New York, creating a new direction for her story. And, unless she was sadly mistaken, she was almost to the good part.

She put the tumbler of wine to her lips, only to find it empty.

It was time for bed.

She shuffled into the closet that served as her bedroom and crawled beneath the sky-blue goose down duvet that was her biggest extravagance. Her bed was her sanctuary, and normally her lavender-scented sheets relaxed her within minutes.

Not tonight.

Tonight she could only toss and turn, searching for a comfortable place to lay her head.

She was tormented by images of the flowered treasure box that lay hidden under her bed. The one that contained memories she couldn't stand to destroy—and that destroyed her to remember.

Sighing, she twisted the knob on the delicate crystal lamp on her nightstand and clambered out of bed.

With the box settled in her lap, she gently lifted the cover.

Resting there was a picture of her, snuggled against Pence's broad chest at sunset aboard a sailboat. The camera had caught him midlaugh, his blue eyes crinkling, looking happy and relaxed. She could remember the exact moment. She'd felt so safe. So loved. So incredibly sure she was right where she belonged.

The ruby promise ring he'd given her was also there, nestled in its green velvet box. As was the long gold chain he'd insisted she hang it on, so she could wear it "next to her heart." She'd loved to feel it hanging between her breasts, imagining it was him touching her every time the ring had brushed a sensitive area.

There were other pictures, including one taken at the dinner held in honor of her first award-win. He was scowling darkly at the camera, unhappiness obvious in every line of his body.

That was when things had started to go wrong. He hadn't liked it when she'd started succeeding on her own.

At the bottom of the box was the memory she was most dreading. A grainy black-and-white photo of the peanut-size blob that had been her baby at eight weeks.

The baby she had aborted a week later.

She remembered the day the picture had been taken as if it was yesterday. She'd known she was pregnant for three weeks. After the first test had come out positive she'd bought an economy-size pack of pregnancy test strips and taken a new one every morning. The little pink line indicating the baby's existence had got darker and thicker with each passing day, but it hadn't been until her doctor had shown her the blurry black-and-white ultrasound image on a video monitor that she'd allowed herself to believe it was real.

And when he'd found the heartbeat her soul had melted, reforming itself around the tiny little being growing inside her. She'd promised the little peanut that she'd take care of it. That she'd be the best mom ever.

What a joke *that* had turned out to be.

The next night she shaved every last hair from her body and perfumed every crevice before sliding into the sexy white lace lingerie Pence loved. She'd donned silky back-seamed thigh-highs and a skintight black dress that showcased her newly voluptuous breasts.

Her one and only pair of Manolos had been the finishing touch.

When she'd arrived at the intimate French restaurant where she'd arranged to meet Pence she'd known by the slack-jawed look on the face of every man she'd passed that she'd done well.

But by the time the *maître d'* had shown her to the table and helped her settle into a chair under Pence's watchful gaze, her confidence had already been taking a nosedive. His eyes had scraped over her body, taking in the size of her breasts and the curve of her hips.

"Have you gained weight, Becky?" he'd asked.

"N-no," she'd stuttered. "It's just this dress. It forgives nothing."

"Good. You look great, but you know how important it is to stay thin if you want to make it in advertising."

Becky had nodded. "I know," she'd said quietly.

But inside her mind had been screaming. Pregnant women got fat. Would Pence love her when she was fat? It would only be temporary, but his attention span was notoriously short. By the time this baby was born and her body had returned to normal he might have forgotten all about her.

Then what would she do?

"What's wrong?" Pence had asked, reaching out to stroke her hand. "Did I say something to upset you?"

"No, not at all," she'd said with a small smile. "I've just got a lot on my mind."

"That's right." He'd groaned. "You wanted to 'talk.' What is it this time? Is your mom after you to get married again?"

She shook her head. "No, not so far this month," she'd said.

Just then their server had arrived, giving Becky a reprieve. He'd offered Pence a sample from a bottle of freshly uncorked Syrah. Pence had inhaled deeply, then swished the purple liquid around in his mouth. After a long moment he'd given a sharp nod. The waiter had smiled and filled their glasses before fading away.

Pence had looked at her over the rim of his glass. "So what is it?"

Becky had taken a deep breath and reached into her black sequined bag with a trembling hand. "I have a surprise for you," she'd said.

He looked at her suspiciously. "I don't like surprises," he'd said.

She'd pulled out the small silver-wrapped package she'd stowed in her purse and handed it to him.

"I think you'll like this one."

Lord knew he'd talked about his longing for children often enough.

"Humph," he'd muttered as he undid the bow. "We'll see about that."

He'd torn off the wrapping paper in one fell swoop. Becky had felt her heart rise into her throat as he lifted the lid of the box, unsure of what his reaction would be. He'd frowned when he saw the framed picture inside.

"What is this?" he'd demanded.

"It's a picture," she'd said. "An ultrasound."

"An ultrasound? What? Do you have a tumor?"

"N-no," she'd stuttered, taking a deep breath. "I'm pregnant. That's a picture of a baby. *Our* baby."

Pence fell back in his chair. "Pregnant? But how could that be? We take precautions."

Becky had shrugged her shoulders, knowing full well that she wasn't as religious about taking her birth control pills as he supposed she was.

"Apparently not enough," she'd said.

"So this is real? You're not joking?"

"No," she'd whispered. "I'm not."

"But this can't be. You *can't* be pregnant. I have a *wife!*"

Her heart had plummeted, smashing into the polished cement floor at their feet. "You're *married?*" she'd whispered.

"Of course I'm married. I thought you knew that? Didn't you ever wonder why I never spend the night? Or why I never invite you to my house?"

"N-no. I just thought… Well, I didn't think. You said you loved me! You talked about getting married!"

He'd taken her hand again, stroking it gently. "I do love you. And I would love to marry you. But I can't divorce my wife. Her father owns the agency. If I left her I'd lose everything."

"But what about our baby?"

"There can't *be* a baby. Don't you see? You have to get rid of it. It's the only way."

"Get rid of it?"

"Yes. Have an abortion."

"But I don't want an abortion," she'd said. "I want to keep it."

"Then you're on your own," he'd said. "I won't have anything to do with it. If you don't take care of this problem we're done."

"But you just said you love me," she'd whispered.

"Love has nothing to do with it. This is business. And I can't let a little accident like this jeopardize my position with the agency," Pence had said. "Please, just think about it?"

At a loss for words, she'd nodded.

"Good," Pence had said. "Now, if you'll excuse me, I have to attend a dinner party. With my wife."

And with that he was gone.

Becky had stared after him, mouth agape. What was she supposed to do now?

The next week had been a nightmare. She'd crunched numbers, searched the internet and racked her brain, trying to find a way through the predicament she had suddenly found herself in.

Eventually, though, she'd admitted the truth to herself.

She was twenty-three. She had seventy-five thousand dollars in student loans and only made twenty-four thousand dollars a year. There was no way she could raise this baby on her own. And there'd be no help coming from the man she had thought loved her.

Worse, if she kept the baby her career would take a nose-dive just when it was starting to get off the ground. The financially secure future she had imagined would disappear in a puff of smoke.

She'd end up like her parents, working two jobs and worrying over every penny she spent for the rest of her life. That was no way to live—or to raise a child.

There was only one choice she could make.

When she'd arrived for her appointment at the family planning clinic it was with cold anger and hot despair stomping on her heart. Rubbing her still-flat belly, she'd made her soon-to-be-aborted baby a promise.

She would never forget him—for it had become a him in her mind—and Pence would pay dearly for this betrayal if it was the last thing she did.

Hot tears leaked down her face now, as she stroked the image. She'd never forgive herself for not standing up to him. For allowing him to control her and for letting him convince her to do something that had felt so wrong.

No man would ever have that much power over her again.

Wiping her tears away with her sleeve, Becky slid the box back under the bed. She had to get to sleep. She had a competition to win—and a living nightmare to defeat.

CHAPTER FOUR

MARK ARRIVED AT the office bright and early, doughnuts and coffee in hand. After the relaxed evening they'd shared he was looking forward to working with Becky today.

Tucking the breakfast items under his chin, he opened his office door, expecting to see it empty. But Becky was already there, pounding away at her computer, punishing the keys with every clack.

"Good morning, early bird! I brought breakfast."

Becky looked up. If the dark circles under her eyes were any indication, Mark thought, she'd never left the office.

She smiled frostily. "Nice of you to make an appearance. Considering how much work we have to do, I thought it would be best to get an early start."

Whoa. Okay. Apparently they were playing a new game.

"Sorry. I thought eight-thirty on a Saturday was plenty early."

"And that's why I'm going to win and you're not," she snapped. "This job takes dedication."

"I've got news for you, princess. Neither one of us is going to win if we can't find a way to merge these two campaigns."

She waved dismissively at him.

"I'm working on it. Why don't you go over there and look for some pretty pictures or something?"

All right. Enough was enough.

"I'll tell you what I'm going to do. I'm going to go over there and come up with another, even more kick-ass idea.

And when David asks what your contribution was I'll tell him you didn't make one. How's that sound?"

She rolled her eyes. "Whatever. Just be quiet about it."

Mark stomped over to his desk and slammed the coffee down. Forget quiet. He was going to work the way he always did. With music blaring.

Seconds later, the discordant sounds of a heavy metal guitar filled the room.

She glared at him, then reached into her drawer and pulled out a pair of headphones.

He loaded up his photo editing program to look at the images he'd already created, but the glare from the overhead lights was killing him. He got up and flipped the lights off. He'd hardly even sat down before she was turning them back on.

"Do you mind?" he said. "I can't work with all that glare."

"Well, I can't write if I can't see the keys," she said,

"Come sit by the window," he said.

"Go work in a cave," she retorted.

He sighed. "Fine. Have it your way. It's not worth fighting about."

She huffed and put her headphones back on.

Mark turned to his computer to get started, but his mind refused to cooperate.

Maybe looking at the existing boards would help. He grabbed the pile from where it lay by the office door and spread the boards out on the plush red carpet, laying the two campaigns side by side.

Then he began to pace back and forth down the line, looking for common ground.

They both featured strong women. And used humor. Maybe…

Becky sighed angrily. "Really? Are you going to pace all day? Because it's really distracting."

He turned to look at her. She was standing with her

hands on her hips, completely unaware of how ridiculously her angry expression contrasted with the giant happy face emblazoned on her oversize T-shirt.

Unbidden, the image of her standing in exactly that position, laughing and naked except for a pair of cheetah-print heels, rose to the front of his brain. How could that free spirit belong to this completely aggravating woman? There had to be a way to get past her anger.

Suddenly he had an idea. Grabbing his jacket, he turned to leave.

"Where are you going?" she asked.

"Out," he said. "See you later."

"But what about—?"

"We can't work together like this. So I'm leaving," he said, shutting the door before she could see the smile on his face.

That would give her something to stew about.

Becky stared openmouthed at the shut door.

Her so-called partner had bailed on her. *Now* what was she supposed to do? True, she hadn't exactly been welcoming, but that didn't give him the right to just quit.

Of course if he didn't come back the promotion would be hers by default. At least it would if she could find the brilliant idea that would allow her to win the competition.

And she *had* to win this. She didn't even care about the promotion so much anymore. She just wanted to kick Pence's pompous ass.

Sighing, she collapsed into her chair and put her head in her hands.

If only Mark wasn't so damn hot. Just being in the same room with him made her think inappropriate thoughts. Thoughts of unbuttoning the faded blue shirt he'd been wearing and licking his chest. Of sliding her hand down the front of his jeans. Of letting him roll down her leggings and take her—right on top of the desk.

She was sorely tempted to do just that. To scratch the itch and move on. After all, she was an empowered, independent woman. Why shouldn't she take what she wanted when he obviously wanted it, too?

Because once would never be enough, that was why. And she knew better than to get involved with a coworker—even a temporary one—ever again.

If sex was out, there was only one thing to do. Work.

An hour later she was still typing indecipherable garbage when the door opened. Mark walked in, carrying a giant F.A.O. Schwartz bag. Trying hard not to feel relieved, she looked at him with a raised eyebrow.

"You went to the toy store?"

"Yep."

He waltzed over to his desk and turned his back on her. She heard a great deal of rustling, then boxes being ripped. Unable to hide her curiosity, she walked up behind him and stood on her tiptoes, trying to see what he was working on.

He turned and she quickly stepped back, nearly falling in the process.

When she caught her balance she saw that he was holding two...*plastic swords?*

Mark looked at her, a serious expression on his face.

"I would like to challenge you to a duel," he said.

"A what?"

"A duel. To settle the problems we seem to be having this morning. If I win you have to give up the attitude. If you win I'll...well, I'll do whatever you want. Leave. Stay. Draw pictures of monkeys. Whatever."

Becky wanted to laugh, but he didn't seem to think what he was proposing was funny.

"Are you serious?"

"As a heart attack."

She licked her lips. "All right."

"Good," he said, a smile quirking at the corners of his mouth. "Do you want to be red or blue?"

"Um…red."

She reached out to take it. "This is actually kind of cool," she said, taking a few test swings.

He nodded, and brought his sword up into fighting position.

"Ready?"

"Sure," she said, imitating his stance.

He started to advance and they circled each other warily.

Suddenly he struck, aiming for her stomach. She moved her sword into position just in time, batting his out of the way before striking back.

He parried her blow and the fight was on. Soon they were whirling around the room, their swords crashing and crackling. Mark kept his expression serious, but Becky felt herself grinning.

She couldn't remember the last time she'd had this much fun with a guy. Or at all.

Mark lunged forward and she backpedaled before stepping on something sharp and cold. The award she'd thrown last night. She cursed at the sudden pain, then grabbed Mark's arm to try and keep herself from falling. Instead she overbalanced, and they fell into a heap, Mark's big body pinning hers to the ground. He pulled one arm free and lightly tapped her forehead with his saber.

"You're dead," he said.

Becky gave in to the laughter frothing in her throat.

"I guess you won, fair and square," she said between giggles.

He grinned down at her.

"Yep. No more attitude from *you*, Sir knight."

"I don't think I could frown if I tried right now," she said.

"Good. I like you better when you're laughing." His

dark eyes took on a liquid sheen. "In fact, there's only one expression I'd rather see," he said.

And without warning he took her lips with his.

His lips crushed down on hers with an urgent demand that she give in to the heat that had been building between them—not just today, but every day since she'd returned from Vegas. And, God help her, but she couldn't ignore it. Couldn't say no.

She let her mouth fall open in silent surrender, giving in to the hunger his searing kisses awakened in her. His tongue plundered her mouth, claiming every inch of it for his own.

She twined her hands in his dark hair and pulled him closer, wanting all that he had to give. She gave up on thought, letting instinct drive her as she arched her body upward, wanting still more.

He took that as the invitation it was, sliding one hand down her body to cup her through her panties.

"Mmm..." he rumbled. "You're already hot for me."

Becky heard herself moan as he slid his hand back up, leaving the sensitive nub of nerves that she wanted him to touch so badly. She grabbed it and put it back, whimpering.

"Wait. Not yet," he said. "I want you naked first."

"Then help me get my clothes off," she growled, starting to squirm out of her shirt.

He pulled it quickly over her head, then whipped her leggings off.

"Yours, too," she said, and within seconds his clothes had joined hers on the floor.

Clothes gone, he lowered himself on top of her and kissed her lips again. She let him in, losing herself in the feel of the intoxicating hardness of his body. She pressed upward, moving her hips against his, almost delirious in her need to connect with him in the most primal way.

"Mark, *now,*" she begged. "I need..."

"Hold on, baby," he said. "I want to taste you first."

In seconds his mouth was on her, licking and nipping at her most sensitive parts.

"Damn, Becky, you have no idea how long I've been wanting to do this," he growled, from somewhere at her center.

She wanted to ask him how long, but the ability to form words left her as he began to suck. She could think of nothing other than the waves of pleasure he was creating. At that moment she would have given anything to keep him right where he was for as long as possible.

Seconds later she peaked, crashing into an abyss of pure sensation.

Mark kissed her as she came down, his mouth even more urgent than it had been before. Knowing what he needed, what they both needed, she wrapped her legs around his waist.

"Mark…now," she whimpered against his mouth.

"Yes, *now*," he said, and sheathed himself inside her with a quick flex of his hips.

She groaned and clenched her body around him, wanting to keep him there forever.

She let her eyes drift closed as he started moving, losing herself in the sensation.

"No, don't," he whispered. "I want you to look at me."

When she opened them he was looking at her fiercely.

"I want you to see. To know it's me that's doing this to you," he said as he thrusted, pressing against all the right spots.

"Only you," she gasped as he moved inside her. "You're the only one that's ever done this to me."

"God, Becky," he rumbled, heat flooding his gaze as his pace quickened. "You're amazing. Where have you been all my life?"

"I'm. Right. Here. Now," she said.

The heat stabbing through her from his thrusts and the

weight of his gaze melded together into a hot haze of perfection, and she felt her world beginning to splinter.

"Mark, I'm going to…"

"Come for me, Gorgeous Girl," he said, smiling down at her.

And she did, waves and waves of sensation swamping her psyche and blurring his face in front of her.

His expression turned fierce and with a guttural moan he followed her over the cliff.

Afterward they lay twined together, their hearts beating in time. Becky lost herself in the perfection of the moment, unwilling to move and let the real world in again. If she knew the sex would always be like that she'd never let this man go…

When she could put words together again, she said, "You know, until very recently I thought I was bad at that."

"Why on earth would you think that?" Mark said, genuinely shocked. "Becky, you're amazing."

He watched as she flushed, the rosiness reaching all the way down her chest.

"Oh, I…uh…shouldn't have said that out loud. My internal filter must be busted."

He pulled her into his arms. "But you did. Must've been on your mind. Why?" He was surprised at how much he wanted to know.

She looked down at her hands and picked at her fingernails. "Oh, you know. Heard from an ex. Stirred up bad memories."

Judging by the way she was closing in on herself, they must have been spectacularly awful memories. Then he remembered a snippet from the night he'd found her asleep in the kitchen.

"This wouldn't have anything to do with that Pence guy, would it?"

She looked at him sharply. "How would you know that?"

"You were talking in your sleep. That night in the kitchen."

Realization dawned on her face. "Oh. Right. Well, yeah, that's the one. But you know… Every girl's got one."

"Got one what?"

"A voice. One that points out her flaws and harps on her inadequacies. Mine sounds like him."

Mark felt a wave of anger roll across his brain. "If I ever meet this guy I'm going to have a thing or two to say to him. He sounds like a piece of work."

Becky looked at him, a wry smile on her lips.

"Well, you might get your chance."

"Chance to what?"

"Talk to Pence." Her lips twisted, the smile turning into an unconscious snarl. "His agency is pitching to Eden, too."

Mark sat up straighter, surprised.

"How long have you known?"

"Oh…" Becky said, looking up at the clock. "About fifteen hours or so. He emailed last night."

Suddenly her earlier behavior made a lot more sense. Wishing he could save her from her obvious pain, he pulled her close and kissed the top of her head.

"We'll beat him, you know," he said. "Together. That jerk doesn't stand a chance against us."

She murmured her assent, but when he looked at her he could tell her brain was busily working on another problem. Pulling her shirt over her head, she paced over to the whiteboard on the wall.

"We've been going about this all wrong," she said. "Women aren't going to buy our yogurt just because we recognize their awesomeness. That doesn't do anything for them. They're going to buy it if it solves a problem for them. So if the problem is insecurity, we need to position ourselves as a solution."

He watched as she scratched silently on the board with a red marker. Her butt jiggled ever so slightly with the movement, and he found himself wanting to feel the weight of it in his palms again.

She turned to look at him, triumph lighting her eyes.

"I've got it. Check this out. It could be something like, 'Working mom guilt weighing you down? Take an Eden moment and believe.'"

Mark's brain kicked into gear. "Maybe. Or what about, 'Eden. Your shortcut to a more perfect you.'"

Becky wrote it down.

"Good thought. But what about…?"

And they were off and running.

The next time Mark looked up, the sun was setting.

"Wow. We've been at this all day," he said. "You hungry?"

Her stomach growled loudly in response. Laughing, she said, "I guess so!"

"How about I take you out somewhere? My treat."

"I don't think so," she said, crossing her arms over her chest. "I've got laundry and stuff to do tonight."

"Oh, come on. Laundry on a Saturday night? You're not fifty. I'll take you back to my place for dessert," he said, winking suggestively.

She smiled sadly. "Mark, what happened before…it can't happen again. The situation's too complicated. Besides, I don't date people—"

"You don't date people you work with. I know. You keep saying that. But who said anything about dating?"

She flushed. "I don't do what we did this afternoon with coworkers either."

"We were enjoying each other. There's nothing wrong with that."

"You say that now. But if we keep it up before long there will be feelings, then hurt feelings, and eventually heartbreak. I don't do heartbreak," she answered.

Mark felt himself getting frustrated. "You don't do heartbreak. I don't do relationships. So we should be well matched."

"I don't think so…" she said, looking everywhere except at him.

Mark gently turned her to face him.

"Listen to me. This situation *is* complicated. We don't need to add sexual frustration to the mix. After all, we didn't get anywhere today until after we let that go. Right?"

She gave a slight nod.

"And you have to agree the sex is amazing. Probably some of the best I've ever had."

She looked up sharply. "Really?" she said.

"Really."

"I thought it was just… I mean you've been with so many… And I…um…haven't…"

"Becky?"

"What?"

"You're amazing. Period."

She smiled, her cheeks flushing pink. "Thank you."

"You're welcome. So let's just agree to enjoy each other until this—whatever this is—is over and decided. Then we'll go our separate ways. No harm, no foul."

She looked at him. "Do you really think it can be that easy?"

"I know it can," he said. "I won't let it be any other way."

She stared at him for a long moment, an unreadable expression on her face. "I'll think about it," she said.

He nodded, knowing that was probably the best answer he could hope for at the moment.

"Don't think too long," he growled.

She just smiled in response, blowing him a kiss as she walked out through the door.

He knew she'd eventually agree to his proposition. The chemistry they had was too incredible for either of them to walk away. And as long as they kept it to the physical realm no one would get hurt.

Heck, he didn't have enough cash to make her want anything more permanent anyway. She might not *seem* interested in his wallet, but he knew from experience that even the sweetest girls were ultimately moved by money.

For the first time he found himself wishing they weren't.

CHAPTER FIVE

"THIS IS GOOD. Really good," David said after Becky and Mark had pitched their concept to him. "Which one of you came up with it?"

Nice try, Becky thought. She wasn't going to let him knock one of them out of the competition that easily.

"It was pretty organic," she said out loud. "I couldn't tell you which one of us nailed the final line. Could you, Mark?"

"No, not really," he said. "We make a surprisingly great team."

"Good, good—glad to hear it," David said, leaning back in his chair, hands behind his head. "Now we just have to decide how to proceed."

"When is the presentation?" Becky asked.

"October thirtieth at ten a.m."

"Oh. Good. We've got some time, then," she said. More than three weeks, as a matter of fact.

She looked at Mark. He looked back at her, his face pinched with uncertainty. Okay, since he didn't seem to be willing to take charge they were going to do things her way.

"Here's what I think," she said. "I think we need to overwhelm the client with our awesomeness. We need to go in there with print, digital, TV—the works. Obviously we're going to need everybody's help. Mark and I will act as creative leads and work on the big concept stuff—I'm thinking we should tackle TV first—and we'll break everybody else into small teams to handle individual projects. We'll meet with the teams daily, to check their progress and keep everyone on task. When we're satisfied with a project, we'll bring it to you for final approval. Sound good?"

David leaned forward, reluctant admiration showing in every line of his face. "That's a good plan," he said. "If I didn't know better I'd think you'd been handling assignments like this for years."

Don't blush, she told herself. *Don't you dare blush.*

"Thank you," she said. "I've been waiting a long time for an opportunity like this."

"Better get to it," David said. "You have a lot to accomplish in a very short amount of time."

Becky nodded at Mark and they rose, walking silently across the office.

"Good luck," David called as they closed the door. "I'll be watching you. Remember, this is still a competition!"

It was well after eight p.m. before Becky was finally able to sit down at her desk.

It had been a long day of kick-off meetings and strategy sessions, but the teams now had their marching orders and were ready to move forward.

Groaning, she kicked off the patent leather heels that had been torturing her feet all day and massaged her toes. If this was what her life was going to be like from now on she was going to have to invest in some more practical shoes.

And some protein bars, if the tormented sounds issuing from her empty stomach were any indication.

She was seriously considering eating the wizened apple she'd found at the back of a drawer when Mark walked in, carrying a delicious-smelling pizza.

"Dinner is served, my lady," he said, presenting it to her with a flourish.

Becky tore open the box and grabbed a slice of the pepperoni-studded goodness. "It's official," she said, practically moaning as the heavenly mixture of cheese, tomato sauce and bread hit her tastebuds. "You are my hero."

"I try," he said, snagging a piece for himself. "Some days it's easier than others."

They chewed in companionable silence.

"What do you think?" he eventually said. "Can we pull this off?"

"'This' meaning…?"

"The pitch. Three weeks isn't a lot of time to finish everything you proposed."

"Oh. Well, yeah, of course we can. Especially since we've got an entire department of talented people at our disposal."

"That does help," he said between bites. "I've never experienced this level of support before. I'm usually the guy they bring in to salvage a project that's gone off the rails or save an account that's in danger. No one ever really *wants* to work with me."

She thought that sounded kind of lonely, but didn't think he'd appreciate it if she told him so. "It is a pretty unique thing you do. How on earth did you end up being a modern-day dragon slayer?"

"I'm not sure. Just luck, I guess."

"That's some luck you have. You've worked with some of the best agencies out there," she said, eyebrows raised.

"Yeah, well, I've got some connections. It's all about who you know in this business," he said, looking off into the distance.

The sour look on his face was one she'd seen only once before.

"Let me guess. The stepdad?"

"The one and only." Mark grimaced. "He'd do just about anything to keep me out of his house and away from his wife."

"What does he do, anyway?" For some reason, Becky

imagined Mark's stepdad as being some kind of modern-day nobility, living off his inheritance and not doing much of anything.

"You've heard of Kipper, Vonner and Schmidt?"

She snorted. "Of course. They're only the largest ad agency in New York."

"My stepdad's the Kipper. And he bought out Vonner."

"Oh," Becky said, trying not to be impressed. "I guess he *would* have connections."

"Yep. He's the only reason I ever got any work. At least to begin with."

Becky was willing to bet there was more to the story than that. But she wasn't in the mood to push.

"Well, connections or no, you're really good at what you do—at least according to the internet. You've got almost as many awards as I do."

"Ah, so you cared enough to look me up, huh?

"Of course. You didn't think I'd let you back into my pants without making sure you weren't a serial killer first, did you?"

"I wasn't aware that you'd put much thought into the situation at all."

She lowered her eyes, suddenly unable to meet his penetrating gaze. "Well, I may have done it post-pants-getting-into. Last night."

"I see. And what did you decide?"

She smiled. "Well, it was quite a debate. On the one hand, you're great for stress relief."

"Sure—I'll buy that."

"But you're bad for the rep. I had an ice-queen thing going, you know."

"Well, it's too late to save her," he teased. "I distinctly remember seeing her melt Saturday afternoon."

"You might be right. But I was a little worried I might lose my competitive advantage by sleeping with you."

"A valid concern."

"But then I realized engaging in pillow talk is a great way to gather intel."

"True enough."

"There's also the brain goo problem."

"Brain goo?"

"Yeah, when I'm around you and start thinking about what we could do to each other my brain turns to goo."

"Oh," he said, looking devilishly pleased. "Well, that's a good problem to have."

"It is. Especially since the best way to fix it is to do the things I'm thinking about."

"Which means…?"

"Which means you should probably stock up on condoms. I have a very good imagination."

He grinned. "I already did."

"Good. Because you know what I'd like to do right now?"

"What?"

"Have sex in an elevator."

"Did you just…? You want to have…?"

"Sex in an elevator. Yes. It was all I could think about on the way down from David's office this morning."

He shot up from his chair, excitement and desire dancing in his eyes. "Let's go, then. I wouldn't want your brain to be clogged with goo any longer than it needs to be."

A short time later, Becky hit the lobby button so their elevator could resume its descent. Her brain was magnificently clear—and her thighs were wonderfully achy.

Elevator sex was much more acrobatic than it looked in the movies. If Mark hadn't been so wonderfully strong it wouldn't have been possible at all.

Becky peeked over at the man in question just in time to see him rubbing his biceps.

"I guess you got your workout for the day, huh?"

He smiled at her ruefully. "I think I did. Totally worth it, though."

Feeling strangely shy now that the deed was over, Becky blushed and looked up at the ceiling to avoid his eyes—only to find herself looking at a different kind of lens.

"Oh, crap," she breathed. "There's a camera up there."

Mark's jaw dropped. "What are you talking about?"

She pointed. "There's a camera. In the ceiling."

"Oh, well…" he said.

"*Oh, well?* I tell you we were just filmed having sex and you say, *Oh, well?*" she squeaked.

"Becky, look at me," Mark said.

Reluctantly, she did. The intensity in his gaze was almost too much to bear.

"I'm not ashamed of what we've done here. If someone wants to watch, let them," he said. "Besides, no one ever looks at those tapes unless there's a robbery or something."

Looking into the bottomless pits that were his eyes as she was, she couldn't doubt his sincerity. He meant what he was saying. Deciding there was nothing she could do about it anyway, Becky nodded.

"I guess you're right," she said, and reached up for one last kiss.

Just then the elevator bell dinged.

"Well, I guess that puts an end to the evening's festivities," Becky said as she pulled away and stepped out through the open doors into the marble lobby.

"It doesn't have to," Mark replied. "You could come home with me."

For a brief moment Becky found herself wondering what it would be like to fall asleep in his arms. Heaven, probably. Better not to think about it.

"Nah, I don't think so," she said, wrapping her arms tightly around herself. "I'll leave you to your dreams.

They're bound to be steamier than anything I can come up with."

Mark let out a bark of laughter as he held the glass door open for her. "This from the woman who just propositioned me with elevator sex? I don't think you give yourself enough credit, my dear."

"Well," she said as she breezed past him, "I guess it's up to you to top my idea, then. Better put your thinking cap on."

Blowing him a kiss, she strode off into the dark night, waiting until he was out of earshot to give in to the hysterical giggles that were bubbling at the back of her throat. Her sex-kitten act was going to need work if they kept this up very long.

Mark collapsed into the black leather massage chair in the creative conference room and closed his eyes, groaning out loud when the vibrating knobs found the tight spot between his shoulder blades.

It had been another long day spent in meetings and reviewing his team's work. He and Becky hadn't even had a chance to think about their own assignments.

This creative directing stuff was hard.

He was just starting to relax, the tension in his back mostly gone, when his phone rang. When he saw who it was he groaned again. His stepfather always had had impeccable timing.

Mentally steeling himself for a lecture, he hit the answer button.

"Hi, Bill."

There was a pause as the man on the other side of the line took a sip from a clinking glass. "Hello, son."

Mark cringed. He hated it when Bill called him that.

"What can I do for you, Bill?"

"Oh, nothing…nothing. Just checking in to see how the Eden thing is going."

"You know about that?"

His stepfather snorted. "Of course. I know everything that's going on in this industry, son. So, have you closed the deal yet?"

Mark sighed. "No, we haven't even gotten to the pitch stage yet. But it's going very well. In fact, I'm acting as creative director on the campaign…"

"That's right. You and that Becky girl. I hear she's pretty hot stuff."

"You have no idea," Mark said.

"Yeah, well, you'll keep your hands to yourself if you know what's good for you," Bill said. "It's never a good idea to mix business with pleasure."

Now it was Mark's turn to snort. "Is that what you told my mom? I seem to remember she worked for you before she married you. Unless that was a business arrangement too…"

"Just keep your hands where they belong and do this right," Bill snapped. "Our family's reputation is on the line here."

"How do you figure? I never tell anyone we're related unless I have to."

"Maybe so. But the ad world is a small place. Those who matter know you're my son."

"Stepson," he snarled. "As you never failed to remind me when I was living under your roof."

"Yes, well, that was then. This is now. There's a place for you at my agency anytime you want it. Especially if you can bring—"

"I assure you, I never will," Mark broke in, and hung up.

He couldn't take any more of his stepfather's asinine advice today. Although he had deflected the question, Mark knew that love had very little to do with Bill's marriage to his mother. She had told him so herself—on their wedding day.

He had found her pinning a flower in her hair in her opulent palace of a bedroom at Bill's house. She'd looked more beautiful than he'd ever seen her.

She'd seen him in the reflection of her mirror and smiled. "Come here, handsome," she'd said. "Let me look at you."

He'd moved to hug her, then asked the question that had been driving him crazy ever since he'd heard about their engagement.

"Mom? Why are you marrying Bill?"

"Because he asked me to," she'd answered.

"But you don't love him."

"I don't have time to wait for love," she'd said as she straightened the gray-and-white striped tie of his morning suit. "I'm not getting any younger, but you *are* getting older. And more expensive. This way I'll have a partner I can count on—and you'll have a father."

"But I don't want him to be my dad," Mark had said. "He doesn't even like me."

"He does, too. He just doesn't know you very well. Be your usual charming self and everything will be fine," his mother had said.

She couldn't have been more wrong. Bill had never shown him anything other than complete and utter disdain. Mark was sure that his stepfather considered him to be nothing more than an annoyance—a piece of unwanted baggage that unfortunately could not be parted from his wife.

He would have been better off growing up poor and fatherless.

Suddenly a soft hand landed on his shoulder.

"You look lost in thought," Becky said.

Mark shook his head to clear it. "Just relaxing," he said, and pulled her down on his lap.

She put her head on his shoulder and for a moment they just sat together, the vibrations from the still-operating massage chair the only noise.

Then she sighed. "Being a creative director is way less fun than I thought it would be."

He laughed. "You know, I was just thinking that. I haven't done any actual work today, but I'm completely exhausted."

"Me, too," she said. "But I was thinking I should try to write now that it's quiet."

She shifted on his lap, preparing to get up. But when Mark caught a glimpse of a black lace stocking as her skirt crept up her thigh all thoughts of work vanished from his brain.

"What's this?" he said, running his hand up the silken material and under the lace top.

"Oh, you know... Just a little something to keep you wondering," she said, blushing.

"Oh, I'm wondering, all right," Mark growled, mentally picturing her riding him wearing only those stockings. "I'm wondering what else is under that skirt."

She shrugged. "A lady never tells. You'll have to find out for yourself."

That was all the encouragement he needed. He let his hand wander up her smooth thigh, tracing the elastic of the garter up to where it met the satiny belt. Then his hand drifted down, toward the middle, looking for the top of her panties. But nothing blocked his way, and soon he felt the soft roundness of her mound under his fingers.

"You're not wearing any underwear," he said, and a bolt of lightning struck his groin, leaving him rock hard and aching for her.

She put a mocking hand over her mouth, unable to hide her grin. "Oops, I must have forgotten. Silly me."

"You. Are. So. Hot," he said, stroking her bare center and grinning when he saw her expression liquefy.

He plunged one finger slowly into her core, enjoying teasing her. But it wasn't enough. He knew he had to have her.

He drew his finger out and nipped her ear. "Stand up for me, Gorgeous Girl."

She did, her legs shaking the tiniest of bits.

"I'm standing," she said, her voice husky with desire. "Now what?"

Mark remembered where they were and paused. "Hang on just a second," he said, and pushed a chair under the door handle. It wouldn't do to have one of the cleaning people walk in on them.

Crossing the floor in two strides, he returned to where Becky was standing, looking beautiful and unsure. "Now, where were we?" he growled.

She smiled. "I think you were trying to get a better look at my stockings."

"Oh, yeah." He grinned. Reaching behind her, he pulled her zipper down and her gray wool skirt fell to the floor, leaving her wearing only the stockings and heels on her bottom half. He paused, taking a moment to appreciate the perfection of her body. Overcome with a fierce sort of want he couldn't remember ever feeling before, he pulled her toward him.

"I want you right here, right now," he said, sitting down again.

"In the chair?"

"You better believe it," he said, freeing himself from his pants and boxers as quickly as he could. "Get over here."

Smiling, she straddled him, plunging on top of him the second he had a condom on. They both groaned, and Mark grabbed her hips, helping her to find her rhythm. He'd never met a woman who fit him so perfectly. So deliciously. If only relationships depended solely on sexual compatibility…

In no time at all she was arching backward, pushing her breasts into his face as she rocked. He kissed the tender swell of them, feeling grateful that such an amazing woman was giving herself to him.

To show her exactly how grateful he was, he slipped a finger into the place where their bodies met, searching for the nub that brought her so much pleasure.

"Oh, God, I think I'm—"

The last bit of her sentence became a wordless yell as she spasmed over him. Seconds later, he allowed himself to follow her over the edge.

She collapsed on top of him and they sat quietly, catching their breath. Just then, his stepfather's unwanted voice echoed in his head. *Keep your hands to yourself if you know what's good for you.*

Clearly the man had no idea what he was talking about. Nothing could be better for him than this. If there was a more satisfying way to relieve stress he'd yet to find it.

Kissing her neck, he said, "I want to do that again."

"Already?" She laughed. "Give a girl a moment to recover."

"Not here. I want to take you home and love you properly."

She bit her lip, clearly trying to think of an excuse not to go.

Taking her head in his hands, he looked deep into her eyes. "Don't overthink it. I just want to spread you out on a bed and do you right. Just this once."

"All right. But just this once."

CHAPTER SIX

BECKY COLLAPSED ONTO a fluffy white pillow, letting out a deep breath as her heart rate returned to normal.

"I've said it before, and I'm sure I'll say it again, but you really are Magic Man," she said. "I can't remember the last time I felt this relaxed."

Mark raised himself up on one elbow and grinned. "Glad to be of service," he said. "Think I should go into business?"

Becky giggled. "Sure—I can picture the ad now. It could read something like, 'Forget the massage. Spend an hour with the Magic Man.' And there'd be a picture of you, wearing nothing but a top hat and holding a wand."

He groaned. "Don't quit your day job, babe."

At the mention of work Becky felt some of the tension return. "Day job? Try twenty-four-seven job. I never stop thinking about the pitch. Do you?"

"Only when I'm otherwise occupied by you," Mark said, eyes smiling. "Hey, think we could work orgasmic sex into the Eden campaign?"

Becky laughed as her stomach growled. "I don't know. I'm too hungry to think. But maybe if you feed me I'll think of a way."

Pulling on his boxers, Mark said, "Message received. Let me see what I can rustle up."

As he padded the short distance over the hardwood floor to the kitchen area Becky couldn't help but admire the gorgeous contours of his muscled body. He was by far the best-looking man she'd ever slept with—not that there'd been that many.

She hadn't had time for boys in high school, and had spent her undergrad years being too afraid of making the same mistake her mother had—dropping out of college to get married—to allow herself to have any real relationships.

In fact, other than a few drunken encounters, there hadn't been anyone until Pence. And there certainly hadn't been anyone after him.

She sighed. What a waste of a decade. If Mark had taught her anything, it was that sex could be lots of fun—especially when there were no strings attached.

Mark's voice brought her out of her reverie. "What do you want? Chinese, Thai, or pizza?"

She blinked. "You have enough stuff in that tiny refrigerator to make all of that?" It didn't look big enough to house much more than a six-pack of beer.

"Nope. I've got exactly five green olives, two hunks of moldy cheese, and one gallon of expired milk. We're getting takeout."

"Oh. Thai, I guess," she answered, leaving her cozy nest on the futon to peek at the menus he was holding out. He pulled her against his chest so they could look at the menus together, but all she could think about was the delicious way he smelled: a little bit spicy, a little bit outdoorsy, and all male.

Suddenly an idea struck her. "Maybe we could work orgasms into the campaign," she said.

"What?"

"Orgasms. Eden. I bet we could do some funny videos linking them."

He blinked. "I thought you had to eat before you could have any more brilliant ideas?"

"Yeah, well, get me some of that pineapple curry and I'll be even more brilliant," she answered.

"Coming right up," he said, and punched the number into his phone.

* * *

A couple of hours later the block of granite that did double duty as a table and a kitchen counter was littered with take-out boxes and crumpled sheets of paper.

Becky yawned and stretched. "I think we've got some pretty solid scripts here, don't you?"

"I think we've got some award-winners here—that's what I think," Mark said.

"Me, too," she said, yawning again. "Which is good, because it's definitely time for me to go home."

Mark glanced up at the clock on the microwave. "It's practically morning already. Why don't you just stay?"

A small ping of alarm sounded in her brain. Coming over for a quick hookup was one thing. Staying overnight was definitely relationship territory.

"Two o'clock is hardly morning," she said. "Besides, we've got work tomorrow. I'd rather not be seen wearing the same clothes two days in a row."

"Nobody will notice," he said, his voice softly cajoling.

"No? Not any of the fifty bazillion people I have meetings with tomorrow? I think they will."

"Well, you could always stop at home in the morning. Before going to work."

"I've got an eight a.m. meeting. No time." It was just supposed to be a quick gab with Jessie at the diner. But she'd put it on her calendar, so it counted.

Mark looked at her for a long moment. She wasn't sure what he saw, but finally he sighed and looked away.

"Fine. I'll call you a cab."

"I can walk."

"No. You can't. Not at this hour."

"Really. I can!"

"Just let me do it, okay? I'll worry about you otherwise."

She shut her mouth with a snap, unsure of what to say.

No one had worried about her in a long time. It felt good to know that he cared.

But he wasn't supposed to care. And neither was she. Caring led to relationships, which led to heartbreak—and she was sure as hell never going through that again.

"Okay," she mumbled. "Call me a cab. I'll go get dressed."

Becky poured milk into her coffee and watched the cheerful chaos that was morning in the diner, waiting for Jessie to digest what she'd told her.

"So you went to his place? Big deal," Jessie said, leaning back against the red vinyl booth.

"I thought you said that was out of bounds in office affairs?" she answered.

Jessie shrugged. "I just said that to make you feel better. Think about it: most people have to have sex in their homes. We don't all have a private office to escape to when we decide we're in the mood for a booty call."

"We've only actually done it in our office once…"

Jessie covered her ears. "*Eww.* That's enough. I don't want to know where else you guys have been. I have to work there, too, you know."

"All right, all right, I won't tell you. It's just that, well, it feels safe at work. Once we venture beyond the building it all starts to feel too relationshippy," Becky said.

Just then Rachel, their favorite waitress, arrived and slammed down their pancakes. "Here you go, ladies! Two pancake short stacks, just like usual. Enjoy!"

"Thank you, Rachel," Becky said.

"No problem," the matronly woman said. "Eat up. You're getting too skinny!"

Both women were silent as they buttered the stacks and dived in. After the first bite, Jessie pointed at Becky with her fork.

"You know what your problem is?"

"What?"

"You're overthinking it. This thing with Mark is just like the stack of pancakes in front of you. They're gorgeous to behold, delicious to experience, but when you've had enough you won't be sad, will you?"

Becky shook her head.

"Exactly. You'll enjoy your post-pancake carb coma and forget about them. Until the next time you get a craving."

With that she took another giant bite and grinned. "These are really yummy."

Becky laughed. She had a point.

"I don't think he'd like being compared to pancakes."

Jessie raised an eyebrow. "You don't think he'd like you to eat him up?"

"I don't know. Maybe I'll ask him."

"Good girl. But mind if I give you a tip?"

"What?"

"Don't use maple syrup in bed. Too sticky."

Becky blushed. "I'll try to remember that."

And just like that everything was right in her world again. She wasn't having a relationship. She was just enjoying a good breakfast after a long fast.

That she could deal with.

Mark hovered at the door to their office, afraid to go in. After Becky had left his apartment he'd tossed and turned all night.

It had been a great evening. He'd enjoyed every second of it. The sex, the food, the brainstorming…he'd never experienced anything like it. He certainly hadn't wanted it to end.

But when he'd realized how much it mattered to him that Becky got home safely—and how much he'd rather she didn't leave at all—reality had crashed in. He'd never worried about any of his other bedmates like that. In fact he was usually the one rushing them out through the door.

After Mark had seen her into a cab he'd collapsed into bed, but sleep had been the furthest thing from his mind. All he'd been able to think about was Becky. He could no longer pretend this was a simple office affair. He was starting to have feelings for this woman. Big feelings. And that was no good.

He didn't do relationships. Period. And even if he did want a relationship he couldn't have one with Becky. It was just too complicated.

It had been almost time to go to work when he'd finally faced the truth. As much as he was enjoying their time together, he had to put a stop to it. If he didn't, both he and Becky were going to get hurt.

No matter how cool Becky seemed, he couldn't take a chance on her. Sandra had taught him that love wasn't worth the pain.

Besides, she deserved someone who had enough money to take care of her. Not someone who had voluntarily cut himself off from his rich family's largesse.

Taking a deep breath, he walked through the door. And stopped dead. Becky was sitting cross-legged on the floor in a patch of sunshine, laptop perched precariously on her knees. She was jamming to something on her iPhone, humming tunelessly along to whatever song was piping through her headphones.

She looked relaxed and happy, which was a far cry from the stressed-out ball of nerves he had expected to encounter this morning.

He must have made some kind of noise because she turned. When she saw him she smiled, the grin lighting up her whole face.

It took his breath away. God, she was beautiful.

"Hey, Magic Man," she shouted, clearly not realizing her headphones were in.

He laughed in spite of himself, motioning to her to take them out.

"What?" she yelled. "Oh." Giggling, she removed her headphones. "Oh. That is better," she said, unwinding herself from her spot on the floor. "Okay, let's try this again. Good morning, Magic Man."

He smiled back at her. "Good morning."

She crossed over to him and reached up for a kiss. At the last minute he turned his cheek.

She frowned. "What's with the shy act?"

He shrugged. "I just think we should cool it during office hours."

"You do, huh? That's a first. But whatever…"

She turned and went to her desk, but not before he saw the hurt that flashed across her face.

"I've got our scripts all typed up and polished. If you want, we can go present them to David now."

He took a deep breath, knowing that if he didn't tell her what he had come to say now he never would.

"Good idea. But can we talk for a minute first?"

"Okay," she said. "This sounds serious. What's up?"

"I don't think this is a good idea anymore," he blurted.

"You don't like the campaign?"

"No, I meant this," he said, motioning to the two of them. "Us. I don't think we should pursue a personal relationship anymore."

She blinked slowly. "Wow. Okay, that's a change in tune. May I ask what prompted it?"

He shrugged again. "There's just too much going on right now. We need to focus on the task at hand."

It wasn't a lie. He definitely did need to focus on his career right now. And so did she. The fact that doing so would keep all those pesky feelings at bay was just a fringe benefit.

"I thought we decided that the best way to stay focused was to give in to our personal desires," she said, in the same carefully professional voice he had used.

"I changed my mind," he said.

She shook her head as her face flushed with anger. "You're a piece of work—you know that? First you come on all hot and heavy, begging me to give this a shot, telling me how much fun we'll have, and then, just when I'm starting to enjoy myself, you pull the plug."

"I'm sorry," he said, fighting the urge to grab her in his arms and kiss her until she forgot all about this conversation.

"I should have known better than to trust you to keep your word," she snarled. "You're a selfish bastard, just like every man I've ever known."

Grabbing her computer, she headed for the door.

"Where are you going?"

"To my office. I can't stand to look at you right now."

"This *is* your office."

"Fine. I'm going to Jessie's office, then."

"What about the scripts?"

"I'll email them to you. You can present them to David by yourself."

Then she swept out, slamming the door behind her.

Mark scrubbed his face with his hands, fairly certain he'd made a gigantic mess of things. But at least he'd done it before anyone's heart had gotten involved.

That would have been even worse.

Becky sat nursing a cup of tea in the kitchen, keeping an ear cocked toward the hallway door so she could escape out the back way if necessary. So far she'd managed to avoid Mark for three days, and she had every intention of continuing the trend.

It had been easy enough to do. She'd kept herself busy managing the print and digital teams, and let him take the lead on the broadcast stuff.

It pained her to give up control of her ideas, but the only other option was to sit in a room with him and wonder what she had done to turn him off. And, worse, what it was about her that made men want to run—even when all she wanted was sex.

Her instincts had been right. She was better off without a man in her life, even if the sex was awesome. There were enough adult sites selling sex toys to keep her satisfied for decades—no emotional entanglements required.

The only thing they couldn't do was make her laugh. But as long as Jon Stewart and Stephen Colbert continued to make their nightly TV appearances she'd have plenty of funny men in her life. It would have to be enough.

She was debating whether she should make a second cup of coffee when she heard a familiar roar in the hallway.

"Becky? Becky, where are you?" David shouted. Then, only slightly more quietly, "Just like a woman. Never around when you need her."

She slammed her cup down and strode out into the hallway.

"I'm right here," she said.

He turned, a slippery smile on his face. "Oh, there you are. I've been looking everywhere for you."

"Well, I've been sitting in the kitchen for the last twenty minutes, so…"

"Never mind, never mind—you're here now. Come with me, my dear. We need you in the production studio."

"All right," she said as they hurried down the hallway. "What's going on?"

"It's these videos," he said, holding the door open for her.

"They were brilliant on paper, but they're just not coming together. I want you to have a look."

She stopped just inside the door, waiting for her eyes to adjust to the darkness of the room. When her vision returned she saw Mark frowning into one of the eight monitors, unhappiness etched into every line of his face.

He glanced in their direction, and when he caught sight of her she was pretty sure she saw a relieved expression cross his face.

"Hey," he said.

"Hey, yourself," she said. "What did you do to our videos? I hear they lost their magic."

He ignored the dig.

"I'm not sure. Take a look and tell me what you think."

He hit a button on the keyboard and the videos began to play. Becky tried to pay attention, but found herself getting distracted by the man next to her. She could feel the heat coming from him like a physical thing. It called to her, drawing her in like a moth to a flame.

What *was* it about this man? Why did the very sight of him turn her knees to jelly? It wasn't fair. Especially since he didn't seem to feel the same way.

"So what do you think?" he asked, and she realized the videos had stopped playing.

"I'm not sure. Play them again." This time she would actually watch them.

The problem became apparent almost immediately, but she let the reel play to the end before she gave her opinion.

"It's simple. The actress you hired thinks she's in a porn movie. She doesn't appear to have a funny bone in her body. And those boobs make her look like Jessica Rabbit. The women in these videos are supposed to be way more real and way funnier."

"So what do you think we should do?" Mark asked.

"Start over."

"What?" David yelled. "We can't do that. We've already spent too much. We can't hire another actress."

"We have to," Becky snapped. "These videos are what's going to make people remember Eden. We can run all the polished TV ads we want, but if we don't find a way to connect with people, to entertain them and get them talking—well, Eden's just going to end up being another yogurt in the refrigerator case. And we're going to end up fired."

"But we don't even have the business yet! I can't possibly put up the money to do a whole new shoot—the first one cost almost fifty thousand dollars!"

Mark looked at her, a silent plea in his eyes. She thought about the night they had scripted them. About how excited he'd been. And how badly she wanted to win this account. She made the only decision she could.

"Fine. I'll do it," Becky blurted.

"You'll what?"

"I'll be your actress…but only for the version we show at the pitch. It's either that or we scrap the whole idea. We certainly can't show these to the client."

David and Mark stared at her, plainly flabbergasted.

"Are you sure you want to do that?" Mark asked.

"No, but I will. Just as long as we all understand that if they like them and want to go ahead with the video campaign, we make them give us the budget to shoot them with real actresses—actresses that I choose."

"Do you think you can pull it off?" David asked.

"Oh, I'm fairly certain I can."

"How certain?"

"Very. I can fake an orgasm right now if you want me to prove it."

David blanched. "No! No, that won't be necessary. I trust you. Just get it done. Quickly."

Then he scrabbled backward out through the door as quickly as he could.

Mark looked at her. "I guess it's just you and me, kid."

"Yep. I guess so," she said, trying to ignore the way her pulse was pounding.

"I've missed you."

He'd missed her? He'd *missed* her? How dared he...? It was his fault they'd been apart in the first place.

"Good," she said. No way was she going to admit that she'd missed him, too.

He looked at her, a rueful smile on his face. "I guess I deserved that," he said.

She nodded. "Yep. You did. But never mind that. We've got a video series to film. When do you want to start?"

He sighed. "Well, unfortunately the camera crew we used the first time has moved on to another project, and I'm not sure where to get another one on such short notice."

"Camera crew? Who needs a camera crew? We're both professionals. Let's just do it ourselves."

He raised an eyebrow. "Seriously? You think we can?"

"I don't know if you've seen the agency equipment closet, but we've got some pretty sweet cameras. As long as you can push a button we'll be fine."

"Okay," he said. "You're on. I'll book a room and we can start filming tonight."

Her mind stuttered. "A room?"

"A hotel room, silly. That's how you scripted it, remember?"

Oh. Yeah. She had. But she wasn't sure she felt comfortable being alone in a hotel room with Mark now that their relationship was back to being strictly professional.

Unfortunately she had already volunteered. She couldn't back out now.

"Right," she said. "That makes sense. Okay, you set it up and email me the details. I'll meet you there at seven."

Becky decided to spend the rest of the afternoon getting herself camera-ready. While she'd told David she wanted the videos to look real, she didn't need the client to see her in her current frazzled, haven't-looked-in-a-mirror-in-four-days state.

After three hours at the salon, getting her hair blown out, eyebrows waxed, nails manicured and face professionally made up, she was feeling much better.

Especially since she had every intention of billing it all to the agency. Now all she needed was a few outfit changes and she'd be all set. The scripts she'd written called for both yoga pants and exotic lingerie.

The yoga pants she had. But the other scenes called for a visit to her favorite lingerie boutique. She hoped David had been billing their clients regularly, because this trip was going to cost him.

She wandered around the store, looking at frilly pink confections, slinky red gowns, and black lace fantasies, unable to decide which would be best. Finally she decided to just try them all on.

Once in the fitting room, she was struck by an idea that she knew was both awesome and completely evil. Since she couldn't decide what to buy, she'd snap pics and send them to Mark.

After all, he was the art director. It was only fitting that he be in charge of wardrobe. Before she could talk herself out of it Becky took a picture of herself in a slinky red gown and composed a message to send to Mark.

Can't decide what wardrobe choices to buy for the shoot, she texted. Should I get this one?

After hitting Send, she quickly changed into the next outfit and prepared to repeat the exercise. But before she could even take the picture, her phone pinged with Mark's return text.

Hell, yes.

She grinned and sent the next picture.

How about this?

Please do.

After sending the third picture, she sat back and admired her reflection. The push-up cups in the black lace chemise made her breasts look huge…making her waist look tiny by comparison. Her hair was thicker than she'd ever seen it, and her face practically glowed under the makeup.

She might not be a porn star, but she looked pretty damn good.

Finally, her phone pinged.

GET THEM ALL, his text read.

Her veins buzzed with triumph. Hopefully, he was sincerely regretting his hasty decision to end the physical side of their relationship right now. He certainly would be by the time the night was over if she had anything to say about it.

CHAPTER SEVEN

MARK DRUMMED HIS fingers impatiently on the glass table-top. Everything was ready for the shoot. Now all he needed was for his talent to show up. Hopefully with her clothes on.

He'd chosen to rent a suite instead of a hotel room. He'd told himself that it was so they'd have plenty of space to set up their equipment, but if he was being honest he knew it was so he'd have somewhere to retreat if the temptation to touch her got to be too much.

Lord knew the pictures she'd sent this afternoon had been enough to get him rock hard. She looked like something out of his fantasies, her innocently mischievous expression contrasting wildly with the siren's body underneath. He was certain better men than him would fall victim to the silent promise in every pixel of those images.

But he wouldn't. Couldn't.

If he touched her again he wouldn't be able to stop. And if he didn't stop touching her, their hearts would get involved. And then, if he wasn't careful, he'd find himself with a life full of... His mind showed him pictures of weddings and babies and laughing families. But he shook his head, rejecting the images.

It would all end in heartbreak. Even if they made it to the altar, love never lasted. She'd get bored, find someone better and wealthier, and he'd end up crushed. It was better not to go there in the first place.

He jumped at the sudden knock on the door.

Becky had arrived. After taking a moment to push all

his inappropriate emotions back into the box where they belonged, Mark opened the door.

And felt lust roaring to life all over again.

Gone was the fresh-faced woman he worked with. In her place was a primped and polished beauty who looked as if she'd just stepped out of a magazine cover.

"Wow," was all he could say.

She raised her eyebrow. "Is that your new version of hello?"

"No. Sorry. Come in. It's just…you look fantastic."

"Well, it's not every day I find myself starring in an advert," she said as she breezed past him. "I thought I should look the part."

Once inside the door, she stopped dead and whistled.

"Whoa! When you do something, you don't believe in going halfway, do you?"

The suite *was* pretty spectacular. Dark mahogany wood covered the floor and supported the sky-high ceiling. The bed was king-size and ultraplush, with what seemed to be a mountain of fluffy blankets and pillows piled on top. Through a door to the right there was a kitchen area that gleamed with stainless steel appliances and sparkling granite counters. At the back, just in front of the two-story-tall windows, was a living area outfitted with a white leather couch and vivid red club chairs. And, although Becky couldn't see it, Mark knew she'd die when she saw the bathroom. It had a tub big enough to swim in, a two-person shower, and more complimentary beauty products than he'd ever seen.

"Well, you know… This is on the company. I figured why settle for anything less than the best?" he said, grinning.

She laughed. "We're on the same wavelength, then. I don't even want to tell you how much I spent in the lingerie store."

A strange kind of hunger growled to life in the pit of his stomach. "Well, if the pictures you sent were any indication, I'd say whatever you spent was well worth the cost."

"Well," she said with a wicked smile, "you'll be seeing them in the flesh in just a few minutes. Where do you think we should start?"

The bed. That was where he wanted to start...and finish. But only if he was in it with her. Unfortunately, that was the one place he couldn't go.

"Maybe we should tackle the 'before' parts of the skits first, then tackle the 'after.' That way you don't have to keep changing back and forth."

Plus, that way, he wouldn't have to see her in that sexy lingerie for a while.

"Okay," she said. "Why don't you get set up? I'll get changed."

He nodded, wondering if he should take a cold shower or slam his hand in a drawer or something while she was gone. He needed to do something drastic or there would be no way to keep his libido under control.

Three hours later they were done with every yoga-panted scenario the scripts called for, plus a few more Mark had thrown in just for good measure. It was time to move on to the sexy stuff.

God help him.

He busied himself setting up lights in the bedroom area, telling himself that it was no big deal. After all, the woman who'd been their lead actress in the first version of these videos had been a bona fide porn star.

He'd made it through *that* shoot with barely more than a tingle in his nether regions. Surely he could do the same now? It might be Becky playing the part, but it was still business. Sex had no place here.

None.

"All right, I'm ready," Becky called from somewhere behind him. "Where do you want me?"

Mark turned, his most professional smile on his face. "Did you remember to bring the yogurt con…?"

The sentence trailed off as his mind registered what Becky was wearing. She looked like sin made flesh. Her blond curls tumbled over shoulders covered only by a pair of spaghetti-thin red satin straps.

His eyes traveled farther down, noticing that the straps led to a slinky red gown that made the most of Becky's perfectly mounded breasts, begging him to touch them. Then it followed the contours of her itty-bitty waist before splitting into a thigh-high slit.

The leg that peeked through was wrapped in a matching red fishnet stocking, and was made to look all the longer by the spiky cheetah-print stilettos.

"Hey, I remember those shoes," he said, cursing himself for his stupidity the moment the words were out of his mouth.

She laughed. "Yeah, I figured I was spending enough of David's money without going shoe shopping, too. And these babies certainly had the desired effect the first time around."

Inwardly he groaned, remembering that first night. He hadn't thought she could possibly look any hotter than she had when he'd met her in Vegas. He'd been wrong.

"You look amazing," he said. There. That was innocent enough. He was just giving the lady her due. She didn't need to know how very close he was to ripping those amazing clothes off her body and throwing her on the bed.

She grinned happily and did a pirouette.

"I know. I really should buy things like this more often. It does wonderful things for a girl's self-confidence."

Then she swished over to the bed, crossing her legs seductively after she dropped onto its surface.

"In answer to your earlier unasked question—yes, I did bring the yogurt container. And now I am prepared to do nasty things with this spoon," she said, holding out her intended weapon.

Mark watched helplessly as she brought it to her lips and licked it seductively, then plunged it deep into her mouth. Throwing her head back, she pulled it slowly out, then traced it down her neck to linger at the top of her breasts.

Mark groaned involuntarily, every muscle in his body aching with the need to kiss her everywhere the spoon had touched—and in many places it hadn't.

Her head popped up and she grinned.

"Guess I'm doing that right, huh?"

"I'd say. You may have missed your calling as a porn star."

Her nose wrinkled. "Nah. Too many scary dudes. But maybe I could moonlight as a pinup girl. At, like, an ice cream parlor or something. Ice cream really does make me hot."

He laughed. It was good to know that the Becky he knew was still in there somewhere.

"All right, let's not get ahead of ourselves," he said. "First we've got to make you a video star."

She nodded. "Okay, let's do it."

"So, in one script you have yourself taking a bite while in bed, then having a screaming orgasm. Want to start there?"

She blushed. "Um…let's start with something tamer, shall we? I think I need to work up to that."

"Okay," he said, flipping through script pages. "Well, that thing you were just doing there was pretty close to what you've got here. But at the end you've got to call to your husband and tell him to—and I quote—'Get in here and take care of business.'"

"Right," she said, a worried look on her face. "That seemed like a much better idea when someone else was doing it, but what the hell? I said I wanted this to seem sexy and real and kind of funny, right? I can do funny sexy stuff. I'm almost sure of it."

"Based on what I just saw, I have absolute faith in you," he said. "Let's give it a try. Ready?"

"Just a minute," she said, and paused to plump her hair and her breasts. "How's my lipstick?"

"It's...fine," he said, although it took everything he had to tear his eyes from her chest.

"Good. Let's do it."

He nodded and began the countdown. "Three, two, one...action!"

At his signal she began her routine with the spoon again. But this time she added in strategic little whimpers and moans.

Mark felt himself growing hotter and harder as the seconds ticked by. Just when he thought he couldn't take it anymore, she sat straight up in bed.

"David!" she shouted. "Turn off the TV and get in here. I need you to take care of some business!"

The last part was said with a comically suggestive waggle of her eyebrows and Mark just barely managed to shut the camera off before giving in to the gut-deep laughter that was begging for release. "Oh. My. God," he said between laughs. "Did you have to use David's name?"

"You're darn right I did," she said. "Revenge is sweet." But she was smiling as she said it, and soon she was laughing, too.

Mark collapsed on the bed next to her and she let herself sag against him, still giggling. They sat like that for what felt like forever. As soon as one stopped laughing, the other would erupt in a contagious peal and they'd both be off again.

At long last the laughing fit ended and they sat, gasping, trying to catch their breath.

Mark looked in her sparkling green eyes and felt something shift way down deep in his stomach. He'd never met a woman he could laugh like that with before.

Refusing to put a name to the emotion that threatened to make itself known, he kissed her forehead. "I really did miss you, Gorgeous Girl. You're one funny lady."

She jerked back, anger suddenly sparking in her eyes. "Well, I'm glad I can make you laugh, if nothing else," she said.

Whoa. He wasn't sure what he had said that was so wrong, but he definitely wished he hadn't said it. Time to get back to business.

"All righty, then. I guess we should move on, huh?"

"Give me just a minute to change into the next outfit," she said, and clacked angrily out of the room.

Mark took a deep breath. One sexy scene down, three to go. It was going to be a hell of a long night.

Becky slathered on one last coat of crimson lipstick. They were down to the last scene. The faked orgasm scene. The one she was least sure she could pull off.

But the rest of the shoot had gone much better than she'd ever dreamed it would, so there was hope. She looked at her artificially rumpled reflection and took a deep breath. So far she'd done well, both in front of the camera and in the psyche of the man who was trying to resist her. Now all she had to do was bring it home.

This black lace get-up could only help.

She stalked out to the bedroom area, trying to remember exactly how the orgasm scene had gone in *When Harry Met Sally.* Surely it couldn't be that hard?

A low whistle brought her back to the present.

"Damn, Becky, what are you trying to do? Kill me?" Mark asked in a strained voice.

Becky raised her eyebrow. "You're the one who decided

you didn't want to touch me anymore," she said. "So, if you die from what you're seeing here tonight, I'm thinking they'd have to rule it a suicide."

He sighed and waved her over to the bed. "*Touché*. Let's just get this over with, okay?"

As Becky crossed to the bed she swished her hips as much as she was able. Then she spread her golden hair out on the pillows and prepared to play her part.

"Ready?" she called to her reluctant cameraman.

He shook his head. "No. You still look too controlled. Let your limbs go a little."

She tried to let her arms and legs relax, but felt strangely tense under Mark's dark-eyed gaze. "How's this?"

He moved forward. "No. That's not how you look when you're…in the moment. May I touch you?"

She could only nod, her mouth suddenly dry.

Gently he cupped her knees, splaying them apart slightly. The fabric of the black lace chemise fell to the side, revealing the matching panties underneath. Mark's eyes flashed, dark with desire.

"There. That's better. Now, channel your inner porn star."

Feeling too exposed, she moved the chemise so it again covered her fully. Then she looked at Mark from under her eyelashes and smiled as she lifted her hands to cup her breasts.

He hissed in response, then disappeared behind the camera.

"That's the spirit," he said. "I'm going to start the countdown now."

By the time Mark said "action" she was already turned on. She let her eyes flutter closed and sank deep into the alternative reality she wished she was living in right now. The one where Mark abandoned his camera and came to kneel at her side, gently caressing her breasts and stomach before finding his way lower, to the heated mound that hid beneath the black lace of her panties.

She moaned loudly for Mark's benefit and grabbed the yogurt container from the bedside table. Running her hands up and down its smooth surface, she tried to imagine it was Mark's penis she was stroking.

She let her moans come faster as she pictured Mark putting his mouth to work in her hot wet folds, flicking and sucking and bringing her right to the brink…

"Oh, yes," she groaned. "Oh, please. Oh, God…"

She was wondering how much longer she should continue when she felt a rough, masculine hand fumbling with her undies.

Opening her eyes, she saw Mark hovering over her, desire blazing out of his eyes.

"Oh, Mark," she breathed, seeing that victory was within her grasp. "Oh, please. Please make me come."

A primal growl rumbled in his chest as Mark tore the black lace panties off her body. Seconds later he was plunging a finger deep into her core, a ferocious look on his face. Although he was only touching her in that one sensitive place his gaze pinned her down, making her feel strangely, wonderfully helpless. This wasn't a man giving a woman what she wanted. It was a man taking what he needed— and she was happy to give it to him. Feeling the delicious pressure mount inside, she let her knees slide out to the side, giving him even better access.

"Come for me," he said gruffly. "I want to see you do it."

As soon as the words were out of his mouth she felt herself doing exactly that, her body clenching around his hand in an orgasm so intense that it left her shivering and shaking.

Quickly Mark shrugged out of his own clothes and fumbled with a condom, hands shaking as he rolled it on.

Desperate to feel him inside her, she scooted to the edge

of the bed and tried to wrap her legs around him, but he shook his head.

"No. Not that way. Flip," he said, still using that strangely authoritative tone.

She just looked at him, confused.

"Like this," he commanded, rolling her on to her stomach and propping her up on her hands and knees. Becky found herself looking down at the bed, unable to see what was going on behind her. The suspense thrilled in her blood as she waited, her whole body crying out for his touch.

Suddenly she felt his hands on her hips, grabbing the tender skin possessively.

"I want you to feel how deep I can go," he growled from somewhere behind and above her, his manhood nudging at her sensitive folds. "I want you to know that it's me, reaching into the center of you, making you mine."

He slid deep inside her core, burying himself to the hilt. She gasped, loving the feeling of complete possession, wanting him to take even more. He was claiming her, and every cell of her body celebrated, wanting to feel his imprint on her.

She rocked back against him, signaling her silent acceptance. He slammed into her, filling her to capacity, his hard thick length rubbing against all her most sensitive spots, and as he did something primal roared to life inside her. This man was hers, and she was his, in every way that mattered.

He reached down and grabbed her hair in his hands, pulling her head back. "You. Are. Mine," he said, thrusting even harder, and she shattered into a million tiny pieces, her orgasm hitting her more strongly than any ever had.

With a tortured-sounding moan he let himself go, shuddering as he came apart inside her. Then he collapsed sideways on to the bed, their bodies still connected.

She followed him down, breathing hard, trying to wrap

her head around what had just happened. She had intended to get through his defenses and get him to touch her. And, boy, had she succeeded. If only he hadn't managed to get through so many of hers, as well...

Something monumental had happened here tonight. She only hoped she had the strength to cope with whatever came next.

Suddenly exhausted, she closed her eyes and started to drift into sleep.

"I don't think we're going to be able to use that take," a sleepy voice said behind her.

Alarm bells rang in her head. "You filmed that?"

He laughed. "No. Of course not. That would get us both fired."

"Oh. Good," she said and yawned.

"Close your eyes, Sleeping Beauty," he said. "It's time to rest. It'll all still be here in the morning."

That sounded like the best idea she had ever heard.

The next thing she knew it was morning. She yawned and stretched, reaching for the warm male body she knew must still be beside her. Except...it wasn't. His side of the bed was empty and cold.

She sat up, alarmed. "M-Mark?"

Surely he hadn't run again. Not after what had happened last night. "Mark? Are you here?"

For a long moment there was silence and she began to panic. He couldn't be gone. They needed to talk. She needed to make sure none of those last scenes had been captured on film.

"Mark?" she yelled. "Where are you?"

Still nothing.

She was fumbling for her flimsy excuse for a nightgown, swearing quietly to herself, when she heard the suite's door open. "Mark?"

"Yeah, babe. I'm here," he said, coming to stand in the bedroom door. "I just went to get you some coffee. Venti soy, right?"

Relief flooded through her system. "Yep. I'm impressed that you remembered," she said, padding over to where he stood.

He handed her cup to her, then swooped down to give her a tender kiss. "I try to remember everything about the people who are important to me," he said.

Important? She was important to him? That was a switch. Suddenly she felt vaguely ashamed of her behavior the night before.

"Look, I know you didn't want to be physical anymore," she said, looking down. "So if you want to forget what happened last night I understand."

He sighed.

"I couldn't forget it if I wanted to," he said. "Becky, look at me."

Reluctantly, she looked up, expecting to see derision in his eyes. Instead there was only happiness.

"Look, I know I've been an ass. And I don't blame you if you want to forget *me*," he said. "But that's not what I want."

"It's not?" she asked.

"No. Truth is, I did nothing for those three days other than wish I could be with you, and laugh with you, and touch you. I was useless. You had it right all along."

"Well, of course I did," she said, trying to catch up to him. "What was I right about, exactly?"

"There's no harm in what we're doing. We're just making the best of a crazy situation and enjoying ourselves along the way."

"So you want…?"

"I want you. For as long as we're both into it. No strings, like you said. Just fun."

Just fun. That was definitely what she had wanted. But,

remembering the way her heart had flipped the night before, Becky was pretty sure she was getting into deeper waters.

But he didn't need to know that.

"Okay, you're on," she said, injecting a smile into her voice. "But if you freak out on me again, I reserve the right to do serious damage."

He raised an eyebrow. "What kind of damage?"

She gently caressed his penis through his pants, bringing it roaring back to life.

"I'm not going to tell you. Where's the fun in that? But it would be in an area that's precious to you."

She waited for the shocked expression to cross his face, then turned her back.

"Last one in the shower's a rotten egg," she called as she pulled the gown free of her body and headed for the bathroom.

Seconds later, Mark sprinted by. "Nope, last one in the shower's the first to get taken advantage of," he said, laughing.

At that, Becky slowed. She'd never heard a better reason to take her time.

Becky plopped down on to the red vinyl seat across from Jessie, unable to keep the smile from her face.

"Wow, you look happy," Jessie said. "Did Mark suddenly drop out of the competition?"

Becky laughed. "Of course not!"

"Did David finally come to his senses, realize you're the most amazing copywriter who ever lived, and promote you?"

Becky could only snort. "As if."

"Did he have a heart attack and die and leave the agency to you?"

"Who?"

"David, of course," Jessie said. "Who else?"

"Oh," Becky said. "No. Which is good. I wouldn't want someone's death on my conscience. Besides, I want David to have to admit that I'm talented and worthy of promotion before he kicks the bucket. If he doesn't, I may have to chase him into the afterlife."

"All right, then, I give up. Why are you so smiley? Did you forget you have the biggest pitch of your life in less than two weeks?"

"I wish I could," Becky said, scooting to the window side of the booth and stretching her legs out on the seat. "But there's not a chance of that."

Their favorite waitress bustled over with a gap-toothed smile. "Well, if it isn't my two favorite advertising ladies," she said. "You're looking good today."

Becky giggled up at the matronly woman. "Thank you, Rachel. Your uniform looks pretty fetching today, too!"

Rachel cocked an eyebrow at Becky. "You look different," she said. "All glowy and stuff. Are you in love? Are you finally going to bring me some eye candy? We could use some good-looking man flesh to pretty up the place around here."

Becky felt herself pale. "In love? N-no. Farthest thing from it. I haven't got time for anything like that," she sputtered.

"Mmm-hmm," Rachel said. "Whatever you say. Should I bring you two the usual?"

Becky felt her stomach flip uncomfortably at the idea of pancakes.

"I'll just have a piece of dry toast, if you don't mind. And maybe some tea?"

Rachel gave her another piercing look, but just nodded and turned to Jessie. "How 'bout you? Are you going all rabbitlike on me, too?"

Jessie shook her head. "Nope. In fact, you can bring me

her stack of pancakes, if you want. Working all these hours has made me hungry!"

"You got it," Rachel said, and walked away.

"So what did you do this weekend?" Becky asked, desperately trying to deflect the question she knew was coming.

"Doesn't matter. Right now, I'm interrogating my best friend. *Are* you? In love?"

"No," Becky said, "I most definitely am not. I'm making plenty of love, but not falling into it."

"Ah. So you and Mark are at it again, huh? That didn't take long."

"No," Becky said, "It didn't." Even though it had felt like an eternity.

"And how is it? The sex? Still good?"

"It's…amazing."

Truth was, since the night of the videos they'd spent almost every nonworking hour together—and some working ones. On Friday she'd cooked him dinner in her tiny apartment and fed him dessert in bed.

Then, on Saturday, he'd taken her to his favorite Vietnamese restaurant, fed her drinks in his favorite dive bar and introduced her to the dirty high that was sex in a public bathroom.

And they'd spent yesterday in the production studio, editing videos and teasing each other. It had been the most amazing weekend she could remember having in a very long time.

"Hey, space cadet?"

Becky blinked, bringing herself back to the present. "Yeah?"

"You sure this is just a fling?"

"Yes. Positive," Becky said, trying to convince herself it was true. "We both know the rules. We're having a lot of fun."

"Hmm," Jessie said. "It's just I haven't seen you look this happy…well, ever. Maybe you should rethink where you're headed with this thing. This guy's good for you."

Becky glared at her friend. "No. When this pitch is over, this thing with Mark and me ends, too. I'll be too busy after I get promoted to bother with a man."

"All right, you know I support you, girl. But there's more to life than work."

Unfortunately that was something Becky was becoming all too aware of. Good thing she knew that Mark had no intention of starting a "real" relationship…

Otherwise she might find herself tempted to take Jessie's words to heart.

Mark hit Stop on the remote and flipped the lights back on, pride snaking through his belly. The videos had turned out well. Really well. If David didn't like them—well, he was an ass.

"So what do you think?" he asked.

David blinked slowly for a moment, silent. Then he smiled.

"I think you two deserve congratulations. If Eden doesn't sign on the dotted line after seeing these, then nothing will convince them. These are deal-closers," David said.

Mark looked at Becky and grinned. "I'm glad you like them. We worked hard to put these together."

David looked at Becky.

"I had no idea you had it in you to act like that, my dear," he said, leering slightly. "If you didn't work for me, I'd be tempted to ask you out for dinner."

Mark felt his hackles go up. Instinctively he moved closer to Becky, even though he knew she didn't need protecting.

"Wow, David, that's quite the compliment," she said. "But if you asked me I'd say no. I don't date married men."

David flushed. "Well, uh, I was just speaking hypothetically," he stuttered.

Mark decided it was time to step in.

"I'm glad you liked the videos," he said. "But we've got a lot more work to do. Far too much to think about even hypothetical dates."

David took the out he'd been offered.

"I'm sure you do," he said as he headed for the door. "So, uh, I'll leave you to it! Keep up the good work."

After the door closed Becky kissed him on the cheek.

"Thank you, Magic Man."

"No need to thank me. You were doing a fine job of putting him in his place."

"Yeah, but if you hadn't spoken up it may have come to blows," she said. "And I don't feel like going to jail today." She stretched and yawned. "But you know what? I *do* feel like I need a break."

"One that involves taking your clothes off?" he asked, waggling his eyebrows suggestively. He hadn't had her in his arms in…almost eighteen hours. They were overdue.

Becky laughed. "Nice try. Actually, I'd like to go on a picnic."

"A picnic?" That was definitely not what he'd had in mind.

"Yeah. Have you been outside today? It's beautiful," she said, opening up the window shades.

He turned to look outside. Sure enough, the sun was shining, and if he looked down he could see that the people below seemed to be wearing warm weather gear.

"Well," he said slowly, "it has been several days since I've seen the sun. But I have to admit I've never been on an actual picnic. How does this work?"

"You're a picnic virgin? At your age? Huh! Leave it to me, big boy. I'll take good care of you," she said, smiling.

* * *

A short time later they were outside in the warm October sunshine.

"First we need to get some eats," Becky said, pulling him into an upscale bodega. Grabbing a shopping basket, she headed for the dairy section. "Cheese," she said. "We need cheese."

"How 'bout this?" Mark asked, holding up a package of precut artisan cheeses.

"Perfect," she said.

"Next up, bread," she added, placing a warm baguette in the basket. "And these strawberries will do nicely." Then she headed to the deli case. "Are you hungry? Because I could really go for some meat."

She motioned to the butcher, and soon a hefty packet of sliced deli meats joined the treats in their basket.

"Oh, and wine! But I'll let you choose."

Mark grabbed a bottle of Chardonnay, adding a bar of dark chocolate for good measure. He felt himself getting absurdly excited about their upcoming picnic. It was the kind of thing he'd always wanted to do with his mother. But she'd never had the time or the inclination.

Becky found him and he snapped out of his reverie.

"Ready?"

He nodded.

They paid and rejoined the happy throng outside, everyone seemingly intent on getting the most out of what could be the season's last warm day.

"We've got our food. Now where to?" he asked.

"That's for me to know..."

"And me to find out?" he finished.

"Yep." She grabbed his hand and tugged. "This way."

They walked in companionable silence, enjoying the warm breeze and rambunctious crowd. A toddler raced by, giggling gleefully.

"Josh! Josh, get back here, or so help me God..." a frantic voice yelled from somewhere behind them.

Mark jogged forward and grabbed the hood of the child's sweatshirt.

"Hey, little man, I think you're forgetting someone," he said, smiling.

Scooping him up, he carried the boy back to his petrified mother.

"I take it this is Josh?"

She took the boy from his arms, relief flooding her face.

"Yes. Oh, thank you. He was right there and then...I thought I'd lost him!"

"Hey, no problem," Mark said, squeezing her shoulder. Tapping Josh's nose with his finger, he admonished him. "No more running for you, young man. Don't you know that there are alligators in the sewers, just waiting for a tasty morsel like you to run by?"

The boy's eyes grew wide.

"Really?"

"Really. Your mom will tell you all about it," he said, and jogged back to Becky.

"That was really nice of you," she said, a thoughtful look on her face.

"I am the child of a single mom—or at least I was when I was young. I remember doing things like that to her. This was my penance."

"That's right. You said your mom didn't remarry until you were a little older?"

"Marry. Not remarry. I was born a bastard."

Becky winced. "That's pretty strong language. I'm sure she never thought of you that way."

Mark smiled bitterly. "Oh, I'm sure she did. Her pet name for me was Mr. Mistake. I pretty much ruined her life."

Lord knew, he had enough memories of his mother looking tired and worried, massaging her temples at the kitchen table.

Whatever you do, Mark, she'd say, bending over her calculator, *don't have kids. Life's hard enough as it is.*

He certainly never intended to. Especially since he had no desire to get involved enough with a woman to make a child. No relationships, no children, he chanted to himself. No relationships, no...

Becky squeezed his hand, bringing him out of his daydream.

"I'll bet you were her favorite mistake," she said. "You're definitely mine."

He smiled, which he was sure was the effect she had intended. "Oh, so I'm a mistake, am I?" he asked, one eyebrow raised.

"Oh, most definitely. One I enjoy making over and over again," she answered, her hand sliding into his front pocket and caressing his suddenly hard penis. "In fact, I'd like to do it again this afternoon."

"Mmm," he growled. "Keep doing that and you'll be making it in the next alley I can find."

"Now, now," she said. "Have a little patience. We're almost there."

"I guess we are," he said, suddenly realizing they'd arrived at Central Park.

A short while later she tugged at his hand again, urging him off the blacktopped path they'd been following and onto a carpet of green grass.

They were standing on a gentle slope. At the bottom was a peaceful lake, its waters reflecting the blazing reds, golds and oranges of the trees that surrounded it.

"This is amazing," he said.

"Isn't it? It's just about my favorite spot in the whole park."

She sat down under a fiery red maple tree and started unloading their picnic.

"What do you want to try first?" she asked, looking up at him.

Mark sat down next to her and gathered her up in his arms. "You," he said, and kissed her.

As always, the gentle kiss he'd intended to give her quickly morphed into something more. Her mouth opened under his and he moaned.

"Becky," he said, nibbling at her neck, "you make me crazy."

"Mmm," she murmured, tilting her head to give him better access to the sensitive pulse point, "I could say the same thing about you."

Mark glanced up. For the moment, at least, they were alone. He pushed his hand underneath her brown corduroy skirt, his fingers seeking the place his mouth wanted to go.

He stroked the edges of her cotton panties and said, "I want to make you come."

"Do you think it's safe?"

"Don't worry. Nobody will see."

Panting slightly, she nodded. "All right. If you're sure."

"I am," he said, scooping her up into his lap.

He stroked her silken folds through her underpants, smiling when she moaned. He loved that it was so easy to get her going. Slowly he increased the pace, his heart rate increasing as her breath sped up. Finally, when he couldn't take it anymore, he reached underneath to caress the tiny knob of pleasure at her core. In seconds she began writhing silently on his lap as she climaxed, then collapsed against his chest. He smiled with satisfaction, knowing she'd never trust anyone else enough to let go like that in public.

"You are amazing," she sighed.

"I thought the word was *magic*?"

"That, too."

He lay back on the grass, keeping her snuggled securely against his chest.

Looking up at the scarlet leaves above them, he sighed contentedly. "You were right," he said. "This was a fantastic idea."

"I usually am." She grinned.

"True enough."

He closed his eyes and relaxed, letting the sound of the wind in the trees lull him to sleep.

He woke up with a start when his phone burst into life.

Groggily, he reached into his pocket and grabbed it, hitting the Talk button without even looking to see who it was.

"Hello?" he said sleepily.

"Forget hello. Where the hell *are* you?" David said.

He sounded furious.

"Becky and I decided to take advantage of the nice weather and do a little brainstorming off-site," he said.

"Well, get your asses back here. The client has decided to move up the presentation by an entire week. That means we have three days."

Crap.

"We're on our way," he said, and hung up.

"What was that about?" Becky asked, blinking sleepily.

"Eden has moved the presentation up. We've got three days."

"What?" she said, rubbing her face sleepily. "Okay... okay, we can do this. We just need to get our asses in gear."

She stood and gathered up their food.

"We never got to eat," he said sadly.

"No worries. I have a feeling the food's going to come in handy. Sounds like we're not going to be leaving the office much for the next little while."

"You're right about that," he said, leaning down to give her one last kiss.

"What was that for?"

"I don't think we're going to have much time for fun and games," he said. "That's to tide you over."

The next three days passed in a caffeine-fueled blur. Mark and Becky worked nonstop, pausing only to sleep when it became absolutely necessary.

Their teams toiled beside them, and against all odds they created a stunningly good campaign. When it was over, Mark was proud of the work they had done—and even more proud of the woman who had worked at his side.

She was the heart and soul of the team, doling out encouragement when needed, praise when deserved, and tissues whenever the occasion seemed to call for it.

It was obvious that everyone loved and respected her, and Mark realized that if there was any justice in the world he'd have no shot at the creative director title. She deserved it far more than he did.

Mark had sent her to get some rest and was just packing the last of the boards away when David found him.

"You've done great work here, Mark," he said.

"Thank you, but it was a team effort. I couldn't have done it alone."

"Still, I've been watching you and I've been impressed by what I've seen. You have the makings of an outstanding creative director."

Mark couldn't help but be pleased by the praise.

"Thank you. I hope to be when my time comes."

"I have a feeling your time will come tomorrow," David said. "There's still a promotion up for grabs, remember?"

"I do, but I don't know how you're going to decide who gets it. Becky has worked just as hard as I have."

"She has," David agreed. "But I'm just not sure I sense the same potential for leadership in her."

Obviously the man was blind.

"Are you kidding? The team would follow her right up to the gates of hell—and even beyond—if she asked them to."

"You're right. The power of a pretty face can't be underestimated," David said. "Don't sweat it. I'll find the right place for her."

Mark stared hard at David's retreating back. How could the man be so willfully obtuse? He had one of the industry's most talented women working for him and he didn't appreciate her at all.

One thing was for sure. When he was in charge things would be different.

CHAPTER EIGHT

AS THEY RODE the elevator to the twenty-sixth floor of Eden's headquarters Becky checked her reflection in the shiny metal door, nervously tucking a stray hair behind her ear and checking her teeth for lipstick for the hundredth time.

"Babe, don't worry," Mark said. "You look great."

She knew she did. Her hair shone like gold against the navy blue of her suit jacket. The A-line skirt flattered her curves, and her heels were a to-die-for shade of ruby-red—not to mention dangerously high.

"We're a pretty good-looking team, if I do say so myself." She grinned, enjoying the sudden rush of adrenaline that flooded through her veins.

"You better believe it. Flash those pearly whites at them and they'll be ours before we even say a word."

"I hope you're right," Becky said.

"I know I am," Mark answered, bending down to give her a quick peck on the mouth.

Just then the elevator doors dinged open and Mark straightened.

"You ready?"

"As ready as I'll ever be," she replied.

They made their way through an empty oak-paneled lobby and headed for the conference room labeled Agency Pitch.

They hesitated outside and Mark squeezed her hand, a question on his face. She winked up at him and whispered, "Let's do this thing."

He nodded and stepped inside. Becky followed.

There were twelve business-suited men and women sitting around a long oak table. They were making polite conversation while noshing on coffee and doughnuts, but all chatter ceased when they noticed Becky and Mark standing there.

"Ah, there you are," David said, rising from his chair. "Ladies and gentlemen, this is Becky Logan and Mark Powers, the creative masterminds behind today's presentation. Between the two of them they've won more than a dozen major advertising awards and worked for some of the hottest brands around. I selected them for this project specifically because I knew they had the fresh attitude and unexpected creative flair you need. I know normally we'd do a round of introductions, but we have a lot to cover, so if it's okay with you I'd like to just let them dive in."

There was murmured assent from around the table.

"Great," David said. "Mark, Becky—take it away."

Mark looked at Becky and she nodded. They'd already agreed that he would start the presentation.

He took a deep breath and strode to the head of the table.

"Good morning, ladies and gentlemen," Mark boomed, smiling at the multitude of gray suits in the room. "I hope you brought an extra pair of socks, because we're about to blow the ones you're wearing right off."

"That's right," Becky chimed in. "The campaign we're about to present to you is like nothing you have ever seen. It will change the way business is done in your industry— and make your competition green with jealousy."

"She's not kidding, folks. Tell them how you came up with the idea."

"Well, I was sitting at my desk late one night, thinking, *Now, why would a woman buy our yogurt? What does it do for her?* What do you guys think? Why does a woman buy yogurt?"

A tall redhead raised her hand.

"Yes?" Becky said, waving in her direction.

"Well, because it tastes good," the woman answered.

"Yeah, it does—but so does ice cream. Anyone else?"

"Well, she buys *our* yogurt because it's all natural, high in protein and low in fat," a gray-haired man said.

"Ah-ha, now we're getting closer to the truth. Women buy yogurt because it makes them feel good about themselves. Not only are they making a healthy choice, but they're making a decision even the most critical part of them can appreciate."

"So you're saying we should market our yogurt as a diet aid? That's already been done," the redhead said.

"No, not as a diet aid," Mark said. "As a portal to another world—one where every woman achieves her version of perfection. Show them the concept, Becky."

Becky uncovered the first board.

A woman sat in a classic yogini pose, looking calm and Zen, while surrounded by screaming kids and spilled milk.

"Eden. The snack for the perfect you."

Over the next hour the two of them bantered back and forth effortlessly, trapping the client in a silken web. When the presentation was over, everyone at the table clapped.

The graying middle-aged man who had chimed in at the beginning stood up.

"I'm sold. David, get your team moving, because I want to get this campaign in market by January one."

"You've got it, Larry," David said, clapping the paunchy man on his back. "We look forward to it."

"Great. And, just to be clear, I want these two in charge," he said, pointing at Becky and Mark. "No one else. Don't foist me off on your B team—you hear me?"

David smiled his sleazy salesman grin. "Not to worry, my man. After all the work this team has put in, we wouldn't dream of giving it to anyone else."

The man nodded his satisfaction. Turning his attention to Becky and Mark, he said, "I look forward to getting to know you two better. I know we're going to do wonderful things together."

Becky gave him her brightest smile, her heart soaring. "We certainly will. Thank you for your confidence in us."

"Yes, thanks," Mark chimed in. "We'll try to knock your socks off every time we meet."

"I'm counting on it," said Larry. "Now, if you'll excuse me, I have some business to take care of. Where's Mary?"

A tall woman rushed to his side. "Yes, sir?"

"Is that other creative team still waiting downstairs?"

"Yes, they are. They're scheduled to begin presenting in fifteen minutes."

"Send them home. I have no use for them now. Can't stand their creative director anyway."

"Right away, sir," she said. Then she turned her attention to David. "Can you see yourselves out? I really need to take care of this."

David nodded. "Of course. We'll get everything cleared up and be on our way."

"Great," she said, and hurried out.

Becky busied herself with the boards so no one would see her triumphant smile. Inside, though, she was jumping up and down with glee.

Take that, Pence, she thought. *You've just been schooled by your former student. Booyah!*

When the last bigwig had left the room, David came over and clapped them both on the back.

"Well, team, I believe congratulations are in order. You pulled it off!" He looked down at the gold Rolex on his wrist. "Let's see. It's noon now. Meet me in the large conference room at four and we'll make it official."

"Make what official?" Becky blurted.

David gave her a sly smile. "I guess you'll have to show up to find out."

He waved goodbye and left, leaving them alone in the conference room.

Mark held up his hand. "High five," he said, grinning. "We did it."

She slapped it enthusiastically.

"What do you think David will do? Larry specifically said he wants both of us on the team."

"I have no idea," Mark said. "And I'm not really in the mood to worry about it. Let's go have us a Midwestern carnivore kind of lunch—and charge it to the company."

"That sounds fantastic," she said. "But let's go see if we can find Pence's team and gloat first."

The moment they stepped off the elevator Becky heard the sound of raised voices. One definitely belonged to Pence.

Becky grabbed Mark's hand and followed the squawks into the central reception area.

"What do you mean, he won't see us? I flew my entire team from Detroit for this meeting!" Pence sputtered, his face flushing beet-red as he gesticulated wildly. "I demand that he make good on his promise to meet with us!"

Mary was doing her best to calm him. "I'm sorry, Mr. Britton, but there's nothing I can do. Mr. Richards has left for the day."

"Left for the day? How can that be? I—we…"

Becky knew she'd never have a better chance to exact her revenge. Stepping forward, she said, "Mary? I'm sorry to interrupt, but can I steal you for a second?"

Relief flooded the other woman's face. "Yes, Becky? What can I do for you?"

"David had to leave, but he wanted me to make sure to tell you that he'll be emailing over some contracts later this afternoon. In order to stick to the timeline Mr. Richards has requested we're going to need to move fast."

"Of course. I'll be on the lookout for them. Tell David he'll have the signed contracts by the end of the week."

"Wait. What?" Pence squawked, his blue eyes flashing with anger as he moved to stand in front of Becky. "Are you telling me *your* team won the business?"

"As a matter of fact I'm not telling you anything at all. You can read all about it in the next issue of AdWorld."

"You little…" Pence said, rage suffusing his face.

Before he could finish the thought, Mark stepped forward.

"Is this your old boss, Becky?"

She nodded. "The one and only."

"I've heard a lot about you," he said, extending his hand. "None of it good."

Pence reluctantly shook it. "And you are…?"

"Mark Powers. Becky's teammate. You have no idea what you missed out on when you let her go, buddy. This woman is brilliant."

Pence's already scarlet face turned even redder.

"I don't know what she's told you, but it's almost certainly not what actually happened," he said.

"I'm not interested in your opinion," Mark said. "Come on, Becky, let's get out of here."

But Becky wasn't done yet.

Turning back to Pence, she smiled sweetly. "If you get canned, give me a call. We might be able to find a job for you. In our mail room."

Then she turned on her heel and swaggered out, leaving Mark to follow.

When they were clear of the building he pulled her to him and kissed her soundly.

"That," he said between kisses, "was amazing."

"I know," she said smugly. "You have no idea how good

that felt. It's like a million-pound weight has been lifted off my back."

"Wanna celebrate...in bed?"

"I do. But not until we know for sure what we're celebrating," she said, stepping backward out of his arms. If David announced he was giving the promotion to Mark, she didn't want to hear the news while still tingling from his touch.

"Okay, then. Still up for lunch?"

She shook her head. "I'd like to be alone for a little while. It's been a big morning. I need some time to process it, you know?"

He nodded, a sad smile on his face. "I get it. See you back at the office, then?"

"Yep," she said, then reached up to give him one last melting kiss.

"What was that for?"

"Just a little something to tide you over," she said. Silently she added, *And something for me to remember you by.*

Mark jogged around the corner, his dress shoes slipping on the polished cement floor. If there was one meeting he didn't want to be late for it was this one.

Once the frosted glass doors were in sight he stopped for a second to catch his breath and straighten his tie.

This was it. If he got this promotion he could finally feel as if he'd made it. That he'd gotten where he had in his career because he was talented—not because his stepfather had greased the wheels. His mother might even be a little bit proud of him. Maybe she'd stop thinking of him as a mistake.

Taking a deep breath, he stepped through the conference room doors.

It was crowded. And hot. Everyone in the whole agency

seemed to be there, and the air was quickly growing stale. David stood at the head of the big table, with Becky on his right.

"There you are, Mark. We were beginning to wonder if you'd gone off somewhere to celebrate without us."

"Just staying true to form. You know how I like to make an entrance," he joked.

Becky rolled her eyes at him.

"Yep," she said. "He's the diva on this team. I'm the brains and the brawn."

The assembled crowd laughed appreciatively.

"All right, enough monkey business," David said. "Come on up here and we'll get this show on the road."

Mark made his way to the front of the room, taking his place at David's left.

Once the audience had stilled, David launched into his speech.

"As you all know, we delivered our pitch to Eden this morning. Mark and Becky led the presentation, and I must admit they did a fantastic job. They had the client eating out of their hands. They even got a standing ovation."

There was a smattering of applause in the room.

"In fact," David said, "the client bought into the campaign on the spot. We're the new marketing partner for Eden Yogurt—and about to be two hundred and fifty million dollars richer as an agency!"

The room broke out into riotous applause as their colleagues cheered their victory.

"That's not all," David continued. "As you may remember, Becky and Mark have been involved in a competition of sorts. The prize was a creative director title and a hefty bonus."

The room stilled as everyone waited for the next part of the announcement.

"But choosing one over the other has proved to be surprisingly difficult. They're both incredibly skilled creative geniuses. They both worked on the winning concept from beginning to end. And they both gained the respect and admiration of the client."

Mark drew in a breath and held it.

"So in the end I decided to create a new type of position. One that gives them each their due. Mark and Becky, you're now creative codirectors. You'll function as a creative director team, splitting the responsibilities for the Eden account according to your skillsets."

Mark blinked, trying to connect the dots.

Next to him, Becky said, "So there's no winner or loser? We're both getting promoted?"

"That's right," David said. "Eden is a new kind of account for us. It's only right that a new type of team heads it up."

The room exploded with cheers.

Becky shrieked happily and threw her arms around David. "Thank you," she said. "Thank you so much!"

He chuckled and patted her back uncomfortably.

"I'm the one who should be thanking you, my dear. You've just secured my retirement. Which brings me to my last announcement... If this were a television show I'd have a giant check sitting here. But, since it's not, you'll just have to make do with these regular-size ones."

He turned to Mark.

"One fifty-thousand-dollar check for you," he said, and, to Becky, "One fifty-thousand-dollar check for you."

Stunned, Mark looked down at the check in his hand. This was really happening. The check was his. The job was his. And, he thought, looking at Becky's laughing countenance as she accepted congratulations from her friends, at least for now the girl was his.

He was surprised to discover that it was that last ingredient that made him the happiest.

Maybe it was time to rethink the no-relationship clause.

* * *

By the time Becky managed to break free from her excited colleagues and escape to their office, darkness was falling over the city.

She closed the door and leaned against it, reveling in the blessed quiet.

She jumped when Mark's voice rang out in the darkness.

"Congratulations, creative codirector," he said. "You did good today."

"Mark? Where are you?"

"Just admiring the view," he said, clicking on a lamp by the windows. "And enjoying the fact that I'll get to look at it every day from now on."

Becky crossed over to where he was standing. Time to reintroduce reality.

"What if I want this office?"

He blinked. "What?"

"Now that we're both creative directors, or at least codirectors, David will probably give us each our own office. What if I decide I want to keep this one?"

"I guess I assumed we'd continue to share," Mark said. "Since we're heading up the same account and all."

"I doubt it," she said. In fact she hoped not. It would be almost impossible to keep her distance from him—something she knew she had to start doing—if they were in each other's physical space all day.

"Do you want your own office?" Mark asked, a dark look on his face.

She sighed. "Yes and no. Mark, these last few weeks have been fun, but we've known from the beginning that this couldn't last. Remember what you said?"

"I said that we could both go our own ways after this thing between us had run its course."

"Right," she said. "No harm, no foul."

"But, Becky," he said, looking deep into her eyes, "I

don't think it *has* run its course. I'm having a lot of fun with you—even when our clothes are on. Let's not give up yet."

Uh-oh. Unless she was very mistaken, he was talking about more than the occasional sexual romp.

"That was never the deal, Mark. You don't do relationships, remember?"

He sighed and ran his fingers through his dark hair. "No, Becky, I don't. Or at least I never have. But this... It's different somehow."

She knew exactly what he was talking about. Somewhere along the way they had crossed the line from being sex buddies to...something more. Something that scared her even to think about.

"I know," she said. "But we can't keep going on as we are—hooking up in the office on the sly and slipping out of the building when no one's looking. We're in charge now. Role models. We're going to have to try to act like we realize that."

He wrapped his arms around her and pulled her close. "Well, what if we try something different? Something normal and grown-up-ish. Like, you know, going out on actual dates. And spending the night together whenever we want, rather than heading home after a hookup. That could be fun."

"Mark..." she whispered. "What you're talking about sounds an awful lot like a relationship."

"I know," he said. "But I bet we can make it work."

"You and your bets," she said, smiling. "Nothing is worth doing unless you can bet on it."

He grinned and lowered his lips to hers.

"So what do you think?" he said. "Are you in?"

"I don't know. I'll think about it."

Then he claimed her with his mouth and she stopped thinking at all.

The next thing she knew someone was knocking. She

jumped backward—but not before the door opened, admitting David.

His eyes darted back and forth between her and Mark, taking in their slightly disheveled clothing and flushed faces.

"David," she said. "We were just, uh, I mean, we were—"

"We were just cementing the official end of our feud slash competitive relationship with a hug," Mark broke in.

"Oh. I see," David said, twitching his tie. "Well, that makes sense. Especially since you're going to be working together every day. It's important to present a united front."

"Exactly," Becky said, glancing at Mark.

"Well, I was just coming in to congratulate you one more time," David replied. "Make sure you get some rest this weekend. We're going to hit it hard on Monday. Becky, you'll be moving into the office next door to this one—Fred Sutherland's old digs."

She nodded, relieved that he seemed to be buying their story.

"Sounds good," she said.

"See you Monday," Mark chimed in.

"Right you are," David said, giving them one last suspicious glance. "Have a good one."

When the door was once again closed Becky whirled on Mark. "That," she hissed, "is why an 'us' is not a good idea. I just got promoted. I don't want to get fired."

"I don't remember signing anything that said we couldn't date coworkers."

"Maybe not, but I'm sure David wouldn't approve of the two of us getting together. And you know how tough it is for him to treat me like a creative professional. He'd find a way to use our relationship as a way to discredit me."

"I think you're being a little tough on the guy. All he cares about is the bottom line. And you just tripled his income. I don't think he's going to give you a hard time about anything."

Becky shook her head. It was no use. Mark would never understand how tough this business was for women. Or how biased David was against female employees.

"Well, whatever. Only time will tell," she said. "But I just don't think he could handle the thought of us as both a couple and a working team."

If she was being honest, she wasn't sure if she could, either.

"Just promise me you'll think about it," Mark said.

She sighed and stood on her tiptoes to kiss him good-bye. What she wouldn't give to be able to throw caution to the winds and just say yes. But she had to start focusing on her career again.

"I will," she agreed. "But don't expect me to change my mind."

CHAPTER NINE

BECKY WAS JUST sitting down with a steaming pot pie and a glass of her favorite Pinot Grigio when her cell phone began to whistle cheerfully.

It was her mother.

Becky stared at the screen. Should she answer it? Probably. If she didn't, she'd just keep calling back.

"Hi, Mom."

"Well, there you are. I was beginning to wonder if you were lying dead in an alley somewhere."

"Don't be so dramatic, Mom. It hasn't been that long since we talked."

"I haven't heard from you since you called to tell me you got home safely from the conference! That was almost a month ago."

Surely it hadn't been that long? But, now that she thought about it, maybe it had. She had considered picking up the phone on countless occasions, but when she'd thought about everything that was going on, and how impossible it would be to explain to her mom, she never had.

"I'm sorry, Mom. Things have been really busy at work."

"Work, work, work. That's all you ever talk about. When are you going to give me something to brag about to the ladies in my book club?"

"Well, actually, something pretty huge happened today," Becky said, suddenly eager to tell her mom. "I got promoted. To creative director."

There was a brief silence.

"That's nice, dear. Does that mean you'll be able to afford to come home more often?"

"I don't know. We haven't discussed salary yet. But I did get a really big bonus."

"Maybe you should use it to buy a place in a better neighborhood. I worry about you, you know. It doesn't seem safe, especially with those tattooed hippies wandering around at all hours of the day and night."

"Mom. I live in Greenwich Village, not Hell's Kitchen. This is a great neighborhood."

"I'm sure it is, but I'd feel much better if you didn't live right in the city like that. There's so much crime."

Becky smacked her forehead with her palm.

"We've been over this a hundred times. I moved to New York because I wanted to live in the city. Not in some cookie-cutter house in the suburbs."

Now it was her mother's turn to sigh. "I know, dear. I know. I just wish you'd move past this wild phase of yours and settle down with someone nice."

Becky snorted. Wild phase, indeed. "I'm only twenty-nine. There's no rush."

"That's what you think, dear. But once you hit thirty, your best baby-making years are behind you. I don't want you to end up in some infertility clinic, trying to get your tired eggs to work."

"I know. I've read every article you've ever emailed me on the subject."

Her mother continued as if she hadn't heard.

"You know, your cousin is pregnant again."

"Which one?"

"Tiffany. This will be her third."

"Well, tell her I said congratulations."

"You could come for the baby shower and tell her yourself."

"I'd rather stick needles in my eye," she muttered.

"I heard that," her mother said, sighing loudly. "Well, I'll let you go. I'm sure you have far better things to do than talk to your mother on a Friday night."

If only, Becky thought. Out loud, she said, "All right. Well, I'll talk to you soon, Mom. Love you."

"Love you, too. Remember to take the pepper spray I bought you if you go out."

"I will."

"And never leave your drink unattended."

"Okay."

"And…"

At long last her mother hung up. Becky flung herself backward on the chaise. Any other parent would be thrilled to hear their child had just gotten promoted. But not her mom. The only promotion she wanted to hear about was one that involved putting a "Mrs." in front of her name. Or the title "Mother of" after it.

Infertility clinic, my foot, she thought, taking a giant swig of wine. She already knew her ovaries worked. The proof was in the box under her bed.

Speaking of ovaries…shouldn't she be getting her period about now? Becky reached for her phone and fired up her period-tracking app. Yep. Her last one had been the week before AdWorld. That meant Aunt Flow should show up…

Damn. It should have come a week and a half ago.

Becky's mind froze.

There were all kinds of reasons why she could be late. She'd been under a huge amount of stress. Not sleeping well. Eating too much fast food and drinking too much wine.

But being stressed out was a way of life for her. And she didn't eat all that well on even the best of days.

And she had been having lots of sex. But they'd been safe about it, right? She thought hard, trying to remember all the moments they'd stopped to put a condom on. Yep. They had. Every single time. Except…

The afternoon of the sword fight.

Neither of them had even thought about a condom. She hadn't even realized they'd forgotten until she'd seen the undeniable evidence in her underwear while getting into her pajamas that evening.

She raced to the bathroom and tore off her shirt and bra. If she wasn't mistaken her boobs did look bigger than usual. She squeezed one, just to see.

"Ow!"

Yep. They were tender.

Time to call in the troops.

She pulled out her phone and texted Jessie.

We have a 911 situation over here.

Seconds later, the phone rang.

"Becky, what's wrong? Are you hurt? Is someone dead?" Jessie asked, sounding breathless and shaken.

"No. Sorry. I didn't mean to scare you."

"Then what was the 911 about?"

"I think I might be pregnant," she said quietly.

"What? How? I mean I know how, but…"

"I'll explain later. Could you come over, please?" Becky asked, hating the tremor in her voice.

Jessie sighed. "I'm kind of on a date."

"Oh. Okay. Never mind. I'll just run out and get a test."

"Keep me posted, okay?"

"I will," she whispered, and hung up.

Knowing she should head right to the drugstore, she instead found herself on her knees in front of her bed, gazing at the old sonogram picture.

How many times had she sworn she'd never put herself in this position again? That she'd protect herself at all costs?

Too many to count.

The first time had been in Pence's office, right after she'd told him she was quitting.

"What do you mean, you quit?" he'd said. "You can't quit."

"Yes, I can. I am. And I'm using my vacation time as my notice. I've got two weeks coming to me," she'd said, hoping beyond hope he couldn't see her knees trembling.

"What will you do?" he'd asked, his voice suddenly cold. "You know as well as I do that I'm the only reason you've made it as far as you have."

"That's not true," she'd said quietly.

"Sure it is. I could've gotten rid of you after your internship was over. But I kept you around. Made sure you got put on the best assignments," he'd said, walking over to his awards shelf. "The only reason you got your award was because I convinced the client to go with your idea."

"They would have chosen it even if you hadn't pushed it," she'd said, anger sparking in her veins. "But you had to feel like you were in control of every part of my life. You never let me do things on my own!"

"That's because you would have failed," he'd said, stalking silently across the plush green carpet toward her. "You screw everything up. Heck, you can't even manage to take your birth control pills the right way."

She'd gasped, his barbed comment tearing open the thin scab on her heart. "Oh, my God, you're unbelievable."

He'd smiled coldly as he came to stand in front of her. "I deserved that, so I won't hold it against you." Then, taking a deep breath, he'd said, "Let's start over. Becky, please don't leave. We've got a good thing going here. Stick with me and you'll be a star."

"I already am a star, Pence. And I don't need you to continue being one."

"No one will hire you," he'd said softly.

"I already have a job," she'd said defiantly.

"Where? Ads R Us?"

"At an agency with more awards than you can count. In a place where they've never heard of you."

"You'll fail," he'd said, turning his back on her.

"No. I won't. I'll knock their socks off," she'd said with more confidence than she'd felt. "But I do have you to thank for one thing."

"What?" he'd said over his shoulder.

"Now I know better than to let some egotistical man get in my head. Or my bed. No one will ever be able to mess up my life the way you have, Pence."

He'd snorted.

"You'll be knocked up and out of the game before the year is up."

"I doubt it. But you'll definitely still be a bitter asshole stuck in a loveless marriage. If she doesn't wise up and leave you."

His answer had been a wordless roar. One she still occasionally heard in her dreams.

Her reverie was broken by a loud buzzing sound. Someone was at the front door.

She got up and shuffled to the intercom. "Hello?"

"Let me in, girl. It's cold out here," Jessie's voice called. 'What happened to your date?"

"You're more important. Now, hit the dang buzzer!"

Becky did, and went to hold the door open for her friend. Jessie bounded up the stairs, plastic bag in hand.

"I come bearing gifts," she said. "Five flavors of pee sticks and two flavors of ice cream."

"I told you I was going to take care of it," Becky protested.

"And did you?"

Becky shook her head.

"Right, then. Pick your poison. Pink, purple, blue, red or generic?" Jessie said, holding the bag out in front of her.

Becky closed her eyes and reached inside.

"Looks like we're going with pink," she said.

Becky sat on the closed toilet lid, eyes squeezed tightly shut. In three minutes she'd have her answer.

There was a soft knock and Jessie came in, her sequined skirt sparkling in the harsh fluorescent light.

"How are you doing?" she asked.

"Well, I won a two-hundred-and-fifty-million-dollar piece of business, told off my ex, got promoted and found out I might be pregnant. All in one day. How could I be anything less than fabulous?" she said.

Jessie squeezed her hand. "It'll be okay," she said.

Her phone alarm shrilled loudly. Becky blew out a big breath of air.

"Do you want to look or do you want me to?" Jessie asked.

"I'll do it," Becky said.

Reaching out with one shaking hand, she grabbed the pink-capped stick from where it sat on the edge of her ugly green tub and looked down.

"Well?" Jessie asked, her voice shaking.

Mutely, Becky held it out for her to see, stomach roiling.

"Oh, no," she breathed. "Becky, I'm sorry."

She was pregnant.

Becky slammed the toilet lid open seconds before her dinner made a reappearance.

"Well," Jessie said, when the heaving had stopped. "That's not the reaction you see on TV."

Becky tried to smile. "Yep, but—as we well know—advertising tells only a selective version of the truth."

Jessie helped her up. "You took the words right out of

my mouth. Now, come on, let's get you out of here. Nothing good comes of extended visits to the bathroom."

A short while later Becky was again stretched out on her purple chaise, a bottle of hastily purchased ginger ale fizzing on the table beside her. Jessie was curled up on her only other piece of furniture—a very faded red couch.

Jessie looked at Becky over the rim of her wine glass. "So, I'm assuming this is Mark's kid, right?"

Becky raised an eyebrow at her. "While I admit my behavior has been a little more reckless than usual, I assure you I haven't been having sex with random men I meet on the street."

"No. I know, I didn't mean… I'm sorry, Becky."

She waved her comment away. "No worries. I understand."

"You know, there's a clinic in my neighborhood. They have a reputation for being very discreet…"

Becky shook her head. "I don't need a clinic. I'm keeping it."

Jessie's jaw dropped.

"Are you sure that's a good idea? I mean, you just got the world's biggest promotion today."

"Positive. I'll figure out how to make it work." She'd made her decision the second she'd seen the plus sign on the pregnancy test. It was the only thing she could do.

Jessie looked unconvinced. "Well, if you change your mind, just let me know. I'd be happy to go with you."

Suddenly angry, Becky glared at her friend. "How could you say that to me? You know what happened…before. Having that abortion almost destroyed me. Do you want me to have to go through that again?"

Jessie paled. "I'm sorry. I…I wasn't thinking. I just don't want you to rush into anything. It's a big decision."

Becky immediately regretted her outburst. Her friend

had never been anything but supportive. And there was no way she could know how concrete her decision was.

"I'm sorry, Jessie. You didn't deserve that. But I'm keeping this baby. I couldn't live with any other choice."

Jessie nodded. "All right. Well, I'll support you, then."

Becky smiled her thanks and the two women sat silently for a while. Becky thanked her lucky stars she'd gotten that bonus check today. She'd be able to buy the baby everything it needed. And, she thought, looking around her shoebox-size apartment, she might even be able to afford a bigger place.

"What are you going to do about Mark?" Jessie asked suddenly.

Her brain stuttered. "Do?"

"Well, you're going to have to tell him. It's not like he won't notice. Besides, he deserves to know."

Unbelievably, she'd forgotten about that small detail. She'd been thinking about the baby as hers, not theirs.

"You're right," she said. "I don't think he's going to be very happy though. He's pretty anti-kids."

"Well," Jessie said, "whatever happens, you know I'll be there for you. I'll even be your labor coach, if you want."

Becky laughed. "I'm not quite ready to think about that yet."

Jessie looked at her watch, then heaved herself off of the couch. "Man, it's getting late. I better get going so you can get some rest. Are you going to be okay?"

Becky nodded.

"Okay," she said, wrapping her rainbow scarf around her neck. "Take care of yourself."

"I will."

After one final hug Jessie was gone.

Becky sank to the floor and hugged her knees, allowing herself to hope for a minute. Mark had been ready to start a relationship this afternoon. Maybe it would all be okay.

Her mind flashed back to the way he'd behaved with that little boy on the way to the park. He was a natural. Maybe he'd jump at the chance to be a dad.

And maybe pigs were getting ready to fly.

Oh, well. No time like the present to get the ball rolling. Pulling out her phone, she texted Mark.

We need to talk.

Almost instantly her phone pinged with his reply.

I'm listening, Gorgeous Girl.

Not over text. In person. Dinner tomorrow?

Sure. Where?

Come over. I'll cook.

This was a conversation that needed to be held in private.

See you at seven?

Can't wait.

A bald-faced lie.

Hopefully tomorrow night would go better than it had the last time she'd had this conversation with a man.

It could hardly be worse.

CHAPTER TEN

MARK WOKE UP on Saturday morning feeling happier than he could remember ever being. For once, all was right with his world.

He swung his legs over the edge of the bed and padded across the hardwood floor of his studio apartment to the granite kitchen island where the fifty-thousand-dollar check was sitting. He ran his finger across the dollar amount. All those zeroes belonged to him. And he hadn't had to beg his stepfather for a penny of it.

On impulse, he snapped a picture of the check and texted his mother.

Your boy done good. Got promoted to creative director yesterday. With this as a bonus.

He hit Send and waited for a response. None came.

Not that he had really expected anything else. His mother had made it quite clear over the years that she'd really rather her son disappeared so she could focus on the family she *did* want.

Shake it off, he told himself. Much better to focus on the things he had a chance of fixing—like his relationship with Becky.

And, although it scared him to admit it, he did want a relationship. He wanted to wander the city with her. He wanted to walk in Little Italy at night and explore Central Park during the day. He wanted to eat with her in her tiny apartment and see her golden hair spread out on his pillows after a night of love.

Not even the fact that they worked together deterred him. They made a crazy good team—both in and out of the office.

All he had to do was convince her to give it a try.

Night had already descended when Mark arrived on Becky's doorstep, bearing a bottle of wine and a bunch of daisies tied with a ribbon that matched her eyes.

Taking a deep breath, he pushed the buzzer.

Seconds later, the door clicked open.

Becky was waiting for him at the top of the dark staircase. "Hey, Magic Man," she said with a smile.

"Hey, yourself," he said, taking the time to appreciate the plunging blue V-neck top and tight black leather skirt she was wearing. "You're looking even more gorgeous than usual, Gorgeous Girl."

"Thank you," she said shyly, turning her cheek when he reached down to kiss her.

Hmm. That was a new one.

He handed her the wine and flowers. "For my beautiful hostess," he said.

"How did you know daisies were my favorite?" she asked.

"Lucky guess," he said.

She ushered him inside, then busied herself in the kitchen, putting the flowers in water. "Make yourself at home," she called.

While small, her apartment felt cozy and warm. The walls were painted a cheerful yellow and decorated with pictures of brightly colored flowers and tropical beaches. Although a tiny dining table was tucked away in one corner, a giant purple chaise dominated the room. It shared the space with a comfortable-looking couch and a plethora of rainbow-hued pillows.

"I don't think I mentioned it the last time I was here, but I really love your place."

"Thank you," she said, rounding the corner from the kitchen. "It's tiny, but I kind of love it."

"From what I can tell, every apartment in New York is tiny—even the ones you pay millions of dollars for."

"That's true," she said. "Although I hear the roaches in the expensive ones wear diamond-plated shells."

"That figures. Roaches are excellent at adapting to their surroundings."

She laughed and reached up to kiss him. "Thank you for coming," she whispered.

When he sensed her backing away, he reached out to pull her closer.

"I wouldn't have missed this for the world," he said. "Maybe later we can have dessert in bed again. This time I'll be the plate."

"Mmm," she said with an enigmatic smile. "We'll see how the evening goes. Are you hungry?"

"Starving."

"Good. I've got lasagna. It'll be ready in just a sec."

"Can I help?"

"No need. Unless you want to open the wine?"

He followed her into the kitchen and took the bottle she handed him.

"Glasses are on the table," she said. "But just pour me a drop."

"Are you sure? The guy at the wine shop told me this was an excellent vintage—whatever that means."

"I'm sure," she said.

She was definitely acting a little odd. He hoped it was because she was trying to get used to the idea of them being a couple and not because she had something bad to tell him.

Mentally he shook his head. No use borrowing trouble before he had it.

Soon Becky brought out plates of lasagna and garlic bread.

"It looks awesome," he said.

"I hope so," she said. "Dig in!"

He picked up his wine glass. "I'd like to propose a toast," he said.

Becky smiled and raised her glass. "Okay, let's hear it."

"To the kick-ass team that is us. Here's hoping this is the beginning of a long and beautiful relationship."

She seemed to wince a little at his words, but gamely clinked her glass with his. "To us," she murmured.

An awkward silence fell, and Mark watched as Becky picked at her food.

He let the quiet go on, hoping she'd be the one to break it. She didn't.

"Becky, what's wrong?"

She looked up, her eyes bright with unshed tears.

"I have something to tell you," she said. "Something I'm pretty sure you're not going to like."

Trying not to be alarmed, he said, "Try me."

She took a deep breath. "There's no easy way to say this," she said. "So I'm just going to blurt it out."

"Okay. You're not dying or married or something, are you?"

"No. Nothing like that. I'm just pregnant."

He heard a distant clatter as his fork dropped from his suddenly nerveless fingers.

"I'm sorry. I think I misheard you. You're what?"

"Pregnant." She made herself say it again. "I'm pregnant. With your baby."

"What? How can that be?" he spluttered.

"Well, you see, there's this stork," she said, trying for

humor. "Last night he flew by my window and told me he'd be delivering a baby to us in about eight months. I told him he was mistaken, but he showed me the paperwork. It was all in order."

"This is no time for jokes," Mark snapped. "I don't understand. We used protection."

"We did. All except for one time."

She could see his mind working busily, trying to connect the dots.

"What? When?"

"Remember the afternoon of the sword fight?"

He paled as she watched.

"Son of a..." Mark swore. "I can't believe we were so stupid. *Damn it!*"

He put his head in his hands. After a moment, he took a deep breath.

"Okay. You're pregnant. It happens. Unplanned pregnancies happen all the time. But we can fix this."

He got up and started to pace.

"How far along are you?"

"Just five or six weeks."

"Oh. Good. That's not very far at all. You can probably even still get that pill from your doctor. The one that causes a miscarriage or whatever."

"Mark?"

He stopped and looked at her. "What?"

"I don't want to do that."

"Okay, well, there's bound to be a good clinic around here somewhere. It is New York, after all."

"No," she said. "I don't want an abortion."

He looked sick—as if she had just punched her in the stomach.

"What are you saying?"

"I want to keep it," she said quietly. Then, with more determination, "I'm *going* to keep it. I want this baby, Mark."

"No. You don't."

"Yes," she said, getting annoyed, "I do. I'm a grown woman, Mark. I know what I'm doing."

"No, you don't!" he said, his face turning red. "You only think you do. But once he's born he'll get in the way. There will be sick days and doctor visits and daycare issues. You'll be exhausted all the time, and frazzled, and run down. Before you know it your career will be in the tank. Soon, you'll start to resent him for being born. You'll wish you'd gotten rid of him while you still could. No kid deserves to go through life like that, Becky. No kid should be stuck with a mother who doesn't want him around."

He gazed down at her, shoulders hunched, and she could see a lifetime of hurt reflected in his eyes.

"Please don't do this, Becky."

Becky's heart broke for the man in front of her, and for the mother who obviously hadn't been able to give him what he needed.

She went to him, cupping his cheek gently with her hand.

"It won't be like that, Mark. I've only known about this baby for twenty-four hours and I already love him with all my heart. I always will."

"You can't promise that, Becky," he said miserably. "You don't know what it's like. How hard it is."

"I won't be alone. I'll be surrounded by people who love me—and him. Heck, my mother will probably try to move in with me. The only question is whether you're going to be one of those people."

"What are you asking me, Becky?"

She pulled him down on the couch next to her. "Yesterday you were begging me to give this relationship a chance. To give us a shot. Now I'm asking you the same thing."

Grabbing his hand, she placed it over her stomach.

"Are you willing to see if we can make this work? To

give this family a shot? The stakes are a lot higher now, but I'm willing to go all-in if you are."

He looked at her with horror on his face.

"Are you asking me to *marry* you?"

She snorted. "As if. No. I'm just asking you not to slam the door shut. To be a part of our lives. To see if you can make room for this baby in your heart."

His face grew cold and he stood.

"No, Becky. I'm sorry, but I can't. If you want this baby it's all on you. I won't be a part of it."

She nodded and swallowed, looking down at her hands so he wouldn't see the tears in her eyes.

"Okay. I understand."

A moment later she heard the door open and shut. She was alone.

She rubbed her stomach absently. "Looks like it's just you and me, kid," she whispered, tears running down her face.

Funny. Yesterday she hadn't been sure she wanted to let Mark into her heart. It was only now that he was gone that she realized she already had. And that when he'd left he'd taken half of it with him.

Mark stomped down the cold dark streets, glaring at anyone who dared to meet his eye.

How could she have let this happen? He had assumed she was on some kind of birth control. That she was behaving like a responsible adult.

It wasn't fair. Just when he'd thought he'd finally found a place where he could make a career he was stuck working with a woman who wanted more from him than he could give. A woman who was pregnant with his baby, for God's sake.

The sound of his phone ringing yanked Mark into the

present. Fishing it out of his pocket, he looked at his screen. It was his mother. Impeccable timing, as always.

He considered flinging his phone into the street, but decided talking to her would probably give him all the confirmation he needed that he was making the right decision.

"Hello, Mother."

"Mark, darling, I got your text. How wonderful!"

"I sent that twelve hours ago," he snarled.

"Yes, I know. But we had a tennis tournament today at the club. And then the Petersons came over for dinner. They send their love, by the way."

"Do the Petersons even know who I am?"

"Of course they do, Mark. They've been coming to the house since you were in the seventh grade."

"Yes, but I was never there," he said.

"Oh, don't be so dramatic. You were home for nearly every school vacation. For months at a time in the summer, in fact."

"Only if you couldn't find somewhere else to send me," he said.

There was a beat of silence. "What is this all about, Mark? I made sure you had the best education money could buy. Was that wrong?"

"Oh, come on, Mom. I know the only reason you sent me to boarding school was because you couldn't stand to have me around. Didn't want to be reminded of your mistakes after you married into money. I didn't belong in your fancy new family."

"Is that what you thought?" his mother said, her voice a horrified whisper. "Mark, you couldn't be more wrong. Why, I—"

"Save it for someone who cares, Mom. I gave up a long time ago."

It wasn't until he hung up that he realized he'd been

shouting. Good thing he was in New York. Nothing fazed the people here.

God, he needed a drink. A stiff one. Looking up, he realized he was standing right across the street from a bar.

He'd get drunk tonight. Then decide what to do about the train wreck that was his life in the morning.

CHAPTER ELEVEN

BY THE TIME Monday morning dawned Becky had bottled up her heartbreak and shoved it into the darkest recesses of her brain. She couldn't afford to be weak.

She was starting a new job: working with a man who would prefer never to see her again and for a man who still had a hard time believing she was anything but a pretty face.

She was going to have to be on her A-game every day from here on out. She'd have to prove she was worth every dime they were paying her and, pregnant or not, could kick the ass of every male creative in the city.

That was the only way she'd be able to get through this with both her pride and career intact.

She spent the entire train ride pumping herself up. By the time she strode through SBD's doors she had convinced herself that she could handle absolutely anything the world cared to throw at her. Even a lifetime of working with Mark.

But she couldn't bite back the sigh of relief that came when she realized she had beaten him to the office. With luck, she could have her stuff packed up and moved into her new space before he arrived.

Becky grabbed a box and got to work. She hadn't gotten very far, though, when there was a knock on the door.

"Come in," she called.

David's executive assistant glided through the door.

"Hi, Pam, what can I do for you?"

"I take it you didn't see the email I sent you?" the elegant woman asked.

"No," she answered slowly. "Is something wrong?"

"I don't think so," she said, looking everywhere but at Becky. "But David did say he wanted to see you as soon as you got in."

"All right," Becky said. "Then I guess I'll head up there with you now."

The two women spent the elevator ride in an increasingly heavy silence. Becky was practically squirming by the time they arrived on the forty-third floor.

"I'll let him know you're here," Pam said. "Why don't you have a seat?"

Sensing it was more of a command than a request, Becky sat down in one of the black leather chairs.

She wished she had some idea of what this was all about. Mark wouldn't have told David about her pregnancy… would he?

Thankfully Pam returned before that train of thought could go any further.

"You can go in now," she said.

Becky thanked her and squared her shoulders before stepping through the heavy oak door.

David was ensconced behind his giant mahogany desk, his chair arranged on a riser so he could tower over the people sitting in front of him. But he wasn't alone.

Mark sat in one of the chestnut-colored club chairs while Cindy, the head of HR, perched on the couch.

No one looked happy.

"Ah, there you are, Becky," David boomed. "I was beginning to think we were going to have to send a search party after you."

"Sorry," she said. "I was downstairs. I just hadn't opened my email yet."

'Not to worry," he said. "We've been having a nice little chat while we waited—haven't we, Mark?"

Mark nodded, his face looking pale and strained.

"Good, I'm glad I haven't inconvenienced anyone. May I ask why we're all here?"

David nodded. "I'm going to cut right to the chase, Becky. It's come to my attention that you and Mark are involved in a relationship."

"Excuse me? We most definitely are *not*," she said sharply.

"Don't try to deny it, dear. I have security camera footage of the two of you engaged in rather passionate embraces in several places throughout the building."

Oh, no.

"Yes, well, that may be true, but I can assure you that any relationship we may have had has already come to an end. Tell him, Mark!"

Mark glowered at her. "I already tried."

"Be that as it may, I am afraid you two are in blatant violation of your contracts with us. Cindy, could you read the relevant clause to them?"

The woman nodded. "It's in section twenty-seven A on page seventeen," she said. "'The employee agrees to refrain from establishing relationships of a romantic or sexual nature with any SBD employee, vendor, client, or contractor. If conduct of this nature is discovered the employee understands that he or she will be considered to have violated his or her contract, and will be subject to punitive action up to and including termination of employment.'"

Becky paled. "I honestly don't remember seeing that in my contract," she said.

"It was there," Cindy said. "I have your initialed copy right here. I suggest you pay closer attention to what you're signing in the future."

She nodded, furiously trying to process the predicament she now found herself in. "Obviously. So where does that leave us, David?"

He took a deep breath and smiled a nasty smile.

"If this was an ordinary situation I would dismiss both of you and wash my hands of the whole thing. But it isn't. As you know, Eden has specifically requested that you both be on their team. Which was why I promoted the two of you to the codirector positions. However, in light of this new information, I cannot, in good conscience, allow that arrangement to stand. Therefore I am going to allow one of you to stay and continue on in a creative director capacity. The other person will be allowed to resign, with the bonus received on Friday serving as a severance package. I'm leaving it to you to decide who will go and who will stay. You have until the end of the day."

Becky blinked. *They* had to decide who got fired? Who *did* that?

"But what about Eden? They want both of us on their team," she blurted.

"I'll tell Eden that whichever one of you resigns has had a family emergency and will be on leave indefinitely, and that you'll return to work on their account when things are squared away. You won't, of course, but by the time they figure that out they'll have forgotten why they thought they needed you both anyway. That's it. You're dismissed," David finished. "Now, get out of my sight."

She didn't have to be told twice. She was punching the elevator button before Mark had even risen from his chair.

Unfortunately the elevator was its usual poky self. By the time the door dinged open Mark was approaching. She stepped in and held the door, unable to abandon her innate Midwestern politeness even in a time of crisis.

"Thanks," Mark muttered.

She nodded.

"Look," he said, "I know we need to talk about this, but—"

"I can't right now," Becky cut in. "I need time to wrap my brain around everything we just heard."

There was an awkward pause as Mark stared at the ceiling.

"I guess I was wrong. Someone did watch that footage of us in the elevator," he said.

"Whoever it was certainly got an eyeful."

"You don't think David saw it, do you?" Becky asked with a dawning sense of horror.

"Oh, I'm sure he did. The man is a horndog, you know."

The elevator dinged again and they arrived at their floor.

"Look, I'm going to go for a walk and try to sort things out," Mark said. "How about we meet for a late lunch?"

"Sure. The halal cart at one-thirty?"

"You got it," he said, and headed off.

Becky knocked on Jessie's office door.

"Come in," she called.

"It still feels weird not to be sitting here anymore," Becky said as she entered.

"You're welcome in my closet anytime," Jessie said. "Your chair is still here and everything."

"Thanks," Becky said. "But I don't think I'm going to be working here very much longer."

"What are you talking about? You're my new boss, aren't you?"

"It's a long story. Let's go get some coffee."

Once they were settled in their favorite booth, with steaming cups of coffee, Becky launched into the story.

"So one of you has to quit?"

"That's the long and the short of it."

"Well, obviously it should be Mark. You're the one who belongs here. He just got hired!"

Becky sighed. "That would make the most sense, I know."

"But…"

"But I think I'm just going to do it. David will never

respect me now that he's seen me in such a compromised position, and I'm tired of fighting to prove myself to him."

"What about your promotion?"

"I don't know. It doesn't seem so important anymore." As soon as she said the words Becky realized she meant them. Although she'd been prepared to fight to keep her job, her heart wasn't in it. It was still lying in pieces on the floor of her apartment.

"It sounds like you've already made up your mind," Jessie said.

Becky sipped her decaffeinated coffee in silence for a moment. Truth was, she'd known in her gut what she needed to do almost before the words had come out of David's mouth.

"Yes," she said finally. "I guess I have."

"I sure am going to miss you," Jessie said sadly.

Becky reached across the table to squeeze her hand. "Don't worry. You're still going to see me. You volunteered to be my birth coach, remember?"

"Oh, yeah. I forgot about that. Cool!"

Taking a deep breath, Becky prepared to launch into the real reason she'd asked Jessie to have coffee with her. "So, listen, I need you to do me a favor."

"Anything."

Mark sat on a bench in front of the halal cart, waiting for Becky.

He'd racked his brain for a good solution all morning, but still didn't know what to do.

Common sense dictated that he be the one to go. After all, Becky had been working for years to get the promotion they'd just been granted. He'd just stepped in.

But he wanted to stay. He wanted to launch the Eden campaign into the stratosphere and make a name for himself. He wanted to earn a steady paycheck, get to know his colleagues, just live like a normal human being for a while.

But Becky was pregnant. She needed this job and the medical insurance that came with it. He might not want the baby, but that didn't mean he wanted the child to be denied basic medical care.

He sighed, hating the fact that at his core he still seemed to be a decent human being. Life would be easier if he could stop caring about other people.

He knew he had to be the one to walk away. He couldn't live with himself otherwise.

"Hi, handsome," a voice said from beside him.

He jumped. "Where did you come from, Jessie?" he said to the woman who had suddenly appeared next to him.

"I've been sitting here for five minutes. You've just been on another planet," she said.

"All right, then, here's a better question. What are you doing here?"

"Becky sent me," she said. "She asked me to give you this."

In her hand was a bright blue envelope. It looked like a greeting card.

"You're to read it, then ask me your questions."

"Okay," he said, hoping he sounded calmer than he felt. What could this be about?

Taking a deep breath, he opened the envelope and pulled out the card. The outside featured a black-and-white image of a magician. The inside was cramped with Becky's writing.

Dear Magic Man,
By the time you read this I will have already submitted my resignation. The job is yours. Enjoy it. Rest assured, though, that I will be watching you. If you don't turn our concept into a showstopping,

award-eating monster, I'm going to come back and kick your ass.

Please don't try to get in touch. Don't call. Don't email. Don't stop by. I don't want to ever see you again. At least not until you're ready to step up and be a dad. Which, let's be honest, will probably never happen.

So this is goodbye. Have a nice life, Mark. You deserve to be happy.

Your Gorgeous Girl

XOXO

P.S. Jessie will know how to find me. Just in case you ever want to know.

Mark read the note three times. Finally, he looked up.

"So, she's gone?"

"Well, not yet. But she's leaving."

"Where is she going?"

"Come on, Mark. You know I can't tell you that."

"Do you know why she's leaving?"

"I'm going to guess it's got something to do with the little seed you planted in her belly," Jessie said, rolling her eyes.

"Hey, that wasn't my fault," he said.

"Whatever, dude. It takes two to tango."

She had him there.

"Right. Well, I'll see you back at the office," she said, hopping up off the bench. "Enjoy your lunch."

After she left Mark waited for the relief to set in. After all, Becky had given him what he wanted. He'd be able to keep his dream job for as long as he wanted.

He should be happy. Instead he was miserable.

She hadn't even left yet, and he already missed her.

That couldn't be a good sign.

CHAPTER TWELVE

BECKY SAT ON the bed in her childhood room, trying to find the energy to unpack. It had been an exhausting week. She'd whirled into action the very same day that she'd quit, burying her pain in activity.

Finding a renter to sublet her apartment and getting her things packed had been the easy part. Making peace with leaving New York had been a good deal harder. She'd always thought she'd spend the rest of her life there. She'd dreamed of having a wedding in Central Park and of raising a family in a brownstone on the Upper West Side. And as for her career—well, she'd assumed she'd spend it in the ad agencies on Madison Avenue.

Returning home to Michigan had never been part of the plan.

But without a job she didn't have a lot of choices. Her fifty thousand dollars wouldn't last very long in New York. And raising a baby alone in the city was a challenge she wasn't sure she was up for.

So here she was, back where she'd started. She sniffed, quiet tears falling down her face. So much for her big plans.

There was a soft knock on the door.

"Come in," she said, hastily wiping the evidence away.

Her mother entered, carrying a laundry basket.

"I brought you some clean sheets."

"Th-thanks, Mom."

"Are you crying?'

"No. Yes. Maybe?"

"Oh, honey," her mother said, perching on the bed beside her. "I know things look bad right now. But it'll get better. Before you know it you'll have a job, and a place of your own, and a baby to love."

"I never meant for this to happen, Mom," she said, leaning her head on her mother's shoulder. "I'm sorry if I've disappointed you."

"You could never disappoint me," she said. "Especially not when you're carrying my grandchild! It would have been better if you'd gotten yourself a husband first, of course. But you're young. It will happen in its own good time."

Becky looked at her mom, flabbergasted. That didn't sound like the conservative Catholic she knew her to be. "I didn't expect you to be so calm about all of this," she said.

"We've been watching a lot of reality TV these last few years," she said. "I know the world has changed."

Becky just barely managed to stop herself from laughing. She could tell her mother was completely serious.

"Well, I appreciate it. You don't know how much."

"Not to worry. It's all part of the job. You'll find out soon enough."

Becky put her hand on her still-flat belly.

"I guess I will at that." The thought filled her with fear. "Mom?"

"What, honey?"

"Do you think I'll be any good at it? At being a mother?"

"Of course you will. You'll be an amazing mother."

"But I don't even like kids."

Her mother laughed out loud. "You probably never will like other people's children. But you'll always love your own. Trust me."

Since she didn't have many choices, Becky decided to try.

Mark scowled as he examined the printout Jessie had brought him.

"Jessie, this is nothing like we discussed," he said.

"I know, but I thought this was better," she said. "No offense, but your idea kind of sucked."

"Jessie, I'm your boss. You can't talk to me like that," he snapped.

"Just look at it," she said. "Please?"

"No. I need you to do what I asked you to do. *Now.*"

She glared at him and stomped out.

Sighing, he sat down in his chair and glanced at the printout. He hated to admit it, but she was right. It *was* better.

He called to his assistant. "Susan?"

She poked her head in the door, looking tense. "Yes, Mark?"

"Can you ask Jessie to come back to my office, please?"

She nodded and left.

A few minutes later Jessie returned, looking even more furious than she had when she'd left.

"You wanted to see me?"

"Yes. Sit."

She did—reluctantly.

"Look, I'm sorry," he said. "This *is* better. I don't know what the hell is wrong with me lately."

Jessie snorted. "I do. Its name is Becky."

"This has nothing to do with Becky," he said, feeling the weight of the lie in his heart.

"Whatever you say, dude. Have you told the client she's gone yet?"

"We've told them she's taking a leave of absence. We didn't clue them in to the fact that it's a permanent one." And if he had his way they wouldn't. At least not until they were happy with what he and his team had put together without her. He owed it to Becky to keep them on board and in love.

"I could dress up in a blond wig and pretend to be her at your next meeting if you want."

He laughed. "Thanks for the offer, but I don't think that would go over very well."

"Okay, but if you get desperate you know where to find me," she said, turning to go.

"Hey, Jessie?" he asked, hating himself for what he was about to say.

"Yeah?"

"Have you heard from her?"

"Her who?"

"You know who. Becky."

"Oh, her. Yeah. She's okay...considering."

His blood ran cold. He'd never forgive himself if something bad had happened to her... "Considering what? Is something wrong?"

"She's pregnant. Unemployed. And the father's being a dumbass. So, yeah. There are some things that are wrong."

He had asked for that, he guessed. Sighing, he motioned for her to go, but she was already gone.

He'd thought it would be easy to forget about Becky. After all, their—well, whatever it was they'd shared had only lasted a few weeks. Just the blink of an eye, all things considered.

But he missed her right down to his core. He'd thought about asking Jessie to give him her contact information on a hundred different occasions, but stopped himself every time. No matter how much he wanted Becky, he did not want to be a father to their child. Which meant he had to respect her wishes and stay away.

Just as he was about to sink into a vat of self pity there was a knock on his door.

"Yeah—come in," he said.

"That's how you greet your guests?" a familiar voice asked. "I thought I had taught you better than that."

Mark looked up and was shocked to see his mother

standing there, looking out of place in her conservative pantsuit and sensible shoes.

"Mom? What are you doing here?" he said, trying not to let the shock show as he rounded his desk to give her a hug.

"Oh, you know. I was in the neighborhood and thought I'd stop by."

"Mom, you live in Connecticut."

"I just came into the city to do some shopping," she said, picking nonexistent dust off her navy jacket.

"You hate shopping in New York," he said, flabbergasted.

"All right," she said. "I came specifically to see you, if you must know."

"Why?" She'd never done that. *Ever.*

"Because I haven't heard from you since that night you yelled at me over the phone. I was worried."

Worried? His mom was worried about him? That was news to him. He couldn't stop the sudden warming of his heart.

"You could have called."

"I did. Repeatedly. You never answered."

Damn it. She had him there. He was behaving more like a spoiled teenager than the adult he was.

"Look, Mom, I'm sorry. Let's start over, okay? It's lovely to see you."

"Thank you, Mark. It's wonderful to see you, too. Do you have time for lunch?"

He really didn't, but he'd have to be a total ass to tell her so.

"Sure. Where would you like to go?"

"I've already booked a table, darling. The car's waiting downstairs."

She had chosen a kitschy bistro in Little Italy, complete with red-checkered tablecloths and traditional Italian music playing in the background.

"This has always been one of my favorites, but your step-father won't come here," she told him as she settled herself into her seat. "The lasagna is to die for, but he can't appreciate it. Too many carbs, he says. As if that's possible."

"He does seem to have a hard time appreciating anything enjoyable," Mark said blandly.

"He means well—you know that. But he takes his responsibilities very seriously. He has a hard time letting go."

"That's the understatement of the year."

"Be nice, Mark," his mother said sharply.

"Sorry," he said. But he wasn't. Not really.

A smiling waiter came to greet them. "Lucille," he said. "How lovely to see you. The usual?"

"Yes, please." She smiled.

Turning to Mark, he said, "And you, sir?"

"I'm told the lasagna is to die for. So I guess I'll try that. In fact, bring me whatever she's having."

"Very well. Two usuals. I took the liberty of bringing your favorite wine with me, Lucille. Would you like me to pour?"

"Certainly. Mark, can you have a glass during working hours?"

"Sure, why not?" He'd probably need it to get through this conversation.

Once the waiter had retreated his mother looked at him with a serious expression on her face.

"I want to talk about our last conversation," she said.

"Look, Mom, I was out of line. I'm sorry. We don't need to talk about it."

"Yes. We do," she said, a hint of steel in her voice. "We need to clear the air. Or at least I do. Now, listen very closely. I love you very much. I always have. I sent you away to school because your stepfather insisted it was necessary to ensure you had the best possible foundation for college. Every family we know did the same thing. It's what people with money do."

Mark squirmed uncomfortably. He so didn't want to have this conversation.

"It felt like he was just trying to get me out of the way. Why would he want to look at his wife's illegitimate child every day if he didn't have to? Especially since everyone knew I was a mistake."

"You probably won't believe me when I tell you this, but he's very proud of you."

"That's not what you said when I was a kid. You told me I was an embarrassment to you both almost every time you saw me," he said, unable to keep the whine from his voice.

"I admit when you got yourself thrown out of three boarding schools in the space of one term I was a bit frustrated with you. Anyone would have been. I probably said some things I didn't mean. But, Mark, I never meant to make you feel unwanted. You're one of the best things that ever happened to me—even if you were, ahem, unexpected."

"Did you ever regret having me?" he blurted, unable to stop himself from asking.

"Never. Not even for a minute. How could I? You're my son. I can't imagine life without you," she said, practically glowing with sincerity.

Mark smiled, surprised to realize how much her answer mattered.

"Thank you," he said. "Thank you for telling me that."

Their food arrived and they applied themselves to the delicious baked concoction, watching the traffic go by on the street outside. A mother passed by with a gorgeous little blonde girl in tow. The child saw them looking and waved, her whole face lighting up as she smiled. Mark laughed and waved back.

"I hope you have children of your own someday," his

mother said, a certain wistfulness playing across her face. "A family makes life worth living."

"Maybe someday," Mark said, trying not to think about the baby currently growing in Becky's womb. "When I'm ready."

His mother snorted. "You'll never be ready. No one ever is. You just figure it out as you go along and hope you don't make too many mistakes."

He nodded. He was pretty sure if he told his mom what had happened she'd tell him he'd already made a giant one.

Becky slammed her car door and hit her fist on the steering wheel. This had been the week's third job interview and it had been just as big of a bust as the last two.

Although her interviewer probably didn't think so. Judging from the light in his eyes when they'd said goodbye, he thought he had found his next senior copywriter. If only the job hadn't sounded so boring.

Her phone blared in the silence. She looked down at the number. It was the recruiter she'd been working with.

"Hi, Amy," she said, sighing into the phone.

"Hey, girl, you rocked another one," an excited voice said. "I just talked to Jim and he said he'll have an offer put together by the end of the week. That means you'll have three opportunities to choose from."

"That's nice," Becky said.

"Really? I tell you you're about to have three offers thrown at you and all you can say is 'That's nice'?"

"It's just—well, I don't want to work on cars," she said.

There was a beat of silence. "Becky. You *do* realize you're in Detroit, right? Cars are what we do here."

"I know, I know. And I'll do it. It just doesn't thrill me."

"Well, I'll bet you'll feel differently when the offers come in. They're going to throw buckets of money at you, honey."

"All right. Call me if you hear anything," she said, and hung up the phone.

She turned the key in the ignition and drove out of the soulless office park. Everything here seemed so sterile. Although cars jammed the streets, there was not a single person on the sidewalk. There was no music. No street vendors. Not even any taxis leaning on their horns. It was as if somebody had hit the mute button on the world.

The leaden skies didn't help, either. The only thing worse than early December in Detroit was late February in Detroit. It was cold. Wet. And eternally cloudy. Only the twinkling Christmas lights that winked into life after the sun went down relieved the monotony.

But that didn't help during the day.

God, but she missed Mark...er...New York.

She put her hand on her belly and sighed. "I hope you appreciate what I'm trying to do here, kiddo. Because I gotta tell you, it kind of sucks."

Mark stepped into the dimly lit bar, hoping a night out with his college roommate would snap him out of the funk he'd found himself in. Quickly he scanned the room, looking for the former football player.

It didn't take long to find him. Although John had blown his knee out the season before, he was still the guy who'd kicked the winning field goal in the Super Bowl a couple of years back. He attracted a crowd wherever he went.

Tonight he was surrounded by a gaggle of beautiful women, as usual.

He strode up to the booth and slapped him on the shoulder.

"Hey, Casanova," he said.

Immediately John turned and grinned. "Mark, you made it! Sit down, buddy. It's been too long."

"It has, hasn't it? We'll have to make up for lost time. What are you drinking? I'll get the next round."

John waved his arm dismissively. "Don't worry about it. Unless you've cozied up to that rich stepdad of yours I've got more money than you do. Still like tequila?"

He nodded.

"All right." He motioned to the bartender. "Jake, I'm going to need a double of Patrón. Fast."

Within moments a large glass of tequila landed in front of Mark.

He downed it, trying hard not to think of the last time he'd done shots of tequila—or who he'd done them with.

Unfortunately his brain insisted on showing him Becky's eyes glittering at him from behind an empty shot glass.

Her voice echoed in his ears. *All right. Let's toast,* she'd said, raising her glass. *To one wild night.*

He'd clinked his glass and locked eyes with hers. *To one wild, scandalous night.*

If he'd known how much that one night would change his life he probably would have walked away after that toast. Although he was really glad he hadn't. Even if what they'd had wasn't meant to last, he was glad he'd gotten the chance to experience it. To experience *her.*

"Hey, dude. You still with us?" John asked.

Mark shook his head to clear it. "Yeah, man. Sorry. Just lost in my thoughts."

"Ri—ight. Dude, the last time I saw you looking this pathetic you'd just found out about Sandra... Oh. This is about a chick, isn't it?"

Mark just looked at him. "I don't want to talk about it. Especially not while you're covered in women."

"Say no more," John said. "Okay, ladies, it's time to shove off. I'll see you later, okay?"

Although they pouted and whined they slowly left the booth. Once they were alone, John turned back to him.

"Okay, out with it. What's wrong?"

"Nothing," said Mark, looking down at his newly refilled shot glass. "I'm just a little off my game tonight."

"Right," he said. "And I'm Robert DeNiro. Try again."

He looked at him and sighed. "All right, but you're going to think I'm a jerk."

John just looked him, one eyebrow raised. "I'll be the judge of that."

By the time the story was done the tequila was long gone. John took one last swig of his beer, then shook his head.

"You were right," he said.

"About what?"

"I do think you're a jerk. How could you abandon her like that?"

Immediately he felt his hackles rise. "I didn't abandon her. It was her choice to go. She left without even telling me."

John stood. "Only after you proved yourself to be an immature cad who runs the second the going gets tough. She did the right thing."

"Where are you going?"

"Nowhere. But you're leaving. You've got no business being here, Mark. Man up and go get your woman. You're too old to sulk because things got too real."

Unable to think of anything to say, Mark got up and left. He didn't want to drink with someone who was lecturing him, anyway.

He wasn't sulking. And he certainly wasn't immature. He'd done Becky a favor by refusing to get involved— better that the child never have a father than have one who didn't really love his mom. He knew from experience how much that sucked.

And he didn't love Becky. He was infatuated, maybe, but not in love.

It never would have lasted.

Even if he did love her she wouldn't have stuck around. A woman like that could have any man she wanted. She'd never be happy settling for a schmuck like him.

Logically, he knew he had done the right thing.

Maybe in a couple more years his heart would believe it, too.

Becky lay back on the paper-covered pillow and breathed out, trying to relax. As the technician moved the gel-covered wand around, trying to get a clearer picture, she did her best to avoid thinking about the last time she'd been in this position, or about the baby that first sonogram had shown her.

"There you are, little bean," the technician said. "It's time to check you out."

Becky looked up at the video screen, trying to identify which of the grainy black-and-white blobs was her baby.

"Mmm-hmm," the technician muttered. "That's good. And there's that…perfect." Then, louder, she said, "Ms. Logan, your bean is in good shape. So far everything looks just the way it should."

Becky still wasn't sure where to look. "Good, but can you show me? I'm embarrassed to say I'm not exactly sure what I'm looking at."

"Oh. Of course. Silly me."

She punched a few keys on the computer and in seconds a peanut-shaped fetus zoomed into focus.

"There's your baby," the technician said. "All curled up and ready to grow. Want to hear the heartbeat?"

Becky nodded.

"All right, here it comes!"

Soon a soft, rapid-fire whooshing beat filled the room.

"That…that's my baby?" Becky asked.

She nodded.

"Oh. Oh. wow." She lay silently for a moment, struggling against tears as a flood of emotions washed over her. Joy. Fear. And a fierce, all-consuming wave of love.

She was going to be a mommy. In fact she already was. And this time nothing would stop her from loving her baby with everything she had.

Eventually the technician cleared her throat. "Sorry to rush you, Ms. Logan, but I have another appointment in just a few minutes. I'm going to have to shut this down. How many pictures would you like?"

For a moment she thought about asking for three. One for her, one for her mom, and one to send to Mark. Maybe seeing the baby would bring him around.

But. No. That was just the hormones talking. Mark didn't want to be involved in the baby's life. And she didn't need him to be.

"Just two, please."

Mark was reviewing the latest round of Eden coupon designs when David let himself into his office.

"We're going to the bar. Come with us."

"Oh, I don't know, David. I have a lot of work to do," he said. Truth was, he had no desire to spend a second longer in the older man's company than he had to.

"Come on. I'm tired of seeing you moping around here. It's time to go out and have some fun."

Fun? With David? Somehow, Mark didn't think that was going to happen. But he knew it was important to appear to be a team player.

"All right," he said. "Just let me get my coat."

A short time later he found himself sitting on a stool in David's favorite dive bar.

"Two whiskeys on the rocks," David said to the bartender.

"Actually, I don't—"

"Every ad man drinks whiskey, son. Buck up."

Mark nodded and fell silent. *Think about the money,* he told himself. *And the job. Thanks to this man, you've finally made it. You can drink a little whiskey if it makes him happy.*

When their drinks came David took a deep swallow. Mark copied him, feeling the burn all the way down into his intestines.

"Listen, Mark, I asked you to come for a drink so I could set you straight on a few things," David said.

"Oh?" Why was it everyone wanted to talk to him all of a sudden?

"I know you think what happened to Becky was unfair. That it was none of my business what you two were getting up to once work was done."

"Well, sort of." The man was a master of understatement.

David continued as if he hadn't heard. "Here's the thing, though. It had to be done. If it hadn't been because of you I would have found another reason to get rid of her."

"But she got rid of herself," Mark protested.

"Oh, please. I knew what she would do when I called the two of you in there. I'd even warned the Eden people that she would probably be taking a leave of absence. Becky's got too big of a heart to let someone else take the fall for her. And you have too much common sense to let go of a golden opportunity like this one."

"I'm not sure I follow you," Mark said slowly, his stomach churning.

"Women don't belong in advertising," David said. "Not in the upper ranks, anyway. They're too emotional. Too distracted. Becky is a damn fine copywriter, but she's incapable of achieving the single-minded focus men like you bring to the table. Eventually she would've found a man. Started a family. And just like that her career would have fallen to third place in her priorities. This agency is too important to me to allow it to take anything less than top priority in the lives of my management team. Advertising isn't a business. It's a lifestyle. I have yet to meet a woman who gets that."

He took a sip of his drink and chuckled.

"Sometimes you have to get creative to persuade them to make the right choice. Like, say, with a 'no relationship' clause."

Mark slammed his glass down on the counter, barely containing his sudden fury.

"Wait a minute. Are you're telling me there's *not* a no-relationship clause in our contracts?" he asked.

"There is now," David said with a smug smile.

It was all Mark could do not to punch him.

"Did you actually have proof that Becky and I were involved?"

"Well, I saw you hugging in your office that day. I didn't need any more proof than that. It was written all over your faces."

Mark's jaw dropped. This man was the biggest ass he'd ever met. And he'd chosen him over the woman he loved.

Loved? Yes, *loved*. As soon as the thought ran through his consciousness he could no longer deny the truth. He loved her with every fiber of his being. No job, no matter how awesome, would ever fill the hole her absence had left in his heart.

Suddenly he knew what he had to do. And it didn't involve wasting any more time with the man sitting next to him.

"David, do you have a pen?"

"Sure," he said, reaching into the pocket of his suit coat. "Here you go."

"Thanks," Mark said. Then he grabbed a fresh cocktail napkin from the pile on the bar. Uncapping the pen, he wrote "I QUIT," in all caps, and signed his name.

"Here," he said, handing it to David.

"What's this?"

"My resignation letter. It's effective immediately. Good luck with Eden," he said and strode out through the door, already punching a number into his phone. "Jessie? I'm going to need Becky's address. I have a mistake to fix."

CHAPTER THIRTEEN

BECKY STEPPED BACK to admire the Christmas tree. Twinkling lights sparkled from its branches, highlighting the perfectly coordinated red and gold ornaments.

"It looks like something out of a store catalog," her mother said, a note of wistfulness in her voice.

"A little too perfect, huh?"

"No, I just wish you'd saved a little room for our family ornaments. I really love that snowman you made when you were five."

Her shoulders slumped. "I'm sorry, Mom, I was just trying to do something useful. I feel like such a mooch."

Her mom hadn't let her do anything since she'd arrived home. She didn't want any help cleaning. Wouldn't allow her to touch a pot or pan. And she refused to accept any money for her room and board—money Becky knew her parents could use.

The forced idleness was driving her batty.

"You're not a mooch. You're my daughter, recovering from a very recent heartbreak and trying to build a whole new life—while making a new life. Cut yourself some slack."

She sighed. "I'll try. It's just that I'm feeling itchy. I need to go back to work. I haven't had this long of a break between jobs since I was sixteen."

"I know. Give it time, Becky. The right opportunity will come along."

"I hope so. Can you bring me the other box of ornaments? I'll fix the tree."

As her mother disappeared into the basement Becky heard the muffled sound of her phone trilling from somewhere in the room.

"Oh, great. Where'd I put the damn thing now?" she muttered, lifting boxes and tossing pillows.

She finally found it, mushed between two couch cushions.

"Hello?" she said a little breathlessly.

"There you are. I was just getting ready to leave you a message."

"Oh, hey, Amy. What's up? Another car agency sniffing around?"

"Nope, I promised not to bother you with any more of those. This one's different."

"All right, I'm listening," Becky said.

"Well, it's a new agency. Pretty much brand-new."

"Uh-oh…"

"Now, hang on. They have some pretty big accounts. And not automotive, either."

"Which ones?"

"I'm not allowed to tell you. You have to sign a nondisclosure agreement first. But they said you're first on their list of candidates. Said they'd pay a premium if I could snag you."

"Hmm. That's flattering."

"It is. *Very.* Why don't you just go and see what they have to say? It could be just what you're looking for."

She looked over at her OCD tree and nodded. "All right. At the very least it will give me something to do."

Becky parked in front of a bright yellow Victorian house, checking the address one more time. Yep, this was where Amy had directed her to go.

Huh? It didn't look like any ad agency she'd ever seen. She had to admit that the surroundings were charming, though. It had the same vibe that all her favorite New York neighborhoods had—young and hip and full of life.

She shouldered her laptop bag and clacked up the carefully manicured walk. As she crossed the covered porch she noticed a small woodcut sign that read 'Trio' hanging from the wreath hook.

Definitely the right place, then.

She was about to ring the bell when a gawky pink-haired girl opened the door.

"You must be Becky," she said, blue eyes sparkling.

"I am. And you are...?"

"Izzie. I'm just a temp, but I'm hoping to convince the owner to keep me on," she said conspiratorially.

"Ah," Becky said, at a loss for words.

"Come on in," she said. "He's expecting you."

She stepped inside and handed Izzie her coat, taking a moment to check out her surroundings. The house looked fabulous—contemporary furnishings contrasting nicely with ornate woodwork and jewel-toned walls.

"It's this way," Izzie said, leading Becky into what must have once been the dining area but what was now a fully kitted-out conference room.

"Have a seat anywhere you like. He'll be right in."

Becky pulled out one of the cushy wood chairs and sat down, realizing she had no idea who she was about to interview with. No one had ever given her a name.

Oh, well. The mystery would be solved soon enough.

She fired up her laptop and was opening her online portfolio when she heard a familiar rumble.

"There you are. Detroit's hottest copywriter, in the flesh. Thank you for agreeing to meet with me."

Her head snapped up. *It couldn't be.*

It was.

Mark stood in the doorway, wearing a tailored black suit, looking even more delicious than she remembered.

Her emotions spun, unsure whether to settle on absolute fury or melting delight. She stood, fighting the urge to either hug or throttle him.

"M-Mark? What are you doing here?"

"This is my agency."

"Wait. What? No. You belong at SBD."

"Not anymore. I quit."

"You quit?" she asked, fury winning. "After I gave up everything for you? What the hell did you do that for?"

"I had to."

"Why? Did you lose the account?" Surely he couldn't have screwed up that badly that fast.

"No. I brought it with me."

She sank back down in her chair. "Okay, I am completely lost."

Mark stepped into the room and pulled down a white screen.

"Let me do this right," he said. "I put together a presentation to explain everything to you. Will you listen?"

Unable to speak, Becky nodded.

"Okay," he said, clicking a few buttons on his Mac. A picture of a sullen teenage boy filled the screen.

"Once upon a time there was a boy with a nasty attitude. He lived in a big house, and attended the most exclusive schools, but had the world's biggest stick up his ass. He had long ago decided his mother didn't love him, her illegitimate son, and nothing she did could change his mind."

He clicked forward to an image of a grinning Mark in a graduation cap and gown.

"He managed to graduate from college in spite of himself, and soon embarked on a career in the soulless world of advertising. He was quite good. Racked up lots of awards. And he managed to get through his twenties without ever having a real relationship."

He clicked forward to a shot of the famous Vegas sign.

"Then he went on a business trip and met a woman who would change his life forever. They spent only one night together, but by the time she left he was already falling in love. Not that he was capable of admitting it."

He flipped forward again to show the SBD sign.

"Then he got hired to work with and compete against the same phenomenal woman. Although he told himself not to get involved, he quickly did. They worked together, played together and won the account together. Somewhere along the way he fell head over heels, but still couldn't admit it to himself."

He clicked forward to a shot of a pregnant tummy.

"When she told him she was pregnant he reverted back to that sullen little boy and ran for the hills."

He clicked forward to David's headshot.

"Then the evil agency owner cooked up a plan to get rid of the girl. Both the girl and the boy fell for it, and before he knew it she was gone."

He clicked forward to a gray sky.

"Without her, his world fell apart. But it wasn't until he discovered the evil agency owner's dastardly plan that he managed to get rid of the stick still up his ass."

Another click and one of their Eden ad designs filled the screen.

"He submitted his resignation on a cocktail napkin and headed to the Eden company to tell them what he knew. Being decent people, they fired SBD and signed on the dotted line with the boy's as yet unnamed agency—on the condition that he find his better half."

He clicked forward to the yellow house.

"So here he is. Starting over. In Detroit. Betting that the woman he doesn't deserve will give him another chance with her heart and let him be her partner and her baby's daddy."

"Are you serious?" she whispered.

"Do I ever bet when I think I might lose?"

"I don't know," she said, her mind whirling. "This is all so sudden..."

"I have one more thing to show you," he said. "Will you come?"

She nodded and he led her up the ornate wooden staircase. He opened a door and stepped through to the sunny yellow room beyond.

"This is your office," he said. "And this," he went on, opening a door with a placard reading CEO, "is our baby's office."

It was a nursery, done in shades of green and yellow, complete with crib, rocking chair and changing table.

"My office is just over there," he said, pointing to a door on the far side of the room. He turned to her and smiled. "What do you think?"

She opened and closed her mouth, spinning in a slow circle in the middle of the room. "It's amazing," she breathed.

Mark crossed the room in two steps and got down on one knee, producing a diamond ring from his suit pocket.

"Becky, I'm ready to go all-in. I want us to be a family. Will you do me the honor of becoming my wife, partner and best friend?"

Becky thought her heart might explode with joy.

"Yes," she said. "Oh, yes."

Mark solemnly placed the ring on her left hand, then grinned up at her.

"I bet I know what you want me to do now."

"What?" she asked, smiling through the tears streaming down her face.

"This," he said, rising to take her in his arms and claim her lips.

Becky looped her arms around his neck and kissed him back with everything she had.

"You win again, Magic Man," she murmured. "But do you know what I want more than anything right now?"

"No. What?"

"For you to take me to bed."

"I don't have any beds here yet. Will a desk do?"

"Splendidly." She grinned.

He swooped her up into his arms and carried her over the threshold into his office.

"God, I missed you, Gorgeous Girl."

"Prove it," she said.

And so he did.

EPILOGUE

BECKY WAS JUST clicking through to her final PowerPoint slide when a baby's cry echoed through the monitor placed discreetly under the conference room table.

She grinned and nudged the power switch to the Off position with her toe.

"And that's how we'll make the Eden campaign the advertising darling of the new year, fueling New Year's Resolutions across the country."

As applause broke out around the crowded conference table Izzie poked her head through the white-paneled door.

"He needs to be fed," Izzie said in a stage whisper.

Becky motioned for her to come in and gathered the baby into her arms.

"If you have any questions, Mark can field them," she said, moving to the comfy rocker tucked behind a folding screen in the corner.

She listened, baby nestled at her breast, as Mark swung into action. In no time he had sweet talked the Eden people into spending even more money with their tiny agency in the next year.

Trio's future was secured.

When they were finally gone, Mark plopped down on the rocker's ottoman and stroked the baby's cheek.

"Well, I'm glad that's over," he said.

"Were you worried they wouldn't sign?" she asked.

"No, not really. I just want to move on to the day's big event."

"Big event? I know I've been preoccupied," she said, indicating the baby nestled on her chest, "but I thought that meeting was our last piece of client business until after the holidays."

"It was. This has nothing to do with business."

"Then what is it?"

Mark grinned. "It's a surprise. Do you trust me?"

"You know I do," Becky said.

"Good. Then I need you to head up the back staircase into your office and do whatever Izzie tells you to do. Okay?"

"Okaaayyy… I guess," Becky said. "Now?"

"Yep. Now," he said, pulling her to her feet.

"What about Alex?"

"I'll take care of Alex. Hand him over," Mark said, holding his arms out for the baby.

Becky kissed his soft head, then reluctantly gave him to Mark. Even after five months of life as a mom it still amazed her how in love she was with her baby.

"He just ate, so he's going to need a diaper—"

"I know," said Mark.

"And he needs to do some tummy time…"

"Got it. Just go."

"Okay. If you're sure…?"

Mark sighed. "Becky. You're just going to be upstairs. I've got this."

She realized she was being a bit ridiculous. "All right, I'm going," she grumbled, and headed for the kitchen door.

When she opened her office door, she was shocked to see four different people rushing about, setting up mirrors and plugging in hair appliances.

"What on earth is going on here?" she asked.

Izzie's pink-haired head popped up from behind her desk, plug in hand.

"Oh, there you are! We're on a mission to doll you up. Now, hurry up and get in here. There's not much time!"

"Time before what? I'm so confused," Becky moaned.

Izzie grabbed her by the hand and pulled her behind a screen that had been set up in the corner.

"Don't worry about it, boss lady." Izzie grinned. "You're going to love it. Now, just relax and go with the flow."

Realizing she had no real choice in the matter, Becky nodded. "All right, I'll try."

"Good," Izzie said, unzipping a dress bag. "You can start by stripping down to your skivvies. We need to make sure this fits you."

Becky gasped when she saw the confection Izzie was holding. It was a full-length evening gown made of red velvet. Gold and red beaded embroidery sparkled at the bodice and traced a delicate path down to the hip of the A-line skirt, then flowed along the hem. Cap sleeves finished it off.

"It's beautiful," she breathed.

"It'll look even better on you," Izzie said. "Now. come on—off with your clothes."

Two hours later Becky was staring at her reflection in a full-length mirror, not recognizing the gorgeous woman staring back at her, when there was a knock on the door.

"Come in," she called, not bothering to turn around.

"Wow. If that's what having a baby does for your body, sign me up," a familiar voice said.

Becky whirled, unable to believe her ears. "Jessie!" she shrieked when she saw her beloved redheaded friend grinning at her from the doorway. "Jessie, what are you doing here?"

"Oh, you know," she said. "I was just in the neighborhood, so I thought I'd stop by…"

"You are such a liar." Becky laughed, throwing her arms

around her friend. "But I don't care. I'm just so glad to see you!"

Jessie squeezed her back. "Me, too, lady. Me, too. But, hey, we better be careful. I don't want to muss that gorgeous gown you're wearing."

Becky disentangled herself and did a little twirl.

"I know. Isn't it amazing? But I have no idea why I'm wearing it."

"I do. And so will you in a few minutes," Jessie said. "But first I need to freshen up. Izzie? What have you got for me?"

Izzie dragged her behind the screen and Becky went back to gawking at herself in the mirror. Her blond hair was swept up with an elegant mass of sequined hairpins, artfully crafted curls framing her face. The makeup artist had made her emerald eyes look huge, and she was sure her lips were nowhere near that plump.

The dress emphasized her newfound curves, and for the first time since Alex was born she felt beautiful.

Tears welled in her eyes. She had no idea what Mark was planning, but she owed him big for helping her feel like a woman again.

Just then Jessie's faced popped up behind her shoulder. "Hey, hey, hey—no crying allowed! You're wearing way too much mascara for that."

Becky smiled, wiping at the corner of her eye as she turned. Jessie had changed into an elegant green cocktail dress, with the same gold embroidery flashing around the knee-length hem.

"Wow. You clean up good. Wait a minute…" she said, realization dawning. "That looks like a bridesmaid's dress. But we haven't even begun planning the wedding. It's supposed to be in June!"

Just then the lilting sound of a harp playing her favorite hymn floated up to her ears.

"Isn't it?"

Jessie just winked and peeked her head out through the door.

"Mark? We're ready for you!"

Seconds later Mark stood in the doorway, wearing a tuxedo. "Hey, babe." He grinned. "You ready to get married?"

Becky sat down heavily in her chair. "But I thought— I mean, we'd always talked about June!" Not that she'd done anything to put plans in motion.

Mark crossed the room and kneeled down in front of her. "I know, Becky, I know. But it was a year ago today, right here in this house, when we became a family. I thought it only fitting that we make it legal in the same place. Besides," he said, kissing her fingers, "I don't want to wait another six months. I want the whole world to know you're mine *now*. Becky Logan, will you do me the honor of becoming my wife today?"

Becky dabbed at her eyes again, holding back the tears by force of will alone. "Of course I will," she said, joy fizzing in her veins.

"Good," he said. "Then let's do this thing."

From the hallway, Izzie called, "Hit it, guys!" and a string quartet launched into the "Wedding March."

Becky put her hand in the crook of Mark's arm. "Let's do it."

Mark stood in front of Becky's childhood priest, listening to the sermon with half an ear as he gazed at the beautiful woman who had agreed to be his wife. Even the glow of the twinkling white Christmas lights that sparkled around them paled in comparison to the joy emanating from her.

To think he had almost missed out on all of this. Now that their baby had arrived he couldn't imagine life without him. Not to mention his mother.

Becky caught him staring and smiled, love shining from her eyes. "I love you," she mouthed silently.

"I love you, too," he mouthed back.

"If I can get these lovebirds to stop mooning over each other for a minute, we'll get to the real reason you're all here," the priest said, breaking into their silent communion. "But first let me ask all who are gathered here an important question. Is there anyone here who objects to this marriage? If so, speak now or forever hold your peace."

Silence fell, making the sudden outraged shriek from their baby's miniature lungs echo all the louder.

"We'll assume that's his way of objecting to his place on the sidelines and not to his parents' matrimony," the priest joked as the room erupted with laughter.

"Well, let's fix that." Becky giggled, and motioned for her mother to bring the baby forward. "After all, he's part of this family, too."

Once he was settled on her hip, the angry cries turned into contented coos.

"All right. Now that we're all settled," the priest said, "do you, Becky, take this man to be your lawfully wedded husband, to care for him and keep him, in sickness and in health, in good times and in bad, all the days of your life?"

"I do," she said softly, and Mark's heart swelled.

"And do you, Mark, take this woman to be your lawfully wedded wife, to care for her and keep her, in sickness and in health, in good times and in bad, all the days of your life?"

"You bet I do," he said, putting his whole heart into every word.

"Then it is my honor to proclaim you husband and wife. Mark, you may kiss the bride."

Mark gathered her to him, careful not to dislodge the baby from her hip. "Now you're mine," he whispered, and pressed his lips to hers, silently communicating his joy.

"I always was," she whispered against his mouth.

Alex chortled happily as they broke apart, and, laughing, Mark bent to kiss his cheek.

"Ladies and gentlemen, I am overjoyed to present to you Mr. and Mrs. Powers!"

The small crowd rose to its feet and applauded.

Looking around at the sea of happy faces, Mark felt at peace. Love might be a gamble, but he was pretty sure he'd hit the jackpot.

* * * * *

ENEMIES WITH BENEFITS

LOUISA GEORGE

To Nikki Logan, Joss Wood and Charlotte
Phillips – thanks so much for the fun and the
friendship during the creation of this wonderful
apartment and the people in it. It was an absolute
pleasure working with you all – I hope we can do it
again some time.

To #TeamKISS for help with the cocktail
names – many thanks to you all! I hope we all get
to have a Merry Margarita together one day!

This book is dedicated to my fabulous editor
Flo Nicoll. Thank you for your continued support,
help and advice – you are amazing!

CHAPTER ONE

1st December. Operation Christmas

CHRISTMAS MUSIC. CHECK.

Dodgy Christmas tree and decorations from attic. Check.

Decent bottle of red and one extra-large glass. Check... *Oops*...one bottle down. Better make that two bottles of decent red...

Poppy Spencer dumped the years-old artificial tree by the corner window and started to pull back its balding branches, creating a kind of...sort of battered tree shape.

It was about time someone in this apartment got into the Christmas spirit and if that meant she had to do it on her own, then she would. So what if her AWOL flatmates were too busy to care about the festive season? She had to do something to fill the long, empty holiday that stretched ahead of her.

'Never mind, poor thing.' She was talking to a tree? That was what being alone in a flat, which until recently had resembled a very busy Piccadilly Station, did to a reasonably sane woman. 'Looks like it's just you and me. We'll soon have you shipshape and looking pretty and sparkly for when everyone comes home. Cheers.'

She chinked a branch with her glass and took a large

gulp. There were few things in life that beat a good Shiraz. It went down rather quickly, coating her throat with the taste of blackberries and...well, wine. She poured another. 'And here's to absent friends.' All of them. And there appeared to be more going absent every day.

The box of baubles and decorations seemed to have ended up in a similar state to the tree: a nibbled corner, depilated tinsel. Mice perhaps? Surely not rats? She shuddered, controlling the panicky feeling in her tummy... Rats were horrific, nightmare-inducing, disease-ridden rodents and mice their evil little siblings.

So maybe she wasn't alone after all.

Standing still, she held her breath and listened. No telltale scurrying, no squeaks. Quiet. The flat was never quiet. Ever.

Oh, and there was some woman crooning about not wanting a lot for Christmas. Yeah, right, said no woman ever.

Note to self: ask big brother, Alex, to look for evidence of four-legged friends—the man had fought in Afghanistan; he was more than equipped to deal with a little mouse infestation.

Second note to self: Unfortunately, Alex was sunning himself on an exotic beach somewhere with Lara. And Isaac, the only other male flatmate, was...well, hell, who ever knew where Isaac was? He was like a sneaky, irritating nocturnal magician, here one minute, gone the next, probably expanding his über-trendy bar portfolio along with his list of short-term female conquests.

Tori had gone with Matt to South Africa. Izzy had moved in with Harry. That was it, all her friends out, happy, settled. Doing things with significant others—or, in Isaac's case, insignificant others.

Was it too much to want a little bit of their collective happiness? Someone to care if she died alone, suffocated under a box of musty decorations or knocked out by a toppling balding Christmas tree, toes nibbled by starving mice. More, someone to care if she never ever had sex again. Like ever.

She imagined the headlines.

Doctor's body found after three weeks! Nobody noticed recluse Poppy Spencer had died until the smell...

Or...

Miracle of regrown hymen! Autopsy of sad, lonely cat lady Poppy Spencer discovers born-again virgin...

No doubt somebody somewhere who bothered enough to listen would say she had lots of things to be thankful for. A good job—albeit varicose-vein inducing, with long hours of standing. Friends—albeit all absent. A flat—albeit leaky.

And a new, less-than-desirable flatmate, with fur. Which she would tackle, on her own, because she was a modern evolved woman...and not because she was the only person around to do it. Seriously. It was fine.

She took another decent mouthful of wine. Mr Mouse could wait; first, she'd cheer herself up and decorate the tree. Putting a hand into the box, she pulled out a bright red and silver bauble and almost cried. This was the first house-warming present Tori had bought her. Tori always bought the best presents; she had an innate sense of style.

And Poppy missed her.

'No.' More wine fortified her and put a fuzzy barrier between her and her wavering emotions. 'It's okay. I'm a grown up. I can be alone.'

She'd read, in an old tattered magazine in the doctors'

on-call room, about a famous reclusive actress who'd said that once. German? Swedish? Poppy couldn't remember; in fact things seemed to have gone a little hazy altogether.

She picked up two baubles and hung them from her ears like large, gaudy earrings, grabbed a long piece of gold tinsel and draped it round her shoulders, like an expensive wrap over her brushed-cotton, pink-checked pyjamas. Lifted her chin and spoke loudly to the street below. '*I* want to be alone. Or is it, I want to be *alone*...?'

Louder, just so she could feel the words and believe them, she shouted to the smattering of falling snowflakes illuminated by the streetlights, to the dark, cloudy sky, and to the people coming out of the Chinese takeaway with what looked like enough delicious food for a party. A far cry from her microwaved meal for one. 'It's fine. Really. You just go and enjoy yourselves with your jolly Christmas laughing and your cute bobbly hats and fifty spring rolls to share with your lovely friends and don't worry about me. I'll just stay here, on my own, and think about adopting a few stray cats or crocheting toilet-roll-holder dolls to pass the time. Crochet is the new black. It'll be good for my...fine motor skills. I'm fine. I want to *be* alone. I do.'

'Oh,' came a voice from behind her. 'In that case, I'll leave you to it. Goodnight.'

'Ah! What the hell?'

Isaac. She'd know that voice anywhere. Half posh, half street. All annoying. And very typical. Strange kind of skill he had, always turning up at her most embarrassing moments.

She winced, slowly swivelling, bringing her arms down to her sides—had she ranted out loud about her pathetic misery and lonesomeness?

Damn right she had.

The tinsel hung pathetically from her shoulders and the baubles bashed the sides of her reddening neck in a not-quite-in-tempo accompaniment to her heart rate. She probably looked a complete fool, but then, where Isaac was concerned, she was used to looking like a prize idiot.

He, however, looked his usual scruffy 'male model meets bad-boy done good' self. He needed a shave and a decent haircut; his usually cropped crew cut stood up in little tufts making him look angelic—which he wasn't. His cheeks were all pinked-up by the cold winter air. A light dusting of snow graced his shoulders. No doubt some unknowing bimbo would think he looked adorable. But Poppy knew better. Isaac's looks were deceiving.

He'd been part of the Spencer family's life for so long he was almost a member of it, and had a habit of turning up like a bad penny at the entirely wrong time, giving her that disappointed shake of his head he'd perfected over the years. But it didn't affect her quite as much as he hoped because her parents had been doing the exact same thing since she was in nappies.

And now he was here, occasionally living in her lovely flat, because her big brother, Alex, had let him rent a room without asking her first.

Isaac's head shook. Disappointedly.

She feigned nonchalance because any kind of in-depth conversation with him was the last thing on her Christmas wish-list. 'So, the missing flatmate returns.'

'I wasn't missing. I was working in Paris and then on to Amsterdam, checking out some decent bar venues.'

'Oh, lucky for some. The other day I managed to get all the way to Paddington for a sexual-health meeting, and once I even made it to the dizzy heights of Edgware Road.' She loved her job, she really did, but sometimes delving into women's unmentionables lacked any kind of glamour. And definitely no travel—apart from visiting the dark underworld of repairing episiotomies and doing cervical smears. Where she discovered a lot of women were having a lot of sex. Sadly, she wasn't one of them.

He shrugged. 'Oh. You got a whole mile away. Whoop-de-doo. Aren't you adventurous?' The animosity was a two-way thing.

He dumped his large duffel bag on the floor and threw his coat on top, cool blue eyes roving her face, then her ears, the tinsel, her flannelette pyjamas. Which had to be the most sexless items of clothing she owned. Which didn't matter. Isaac was just a flatmate. Her big brother's best friend. Nothing else.

Apart from…weird, his eyes were vivid and bright and amused. And somebody else might well have thought they were attractive, but she didn't. Not a bit. Not at all. They were too blue. Too cool. Too…*knowing*. He gave her one of his trademark long, slow smiles. Which didn't work the way he might have hoped. She did a mental body scan to check. Nope. No reaction at all.

Through her pre-pubescent years she'd done everything to garner his attention—and had probably appeared as an exasperating little diva. Then she'd woken up to the reality that he was not interested, and then neither was she once she'd discovered bigger and—she'd thought—better men to chase. Real men, not teenage boys…and then… The shame shimmied through her and burned bright in her cheeks. Eight years and she still felt it.

Well, and then Isaac had been lost in the whole sordid slipstream.

He took a step forward and plucked the tinsel from her arm between his finger and thumb, gave it a sorry little look then let it drop to the floor like an undesirable. 'I'm very sorry to have to break this to you, Poppy, but I think your Christmas fairy days might be over.'

Grabbing a bauble from her ear, she wrapped it round one of the needleless branches. Then did the same with the other one. In a last act of defiance she placed the tinsel from the floor in pride of place in the middle of the tree. 'Well, gee, thanks.'

'I just think it might be a little unstable.' He glanced up at the wonky, droopy top of the tree, then watched her sway. 'Like you perhaps?'

'Hey, be rude about me all you like, that's normal service. But you do not insult my tree.' She eyed the wine bottle behind him. No harm in a little more. 'Me and this tree have been together a long time, and no one's going to criti…be rude about it. Pass me that glass?' She pointed to the bottle and the glass and then realised that, irritating or not, she should at least be polite to him. Who knew? He might be an expert at rodent removal.

'D'you want to get yourself a glass, too? There's plenty…oh.' There appeared to be a lot of bottle and not a lot of anything in it. 'You want the last dribble? Or we could open another one?' Two bottles downed already? Now she was all out. 'Beer? Eggnog?'

'No. Thanks. I've just been working down at Blue and I've had my share for tonight.' His too-bright, too-blue eyes narrowed as his gaze roved her face again. 'And you look a little like you might have, too?'

'Hmm. I thought there was more in there. I'm just…' His smile made him look like some major celeb. She'd never noticed that before either. Gangly teenager Isaac was now pretty damned handsome? Who knew? And now he was swaying, too. *Oops*…no, it was her… What was she doing? The tree…yes, the tree. 'I just need to finish this decorating. Then I really should go to bed.'

'You need a hand?'

'Going to bed? No. I don't think—' She looked down at his palm. It was a nice hand. Slender fingers, neat nails and the slightly roughened skin of a man who worked with his hands…

Oh, and his brain. Because he was also too clever and too successful—seemed the man just knew instinctively about bars and where to put them and who to market them to. Clever, and her brother's friend. And then he'd found out her deepest, darkest secret…

Stupid. Stupid.

'No. Thanks. I'm just finishing this. You can go.' She wafted her hand to him to leave, *needed* him to leave as that memory rose, scoring the insides of her gut like sandpaper.

She slid her fist back into the decorations box. Something warm banged against it, then darted out of the hole. Something brown. Small. With more legs than she had time to count.

'Yikes!' Jumping back, she stepped on Isaac's booted foot, banged against his body—which was a whole lot firmer than she ever remembered—and ricocheted off him into an armchair, which she scrambled on, all the better to get out of the way of a man-eating furball. Her heart pounded against her ribcage. 'What…the…hell was that?'

Isaac laughed as he ducked down to the floor. 'Shh…it's just a little mouse. Very frightened now, too, by your crazy demonic scream.' He crawled along the carpet, hemming the creature into a corner, then swooped in and grabbed.

It darted away, under the TV cupboard and into a very dark corner. Now the only view Poppy had was of a very firm-looking jeans-clad backside. And a slice of skin between his belt and T-shirt, skin that for an odd reason made her tummy do a little somersault. Seemed Isaac had recently been somewhere sun-kissed as well as wintry northern Europe. 'Have you got it?'

A muffled voice came from underneath the cupboard. 'For an educated woman who uses scalpels for a living you're mighty squeamish when it comes to tiny pests. I think it's escaped.'

'You think? You *think*? I can't live here *thinking* I don't have mice. I want to *know* I don't have mice. I don't like them, they scare me, however irrational that makes me. And where there's one, there's always more. There could be fifty of them.'

'Then at least you won't be alone, right?'

'I'm fine.'

'Sure you are.' He scrambled up, looked at her all hunched up on the chair and grinned. 'So you were yelling at some poor, unsuspecting, innocent bystanders. Very loudly.'

'They were down there across the road and I'm up here behind a window. They didn't hear.'

'No. But I imagine the rest of the building did. Where is everyone?'

She slumped down, choosing not to have any more wine, because, seriously, two bottles were way more than she usually had. The mouse had done a runner, so she shovelled her feet under her backside in case it decided to retrace its teeny steps. 'They're all out. Gone. Holidays, shopping…all insanely happy and…' *Left behind.*

He perched on the arm of the chair, arms folded over his chest—looking as if he was trying to appear sympathetic but inwardly laughing. The way his face lit up when he laughed…that mouth, so nice, so weird. And maybe it was Shiraz-coloured glasses because he was so *good-looking* weird. Attractive weird. *Sexy* weird. Infuriating Isaac was eye candy, too. Who knew?

She'd been so busy being annoyed at him living in her space that she hadn't thought anything else about him at all. Apart from being aware of an electric current every time she was in the same room as him. She'd always assumed that had been caused by her anger at his general class-A irritatingness. 'Fancy them going off and having a nice time without you. Poor Poppy. Lonely?'

And he was a mind-reader, too, but no way would she fess up to such an idea. 'Don't be silly. It's great that they're all sorted—it gets them off my hands. Finally.'

'You love it, though, playing the mum, looking after them all, nurturing them…putting up the tree as a surprise for when they get home. Sweet. You don't want to be alone at all, do you?'

'You make it sound pathetic when really I'm just using you all to pay the mortgage.'

He leant towards her. 'Hey, I was joking—at least you were the sensible sibling and put your money into bricks and mortar instead of partying it away like Alex. And it's a great flat even if it does get a little busy. And leaky. But the company helps, right?'

'*Some* of the company does…'

'Don't worry, message received loud and clear. I'm sorry Alex gave me the room without talking to you first. I wouldn't have moved straight in if I'd known. But I'll be out of your hair as soon as my apartment's done.' Isaac's grin smoothed into that soft smile again and for some strange reason her unmentionables suddenly got hot and bothered.

What? No. It was just unseasonably warm tonight. Or a vasoconstrictive response to the wine. Or something. Whatever was making her body parts flush it was definitely not Isaac Blair. 'Oh, yes, the swanky South Ken penthouse. I've heard it's going to be very nice. Very swish and expensive.' Very uncluttered, too, no doubt. Isaac liked to keep things simple—most notably his love life, which, she'd observed over the years, was more like a revolving door of heartbroken women trying to ensnare him, and nothing stable or serious. Or committed. Ever. 'And the renovations will be finished when?' Hope rose.

'A couple more months, I imagine. There's Christmas

coming and everything shuts down so there'll be no progress made for a few weeks. Mid-February?'

Hope fell, but, God knew, she needed the cash to fund her home loan. Alex might well have spent all his inheritance but he'd had a good time in the process. All she'd got out of ploughing her grandmother's inheritance cash into a bijou flat was a financial noose around her neck, dodgy plumbing and four-legged furry friends. Regardless, she didn't feel overly comfortable being on her own with Isaac and flushing unmentionables. 'Okay, so you stay on longer than February the twenty-eighth and I'll charge you double rent.'

His eyes widened. 'You drive a very hard bargain, Dr Spencer.'

'Indeed I do.' Her eyes locked with his and there was a strange rippling in the atmosphere between them. Was she imagining it or did he feel it, too?

He dragged his gaze away, but not before she caught a glimpse of tease there. Maybe a little heat. Whoa. Isaac? Heat? With her? Maybe she hadn't imagined it.

'So it's just you and me here tonight, then?' he asked.

'It appears so.' And why did that make her feel suddenly nervous? No, not nervous…tingly. Tingly happened to other people. Not her.

She looked across the wooden floor to the dark hole under the TV and tingly mingled with fear. Although she had to admit she did feel a lot better with Isaac in the flat. 'Just you, me and our furry friend, of course…plus his babies, wife, mother, grandparents, probably a community the size of a small tropical nation living in the rafters, the walls…under my bed.'

'I'll get a trap tomorrow from the hardware stall at the market and have a word with the café and let them know we have guests. They'll need to know for their own health and safety measures.'

'Oh, I don't want it hurt, or dead. I just want it gone. Out of here.'

'Like me? Right.'

Got it in one. She couldn't hide the smile. 'You can stay if you can keep the rodent population to a minimum. Humanely. Yes. Yes. The mice. Do things…with them.' Was she rambling a little?

'Is that all I'm good for, really?'

She could think of a few things—starting with that mouth. Her stomach joined her head in all kinds of woozy. Definitely too much alcohol on an empty stomach. 'I'm sure you're good for a lot of things, Isaac…'

'I've never had any complaints.' He stood up, the flash of cheekiness gone. She wondered how it would be to really flirt with him, just a little. But then she didn't know how. He brushed down his T-shirt and strode towards his bag.

There was something she was supposed to ask him. She couldn't remember… Something about work or Christmas… Her head was getting foggy… Oh, yes… She held up a finger. 'Wait. One thing.'

He stopped and turned, the bag still in his hand. 'Yes?'

'I have a problem.'

Smug eyebrows peaked. 'Oh? Just the one?'

'Don't be cheeky. I'm organising the department Christmas party and the venue has double-booked us. Any chance Blue could fit us in? I'm in a bit of a pickle because I'm organising the party…' Had she already said that? He might just save the day. She put her hand on one hip and flashed him her best winning smile. 'Pretty please?'

It appeared to have little effect apart from the eyebrows rising further. 'Now you're just being nice because you want something. Poppy, Poppy, should I charge you double rates, too? What night?'

'Next Friday.'

'I'll check the diary tomorrow. Shouldn't be a problem, though. That's early for a Christmas party.'

'Things tend to hot up the closer we get to Christmas. Everyone wants a Christmas baby so they either try to hold on…or try to get it out early. We want to get the party out of the way so we can focus.' Focusing was a bit of a problem right now, but she figured she'd be fine by Christmas.

'So you're working over Christmas? Not going home?'

She snorted at the thought. 'You're joking, right? I offered to work Christmas Day so the staff with families that actually cared for each other could spend time together. That way I have a good excuse to stay away from the family pile. So do me a favour and make sure my work Christmas party's a good one? I want at least one thing to look forward to this festive season.' *Give me a good time, Isaac?*

Geez, she was funny.

'Okay, I'll see what I can do. And now, I'm definitely going to bed.' He turned again, his back straight, shoulders solid and that backside giftwrapped in jeans, all tight and firm and…her mouth watered.

What in hell was she thinking?

She watched him reach the door and felt an overwhelming desire to talk to him just a little more. She didn't want to be on her own. And for some reason she felt a tingling down low and a need to…to what?

She hadn't been able to think about sex for so long and now…well, right now she was thinking about it a lot. And not just because she was on the obstetrics and gynaecology rotation, although if that job taught her anything it was that women were either doing it a lot or not able to do it and wanting her to fix problems so they could do it some more.

But she deserved a little fun—and some much needed sexperience—maybe Isaac would know how she could find some. 'Hey, Isaac, wait.'

'What now?'

'You have fun, right?'

She couldn't read his expression as he turned to face her. Something between grumpy and irritated. And downright insanely sexy. 'Sure. I work hard so I figure I should play hard, too.'

'That's it...that's just it, right there. I've worked so hard for so long and I just want...*more*. Is there more? What more is there? What am I missing? How do you... you know, have fun without getting messed up in the process? Do you understand?' She wasn't sure she did. Not a lot of anything made sense right now. Except that Isaac had come closer and was looking at her with those bluest of blue eyes—okay, he was a little out of focus... And she wanted to stroke his hair. No, she wanted to breathe in his smell. It was smoky, very masculine. Yummy. She wanted to breathe him in and stroke his hair. 'Is there more, Isaac?'

'Oh. Okay, I see, we're at stage three already.' He disappeared into the kitchen and brought back a pint glass filled with water. 'Drink this.'

She took a sip. He pushed it back towards her mouth and she drank a whole lot more; it was refreshing but nowhere near as nice as the Shiraz. 'Stage three of what?'

'It goes like this. The tipsy stage. The funny stage. The "pondering the universe" stage. Then, the "I love you, you're my bestest ever friend" stage. And finally, the upchuck. We see it all the time at work and, trust me, you do not want to get to stage five.'

She put the glass down on the coffee table. 'I am so not at any stage.'

'Walk in a straight line, then, preferably towards your bedroom to sleep the alcohol off.'

She doubted she could stand in a straight line. 'I don't have to. I'm fine, thank you very much. Very fine indeedy.'

He held her gaze. A challenge. The heat in his eyes was flecked with serious. So nice. So very, very nice.

And very, very Isaac. 'Okay, okay, I'll walk.' Oh, yes, she could do that. She could do that perfectly; show Isaac Blair she wasn't afraid of any challenge from him.

CHAPTER TWO

STAGE THREE. WITHOUT a doubt things could well get messy. After spending hours dealing with this kind of stuff at work Isaac really did not need it at home, too, but he took Poppy's hand and pulled her up from the chair. For the second time that night she bumped against him and he steadied her, feeling the softness of her body as she leaned into him. Cute that she wore old-fashioned pyjamas to bed, but with Poppy's slightly restrained approach to life it wasn't surprising.

The way she felt was, though. She had curves where curves should very definitely be and right now, pressed against him, they certainly chased away the London winter chill.

Hell, she'd grown up. A lot. And even though he'd caught up with her over the years he hadn't really looked at her. Hadn't wanted to—and she clearly hadn't wanted anything to do with him either. Not since the night he'd held her thick dark hair while she vomited into a rose bush and cried for a man who wasn't him. 'Hey, careful.'

'Oops. Sorry.' She looked up at him through a fringe that grazed long black eyelashes and something flashed behind her deep brown eyes. Caution. Poppy's normal mojo. She'd trodden a safe, sensible path for the last however many years—never letting herself get out of control, always steadily working towards her career goal. But there was something else in those eyes, too—something glittering—need? Lust?

First time he'd seen her let her guard down in for ever. Amazing what a bit of wine could do.

'Right.' He stretched a piece of tinsel along the floor. Hell, it wasn't his problem; *she* wasn't his problem. But he had to make sure she was safe. Way he saw it, he could probably do this tinsel line straight to her bedroom and she'd hardly notice. 'Now, walk along this line and we'll see what stage you're at. Then you should definitely get some shut-eye.'

'See. I can do this, *no problemo*.' Her right foot rested on top of the tinsel, scarlet-painted toes pointed as if she were perfecting a gymnastic display on the barre. Left foot. Then the right flailed in mid-air, she wobbled, fell sideways and into his outstretched arms. She grabbed on to his shoulder and he got a whiff of clean citrus, shampoo possibly or shower gel. The woman smelt good. She smiled. 'Oops again. You're a good catcher, Isaac. Thank you for being here. You're very kind. Very nice actually, I think. Underneath that standoffish mask. Very nice indeed. We could be friends, you know… You know a lot about me. More than anyone—'

'Shh. Let's concentrate on the walking thing.' He placed a finger over her lips. Rapidly approaching stage four—he did not want to deal with that. 'Then I think we should get you to bed.'

'Absolutely… Is that…is that an offer?' The heat in her body slammed against his. Her lips parted ever so slightly as she smiled.

Then closed again as he shook his head. 'Thanks. But, no. If we were ever to do anything in bed, Poppy…which we won't…I'd want you to be able to remember it in the morning.'

Sleeping with Poppy? Insane idea. But the thought lingered for just too long, and he hadn't been with a woman in a while.

Absolutely not.

He gently removed her from his arm, and within a nanosecond of that touch his body zinged with a shot of pure feral desire. Here she was offering herself to him, this attractive grown-up woman—although he'd only just awoken to that fact. He could take her to bed and ease away some of the stresses of the past week. Show her the fun she so obviously craved.

Only, this was Poppy and there were a dozen or more reasons why that would be the worst damned idea he'd had in a long time. Not least the fact she was drunk, lonely and, until she'd uttered that last sentence, he would have sworn she hated his guts. He'd been there at her lowest, her weakest and worst moment, and somehow she'd never forgiven him.

Not that he'd ever cared. Impressing women past a flirty dalliance had never been on his agenda. He'd spent enough time watching too many marriages fail to contemplate one himself, and he wasn't about to change that any time soon.

It had been a busy few days—he was tired, was all, having put every ounce of effort into getting the Paris bar up and running. He needed sleep. On his own. 'Come on, let's get you to the bedroom.'

'No! Bathroom first. Teeth. Floss. Wee.'

'Too much information, lady.' For some reason his hand seemed to have slipped back round her waist. She wasn't so drunk that she'd fall over, but he thought it best he should steady her as they walked towards the bathroom. Her head rested against his shoulder and she looked sweet. Smelt great. Felt…sexy as all hell. Was it possible to be jet-lagged from a one-hour flight? Because he couldn't think of any other reason for this strange disorientation.

He tried to keep his eyes on the bathroom decor and

not on Poppy's backside as she dipped to rinse her tooth-
brush. She'd done a reasonable job painting the flat in
bright, light colours. The bathroom still needed a little
TLC as the plumbing was cranky at best but it was clean
and tiled in muted stone. A large skylight shed light from
above although now all he could see were glimpses of stars
in a cloudy night sky.

What gave the room colour were the multi-hued bits of
lace drying on the radiator on the far wall. Still unused to
sharing a house with so many women, he wondered what
the correct response should be to finding flimsy underwear wherever he looked. He doubted it should be the
spike of interest, and trying to match the panties to the
woman. Now he tried not to imagine Poppy in the red
and black number.

Hey, he was a hot-blooded man after all.

After a few moments of brushing her teeth she looked at
him through the reflection in the large mirror. 'You know
it's a medical impossibility to become a virgin again once
you're not. Right?'

'Uh-huh. You're the doctor, not me. But I think it's a
given that once the seal is broken it can't exactly be unbro-
ken. And where are you going with this, Miss Einstein?'
Grabbing the towel, she dried her mouth, then turned to
him.

'I'm a fraud. I advise women every day about their sex
lives and I don't have one. How can I talk to them about
sex when I don't even remember what it's like? I don't
want to be an almost-virgin when I die, Isaac, but I'm
headed that way.'

Like he was the right guy to be having this conversation with. Especially when he was the only person in the
universe who knew why she'd given up sex. Anger started
to rise from nowhere. She'd run away from any kind of
relationship ever since, when she could have been happy.

Happier. 'You really do need to sleep off that wine. There's plenty of time to get a sex life and plenty of men who, I'm sure, would be willing to help you in your…dilemma.'

'Would you?' Those pretty painted toes took a step towards him.

'Would I what?'

But instead of answering in words, she pressed her mouth against his. Pressed her body against his. Made little mewling sounds that activated every hot-blooded cell in his body. And, hell, he should have pulled away, put her straight to bed and left. But she tasted so damned good…

Someone was playing bongo drums in Poppy's head. And someone else was stomping in her stomach. Her throat hurt. Her mouth was dry. She felt like hell.

Worse than hell.

After a couple of minutes stabilising herself she twisted in the sheets about to sit up but her foot collided against something warm. Something large. In her bed. Her eyelids shot open and she managed to stifle the scream in her throat, holding her breath as she tried to make sense of it. Her heart thumped in conjunction with the annoying beat in her head as her toes gingerly tested the object.

A leg. Human. Hairy.

What. The. Hell?

She closed her eyes again until her stomach stopped churning. There was a man in her bed.

Isaac?

It took all of her strength to turn over quietly so as not to waken him up. Yes—same hair, same smell. She clamped her eyes closed again.

Isaac.

A bare leg. Two bare legs. She felt down her front…no cosy pink flannelette pyjamas, but a skimpy silk cami top? No PJ bottoms, but matching silk and lace French knickers? Lara's expensive design—for best times only. What in hell had she done?

Please no.

Surely not?

Surely, surely not? She'd spent the night with a man. With Isaac. First time in eight long years and she couldn't even remember it?

The vodka and Coke she'd had at the pub before she came home she easily remembered. And…ugh…the red wine gifts from her clients. Bile rose to her throat. She was never ever drinking again. Fuzzy flickering images of Isaac arriving while she was putting up the tree gradually came into focus. But how had they gone from that, to…this?

But oh, oh, God…she suddenly remembered kissing him in the bathroom. Remembered how she'd felt bold and brave and very sexy. And how he'd tasted so nice, his kiss so tender… Even now she could smell his scent, firing flashes of heat through her belly.

'Sleeping Beauty finally wakes up.' He turned, naked shoulders peeking out from her sheets, sat up, eyes as bright as the daylight splicing through her curtains. His hair was mussed up and he looked devastatingly hot. 'Sleep well? Eventually?'

'Why are you in my bed?' Bunching the sheet around her throat, she sat up, too. No way was she getting out until he'd gone.

'You don't remember, Poppy? What a shame. It was a spectacular night and you don't remember at all? I'm so disappointed.'

There was that shake of the head she knew so well. Daddy Spencer would be a proud man to see someone perfect that frown, even if it wasn't his own flesh and blood.

'I remember…we kissed.' *Oh, God, kill me now.* 'And

then…' She tried to force the cogs in her brain to work harder, faster, but they were stuck in fog. 'Not a lot else.'

His hands clasped at the back of his neck showing mighty fine pectoral muscles, impressive biceps… Her mouth dried to something beyond the Sahara. Mortified she might have been, but she could still take time out to appreciate a beautiful human specimen when she saw one. She'd touched that? Lain under that? Or had she been on top? Or both? Who knew?

Aargh! Why couldn't she remember?

He appeared to be struggling to keep a straight face. 'You surprised even me. And I'm used to pretty much anything. Not exactly a screamer, more a gasper…'

'A gasper? I didn't… We didn't…?' A flash of him running his hand through her hair emerged through the soup in her brain. No, that had been years ago. But…the image in her head was of her current bathroom. Of safe hands stroking her back. A soft smile as he'd picked her up and carried her across the apartment and into her bedroom.

'You kissed me.' No way would she forget that in a London minute.

'No, Poppy. You kissed me.'

'You kissed me back.'

Those magnificent shoulders shrugged. 'Glad to help out a lady in need. You said you wanted me to teach you a few things. Asked me…begged me.'

Oh, good Lord. Begged Isaac? 'Well, that was the vodka talking.'

'Vodka? No, a couple of bottles of Aussie Shiraz by the looks of it.'

Her stomach lurched with just the thought of it. She swallowed hard. 'Vodka with colleagues in the pub before the wine on my own.' Could it get any worse? He'd kissed her because she'd asked him to help her. Begged him. Not because he'd fancied her. Not because he'd wanted her. He'd kissed her out of pity.

She'd begged him?

'I have to say you are an almost textbook drunk.'

'Good to know.' That'd be right. Usually Poppy did everything by the book, because not doing so caused too much harm and mayhem. And she never wanted to go there again.

'But what is it about me, Popsicle?' His use of her childhood nickname made her cringe, and he damn well knew it, making her pull the sheets more tightly round her cleavage as he spoke. 'Is it something I do? Is it the way I smell? Every time we get a moment alone we end up with your head down, bum up. Gasping. Stage five implemented to perfection. You are a champion upchucker.'

No. Not again. 'I was sick?'

'Yes. Spectacularly.'

'I'm so sorry.' No wonder her stomach hurt.

'Not pretty.'

'So we didn't, er, you know.'

He shrugged. 'Hey, you know me, I never give away our secrets.'

She'd begged him not to before and he'd been true to his word. She threw him a glance—his grin widened and she wasn't sure if he was referring to back then or last night. But he was clearly not going to enlighten her. Irritating.

Over the ensuing years that evening had hovered between them like an ominous dark cloud—would he ever confront her? Would he put her in a situation where she'd have to confess to everyone what she'd done and show who the real Poppy Spencer was?

So far he'd kept schtum on the whole thing—but then she'd never allowed herself to be in any kind of situation where she owed him anything more. And ever since then the all-new shiny reformed Poppy Spencer hadn't put a foot wrong.

But still—he *knew*. And for that reason alone she kept him at a distance.

Fast forward to the second most mortifying moment of her life—if they'd actually done the deed surely she'd know? She'd feel different—her body would feel less nauseated and more…excited. Surely? No, they hadn't had sex, she was pretty certain. Relief flooded through her. 'So why are you in my bed now? Why am I in different clothes? Where are my pyjamas?'

His head shook. Disappointedly. 'Don't panic, I put a quick stop to the kiss and you're still an *almost*-virgin.'

'A what?'

'Never mind. Just something you said last night. Amongst a whole lot of other stuff.' His voice rose a couple of octaves. '*"Please don't leave me, there's a mouse on the run. I'm scared. Too cold. Too hot. I need a drink. Headache. I'm going to be sick again. Please, don't leave me, Isaac, I'm scared."* Eventually your demands exhausted me and I fell asleep right here. You are one hell of a snorer, by the way. I hope for your sake it was just because of the alcohol.' He smiled his slow, lazy smile. 'And now you're wearing the only things I could lay my hands on in the dark at four-thirty this morning during the too-hot phase. Very, very nice, too.'

His eyebrows rose as his fingers plucked the blush-pink lacy straps of her cami. At his touch her body reacted in a very un-Poppy-like way—with a frenzied surge of what she could only describe as lust. And he knew it, too, judging by the glittering in his eyes. 'Must have cost a fair bit.'

She slapped his hand away from her straps, not least because of the effect his skin was having on her skin. 'They did, even with mate's rates. And did you look…did you see…?' She'd learnt to be forthright with her patients;

why couldn't she be forthright with him? She needed to know the extent of her absolute mortification. She took a deep breath, not wanting to hear the answer to her question. 'Okay, so who undressed me? Did you help with that or did I manage it all by myself?'

'Don't worry, I closed my eyes.' He leaned forward and whispered against her neck, making her shiver and shudder and hot and cold at the same time. 'Most of the time.'

'What? No!'

Then he winked. 'All I can say is that someone's going to be a very lucky man one day.' But he clearly wasn't referring to himself because with that he threw the sheet back, revealing a pair of extremely well-toned legs, thigh-hugging black boxers with the outlined shape of something she only allowed herself a moment's glance at before she was totally and utterly lost for words… Wow…just wow. And a body that she could have sworn she saw advertising aftershave in a glossy yesterday. 'Got to get to work, Popsicle. I'll make sure I get a mousetrap on the way back. Thanks for a very entertaining evening.'

Then he was gone.

'Damn. Damn. Damn.' She leaned back against the pillows and breathed out a huge sigh, unsure of what to make of it all. Because, despite the Macarena in her stomach, she could have sworn she should be feeling a whole lot different from the way she felt right now. She should definitely not be feeling turned on. Her breasts should not be tingly, her heart should not be pounding, her lady bits should definitely not be wide awake and singing hallelujah at the mere hint of Isaac's presence. Or at the thought of him seeing her naked. No. She should not be feeling like this at all. Especially when the startling, belittling, humiliating truth of it all was that, without any thought of consequences, she'd got drunk, accosted him and he'd kissed her back *out of pity*.

CHAPTER THREE

'WE HAVE MICE. At least, we've seen one little critter upstairs. I thought I should let you know.' Isaac paid for his coffee and nodded his thanks to Marco, the café owner. 'I've got a couple of traps and we'll sort it out our end. Just keep an eye out down here in case they migrate.'

'Okay, cheers, mate, I'll have a look, but we're usually on top of zeez things. No mices here.' Marco pushed Isaac's coffee towards him and started to serve the next customer.

Isaac took his cup, negotiated the defunct fireman's pole that connected their upstairs apartment with Ignite café, and found a seat, aiming to fortify his strength with a sharp caffeine buzz before he nipped back to the flat. The last thing he wanted was to bump into Poppy and relive the awkwardness of earlier. A coffee shot would help. Plus keep him awake for the long night's work ahead.

He took a sip. Added an extra sugar for luck. Opened his smartphone and reviewed his notes. The only thing of any consequence he'd managed to achieve today was to check the availability of the bar for Friday, for Poppy. Then he'd sorted out a mousetrap, for Poppy. Spoken to the manager at Ignite café, for Poppy. And hidden in the café, *from* Poppy. The woman was invading his every living, breathing moment, not to mention his to-do list.

Which was very interesting. He never allowed any

woman to ever invade anything at all. Work came first. Always. Work was predictable and straightforward. Work didn't change the goalposts or come with an agenda that you didn't understand. He knew where he stood with his business—knew what he needed to do to be the best. And he'd made damned sure he had been, throwing hour after hour, year after year into transforming his bars into award-winning establishments. Being pretty much uprooted and homeless by the age of sixteen, he was used to travelling, liked the challenge of working in different countries, of winning the hearts and loyalty of the Parisians and the Dutch. Next stop, the States, and he'd be a success there, too. That would show everyone who'd ever doubted him.

But despite what he'd said and what he'd tried to convince himself to believe, he'd really enjoyed that kiss. The cheeky glimpse of Poppy's half-naked body bathed in moonlight hadn't been half bad either. Which, hands on heart, had not been his fault. She'd said she was ready, when in reality her silky top hadn't quite covered everything it needed to. He'd turned away...too late.

Hell. He closed his eyes briefly at the mental image; she was definitely all woman. And off every limit he had. So the fact his brain kept wandering back to those scenes last night—the kiss, her body, her smell, even her pyjamas—was very inconvenient.

He added *fast-track the renovations* to his to-do list. He could control his libido, but he couldn't guarantee for how long, so the sooner he was out of that flat, the better. Stupid enough to get in any way involved with a woman, doubly so to get carried away with a woman he had too much history with. That could get all kinds of messy.

Isaac subscribed to the 'no promises, no commitment, no heartbreak' school of relationships. Easy. In his bitter experience commitment usually lasted just until someone *better, richer, younger* came along, leaving chaos and hurt in the slipstream. He didn't need any of that.

The doorbell pinged behind him as someone entered along with the cold December wind-chill factor. Women's voices. His gut pinged, too, as his hand froze, coffee cup halfway between the table and his mouth. Izzy's northern-infused accent. Poppy's hesitant laughter.

So much for avoiding her.

Gulping the too-hot coffee and almost suffering third-degree burns in the process, he put his cup on the table, tugged up his coat collar around his ears, focused on his phone and concentrated on trying to be incognito. Plan A: when they started to order at the counter he'd slip out unnoticed.

'Isaac! Hello.' Izzy dropped a kiss on his cheek, then shoved a stray lock of short blond hair behind her ear, beaming. He'd met a lot of Poppy's friends over the years, as part of a peripheral group that tagged along whenever Poppy's brother, Alex, was home on leave, but never had he envisaged living with any of them. Strange how life worked out. 'Long time no see. Where've you been?'

'Hi, Izzy. Hello, Poppy. I was in Europe for a while sussing out some bar venues. We've just opened one in Bastille and we've another planned for Amsterdam.' He tried to focus on Izzy, but his eyes kept drifting towards the woman he'd spent the night with. She refused to meet his gaze, keeping her focus on the counter ahead, then on Izzy, a small polite wave to Marco. Scraping his chair back, Isaac lifted his plastic carrier. 'I got some traps. I'll head upstairs now and set them up. Do you have any pea-nut butter?'

Finally Poppy looked up at him, her make-up-free cheeks pinking. Instead of her regulation work ponytail her hair hung in loose curls around her shoulders, which normally would have made her look younger, if it hadn't been for the purple shadows under her eyes.

She pulled a thick cream cardigan around her uptight shoulders and stamped black suede boots on the tiles. Her mouth had formed a grim line. Clearly the hangover still hung.

Even so, she still looked breathtaking. He'd never really thought of her like that until yesterday. But breathtaking was the only way to describe her. Yeah...well, she'd certainly taken his breath away with that surprise kiss last night. As she spoke he wondered what could happen next time, if he left his principles at the bedroom door. Which was never going to happen. Because he would never let them get into that situation again.

She frowned. 'I thought mice ate cheese.'

'The guy in the market said to use peanut butter— apparently they love it. If we don't have any I'll head to the shop and get some.'

'No. There's some in the cupboard by the fridge.' She peered up at him. 'Smooth.'

'Thanks. I like to think so.' He grinned.

'Yeah, Mr Big Shot, whatever. I was talking about the peanut butter, not you.' She tutted, her shoulders dropping a little as her eyebrows rose. 'You definitely fall in the crunchy camp.'

'Oh, and now I'm mortally wounded.' Still, it was good to have her at least being able to look at him. Things could get weird in the flat if they couldn't speak to each other. 'Well, I've got to set these traps then get back to work... Oh, talking of...the private room's free at Blue on Friday for your work get-together if you still want it. Do you need to come and view it?'

'No, I don't think—' She looked off-balance and not particularly thrilled at having this conversation.

'Or are you fine taking my word for it?' He could give

them both a get-out if he sorted it all here. Then he could head off to his sanctuary and work out what the hell was going on in his head. Or at the very least try and get her out of it. 'How many will be coming? Do you need food? I can get the chef to make up a specials menu for you all.'

'I think there's probably about twenty of us, including some spouses and partners.' She matched his smile. Not too friendly. 'I'm sure the regular menu will be fine.'

Good, no need to spend any more time with her than necessary. 'Great. I'll see you later. Some time. I'm kind of busy at the bar so I might not be around much.'

Way to go—Poppy's whole demeanour seemed to brighten. 'Oh—okay.'

'Wait. Isaac?' Izzy interrupted and his optimism floundered. 'Maybe Poppy and I should come over this afternoon. I'd love to see your new bar. I'm scouting out places for the wedding reception. And Poppy? How can you organise a party without checking out the venue first?'

'Oh, I trust Isaac,' she said in a voice that conveyed the opposite. 'I'm sure it'll be fine.'

Izzy looked at her friend with growing incredulity. 'It's a cocktail bar, right? And you're on a day off?'

Poppy gave a weak shrug. 'Yes. Actually, just for a change I have some time off. And I was hanging out for a coffee. You know Marco makes a mean espresso.'

'Forget the coffee. What are we waiting for? Blue awaits. Come on, bride-to-be's prerogative.' Blissfully ignorant of the awkwardness in the room as she rode her fluffy happy wedding cloud, Izzy smiled. 'A cocktail will be fun. Happy hour for mates, okay, Isaac?'

Looked as if he had no choice.

Looked as if none of them had a choice. The bride-to-be certainly did hold all the cards.

Poppy shook her head as she wiggled out of Izzy's hold and held up her hands. 'No, I'm sorry, not today, we can go to Blue some other time. Come along with us on Friday if you want—there'll be quite a crowd. But as from today I'm officially on the wagon. I'm never drinking again.'

'Why ever not?' Izzy asked. 'It's Christmas time. We have to drink and be merry. It's the rule.'

'I had too much last night. You know me, I'm a very cheap date and rubbish at holding my booze.'

As Isaac well knew, to the detriment of a sane mind and a decent night's sleep. And that kiss that made his mouth water for more. 'Oh, don't worry, Poppy, I'm sure we can rustle you up a virgin margarita. Or even—' he made sure he had her full attention '—an *almost*-virgin one.'

'Why do you keep…?' Her cheeks blazed and she looked down at her boots. When she lifted her chin again realisation flamed in her eyes. 'Oh, my God. I didn't…?'

'Didn't what?' Izzy's eyebrows formed a V. She looked first at Poppy and then at Isaac. 'What are you two talking about? What didn't you do?'

Isaac saw the pain on Poppy's face and knew he'd stepped too far. She did sarcasm like a pro, but had also relied on him to hold her secrets close to his chest, and he'd never been tempted to share them so he wasn't going to start now. Although sometimes she was a little too damned serious for her own good. Honestly, she didn't need to repent for ever. Everyone had at least one thing in their past they regretted. And being sexually inexperienced wasn't exactly a crime. Some man would be very lucky indeed to reintroduce Poppy to the dating scene. Isaac only hoped it wouldn't be a jerk like the last one.

And why did the thought of Poppy with another man make his blood pressure hike? Things weren't making sense today. 'Didn't…get to sort out the rest of the tree decorations. Right, Poppy? Maybe you and Izzy could finish them this afternoon.' *And stay out of my way.*

Izzy picked up her bags and shook her head. 'Rubbish.

We'll come with you to set the traps. I'm so glad you've chosen the humane ones—I'd hate to see anything get hurt. We can be The Three Mouseketeers, releasing the mice into their true habitat outdoors. You must call me if you catch any. I'd love to see them. Then we'll tag along and see what an amazing bar you've created, Isaac. I've heard so much about it.' She turned to Poppy. 'Come on, please? I don't get the chance to do this very often. I feel like living dangerously. Okay?'

'Oh, okay. Just a quick drink, but I'm on water.' Poppy sighed.

And for just a second he was back in that bed watching as she fell asleep. How many times had he shared his bed? Too many to count. And no woman sleeping had made his heart squeeze as she had last night, as if he'd wanted to protect her, to stop her feeling as rotten as she clearly felt. To stop her needing to outright ask for a sexual experience. The accidental glimpse of a woman's nipples hadn't ever before made him feel so aroused.

No woman had looked so damned hot with a hangover either.

His groin tightened as he watched her. Goddamn—he needed a bit of distance, not to give her a guided tour of his bar.

Catching Isaac's eye, she frowned and shook her head minutely, but just enough for him to understand. He got the message loud and clear. *Don't mention it, don't think about it and definitely don't ever consider spending another night in my bed.*

Which was one hundred per cent fine by him.

Blue lived up to the hype. Even through foggy hangover vision Poppy could see why Isaac had won the Best New Bar Award this year. Decorated in vivid midnight blue with a wall of cascading turquoise water in the centre of what used to be a bank it was startling, edgy and yet a very comfortable place to be with soft, plump easy chairs she sank into.

Or would have been comfortable if she hadn't been in direct eye line of Isaac all afternoon, on tenterhooks wondering what the heck he was going to say and how she was going to answer. He'd always had slick one-liners, been far too cocky for his own good and she was so out of her league here—tongue-tied with embarrassment.

As it was mid-afternoon the place was quiet with just a couple of other customers sitting up at the long mahogany bar reading the extensive cocktail menu. Izzy tapped her martini glass against Poppy's sparkling water. 'Cheers. I'm very impressed—no wonder he's doing so well if all his bars are like this. He's a bit of a mystery, though, isn't he? Flitting in and out of the country... He's sort of been vaguely around the edge of our group on and off for years, then he's suddenly rich and successful and renting a room at yours.'

Poppy nodded. 'Believe me, the renting's only temporary. He wouldn't have been my first choice of flatmate. But when Alex offered him your old room I couldn't exactly say no. I guess Alex thought he was doing us both a favour.'

Izzy winced. 'Sorry. I didn't mean to leave you in a mess.'

'Ah, look, I'm a landlady, I have to expect these things to happen. Funny, though, we were so settled for all those years, just you, me and Tori in our lovely flat.'

'*Your* lovely flat.'

'Yes, well, I always thought of it as ours really—you helped me find it and decorate it. I just bankrolled it. But then in the space of two months everything's changed so much I can barely keep up. Tori moved out to be with Mark, and you moved out to live with Harry. Alex moved in, Tori moved back into the box room, Isaac took your old room. And just to spice things up a bit, we had Matt for a month. I'm getting a bit dizzy. It's like the place has a revolving door at the moment.' If only Isaac could see fit to revolve out permanently instead of staying over for a few nights here and there…usually unannounced. Still, paying full rent in advance meant his contribution to the mortgage was a big relief to her money worries. In the short term. 'Besides, with his job he's hardly around.' Until recently. Now it felt as if he was around rather too much for her liking.

'And he hasn't got a girlfriend? Or at least no woman to stay with until his flat's ready.'

'Oh, trust me, he's had plenty of women.' Poppy sipped her water and thought briefly about exchanging it for something stronger so she could find some of the bravado she must have had last night. Kissing someone—not even asking, just kissing—took guts. She hadn't known she had any. Not those kind of guts, anyway. Asking for what she wanted, taking what she wanted. Typical it had ended in disaster.

Izzy clarified, 'No long-term woman.'

'According to Alex, Isaac's dating record is a month. Thirty days. That's not enough to give anything a chance. I've heard of the kind of things he used to get up to with Alex and it's not pretty. The man's just a flirt. No self-respecting woman would want long term with him, anyway, not that he'd ever offer. I think watching his mother have failed marriage after failed marriage has put him off any kind of commitment.' So said the ex–junior psychiatrist in her.

She watched him so comfortable there behind the bar with his colleagues, laughing and joking. The smart shirt accentuated the pecs of steel she'd seen this morning. Her mind drifted back to the tight boxers and her heart rate escalated. She swallowed another gulp of water to douse an unexpected heat rushing through her. *God.* Hot and bothered just by looking at a man. This never happened. Never. Was she eighteen again?

Ugh. She shuddered. She damned well hoped not.

'There's a funny vibe between you two. There's always been a funny vibe, but it's getting more *vib*rant.'

Bless Izzy and her wishful happyed-up thinking. 'There's no *vibe*.'

Her friend touched her arm. 'Just be careful.'

This was the girl Poppy had known for ever. Only once had she ever kept a secret from her; every other single thing about their lives they had shared. Openly. Everything. And yet she didn't want to tell Izzy about last night, about kissing Isaac and the weird sensations he was instilling in her. Didn't want to confess about the hole she felt she had in her personal life and the inadequacies in her professional one. All of which could be fixed by one kind, considerate and caring man and a little sexperience. Isaac did not fit that bill.

But inside her head the only image was of naked shoulders peeking out of her sheets. Too-blue eyes teasing, hot breath on her neck, and tight black boxers. Always the black boxers.

Everything tingled. Every damned thing. 'Me and Isaac? I don't think so. Seriously.'

Izzy nodded. 'You're probably right—too close to home. Too weird after all these years. He's definitely good to look at though.'

'Says the married-woman-to-be.'

'Hey, I'm getting married, not joining a convent.' Izzy drained her glass. 'I said be careful, I didn't say don't act on the vibe. You could always just have a little…' her eyes widened '…fun.'

Sexual fun? She'd have to look that up in the dictionary.

A crash and the sound of breaking glass had them turning to look back to the bar. Isaac was holding a towel over one of the barmen's hands. He turned to look at her directly, raised his eyebrows summoning her over. The day was rapidly spiralling into disaster. This was not how she'd planned to spend her holiday.

She stood, wishing that she'd chosen flower arranging instead of medicine as her vocation, then she wouldn't need to be near him. Smelling him. Thinking about the black boxers. *Ahem. Medical emergency?*

She dragged on her game face. 'Looks like I'm needed. Duty calls.'

Izzy stood, too, and grabbed her bags. 'Do you want me to stay and help?'

'No. I'll be fine. You go. Aren't you supposed to be meeting Harry?'

'Yes, but…I don't want to leave you.'

'Seriously, I'm a doctor, I can manage. You go, this could take a little time. See you later.'

'Hey, thanks for coming over.' Isaac looked at the grimacing man and then back to Poppy. 'My friend Poppy, here, is a doctor, very handy to have around. Jamie's my business partner and he's just had a contretemps with a glass. Got a nasty cut—do you think it'll need stitches? I've got a first-aid kit.'

Ignoring the *thud-thud* of her heart as she got closer to the one person she should have been far away from, she pulled back the towel and peered at the gash. 'It's pretty deep. Yes. Yes, it needs sutures and I don't have anything with me. Your first-aid kit probably won't do. You'll have to go to A and E or a GP surgery, I'm afraid.'

Isaac walked the barman to the seating area out front. 'Okay, Jamie, sit down, mate. I'll call a cab and come with you.'

'And close up the bar? Don't be daft.'

Poppy shook her head, grasping the 'get out of jail free' card. 'I can go with you if you like? This is my kind of territory. I might be able to fast-track you through.'

Jamie looked at them both in turn. 'Er…seriously? I stopped needing a nanny in primary school. It's a cut hand, is all. Just get me a taxi and I'll sort the rest. It'll leave you short for tonight though, Isaac. Sorry, mate.'

'Not your problem. Just get it fixed. I'll be fine.'

'With the Christmas cocktail lesson starting in thirty minutes? You reckon? How about you call Maisie in?'

Isaac frowned. 'She's gone to Oxford with her boyfriend.'

'Carl?'

The frown deepened. 'At some uni event. No worries, I'll be fine. I can manage.'

Jamie turned to Poppy, holding his hand close to his chest. Blood seeped through the towel, vivid red contrasting with his blanching complexion. He needed to be gone and quick. 'I know this is a long shot, but I don't suppose you have any bar experience, do you?'

Spend more time with the man she'd shared a bed with? And who her body appeared to want a repeat performance with. This time, with full body contact?

No way. 'Me? No. Not really.'

Jamie's shoulders slumped. 'Just for a couple of hours until I get back, or Isaac can get reinforcements?'

She looked at them both staring at her. Jamie hopeful. Isaac not so much. But heck, she had nothing to do for the next few hours…days…and no one to do it with. She might as well stay and be of use to someone as sit at home with four-legged furry friends and a bent Christmas tree. 'I… well, I could collect glasses and take orders, I suppose.'

Isaac looked less than thrilled but relieved. 'Are you sure? Thanks. Most excellent. That would be a great help. I can teach the class, no problem, it's just the serving I need a hand with.' He pressed a chaste kiss to her cheek that sent shock waves of lust shivering through her. This was such a bad idea. 'You're a star.'

'I know.'

As they watched Jamie leave in the taxi, Isaac stepped closer, eyes twinkling. 'You never know, Popsicle, you might learn a few things. Cocktails are my speciality. Especially virgi—'

'No. Don't say it. Don't even go there.' She stabbed a finger into that hard wall of muscle he had for a chest, resisting the sudden urge to fist his shirt and pull him closer and press her lips to his again—just to remind her what he tasted like. 'I'm doing this because you looked after me last night. Because you're letting me have the private room for my party. And because you bought a mousetrap. After this we'll be even. But be warned...' She fought the urge to either slap or kiss his now teasing, grinning face. 'One mention of virgins, almost or otherwise, and I'm gone.'

CHAPTER FOUR

'ONE RED-HOT RUDOLPH, two Christmas Kisses and a Candy Cane Caipirinha, please.' Poppy shook her head as she gave the order to Isaac. Two hours of cocktail chaos and she was still getting used to the names of these things, and to carrying and fetching.

'Righto, you're getting the hang of this.' He nodded and reached for a bottle of rum. 'I wasn't sure you'd be any use at all.'

'Well, gee, thanks. This may surprise you, but I'm a woman of many talents. Mind you, it is very different from what I'm used to. I'm usually the one giving the orders, so being on the other side of them is a big smack to the ego. Keeping me real.' She did quote marks with her fingers for the *real*. Because nothing kept you more real than assisting at a birth and seeing new life come into being. 'But it's a great crowd. I'm stacking up my good karma points and having fun. Surprisingly.'

Apart from having Isaac's eyes following her around the whole time.

He might well have been just watching to make sure she was doing her job okay, but it felt strange. Intense. She felt scrutinised under his gaze and, every which way she thought about it, she came up wanting. Every sorry experience with him had shown her as an inadequate ingénue, even now after all these years. Had she really blurted out her stupid worries under the influence of way too many wines?

Still, at least the early rush was starting to die down and she could catch her breath. Shame, then, that it only ever seemed to stall when she was around Isaac. 'Clever names. Who came up with them?'

He gave the cocktail-shaker thing a good shake, then poured a bright pink drink into a highball glass, leaned over the bar and popped it on Poppy's tray along with a smaller, salt-rimmed lime-coloured drink. His shirt shifted over his body as he moved, straining across muscles that could not possibly have been honed just by making drinks in a bar. She knew he boxed with Matt and Alex when he was in town, other than that, she realised, she knew very little about his life. Apart from the colour of his boxer shorts. The width of his thighs. And the length... She nearly dropped the tray.

Lost for words, she dragged her eyes away and steadied herself. This was not like her and it was getting out of control.

He didn't seem to notice. 'The whole team had a brainstorming session and came up with the cocktail names. In a couple of weeks we'll be running daily specials on the twelve cocktails of Christmas, so we needed twelve half-decent-sounding ones.'

'That must have been fun. How refreshing to have a job where you can do fun stuff.'

'You don't have a laugh at work?'

'Oh, yes, sometimes, of course. The clients are usually all gorgeous. But this is so...carefree. Making up names for drinks, choosing which music to play, picking out wall colours and decor.'

His eyebrows rose. 'Running an internationally successful business is carefree? Wow, I'd love to see what you mean by intense? Hectic? Challenging?'

'You know what I mean. It's not life and death—and that's just great.' She pigged her eyes at him and enjoyed watching him laugh. 'I love how you've given the clients a couple of recipes to take away and try at home, too. They seem really pleased with that.'

'It always pays to give them an extra something. It's good business.' He pointed at the glasses. 'This is a Christmas Kiss for table two and a Merry Margarita for table six. When you've delivered them you can take a break. The night shift staff are arriving soon so we'll be a little less busy.'

Thank goodness. Being a busy registrar at the hospital was hard enough on her feet, but, despite the fun, waitressing made her back and shoulders hurt, too. She'd have a lot more respect for waitresses in the future. She walked towards what she thought was table six. Had an uncharacteristic mind melt. Was it over in the right corner? Left?

Suddenly a hand clamped round her backside making her jump and nearly lose the glasses onto the floor. 'Hey, little lady. Right in the perfect spot. You looking for someone, because I'm right here. Christmas kiss?'

What? She turned to find a short man with a nasty skin disease, which she'd definitely be looking up in a textbook later, and hair that needed a serious wash, violating her personal space. He reached out for the Merry Margarita and as she watched him she realised she'd been standing under a sprig of mistletoe. The groper grinned. 'These for me? Keep 'em coming.'

'Not unless you're from table six and the last time I looked there were two women sitting there.' She eased her bottom away from his hand. 'Unless you've had a sudden sex change? Or would you like me to give you one? I'm a dab hand with a scalpel.'

He didn't move, but his hand hovered perilously close. 'I was just being friendly. It is the season to be merry.'

'*Jolly*. It's the season to be jolly. Now, walk away from my bottom.' She found him her best sarcastic smile and looked down at his now empty hands. 'Well done. Now, the bar's to your left, the exit to your right. You choose. But any more groping and I'm choosing for you.'

'Well, wow. Nicely done.' This time the voice came from close to her other ear and her bottom remained hands-free. The groper took Isaac's arrival as a sign to head to the bar. 'I was coming over to help—I could see him honing in on your backside from over there. But clearly you have no need for a knight in…' he looked down at his clothes and shrugged '…jeans and a work shirt. Next time I'm looking for a bouncer I'll know where to come.'

He'd come to save her? Cute. Disturbingly sexy. 'Sorry, boss, was I too brutal, out of line? It's just that every Christmas and New Year's Eve there are men like him stalking single women for a quick grope and a snog. The mistletoe's always their excuse. Sad, really.' And, hell, she should know. She was always the one copping the attention from the geek in the corner. And never—never, ever—from someone like Isaac.

'No, you were very in-line. And yet so not the Poppy I know. I'm impressed.' He tugged a hand through his hair. 'So, little mice scare you, but grown men don't? Go figure.'

'I used my work voice. Six months of working in A and E on a Saturday night teaches you how to deal with people who've had too much alcohol…oh.' She felt the blush steal into her cheeks and down her neck. 'I…er…I'm not one to talk.'

'I guess not. You know all about drunken misdemeanours, Dr Spencer. They get you into bed with all the wrong sort of people.' His mouth creased into one of the most breathtaking smiles she'd ever seen. He leaned in close enough that she could smell him. That scent had haunted her all day. His mouth came closer, into full focus… 'Now, about that Christmas kiss…'

'What?' *No.*

Yes. Yes, please! Her body thrilled with a sudden rush of heat, no doubt turning her cheeks from pink to hot Rudolph red. The thought of doing more misdemeanours, preferably with him, and definitely naked, made her hot all over.

Isaac tapped the tray. 'The ice is melting. If you don't get it over to the table soon I'll have to make another one.'

'Of course. Yes. The drink. Right away.' Duh! The cocktail Christmas Kiss. Not the mistletoe. She looked ruefully up at the white berries over her head, shrugging off the shivers of lust skittering down her spine. So inappropriate. Her body screamed disappointment as she watched him walk away. What the hell was happening?

She served the drinks, dodged the groper, removed her apron and headed to the little lounge out back reserved for staff only. Ten minutes would be long enough to get herself together and shake off that weird Isaac-induced vibe.

Okay, so hands up, Izzy was right: there was a vibe. Poppy hadn't really thought of it before, but there was. She'd always felt out of sorts when he was around. Jittery. Nervous. And yet, stupidly anxious to make him see her in a favourable light. There was no one, no one else she ever felt like that with.

In here the seats were the same square, soft, couch types as outside, but the lighting was brighter, making her squint as she walked in. She hadn't been expecting to see Isaac there, kettle in one hand, cup in the other. 'Oh, are you taking a break, too?'

'I was just going to offer you a cuppa, then head upstairs to the office to change the roster now Jamie's likely to be off. It's the least I can do after you've helped me out.' He flicked the kettle on, threw a teabag into a mug. 'Maybe another night you could learn how to make some of the drinks? They'd make your infamous house parties go with a bang.'

'Another night? Not likely, I've done my good Samaritan dash. This was a one-off thing only. I do have a proper job.' Kicking off her shoes, she gave her toes a little massage to ease out the knots and tension. But realised that most of it was coming from inside her gut and not her feet.

Leaning against the counter, he looked relaxed. Easy. In his own space. A direct contrast to how she felt. Getting it together could take a little time. 'I'm well aware of your meteoric rise in the lady-doctoring world, Poppy, and your skills were greatly appreciated here earlier on. Thank you for helping me out with Jamie. But if the challenge ever gets too hard for you and you're just too far out of your *sexperience*-zone…or you just feel like a change of career, there'll always be a place for you here.'

Sexperience? God, beam me up now. 'Hmm, doctor versus barmaid? Tough call.'

He handed her a cup. 'Seriously, I'm grateful you're here. As you can see things get a bit hectic and it'll only get worse as we get closer to Christmas.'

Putting his own drink down, he sat opposite her. No chance of Isaac-free space here. She tried to find some inane non-controversial subject to chat about. 'So are you heading off home for Christmas?'

'Nah.'

'Won't your mum want you home?'

'What? When she has Archie and Henry to fuss over? I don't think so.'

'They're your stepbrothers, right? Won't they want you to be there? Won't you all be doing the Santa Claus thing?' She hoped for their sakes it wouldn't be like the cold, loveless festive time she'd had growing up.

'They will. At eight and six they deserve a decent Christmas.' He shrugged. She'd had the impression he was a little more sympathetic towards his mum now she'd shown she could actually settle down and stay with a man for longer than a few months. Clearly not. He shook his head. 'It's just easier if I stay away.'

'Easier for who?'

Silence stretched between them. He stared into his cup. Eventually his head rose and he met her gaze. 'Easier for us all, to be honest. She has asked me to go down this year for the first time in a long time, but I'm not really into the happy family pretence thing. And since when has my life been of any interest to you?'

Since I kissed you. Saw you half-naked. Almost naked. Lots of bare skin...too much. Not enough.

Since she'd suddenly become overly intrigued by him. 'Just making conversation.'

'Yeah...well.' *Back off.* 'That's weird.'

It was. Yes. But pre-kiss she would have been able to have some kind of conversation with him without thinking about sex. Although clearly not about anything remotely personal to Isaac. Resting her weary feet, she sipped her drink and changed conversational tack. 'I'm surprised you're here doing the actual physical bar work. I imagined you'd have people to do that while you pushed bits of paper around being important.'

'Usually I do—although we're trying to be paper-free so I have to find other ways to look important. But it's early days for this bar and I want to make sure we have the right feel. The only way to do that is to be here when the action happens.'

'And how do you know if you have the right feel? What are you aiming for?'

His eyebrows rose and he carried on chatting, obviously passionate about his work. 'It's hard to quantify. I guess it's more of an instinctive feel. We have a good buzz, the right music and decor. Great service is always important—and, thanks to you, that's happening tonight. Ultimately I'd like this place to be a destination bar like Red and Aqua. Things are going well so far. The takings are brilliant—but then if you can't make a killing in the silly season you're doing something wrong.'

'So how many bars do you have now? Obviously I know about Red, Smoke and…Aqua…in Westbourne Grove, Brixton and…?'

'Newcastle. Five in the UK, six including Bar Gris in Paris. Hopefully one in Amsterdam in the late spring—that's what I was negotiating over there. We have a venue, the fit-out has started. Then it'll be Berlin, possibly New York…'

'And you want more?'

'I always want more, Poppy. Don't you?' His slow smile spread across his face, eyes lighting, too. He shifted forward in his seat, his gaze meeting hers.

Her mouth dried. More? Did he mean what she thought he meant?

Everything had been tipped sideways. But she knew she wanted to touch him again. Definitely more touching.

God, really? Her stomach twisted into a tight knot.

She fancied Isaac? The strange feelings weren't just embarrassment at last night's shenanigans. Or mortification that he knew her deepest truth. She really, truly, bolt-out-of-the-blue wanted him to touch her. Here. Anywhere.

This was not happening.

'Okay, let's get back to work.'

He didn't move an inch but his disconcerting gaze finally left hers and flickered to the back window. 'Ugh, look, it's starting to snow. That'll mean either we get a last rush of punters or they'll all start to leave.'

She ran to the window and watched the tiny swirls of snow, illuminated by the bar's outside lights, falling to the ground. Only a smattering of it had stuck to the pavement, but it was a truly wonderful Christmassy sight. 'Oh, wow, look at that. I love it when it snows.'

He joined her. 'Really? All that sludge and sleet and cold?'

'Scrooge, much? What about making snow angels and snowball fights? Tobogganing? I love it all. We used to sneak out of the boarding house after lights out and have massive snowball fights in the park.'

'Oh, at school? Not target practice with Alex, then?'

'Oh, sure, when we were at home we did, too, but the best fun was at school. Always. Don't you think? Wasn't it for you? I met my closest friends there. And Alex loved it, too—but then it could have been because he wasn't at home. Anything was better than that.'

Isaac shrugged again. His answer for any difficult conversation. But then she realised she'd inadvertently strayed into rocky conversational ground. He'd had to leave boarding school because his parents divorced and his mum couldn't afford to send him any more—meaning he'd enrolled in a local school where he'd allegedly fallen in with a bad crowd. Even though Alex had kept in touch with Isaac, Poppy hadn't seen a lot of him after that. Until the night of her school ball.

The realities of where they stood, what they'd shared, came sharply into focus. He knew her. And she knew him. Knew what his track record with women was like. Knew what he was prepared to give to a relationship and how little that was. Knew he was a lot more experienced than she was and that fact alone scared the hell out of her.

It was one thing to like the look of him, the scent, the feel. But another altogether to even think of anything more.

'Okay, time's up. We should get back to work.' That would be a whole lot better for the both of them.

CHAPTER FIVE

TWO HOURS LATER Isaac watched from the bar as Poppy buttoned up her heavy coat, pulled on a beret-style hat and gloves and tied a scarf around her neck. Instinct made him want to stop her wrapping that gorgeous body up, and then slowly unwrap her, layer by layer. Not just her outer clothes but the ones underneath. To see whether he'd matched the right undies to the right girl. And then to get another glimpse of her clothesless body. To shed layer after layer of the pretence they'd lived with for years—the unspoken scenario that had kept them at arm's length—and see more of the real woman. He'd glimpsed that, too, the other night—amazing how alcohol could lower a person's guard. She was successful, professional and yet vulnerable. Lost and naive. And ever since their conversation in the staff lounge she'd been detached, too.

Interesting. As was the sharp sting of lust every time he got a whiff of her scent. Which meant he really did need a little geographical distance.

She gave him a weak smile, or at least he thought she did—he couldn't really tell as her mouth was hidden by the layers of wool round her neck. Her voice was muffled. 'I'm heading off now. I'll see you at home?'

He'd be in Alex's bad books for ever if he let his sister walk the snowy London streets on her own at this time of night. He figured offering to ride home with her might get a more favourable response to offering her just a ride. 'Wait, I'll come with you.'

'It's okay. I'll be fine.' She walked towards the door.

He finished wiping down the counter tops, flicked on the dishwasher. 'I know that you'll be fine, but if you can wait for a few minutes while I close up we can go together. It seems stupid to trudge all that way on your own for the sake of a couple of minutes. Or are you in a hurry for some reason?'

After a couple of seconds' thought she came back and leaned on the bar counter. 'You know very well that I have nothing to get back for, or to get up for tomorrow. I get a lie-in until the week after next if I want to.'

'Strange way to spend a holiday if you ask me.' Although spending a week in bed with Poppy could be very interesting indeed.

And this was the guy trying to avoid those kind of thoughts.

She gave him a smile that lit up her face. 'Why, Big Shot Bar Man? What rates as a good holiday for you?'

'Not staying in my flat in London on my own in the cold, for a start. I'd prefer surfing somewhere, travelling around South America, exploring new places.' Roots weren't something he craved. Home wasn't a place he'd had much experience of for quite a few years.

'Sounds wonderful, if I ever got the chance. Travelling is on my bucket list, but there's a lot of medical training to get through first.' She huffed out a breath. 'I can't afford to go anywhere, so there it is. I'm planning a couple of days shopping for presents. Chilling out a lot. And Izzy said she'd come ice-skating with me. That'll be fun.'

'Geez, yes. More cold. I bet you love Christmas, too.'

'Don't you?'

'I'd love a South African Christmas, or surfing at Bondi.

That way I don't have to think about all that…mushy sentimental stuff.'

'What, family and friends and being together?'

'Yeah.'

'And now you're Scrooge, too. Who the hell have I let into my flat? Don't let your night-time visitors from Christmas past keep me awake with their clanking chains. I have enough to contend with, with those damned mice.' She tutted and laughed but hung around until he'd dragged down the shutters and locked up. Then slid into step with him towards the Angel Islington tube station. The road was eerily quiet, the snow deadening their steps. Thick dark clouds above threatened more snow as tiny flakes fluttered around them. Walking alongside Poppy in such an ethereal landscape gave him a strange kick beneath his ribcage. Okay, he had to admit, it looked nice. But it was nothing to get excited about.

'Aw, come on, don't tell me you don't like this? It's like magic.' She caught a snowflake on her tongue and stuck it out at him. 'Yum.'

His gaze lingered on her mouth as he thought about all the things that tongue could do, then he shook his head minutely. Once again it was late, he was tired—he didn't need the whole 'wanting Poppy' thing going on. Although, his body obviously had different ideas. Bad ideas. Good bad ideas. In hindsight he should have let her go home on her own, but what self-respecting man would let a woman walk the streets of London on her own in a snowstorm?

Although, judging by her dealings with the groper, she'd probably fare pretty well. Annoying little pre-pubescent Poppy had turned into a surprisingly strong woman. 'It's weather, Poppy. Not magic. You're the scientist, surely you should know that.'

'And you're the least romantic person I've ever met. And I don't mean cutesy, soppy, happy-ever-after stuff—I mean deep, wondrous, meaningful, secrets-of-the-universe stuff. Nature makes these amazing things.'

'You've been spending too much time with loved-up Izzy.'

She did an irritated eye roll. 'Where's your heart and soul? Can't you see past reality and dream a little?'

'Dreams? Romance? Hello? Where's the scientist gone?' Romance was for bleeding hearts. He'd never been into the wooing gig. Never found a woman he'd wanted to spend much time on, to be honest. What he knew about women, to date, was that most of them got turned on by a platinum credit card. His mother included, it seemed, with her relentless pursuit of richer, younger, better.

He hadn't needed, or cared enough, to worry about anything past that. 'Dream about what exactly? Ice particles melting on my *filiform papillae*?' At her impressed eyebrow-raise he grinned. 'You weren't the only one who aced biology. But it's a strange thing to get soppy about.'

'It's way more than just melting ice, Isaac. Each snowflake has a unique pattern created depending on specific humidity and temperature of the atmosphere. Made at cloud level, and not, as some think, as they fall to earth.' Aaand…there was the scientist. Hallelujah. 'Oh, and they look pretty.'

And…gone again. 'Huh? *Magical*. If you like that kind of thing.'

'How can you not? You've got to take time out to enjoy the small stuff.' Seemed the life philosophising wasn't just restricted to a drunken stage—she was at a point in her life when she was questioning what it was all about. He got that. Occasionally he looked at what he'd achieved and wondered if that was it. Six bars, a very healthy bank account and a penthouse apartment. The sum total of his life, which was pretty full and, some would say, very successful. But when he looked deeper he recognised that just maybe there was something missing, too.

He chose not to dwell on that.

They reached the station and began the long process of descending deep into the underground. She stood in front of him as the first escalator moved slowly south. He could see her profile; snowflakes dusted her hair, eyelashes, the tip of her nose. Now that was the kind of licking off melting ice he could live with. Her nose crinkled as she spoke. 'You've seen lots of romance around you—don't you think some might have rubbed off a bit? How long have you lived in our flat and how many chick flicks have you watched?'

'Not watched, endured. As few as possible. Why do you think I spend so much of my time at work?' One mention of a chick flick and he'd always left. Just one downside of living with a bunch of women.

'So what do you dream about?'

He thought back to lying in her bed—in those half-moments between being asleep and awake—and the sudden hitch in his breathing as he'd watched her, the strange unexpected emotion, the need to protect her, to hold her. Not that he'd wanted to make love with her then, because he would never have taken a woman who wasn't in any state to remember it, or who would regret it the instant it was over. But he'd thought about what sex with her might be like…some time. One time. Oh, yes, a man *could* dream—just not the kind of dreaming she meant. 'Believe me, sweetheart, you don't want to know.'

She stared up at him, for a second, two. Three. His peripheral vision closed down and all he could see was her face, those shining cautious eyes, pink cheeks. That mouth that he wanted to cover with his own. There was something about her, beyond attractive, something bone-deep that intrigued him. She wasn't the person he'd thought she was. She was different, matured, strong but yet innocent.

She gave him a very shy and very faint smile. 'Maybe I do, Isaac.'

At least that was what he thought she said. Before he could clarify she'd turned away, almost running down the second escalator without looking back. And he let her go, because he clearly wasn't the only one confused as all hell, and turned on, to boot.

She eventually stopped to work out the correct platform. 'This one?'

'Sure. Now, don't go too close to the edge.'

'Aww, that's kind. But I've been riding the tube for a long time. I know the drill.'

He laughed. 'Kind? Not really…well, not to you, anyway. I just saw a mouse running along the side of the track and I didn't want you to give it a heart attack with your banshee screaming. Poor thing, minding its own business. It doesn't deserve that.'

'There are always mice or rats in these kinds of places. I came to terms with that a long time ago. I just don't like them in my house. Under my couch. Or my bed.' She closed her eyes and he just knew she was drawing on some kind of inner strength. But she edged a little closer to the platform edge and he almost wrapped an arm round her. For the sake of mouse protection. But stopped himself.

She was having a strange effect on him. Last night as she'd told him about her insecurities at work and her sexual inexperience he'd felt a mix of rage and…empathy. She'd guilted herself, limited her own personal growth because of the actions of one selfish, stupid man who had used his position of power to hurt her. Isaac surprised himself by genuinely wanting to make her feel better.

That was strange.

He read out the LED display to distract himself, wanting to get away from any more deep and meaningful. It freaked him out. 'Two minutes until the next train.'

'Yep. What'll we talk about?'

He looked up and down the platform. At the far end there were two guys sitting on a bench. That was it, no one in any kind of proximity. He scrabbled around trying to find something to lighten the tone. 'I could fill in a few gaps in your knowledge for you, if you like?'

She frowned. 'What do you mean?'

'Last night you told me you feel a little…er…unprepared for some of the answers to your clients' questions? What exactly do you need to know?' Okay, so distraction therapy wasn't working.

Her eyes did a funny widening popping thing. Not necessarily a positive reaction. 'I beg your pardon? You want to talk dirty to me?'

'If you say so. What is it about sex that you need to learn? I can help. Either a nice quiet chat where I fill in the gaps—or, I could do the whole show and tell thing. Your choice.'

'As if I'd ask you.' But she didn't deny she wanted to learn. What he could see of her cheeks bloomed bright red.

'Hey, you did me a huge favour tonight. So go on. Ask. Ask me anything. I can pay you back in answers. And I pinky promise I won't laugh.' He held out his little finger.

Shoving her hands deep into her pockets, she squared up to him. 'Just forget whatever I said last night, okay? I was rambling and drunk. I don't need to learn anything. I'm quite capable of understanding the mechanics. I'm doing obstetrics—believe me, I know where babies come from.'

'Okay. Whoa, call off the cavalry. I'm sorry.'

The train arrived and they clambered on, took a seat in a carriage where they were the only people. Even so, she kept her voice a low hiss. 'You have the problem with sex, Isaac. Not me. How long has your longest relationship been? A month? Thirty whole days?'

He really regretted bringing this up. It had been a joke. But, 'Hey, I can't help it if I'm in it for the long haul.'

Her eyes widened again. 'You think long haul is a month?'

'It isn't? Really? That's where I've been going wrong?' He laughed. 'I have no problem with sex. None at all. But commitment is seriously overrated.'

'Men. Typical bloody men.' She sighed. This time it wasn't soft and sleepy; it was downright narky. And it told him to back right off.

And there was the fundamental issue. Poppy believed sex and relationships had to be intertwined, inextricably linked, which was probably why she'd backed away from any hint of any since her first disastrous relationship. Whereas he made sure he only ever dated women who wanted a little harmless fun and relaxation.

The train finally rattled to a stop and they disembarked, lungs filling with the thick metal smell of the underground air. She stomped off ahead and, once out of the station, stalked off through the snow, arms crossed over her body, a niggly line on her forehead.

'Poppy, wait. Come on, it was a joke.'

'Ha-bloody-ha.' She quickened her pace.

As they stomped he scuffed his hand along the top of a wall and collected enough snow to form a snowball. Then stopped and grabbed his ankle. 'Ouch. Ouch.'

'What's the matter?' Bingo. She turned, ran back to him. God forgive him, he almost felt guilty. But not enough. She bent to look at his leg, all concerned and serious. 'What is it?'

'It's a ball made up of pretty magical unique ice crystals. Apparently.' He stuffed it into the collar of her coat. 'Gotcha.'

She screamed. Shivered. Turned. 'What the...? You are the most irritating, stupid, insensitive...' Chasing after him, scooping snow as she ran, she threw a hard ball at his back, the smile finding its way back onto her mouth. 'One more time, Isaac, and I swear...'

He threw one back at her. Missed by a mile. On purpose. 'What? You love snowball fights? What you going to do? Go on. I dare you.'

She threw another one. It lamely hit his leg. He ran and caught her up, reached out for her arm, grabbed it.

She spun around in the snow, dark eyes flashing with anger, frustration.

Heat. It slammed through him like a thousand volts as he touched her.

Her body shook and she glanced down, surprised, at her trembling hands. Looked up at him for answers. He didn't have any. He didn't know what the hell was happening here either.

Her voice was thick and hoarse. 'No. No. You're not worth it.'

'Oh, really?' The electric force that had shimmied between them all evening spiked, stole his breath. He pulled her to him, slamming his body against hers. He needed to kiss her. To taste her again. Because one tiny kiss had been in no way enough last night.

If she had given him any indication that she did not want this as much as he did then he would have walked. But she kept staring at him, searching his face. Confused. Hungry.

'Really. You are so not worth it. Not worth it at all.' But this time her voice was hushed and thick and told him exactly what he needed to know.

He watched the movement of her throat as she swallowed, brushed a snowflake from her cheek. 'Poppy...'

'Yes?' She stuck her tongue out again and caught another one, smiled in a way that shot hot spikes of need through him. Ran her tongue along her top lip leaving a wet trail that he ached to taste, and half drove him mad with desire. Her eyes widened and he was sure she didn't realise the effect she was having on him. Either she had to stop or he had to... 'You have got to stop doing that with your tongue.'

'Why?' Her breathing sped up, her lips parted just a little.

He tipped his head closer to her mouth, unable to do anything else but stand here, with her, holding her. 'Because I have other ideas for it.'

Poppy heard the catch in her throat and felt the shiver run the length of her body as he pulled her to him by her coat lapels, pushed away her scarf and slid his mouth over hers. Felt her body ease against his. Felt the thick outlines of his heavy coat against hers—frustrated by the barriers. Grateful for the barriers.

Because she knew they were on different planets of experience, of expectation. She didn't want to kiss him. Didn't want to want him.

But she did. She wanted him to run his hands over her body. Wanted to see what it felt like to feel desirable, to *be* desirable, to Isaac.

And hell, she needed to stop hiding, stop processing. Start living. Start feeling—but she didn't know how. She wanted him to show her the way, but was afraid of what he'd think of her. And she sure as hell couldn't ask.

As he slowly licked across her bottom lip, any further thought fled her brain. Her body stopped processing anything beyond its innate feral response; the flashes of light and heat in her belly, the tingle in her breasts, the wet of her mouth.

She opened her mouth, unable to resist the pull of him any more, wound her arms around his neck. Felt a strip of bare skin against her arm—that one inch enough to fire more light. More heat. Lost herself in touch, smell. Taste.

And man, he tasted good. Of sin and sex. Of chaos. Of ice and snow and fire and heat. It was an open-mouthed kiss—gentle. Soft. Not greedy or sloppy, as she'd had all those years ago. Not rushed or panting.

His hands cupped her face, as she'd seen on the movies, as she'd seen other couples do—no rampant groping or grasping. No sweaty hands pulling at her clothes. No guilt suffusing every touch. No hurry. No hiding.

Surprising. Delicious. Fresh. Unsullied heat swirled inside her, prickling all her nerve endings, making her feel alive.

But despite the tenderness he was still all male. Confident. Giving. Taking. Making her insides melt away along with her resolve. His tongue slipped into her mouth and at first she didn't know how to react. Too much, too little. Too hard. Not hard enough. A hot rock of panic began to rise from her gut. He was too much for her. She wasn't enough for him.

But gently, gently he coaxed her tongue, stroking, probing, dancing. And she realised she was rocking against him, greedy to feel the contours of his body. Wondering how it would feel to have him inside her.

No.

Whoa.

She pulled away. Those kinds of thoughts made her blood pressure enter the critical range. Memories of destruction roiled back. The last time she'd allowed herself to get carried away she'd almost destroyed too many lives. And even though the logical part of her brain knew that this time there were only two people at stake here—she wasn't prepared to put herself in the firing line. Not with Isaac.

God. Why the hell couldn't she just let go a little? Have the fun she craved? She wanted it. She did.

But eight years of cutting herself off from any kind

of sexual feeling wasn't easy to shrug off. And when she did finally let herself go it had to be on equal terms. She didn't want to feel like a loser, or in any way inadequate.

If she was ever going to have any kind of relationship, which was not on the cards right now, she had to know what she was doing, so she could choose, could have a say in what happened next. She had to have something to offer, and right now she didn't. She was at risk and she didn't like that. Not at all. 'Isaac. Sorry. I…I can't. This isn't me. I don't do this. I need to go home. I'm sorry.'

He stared back at her, confusion written across his features.

He was every kind of wrong. And he knew it, too. Snow turning to cold, damp sleet fell on his shoulders. Down her neck, onto her face. And she began to shiver. He let her go, his breath rushing into the cold night air. 'Crap, Poppy. That wasn't meant to happen.'

'No. It wasn't.' She shoved her hands back into her pockets, ignored the sting of her swollen lips and headed home. Annoyed, frustrated and wondering how the hell she was going to survive until February with him living in her apartment with a *vibe* that was almost palpable.

Mice. Vibes. Isaac. So much for being lonely. The apartment was getting way too full for her liking.

CHAPTER SIX

THE ONLY WAY Poppy was going to get through the department Christmas party was to immerse herself in having a good time. She would chat to everyone. She might even dip her toe into some very gentle flirting if there was a suitable man around. Definitely very gentle.

At the very least, she would try. Try to put the kiss behind her. Try to do what every normal woman her age did—go out with men, brave the waters. Garner a little sexual experience. With all her friends coupled off she needed something fresh to inject into her life, and a date for Izzy's wedding—although turning up single wouldn't be the worst thing she could ever do.

Or the best.

But it would be nice to have someone to share this kind of thing with. Someone safe. Someone who wouldn't stomp on her heart. Who wouldn't lie and cheat. Or, who wouldn't be incapable of giving more than thirty days if that was what they decided they wanted. Together.

A nice reliable doctor perhaps. Suitable. Unlike Isaac. Very unsuitable.

And that would just about give her friends a heart attack! Poor Poppy who had never been seen with so much as a sniff of a man on her arm finally braving the dating waters.

Or was she living in cloud cuckoo land?

She looked across Blue private room, all a-sparkle with sophisticated blue and silver Christmas decorations, which gave the place a mystical feel, and watched as her Obs and Gynae team relaxed into the Christmas spirit—some more than others.

'He's had a few too many Christmas kisses, don't you think?' Tim, the specialist registrar, pointed over to Prof Hartley, obstetrician to royalty and the stars, slumped in a corner, his nose as red as Santa's suit.

Poppy laughed at the prospect of the almost-seventy-year-old under the mistletoe. Or downing the now infamous cocktail. Either seemed a stretch for the big guy. 'In his dreams.'

'And, judging by the snoring, I imagine he's having plenty of them. This is a great party. Well done.'

'Thanks. We managed to pull it out of the hat, I think.' High praise indeed. Pride rippled through her—although she hadn't had much of a hand in prepping for the event. Isaac had sorted out most of the details and left enquiring and confirming notes on the kitchen counter. Or sent short texts.

Fish of the day? Salmon okay?

Yes. Fine.

DJ or just MP3?

MP3.

Champagne or Aussie bubbles?

Cheapest?

She got the feeling he'd been avoiding her as much as she'd been avoiding him.

Where was she? Oh, yes. Tim.

'Do you want another drink?' Tim looked harmless enough. In fact, he was quite attractive, in an understated kind of way. He was quite funny, clever, en route to being a very successful doctor. He had a fairly hot body. Unobtrusive dress sense. And was back on the dating scene after a five-year relationship break-up with a woman who had run off with her dentist a few months ago. He would be a definite catch for someone looking to start dating again. He was stable, had good prospects and made her laugh.

And he seemed quite interested in more than just a drink, judging by the way he'd hung around with her for most of the evening, 'catching up'. She only hoped he wasn't quite a good kisser but a damned fine one. Because he'd need to be if she was going to erase Isaac from her mind.

'I'd love one. Thanks. Just a sparkling water.' Because Lord knew what effect anything stronger would have on her.

'You're being very professional, but you can let your hair down at the end-of-year party, you know. No one will judge you. How about you have just one cocktail?' He had a nice voice, too. Quite calming. Slight northern accent. Pleasant enough. Just not enough to make her heart trip. Maybe he'd grow on her. He looked to be just the type of man she could manage.

'No, thanks.' Cocktails would for ever only remind her of Isaac.

'Go on. I'll grab the menu for you.' Tim leaned across her to the table, accidentally catching her arm. 'Oh, sorry.'

'No problem.' It was just skin on skin. Plain old skin. No problem. No tingles either. 'But seriously, I'm fine with water.'

Maybe he was perfect for her.

'Yes, water is best. You do not want to see her when she's drunk.' That voice again. Her heart jittered. She turned and saw Isaac standing next to her, an old T-shirt skimming muscles that had haunted her dreams. Faded jeans and work boots completing a picture that made her feel very unsafe indeed. And he was grinning that heart-stopping grin that told her he knew he was being a giant pain in the ass, but didn't give a damn.

And hell, if that kiss didn't linger between them now, filling the air with an electricity so intense she felt her lungs empty.

But, if anything, Isaac's entrance certainly cemented Tim as a possible contender. Tim wouldn't leave her lungs empty, or her unmentionables zinging.

She looked back at her colleague, who was smiling, earnestly holding out the menu to her. She took it, ignoring Isaac. Trying to ignore him.

'Why?' Tim turned to Isaac again, his smile fading. 'What is she like?'

Don't say another damned word, buster. But polite was necessary, especially in front of a potential date. 'Oh. Isaac, perfect timing, I didn't see you come in.' Which was mighty strange considering her eyes had been fixed on the door for most of the evening. She spoke through gritted teeth. 'Tim, this is Isaac, an old friend of my brother's. He owns this bar, plus he's my flatmate.'

'Isaac.' Tim stretched out his hand. 'Nice to meet you.'

'Tim.' There was no *nice*. There was, however, a hint of a glower.

And why that gave her a tingling feeling she didn't want to know.

Tim's smile resurrected. 'Thanks for letting us have the bar at such short notice. I know Poppy was very relieved. I hope it didn't put you out too much.'

Oh, good. Tim was polite, too. Another tick.

He leaned in a little closer. Territorial? She got a whiff of his not-unpleasant cologne. Saw his passable jaw in profile. Yes. He was nice. Her heart sank a little.

Trouble was, Tim might well be someone's perfect catch but so far he just wasn't hers. There was no magic. No frisson of electricity. No zinging.

Basically, she didn't want to jump his bones. Which was a shame—because they were probably quite nice, unobtrusive bones, underneath his corduroy trousers and check shirt.

The other trouble was, jumping bones wasn't something she was very adept at.

And there she was over-analysing everything again.

Go with the flow. Magic could grow. She hadn't wanted to jump Isaac's bones for what…twenty years…and that seemed to have just grown out of nowhere. Inconveniently.

Isaac's grin lingered, as if he knew exactly what storm he was causing in her gut. 'Oh, fitting you in was no trouble at all. We had a vacant slot so we were happy to help your department out. Besides, Poppy has a very unique way of convincing a man to do her bidding. We're all powerless to resist.' Isaac patted Tim on the back and then leaned in. 'A word of warning, though. She's a hell of a snorer.'

With that he walked away.

Mortified, Poppy gave Tim a weak smile and shrugged. 'We have thin walls.'

'Thin…?' Tim watched as Isaac sauntered towards the bar. 'Is there anything…you know…between…you two?'

'Me and Isaac? No way.' Why did that have a ring to it? Second time this week she'd denied anything between her and Isaac. Going by the 'repeat it enough and you'll start to believe it' mantra she answered, 'No. There's nothing. He's just my flatmate.'

But she was damned sure you didn't follow *just* your flatmate's backside as he walked away. Didn't spend hours in bed waiting for *just* your flatmate to leave so you wouldn't bump into him and try to kiss him again. And, hell, you never thought about *just* your flatmate naked when you heard him in the shower.

She fired imaginary daggers at Isaac's back. Trust him to come along and spoil her attempt at a relaxed night out. Now she'd have to take a zillion deep breaths and cool off before she could restart her operation fun campaign. With Tim.

She turned back to him, and he held out a glass of water, which she rolled across her chest to try to get some relief. He gave her a startled stare and she realised she hadn't ever thought about him naked. Which surely must be a good sign. 'Now, about that drink?'

Isaac had had enough. Exhaustion ate away at him along with something else that he didn't want to put a name to. But he was damned sure seeing Poppy getting friendly with a *pretty decent chap* might be up there as culprit number one.

Add to the five almost sleepless nights where he couldn't shrug off the unease about kissing Poppy, *twice*, and enjoying it; he was damned well going to sleep tonight if it was the last thing he did.

Shoving the key in the lock, he entered the flat as quietly as he could, relieved that the place was in darkness. He hung up his coat, silently placed his briefcase on the floor, slipped off his boots and—

'You're very late.'

At the sound of Poppy's voice his heart ramped up to a thousand beats a minute. 'Poppy. You made me jump. Not that it's any of your business, but I was closing up and helping some old professor guy get safely home.' All of which he'd prolonged, unsure of how he'd feel coming home and finding Poppy in a clinch with Troy…? Terry…? In the apartment. Worse, if he'd heard things happening in the bed he'd shared with her not many nights ago. Not that it would be any of his business. Not that he would ever have a claim on her. Although, currently, the prospect of seeing her and not touching her was driving him a little crazy. He could only hope it would dissipate and normal service would be resumed. A state where he wasn't über-conscious of her every move, laugh, word. 'Had a good night?'

'Until you came along. Yes.' She was sitting on the couch. His heart steadied. Well, almost. Fully clothed, as far as he could see—his night vision hadn't quite focused yet. Wearing, for the record, a far-too-sexy black dress that skimmed her breasts and her backside and had made every man in that room want her. Shoes with heels that made her legs model-long and very sexy indeed. And her dark hair piled on her head, with swirls of curls around her face. She'd highlighted her eyes with a smoky grey liner and eye make-up that shimmered. *Shimmered.* With lipstick that drew any sensible bloke's attention to her lips. Way too sexy for a Friday night. Or any night that had a Y in it.

But no clinch. No man. He exhaled, deeply. 'Why? What did I do?'

'*We're powerless to resist her.* And…*she snores.*' Poppy snorted. 'Gee, thanks. If that wasn't enough to put him off I don't know what was.'

'If he doesn't want you because you snore then he isn't the man for you. Because, well—face it, you might as well hand out ear plugs.' He looked around the room. 'Where is he, anyway?'

'Turns out, he wasn't the man for me.'

'Like we didn't all know that. But he was very…' He tried to think of the worst insult he could find. The guy had seemed pretty decent. Just so not Poppy's type. Which was? Hell if he knew. He didn't even want to think about it. And she definitely was not anywhere on *his* list of types. But the only thing he could think of was that holding her and kissing her had seemed so far beyond… 'Nice.'

'Yes…he is, very…nice. And that's not a bad thing. I like nice. And safe. And slow. And predictable. And open to commitment. And he's just been in a five-year relationship. Five years, imagine that.'

'And it ended?' Isaac raised his palms towards her. 'Proves my point.'

'Which is?'

'Nothing is for ever.'

'Not if you don't give it a chance. Wait until you find The One. You'll see. What about Alex and Lara? Izzy and Harry? Tori and Matt?'

'They all just got lucky.' He didn't want to add that he'd given himself a silent bet that Izzy would leave Harry at the altar. Alex and Lara wouldn't be talking to each other when they got back from holiday. And Matt and Tori would break up before they even got to South Africa.

'Lucky? It happens to be called love—and they all seem pretty happy about it. Even those who took a bit of convincing.'

Did Poppy just want to be like her friends? All coupled up? 'And I can show you plenty of evidence that love doesn't last, not once there's a roadblock, or the slightest hint of trouble ahead.' Starting with his mother, and…his mother…and his mother…

'You know, your mum seems very happy, currently. And settled. She's been married to Hugo a long time now. See, it is possible to find someone and something that lasts.'

And that was a swift punch to his gut. How did Poppy know he was thinking…? 'Until the next time.'

'You need to cut her some slack. It can't have been easy thinking she was falling in love and then realising and admitting she'd made a mistake. It must have been hard for her, extricating herself from a situation she didn't want to be in. Being less than perfect in front of her son. At least, I couldn't imagine my mum ever admitting she was in the wrong.'

And he hadn't ever looked at it like that. The way his mother had kept him in the dark about her love life had left him reluctant to turn up at yet another one of her weddings. It wasn't as if she'd exactly poured her heart out to him but she'd always seemed happy at first. And she'd never, ever said she'd made a mistake about love. She'd made it all sound as if it was more about cash flow. But then, Poppy could have read it wrong, too—she wasn't exactly famous for her good judge of character.

Which probably explained why she'd tried to kiss him in the first place.

Poppy twiddled one of the straps on her barely-there dress as her speech sped up and her voice rose. 'So, I don't know what your game is, Isaac, but you can butt right out of my social life.'

'I didn't invite myself to be in it in the first place. If I remember rightly it was you. You asked to use my bar. You started all this.' He didn't need to say 'you kissed me...' but it hovered there in the silence.

'Yes, well. Let's finish it.' She clicked on a side lamp, flooding the room with washed orange light. Goddamn, he wished she hadn't. Because sitting there in that dress, her hair half up, half down, mouth still slicked with lipstick, pouting. Pouting, for God's sake. She looked bedready. Sex-ready.

'I don't need you sussing out my potentials, Isaac.'

'Potentials?' She was thinking about dating someone else? Goddamn. He didn't want to think about how that made him feel. *Not your business.* But a tight fist of something speared him in the gut.

'Yes. Potentials. I don't want you frightening them off. I don't want you talking to them, okay? And while we're at it, I think we need a few house rules for while you're here. I don't want you walking around the flat half naked any more. Keep those boxer shorts out of plain sight. Okay?'

He looked down. Huh? Just shirt, jeans and socks very definitely on show. 'My boxer shorts?'

'Yes.'

He stifled a laugh, figuring she wouldn't take kindly to that. Poor little Poppy might be sussing out potentials, but was having a hard time controlling her libido with him. All it would take would be one little spark…

So, he would not be going there. At all. 'Okay. No boxers on show. That works for me, but only if you keep your fancy underwear under wraps. No more knickers and bras on the bathroom radiator. And those pink pyjama things… anywhere.'

She frowned. 'My pyjamas?'

He looked at those shapely shoulders, the skin that he'd run his fingers over, that he knew felt like soft silk. 'Yes. They're too…bed-like. Always wear a dressing gown.'

'Fine.' She shrugged.

So did he. 'Fine.'

'Then, goodnight.' She stood and walked barefoot to the bathroom, slammed the door and turned the radio on. Loud.

Which was a good job because then she wouldn't hear him wince as he thought about her undressing. About what he knew he was missing. And about what he knew he could never have.

CHAPTER SEVEN

LATER—MUCH, MUCH LATER—a wild scream dragged Isaac from a fitful sleep. *WTF?*

Heart thumping almost out of his chest, he jumped from his bed and ran to the lounge, stopping only briefly to pick up a softball bat from behind his door.

'Poppy! Poppy, are you okay? What the hell?'

This time the lights were on and she stood on the couch shivering in those damned pink pyjamas, and, let it be duly noted, no dressing gown…her face pale, her hair messy and knotty at the back, eyes sleep-filled. She pointed to the corner of the skirting board and the small grey plastic box. 'There…there…it's a mouse. In the trap. A mouse.'

'A mouse? Is that all?' An ill-concealed expletive left his lips as he inhaled deeply, filling his lungs with chilly air and Poppy's sweet scent. This woman was responsible for other people's lives? Still, at least she was safe. Thank God. 'Okay, the mouse is captured and can't get out. The trap worked exactly like we hoped. There are no murderers in the flat. All is good.' Not laughing was hard. Stopping himself from hauling her into his arms was a lot harder. 'So, we screamed loudly enough to wake the whole damned neighbourhood, because…?'

'I heard a scratching noise so I got up. I saw the mouse moving around. It made me jump. I screamed. So sue me.'

She peered at the bat in his hand. 'And you think I'm over-reacting. You were planning to do what with that?'

'I thought that the only possible explanation for your blood-curdling screams was that you were being attacked by at least five burglars.'

'And you thought you could fight them off? Sweet. Delusional, but sweet.'

'Hey, honey, I have a lot of expensive stuff. I didn't want them nicking it.' Truth was, he'd become seriously unstuck at the thought of her being hurt and hadn't stopped to think about what might have happened. All he'd known was that for some annoying reason every cell in his body was duty bound to protect her. He held out his hand and tried to talk her down from the soft furnishings. 'Come and say hello to the nice housemate. He won't bite. Or escape.'

'Not likely. No chance.' She looked at his hand and shook her head. 'Just get rid of him.'

'Absolutely. Tomorrow.' Then he realised it already was tomorrow. 'Later. Right now I'm going to try to get some sleep. Please only scream if there is a real emergency. I'm talking blood or fire, okay? Anything else can wait.'

He turned and started to go back to bed.

Her voice made him stop. He was coming to realise that a lot about her made a lot of him stop…his heart, his brain. 'Wait. Isaac. You're not seriously thinking you can leave him here? Like that? He might escape. He might hurt himself.'

'What exactly would you like me to do at silly o'clock?'

'Take him outside? Let him go?'

'It's the middle of the night! The information leaflet said we had to take him at least a mile away and put him in a field with long grass. I'm not walking in Holland Park at this hour, in the snow. Not even for you.' He was surprised to think that he might like to do something for her...to please her. But not this. At her frown he relented slightly. 'Tomorrow. Morning. Okay?'

'Well, if you won't take him, I will. Now.'

No way would he let her, but he wanted to tease her just a little more. 'This I've got to see. You can't even look at him, never mind pick him up. Go on...try.'

She bit her bottom lip, but didn't budge. 'You can't leave him in here.'

'Then I'll put him in my room.'

'Thank you.' She rubbed her eyes sleepily and he found himself mesmerised by the movement of her hands. When she stopped, hands still framing her face, she looked at him, really looked at him. Her gaze roved his face, then his shirtless body, his waist. Lower. And he saw the exact moment when her eyes misted. Her voice was husky and fractured as she spoke and he didn't think it was down to sleep deprivation. 'Hey, the boxers. I thought we agreed? Violating the agreement so soon?'

'I was trying to be the hero. Strangely, fulfilling the flatmate dress code wasn't top of my to-do list.' He flicked the waistband at his hip. 'So, what to do? Punish me? Or do you want me to take them off? Hey, do you want to take them off? Because we should also have an equal opportunities policy, too.'

Her eyes grew wide. 'No way. No. Fully clothed. More clothes, please. More. Clothes.'

He pointed to her body. 'And what's with the pyjamas? We agreed. Although, I won't have the same reaction if you offer to take them off...and I could help. Just putting it out there.'

Her pupils darkened and her lips parted just enough. Then, after she clearly internally debated the pros and cons of having him butt naked in the lounge, she shook her head and pointed to his room. 'Go to bed. I'll see you tomorrow.'

'Okay.' He grinned and walked away, relieved that she'd

had the sense to put a stop to this…this delicious, sensuous game of human cat and mouse, because he had a feeling he was at risk of getting caught, too. 'Goodnight. Get some decent sleep. We have some serious mouse releasing tomorrow.'

'Wait. Isaac?'

'Yes?' Second thoughts? His mouth dried. What little sense had been there before evaporated.

'The mouse?'

Damn. He'd forgotten. He turned, made the few strides over to her and discovered she'd braved enough to peer closer at the box.

'I'll just—' He bent to pick it up but en route his hand banged against hers. She grasped it, whether to steady herself he didn't know, but a shot of raw electricity ripped through him. It was as if he'd gripped a thousand-volt wire. And he couldn't let go.

From this vantage point he was looking down at the top of her head. Noticed the slight tremor running through her body and wondered if she was having the same thoughts and sensations he was. Was she fighting and failing? He noticed, too, that she hadn't turned to look up at him.

Hadn't? Couldn't? Wouldn't?

He needed to let her go. Double quick before they did something they'd both regret.

'Isaac?' Finally she tilted her head, stood up and faced him, her hand still in his. Stepped closer. Raised on her tiptoes, and with her other hand she cupped his cheek, pulled his face closer.

Before he could register what she was doing, what she was asking, what this meant, she'd covered his mouth with hers.

Oh, my God. Her body had begun to shake and she couldn't stop. She'd kissed him again. No surprises there, because the past few days that was all she'd been able to think about. In contrast, Tim's nice attempt at a doorstep kiss had left her cold, which was when she'd explained to him that they needed to keep things platonic.

Platonic.

If only she could feel that about her flatmate, if only she weren't walking into temptation every single time she was here with him alone. But he smelt so good. Tasted so good. And right now those infamous boxers were not concealing how turned on he was. All that rolled up in a guy hell-bent on being her hero, if only for a very short amount of time, made him very appealing indeed. She pulled him to the sofa.

His hands stroked down her back and every inch of Poppy's body strained for his touch. He took too long to reach under her pyjama top and cup her breast. So she undid the buttons, took his hand and placed it there ignoring the flare of concern in his eyes. She wanted him to touch her.

And he did. Which made her stomach tighten and a moan escape her throat. Her nipples beaded as he ran slow circles round them with his fingertips.

'You are so damned gorgeous, Poppy. But slow down a little, eh?' Then his mouth followed his fingers, sucking each nipple, lapping his hot, wet tongue against her skin. Sensation after sensation rippled through her and she bucked against him. She wanted to feel everything. To do everything. To make up for lost time and the last eight years of celibacy. It couldn't be shrugged off quickly enough. She wanted him. Wanted Isaac to show her what she'd been missing.

He took too long to lick back along to her neck. She wanted him now. Pressure built inside her until she felt she was going to explode. She pressed greedily against him relishing his heat and the hardness just inches away from her sweet spot. Her hands twitched to touch him. There. To stroke him. There. To feel him. There.

It wasn't as if she even had to undress him. There was barely a barrier between them. Just those damn boxers.

Should she do something to move him along a little? Her one and only lover had been quick, grabbing at her, in some sort of race to the finish line—and he'd always won. Leaving her dissatisfied and racked with remorse. She only knew quick. And that was how she wanted it now.

As Isaac's mouth left her neck and made its way through mind-melting kisses along her shoulder she reached down to his boxers and gave him a squeeze. He was so big. So hard. So…she closed her eyes at the thought of him inside her…damned scary.

He shifted slightly away.

Plucking up courage, she reached for him again. Squeezed. Looked up to see his reaction.

Which wasn't what she'd expected. He was looking at her again, as if she were some kind of child…his kid sister. The way he'd looked at her too many times—it wasn't a sexy *I want you* look. His hand covered hers and moved it away. 'Hey. Not so fast.' Then he whispered into her neck. 'Or so timid—it won't bite you. But wait. There's no rush.'

'I'm sorry…I thought…' Truth was, she didn't know what she thought. Or what she expected, past having him. But he had a different plan, she could tell. And she'd stuffed up. 'Was I doing it wrong?'

'No.' His eyebrows knotted as he gave her a gentle confused smile. 'But each guy has his own way.'

Obviously not her way. Either that or he was using code for *forget it, baby.* She twisted away from him, put air between them and as she did so she could see the sexual mist clearing from his eyes. He was starting to realise what a ridiculous idea this was. She just knew it. 'You didn't like it?'

'Of course I liked it. I just wasn't expecting it. Not so quickly. People tend to do a little getting to know each other first.'

'Great. I told you I was no good at this.' Suddenly feeling cold and exposed, Poppy stood and buttoned up her top. She'd rushed things and he wasn't ready. Probably wouldn't ever be ready. Was probably kissing her out of pity. Again. After all, she'd made the move, not him. Again. Her cheeks blazed. 'Oh, God, I feel so stupid. I should go. So should you.'

'Hey.' He caught her wrist, one hand reaching out and cupping her face, thumb running along her lip, making her shiver and yet hot again in so many places. 'Poppy, really? You want to leave without sorting this out? You think I can get to sleep now? Can you? After that?'

'I…I don't know.' But she gripped his arm and couldn't let go. Didn't want to let go. A rush of long-dormant hormones threatened to engulf her, definitely made her sway. Just looking at him made her heart jump and jitter and made little flashes in her belly like the twinkling Christmas tree lights. She hauled in breath after breath. This was ridiculous. She'd never felt like this. Out of control. But so turned on. Crazy.

And stupid.

Naive.

Embarrassed.

He pulled her to sit next to him back on the couch, dragged a thick mohair throw over them. Then he ran his hand down the back of her head, snagged into the knots from her fitful sleep. Gave her another of his gentle smiles. 'Now, what's going on in that head of yours?'

'I…I don't know.' A grown woman with a medical degree and that was the best she could do? She needed to try harder. Be honest. Because she did not want to have any kind of anything with a man without wide-open honesty.

That much she was sure about. Hell, she'd just about ripped off what clothes he had on—what could be more embarrassing than that? 'I want to sleep with you.'

'I kind of worked that out.' His smile slipped. 'There were a lot of clues. Nice clues. Very nice. But do I get a say in this?'

'Obviously.'

He tipped his chin upwards. 'Good to know.'

'I know you want me, too.' She looked at his groin, which didn't appear to be quite as hard or as big as a couple of moments ago.

His smile recovered. 'Yes. Yes, I do. That is pretty obvious. And no...I don't.'

'You think it would be a mistake.'

'I think it would be rash. And probably high up in the top sexual rankings of my life.' His fingers combed through her hair, tucking a piece behind her ear. 'You are beautiful and gorgeous and very sexy and very, very desirable. But...I'm not the guy for you. Seriously.'

She wasn't going to beg. 'And clearly I'm not the girl for you.'

'You know what I'm like, you said it yourself—one month is all I can manage—and that's the best I can do. That's not what you need.'

'And you know what I need, do you?'

'Where has all this come from? Why me? Why now? The other night you didn't want to.'

'I did. I was just trying not to. I want to learn about sex.' And, God, if that didn't make her sound pathetic.

He ran a hand over his jaw, one eyebrow raised. 'You want to use me for sex? Interesting.'

'It's not using you, per se. I'd hope you'd have some fun, too. I just want to learn. Stuff. For...later. When I'm back in the dating game seriously. When I'm at work and women ask me things about orgasms during penetration, or games to jazz up their sex lives…I never know what to say.'

'You've never had one?'

'An orgasm? No, not from a man. Not from Tony.'

Isaac's jaw tensed at the name. 'Why does that not surprise me? Did he ever give you anything other than abuse, stress and a lifetime of anxiety?'

Shame. Guilt. She had a list—a long one. 'I guess not.'

'But you must have…had an orgasm from…yourself? Surely? Otherwise it's been a long, long eight years.'

'Of course. I'm a grown sentient woman, Isaac. I have needs. How the hell do you think I've survived the past few years listening through flimsy walls to the comings and goings of my flatmates? Or watching sensuous films?' Geez, and now she was talking about masturbating, with Isaac.

'Ear plugs?'

'Really?' She threw him a frown. 'I get the feelings. I just haven't acted on them…much, at least not with someone else.' And now? Well, now she was almost overwhelmed by them. By him.

There was a subtlety to him—strong and yet gentle. Aloof and yet within reach. Funny and yet serious. Once again she was half-naked with him, in a makeshift bed, his bare shoulders sticking out of the throw. He had a small tattoo in the shape of a Celtic knot on the back of his left arm. A crescent-shaped scar, well healed, just below his shoulder blade. She'd known him almost her whole life and yet never really known him at all. The fine hairs on his arms glistened in the half-light, veins standing out along capable hands. Hands that had instilled intense pleasure. How could something so masculine give such wild sensations? How could that mouth make her wet by its touch? Those were the kind of things she needed to know—the small-print finer details of seduction—what turned a woman on. What did it for a guy.

'What's it like for a man? Can you remove emotion from sex?'

'Me personally? Sure. But only when there's a tacit agreement, otherwise it wouldn't be right. Or...' he searched for the right word '...honourable.'

'I'm not looking for honourable. I want to know what sex can be like. In the one and only relationship I've ever had I was vulnerable and trusting and I was hurt badly.' But he knew all this already. 'I want to enter my next proper relationship equipped with knowledge and skills. I want to know how to behave sexually. I want to feel in control of myself and my desires. I want to be independent. And having little sexual knowledge puts me at a disadvantage. I do not want that.' She shuddered at the memories. 'I don't want to ever be vulnerable again.'

'No. No, you don't. And I can understand you want to arm yourself because that way you can also protect yourself, too. Be in control. But what about afterwards? If I, or another lucky, helpful guy, did agree to sleep with you, then what? You know I can't give you what Lara, or Izzy or Tori have. You deserve better. Hell, you want better, Poppy, don't you?'

'What I'm talking about is exactly the kind of deal you strike with every woman you meet. Short and hot and limited to purely physical. That's all I want from you. No commitment. Because, believe me, I do not want to get involved with you—I'm not so stupid as to think you're a viable option for the long term. Call it a booty call. Friends with benefits.'

'We're friends now?'

She shrugged, aghast at the intensity of desire rushing through her. She couldn't do this with anyone else. It had to be him. If only to stop this physical need. 'Enemies with benefits, then. For a limited time only.'

Again with the hair stroking. 'Poppy, this is torture. It's a dangerous game you want to play. You say you won't care when we stop but you will. I've already seen you get your heart broken once. I'm not going to watch it happen again.'

'Oh, and what makes you think I'd fall for you?'

'How could you not?' He laughed. But then his face grew serious. 'I know you too well. I saw how that sleaze-ball used you. Lied to you. Broke you.' The anger in Isaac's face, in the shadows and lines, was almost as fresh now as it had been years ago. It had scared her then, but she'd been pretty sure he was only concerned that he'd wasted an evening of his precious time. Or was there something else? Some flicker of caring that he didn't want to own up to? She didn't want to think about that, so focused instead on his voice. 'But how would I be any better than him? Using you for sex?'

'You're exactly the man to choose… You know me better than anyone. I know you don't want anything extra. Last time it was all emotion and very bad sex. This time I'd know the score. It would be honest.' With a scathing look of self-loathing she pointed to her heart. 'You think I want to be like this? To be a successful doctor and yet a failure in the most important part of my life?'

'You are perfect as you are. As I said before, any man would be lucky to have you.' But it wouldn't be him, that was clear. He started to pull the throw down. 'But right now, it's time for bed. To sleep. It's late and neither of us are thinking rationally.'

She reached for his wrist, anger mounting—not at his rejection, but at his perception of her that didn't seem to have changed since that stupid day at the school ball. 'Okay, but it's your loss, Isaac. I'm not the same girl as I was then. I'm strong and capable. I'm not going to break into tiny pieces over you. I can survive. I'm a career woman who has poured her heart and soul into saving lives. I see people scraped off the streets and put them back together again. Gunshot wounds. Stabbings. I can deal with drug abusers and alcoholics. I help women give birth, share their joy and, if the worse happens, their sorrows, too. And then I get up and do it again the next day.'

At his open-mouthed reaction she rallied again. 'But you're right, you're not the man for me. The man I need is someone who has the guts to help out a friend. The ability to let go and have some fun. And who can see me for what I am and not for who I was a zillion years ago.'

She bundled herself out of the throw and stood up. 'Goodnight. And don't trouble yourself about getting rid of the mouse. I'll deal with it myself.'

Somehow.

CHAPTER EIGHT

'HEY, HOMEBOY, HAVE YOU seen the email I forwarded to you?' Isaac's right-hand man, Jamie, sauntered into Red with the widest grin he'd had since before he gashed his hand wide open. The white sling contrasted wildly with Jamie's black shirt. 'Another great review for Blue. Oi, cheer up, mate. That's what I call good news. The punters will be flocking in. Edgy, they called it, but with a… cosmopolitan flavour that appeals to the…after-dinner crowd looking for great dance music and a good vibe.'

Isaac forced a grin. Lifted down two beer glasses and poured himself and Jamie a drink. 'Here you go. A celebratory toast. That's great.'

And it was. Everything in Isaac's life was pretty damned epic compared to the dismal picture he'd had growing up. He had a string of successful bars, great mates and a not-too-shabby penthouse apartment, when it was finally finished. Which couldn't be soon enough.

Because, one week after the sex discussion and the atmosphere in the flat had cooled to the sub-zero temperatures of the Arctic Circle.

Trouble was, while his head had been busy debating the pros and cons of sticking his tongue in Poppy's mouth, his body had gone right ahead and done it. The only thing that had stopped him going further had been the look in her eyes as she'd grasped for his groin.

In fact the look on her face for the whole few minutes they'd been locked together had almost killed him. She was terrified. But, with a determination to overcome it, she'd rushed them into a situation neither had been able to handle. Then he'd made everything worse by trying to have a reasonable discussion. How to have a sensible conversation when both parties were turned on as hell?

But the second he'd clamped eyes on her confused and anxious gaze his heart had pinged. Pinged in a way that had happened only once before. And now he understood. Understood that the anger he'd felt for Poppy's first lover had been fuelled by something akin to jealousy. Unadulterated and righteous—hell, the man had been no more than scum—but angry jealousy nonetheless. Then, when she'd tried to seduce him a huge wedge of emotion had lodged under his ribcage. And he still couldn't shake it. Poppy instilled some kind of feeling in him that he did not want to contemplate. Or even acknowledge.

Which was why he'd had to put a stop to anything further happening. It wasn't that he thought of her as still a young girl—it was the opposite. He saw her now as an accomplished, professional, successful woman. Who was beautiful and honest—a little too forthright sometimes, definitely annoying. And who pushed his buttons in so many ways he didn't know what he was doing.

He swirled the last drops of his beer. 'Another?'

'Have you been listening to anything I've said?' Jamie frowned. 'Come on, Isaac. We're talking big bucks here. Focus, man.'

'Sorry. What was it?'

'Electrics. Bar Gris has been having problems with the electrics. They keep short-circuiting. It's a fire hazard. Marcel reckons he has it under control, but I don't think so, I think he's being fobbed off. One of us needs to go over and sort it out.'

Without hesitation Isaac knew he would be a better fit in Paris right now. And he'd get some space, which he needed. 'No worries. I'll grab a bag and get over there.'

'No. Actually, I was thinking you need some downtime. Real downtime. You've been covering for me for too long, zapping between Paris, Amsterdam and London. Why don't I go? You could have the weekend off.'

'And spend it where?' The last thing he needed was extra time in the flat with an angry Poppy. Or a trip home to his mother, which always ended up dysfunctional. And in both scenarios he'd have to spend uncomfortable time experiencing strange emotions swirling in his chest. Nah. 'I'm fine. I want to go to Paris. I like Paris.'

Jamie grimaced. 'Actually, I've already booked a flight. For me. And Steph. I thought I'd take her over for the weekend. You know how things have been between us. We need some couple time before the whole thing implodes. I've also spoken to Maisie and she's happy to take over the running of Blue this weekend—she is the long-term manager after all. We can't babysit her for ever. And this place almost runs itself. Why don't you take some time out and chill?'

'Because I don't need to. I'm fine. We have three bars to run here in London. We can't both take time out.'

'Yes, we can. Two nights, that's all. You've been working yourself ragged. Your head's not in the game at the moment. And the only reason I can think of is that you must be knackered. So go home. Sleep.' Jamie put his arm on Isaac's shoulder and turned him to face the front door. 'Hey, look, there's that girl that was in the other day. Friends of yours?'

'Izzy. And Harry.' Isaac gave a sharp intake of breath and glanced behind them at the swinging door. They were alone. 'Hi. How're you doing?'

'Goodness me, it's cold.' Izzy stamped her feet and

hugged up against Harry, who beamed. 'Oh, nice to see you here, Isaac.' She pulled off her gloves and threw them on the counter. 'Thought we'd have a quick snifter before we meet up with Poppy. We're going ice-skating. Any hot toddies going?'

'Sure. Two? Coming right up.' He poured two large steaming drinks and handed them over. That was the problem with having a bar so close to home—it gave people free rein to pop in unannounced. 'I don't suppose you're meeting Poppy here?'

'No. At the tube station. In ten minutes. She's still off the booze, apparently, so said she didn't want to come here.' Izzy bit her bottom lip. 'She's acting a bit weird. Don't suppose you've noticed anything different?'

What little time he'd spent in her company at the flat he'd noticed every nuance of her stiff shoulders, the aloof tip of her chin. The hesitancy and anger in her eyes. The simmering annoyance and undercurrent of repressed sexual attraction. Hell, he'd felt the same things, too. 'No. Nothing. But then we've hardly seen each other, to be honest.'

'Because he spends way too much time either here or at Blue,' Jamie butted in. 'He's starting to get on my nerves. Don't suppose you can whisk him away for a few hours? Days? Weeks? Maybe he'll come back refreshed and focused?'

And that was the first time anyone had ever accused him of not focusing on his work. He lived for his work. This thing with Poppy was getting to him. He had to speed up the renovations. Find a hotel if necessary.

Izzy clapped. 'Yes. Of course. Why not? Come ice-skating with us?'

'Absolutely not. I'd rather stick pins in my eyes.'

Harry laughed. 'Chicken. Afraid you're going to make a fool of yourself?'

Isaac interrupted the generalised chuckling at his expense, 'Hey, it's not that I can't—' *Much*. 'I just...' Saying he didn't want to would sound churlish; it was a nice offer. 'I'm busy here.'

'No, he's not. Take him. Please.' Jamie joined in. 'Find him a woman, while you're at it. He needs something... I think he's hormonal.'

Harry gave Izzy a fleeting knowledgeable rise of the eyebrows. 'Actually, to be honest you'd be doing us a favour. Poppy really wanted to go to see the Winter Wonderland in Hyde Park and we couldn't refuse her, seeing as it's her only chance of a break before Christmas...and everyone else is away. But, three's a crowd...you know?'

Izzy nudged him. 'Don't you dare say that. I love Poppy to pieces and I want to go ice-skating.' She paused, twiddling a beermat round and round. 'But four would be a good number.'

Yeah, right, if he tagged along as a crowd plumper Poppy would be just thrilled. Not.

Plus, he'd hate every minute.

Harry nodded. 'Hey, come on, mate. Don't let the women gang up on me, two against one. They'll have me making snow angels and looking at ice carvings. Queuing up to meet Santa.' He leaned forward. 'Solidarity, mate. Safety in numbers.'

'Nah. Sorry.'

Harry shrugged. 'Well, poor Poppy, I do hope she can skate. I mean, we'll try to look after her...but a man can only hold up one woman at an ice rink. I hope she doesn't hurt herself too badly.'

That was low, appealing to instincts Isaac hadn't even known he had until a few days ago. Having watched Jamie go through his romance with Steph, and Alex with all his conquests, Isaac had been wingman on too many occasions. So despite every misgiving he had he found himself agreeing, because he didn't want Poppy to be the spare part in what looked like a slightly skewed threesome. And after all the escalating tension in the flat some positive time outside might break the ice. Not literally, he hoped. 'Okay. Okay, I'll come.'

'Well, thank the good Lord for that.' Jamie smiled. 'Peace on earth and goodwill to all men is restored. Well, goodwill to me, anyway.'

'Great. Come on, then. Grab a coat.' Izzy downed her drink, took Harry's arm then paused, turning back to Isaac. 'Oh, did you ever find that mouse?'

And that was another thing. 'Yes. We caught it in the trap. Poppy took it out and set it free in Holland Park. I told her I'd do it, but she was gung-ho to do it herself.' Proving some kind of point. Which really wasn't the point at all.

'Poppy did? I thought she was terrified?'

'She was, apparently. But she wanted it gone and couldn't wait for me to do it. So she did it herself. Quite determined.' By the time he'd woken up the next morning she'd already gone without leaving him so much as a note. And why that had irritated him he didn't know. In fact, when he looked at it there were a hell of a lot of things going on in his head that he couldn't quite fathom. But they all seemed to start and end with Poppy.

Six loops around Hyde Park's temporary ice-skating rink hadn't anywhere near dampened down Poppy's irritation. She dug her heels in as she reached Isaac and covered him with a light peppering of snow. 'I thought you hated being cold.'

He blew into his hands but kept warm teasing eyes on her. 'It's warmer here than in the flat.'

'If you don't like the atmosphere you can always move out. No one's holding a gun to your head to make you stay.'

'No. But I figure if you think it's my life's work to annoy

you I'd better excel at it. At least, until Alex gets back, then he can take over.' He flashed a smile that did something strange to her stomach. Because, despite living the Cold War at home, she couldn't get the weird sensations out of her gut. Head. Lady bits. Although, in an attempt at an entente cordiale she had been at pains to remove her underwear from the radiator. What the heck was wrong with men that they objected to that, anyway? Plus she always tried to avert her eyes if he was dressed in anything less than his full winter overcoat. Which screamed sex, anyway.

She was doomed. And angry.

Bad enough to make a fool out of herself once. But twice? And now her so-called friends had insisted he join them. And then they'd sneaked away to a makeshift beer tavern somewhere on the edges of the rink, leaving her here with him. And the ever-present vibe.

They'd clearly been grateful for Isaac's presence, which meant they had plenty more time for each other. Heck, Izzy and Harry had been touch and go at one point in their relationship; they deserved some good times. Lots of them—particularly Harry, who was now shouldering an international business, and worrying about his father's ill health.

Those kinds of issues put hers into perspective—so she had a fatal attraction with a guy she lived with? It could be a lot worse. Couldn't it?

She looked up at the twinkling lights strewn from the centre pavilion across the rink. In the distance a large Ferris wheel turned slowly, lit up with white lights. It was beautiful, lighting up the dark cloudless sky. She needed to make the most of her three more days of freedom. It hadn't quite been the Zen chill-out that she'd hoped for. But she was going to enjoy this part, the magical Christmassy snowy part; Isaac could go to hell with his frown and his icy words and his…damned beautiful smile.

Sexy legs.

Capable hands, that made her tingle all over... She dragged her eyes away from him. 'Okay, I'm going to go round again.'

'Good. If you happen to pass a kiosk selling good moods, be sure to invest in one. Better still, I'll treat you to one. My shout.' He thrust his hand into his pocket for coins, wobbled, grasped the barrier as twenty or thirty laughing people wearing an assortment of bad-taste Christmas jumpers skated by. Managed to steady himself. 'You know what? I think I'll hang here.'

Pressing her lips together to stop the smile, she skated to him. 'You haven't done much skating?'

'I'm fine. Thanks. Don't worry about me.'

'What's the problem?'

'I don't have one. See?' He stuck his foot out and wobbled. Then the other one. Crashed to the floor. Looked up at her and laughed. 'Finally, a smile. Even if it is at my expense.'

'Well, the frown was caused by you, too. Idiot.'

'Hey. I'm the one hurting on the ice here.'

'Helpless idiot.' She offered her hand, but then withdrew it, preferring to see him struggle. How refreshing to not be the one making a fool of herself. For a change. 'Have you ever skated before?'

'Once. About a zillion years ago.' He pulled himself up by the barrier. 'I'm fine. Just finding my legs.'

She looked down the length of him. His leather jacket skimmed his trim waist. His legs were...perfect. The night sky was perfect. This wonderland of snow and ice, with its lights and laughter, was perfect and it suddenly seemed silly and unimportant to be cross with him any more. Her friends had skedaddled; she might as well make the most of the company she'd been forced to keep. And being better than him at something really gave her a kick. 'You want me to teach you?'

'No.'

'Come on.' She giggled. Actually giggled. Which was a surprise seeing as she hadn't giggled since last century. 'Hold my hand and I'll pull you along. You'll soon get the hang of it, I promise.'

He looked down at her hand and fitted his cold one into it. 'Okay. But be gentle with me.'

She tugged, but he tugged back. Hard. And she lost her footing, tumbling down with him, landing on the ice with a thick whump. Cold seeped through to her bottom. 'Double idiot.'

'Well, that brought you down to my level.'

'Oh, no, matey boy, there's a heck of a long way to go before I get that low.'

Propping himself up on one elbow, he trailed cool fingers lazily along her collarbone. 'And yet you want to sleep with me.'

She blinked. And shivered. And despite the cold she was definitely hot all over. 'Want*ed* to sleep with you. Past tense. I'm so over that. Missed the boat.'

'Oh, so you've changed your mind? Fickle, much?'

'Says the King of Fickledom.' She poked him in the stomach. 'Why are you here, anyway? I'd have thought this would be your worst nightmare.'

He shrugged. 'I needed time out from work. Fresh air… you know. All those late nights and clubbing isn't healthy… yada-yada.'

'Aka, they made you come. Because I can't think of one single thing about this that would tempt you.' And no, she wasn't looking for compliments. It wasn't as if she didn't see the guy every day—he could have offered an olive branch to her any time he wanted. He just hadn't taken the opportunity. In that same token, she could have, too—but

anything past a brief hello had made her blood boil and
her hormones escalate so she'd kept her distance. Something she couldn't do right now. She sat upright, looked for
the barrier to pull herself up. 'Oh, God, don't tell me they
were matchmaking or something equally draconian and
embarrassing? Izzy has this desire to have all her friends
as loved-up as she is.'

'No. Not at all.' He grabbed the barrier, levered himself upright, then offered his hand to her. 'Apparently I've
been distracted. They thought I needed a break. But, I'm
tired, is all.'

Taking his hand, she stood, brushed her jeans down,
wiggling slightly to keep the wet patch away from her bottom. 'Don't you ever take time off?'

'Not if I can help it. I want my business to work.'

'To prove what exactly?'

'To prove nothing at all.' Although the way he said it
made her think otherwise.

'So you ignore all your other…needs. And just work.'

'And that's a bad thing? Says Dr Workaholic, who ignored every need and…worked.'

'I didn't. I have a life.'

His forehead crinkled. 'Really? You have work, you
mean. Your friends, meanwhile, have lives.'

'I… You… Damn.' No one had ever come out and laid
that kind of blunt accusation at her. It was stark and raw
and it hit her hard in the chest. Isaac was good at home
truths. But then he, of all people, knew why she'd lived
like that. Ignoring every need had been easy until now.
Seemed she'd never really been tested. But she'd been running from pain and buried herself in her job—proving she
was worth something. Proving that she was more than a
stupid, infatuated teenager. *Home-wrecker*—the words
made her stomach knot just at the thought of them.

Proving that she could achieve something for herself,

she'd buried the hurt deep inside her and used it as fuel. Was that the way Isaac had been, too? She'd known his home life had been rocky, that he'd almost disassociated himself from his family, but had things been so bad for him? 'I had my reasons for choosing to live the way I do. You know full well what they were. What are yours?'

And yes, she knew she was pressing hot buttons here, but there was more to Isaac than he ever cared to show and she wanted to scratch that fun-loving, too-handsome-to-be-true surface and see what was underneath.

'I like work.'

'Well, it's easier than dealing with deep stuff, isn't it? Family stuff? Stuff you'd rather not face.'

He looked away. Didn't speak.

She lowered her voice. 'You can tell me, you know. I guess it's about your mum?'

'Oh, for goodness' sake. There's nothing.' His eyes darted around to the crowds skating by, to the lights and the sky and the laughter. 'Like this is the right time and place, anyway.'

'Here's as good as anywhere.' She pinned him against the barrier. 'If you want to get away you have to bypass me.'

'What is this, an interrogation?'

'A concerned friend having a chat?' She couldn't help shaking her head. 'How about I give you a head start? Your mum left your dad for a younger man. She married. It didn't work, so she left. Found another guy. Then another?'

The frown deepened, along with a sadness in his eyes that made him look lost. 'Yeah, it's hard to keep up, right? Trading one in for another.'

'Then, she finally settled with a nice guy with a little kid. Then they had one between them. Boys.'

Pushing against her, he gave her a dark look. 'Are we done here? I'm getting cold. You look frozen.'

'And you look angry.' But as she processed what he'd said the penny finally dropped. *Trading one in for another.* Did he feel that his mother had done that with him? 'So you throw yourself into your work, growing your bars and business to feel worth something. To matter. To prove yourself.'

'You really do know how to push my buttons, don't you? Quit with the pop psychology.'

'Getting to the heart of things is my job. Besides, aren't we just two of a kind? Using work to compensate for other stuff.'

His gaze brightened as he looked at her. Her face, her mouth, back to her eyes—as if he was trying to understand something. Then he shook his head. 'I don't think so. We are very different, you and me. Because underneath that bravado you do want what your friends have, what Alex has with Lara. You want someone to love and to be loved and I don't get that. I'm fine on my own. I always have been. I'm fine.' And yet pain laced his voice. He held his hands across his body as a barrier, and he avoided eye contact when he spoke. He might not want to be loved, but he definitely didn't want to be hurt.

'One-month relationships are fine?'

'I've had no complaints so far.'

'That's because you never give them the chance to get to know you. Or to tell you what they want from you. Or to ask for more. Or to tell you you'd broken their hearts.' But she'd seen the odd one or two women, the tears as they'd left him. Or, more usually, he'd left them.

'And that's because I like it that way. And it's working fine. At least it was, until you decided to get drunk and then—*wham*, we're getting down with the touchy-feely stuff. It's not me. It's…well, let's say you definitely win hands down for irritating.' He pulled up the back of her jacket and pressed his cold hand against the small of her back.

'Says you? Get off me!' But a laugh bubbled up from her throat as he swiped his hand across her midriff to her stomach. 'Yeow. Get off.'

'Only if you shut up with the deep stuff.'

'It's hardly…probing…' He was too close. Too treacherous, too perfect. She got the feeling she'd agree to anything if he kept looking at her like that, especially when even though he'd refused to open up his body language had betrayed him, anyway. She scrambled away from him. 'Come on. Skate.'

'I'll give you one loop and unless you have me doing a triple-pike somersault or whatever it's called by the end of it I'll declare you a dud.'

'No duds allowed.' She pulled, tugging hard on his hand, but he didn't budge, his feet forming a tight V shape, toes pointing inwards. He was stuck. 'Come on.'

She skated back to him; he wobbled again, reaching for her. 'Whoa. Sorry. Legs still lost, I'm afraid.'

She wobbled, too, aimed to grasp his outstretched hand but grabbed his left thigh instead. At the top. Her voice thickened. 'No. Legs very definitely here.' And something else, too, very close to her fingertips. Her mouth dried and his name came out on a breath.

'Oh, God,' he gasped, his eyes fixing on hers, lowering to her mouth, back to her eyes. Something passed between them—something tacit. Suddenly her body was awash with awareness. Just to hear his unfettered need stoked the heat in her again.

The way he was looking at her made her think that the only way they'd ever get through this living-together thing was if they slept together, got it over and done with and stopped pretending or waiting for it to go away, because it wasn't going anywhere. He lowered his mouth towards hers. Stopped a few inches away. His breathing sped up, but his eyes…*God*, her heart thumped hard and crazy in her chest…his eyes told her what he wanted. What he needed.

But he was conflicted, too. Because he knew as well as she did that whatever happened next would draw a line under anything they'd done before. Neither was in any doubt as to what was at stake here—where this would lead. He knew what she wanted. She knew what he was prepared to give.

His misted, confused gaze bore down on her.

'Just do it,' she whispered. 'Forget everything else. Forget whatever it is that's stopping us having a little fun. I've been waiting so long to feel this. Just do it. I want you. You want me. Easy.'

'Hell, Poppy. You say that one more time and I won't be able to stop myself.'

She took his face in both hands. He'd rejected her twice—no way would she try a third time lucky. He had to want to do it. He had to make that move. 'Just do it.'

Then his mouth covered hers in a frenzy, a hard, fast, greedy kiss that instilled desire deeper, stronger, further inside her. He pushed her against the barrier, spiked her hair with his fingers. That hot, misted look still in his eyes, focused on only her. Questioning. Surprised. Concerned. And yet, so very, very sexy. 'God, Poppy, the things you make me want to do.'

'Do it, then. Do it all.'

'Just wait until I get you home.'

Her breath came in rasps, her head woozy with adrenalin. She couldn't feel, see, hear anything but him. 'Now? Should we go now?'

And even as she said it she regretted the push. Knew he didn't need to be rushed, knew there was no hurry. Unless, of course, she wanted to wring every last drop of him out before the end of the night, the week…*the month*. And there she was already making things complicated.

She so did not want complicated all over again. She wanted free and easy and fun.

'No, not yet.' But he pulled her close, wrapped strong arms round her as if committed to action. The future, no. Action, yes. But tonight was good enough for now. 'This is your night, your holiday. You can do anything you like here. Then I'll take you home.'

'You'd endure the cold and ice sculptures for me?'

He shuddered. 'Enjoy? I don't think so.'

'Endure.'

'Yup. That's the word. But if that's what you want? More of this place…' He tipped her chin up and took her mouth again, opening her coat and weaving his hand round her back, pulling her tight against him. Against his hardness and his heat. 'Or more of that?'

She could barely breathe for awareness. 'Why not all of it? Everything. And then, seeing as the flat's empty, we can do anything you want there, too.'

'Anything?' She felt his smile against her cheek. And then, just for a fleeting second the nerves returned. What if she wasn't enough? What if she couldn't do it? What if he was too much? What if it wasn't fun at all? Worse, what if she wanted more? 'Hmm, what about Izzy?'

His nose nuzzled in her hair. 'What? Does she want to sleep with me, too? I think Harry might—'

'Shut up. Of course she doesn't. What I meant was, it would be rude to just leave.' She started to undo her skates, the jittery sexy feeling mingling with anxiety. 'Any idea where she and Harry got to?'

'Not a clue. Still in the bar?'

'I'll text them.' But he came closer, sat on a seat and undid the laces on his skates, too. His body brushed against hers and there it was again…the buzz and the whirl in her stomach. Intense. Her phone beeped. 'They couldn't find us, so they've headed back to Harry's.'

'So, Winter Wonderland is your oyster. What do you want to do now?'

Apart from rip his clothes off? But yes, it was a little bit nippy to do that. She pulled a crumpled brochure from her jacket pocket. 'There's so much to do here. We need to pack it all into just this one night.' Work beckoned, and then she'd be too busy with Izzy's hen party and wedding in her downtime—or just too plain exhausted from work. 'We could visit the ice kingdom. Or the circus? Snow sculptures? Heck, let's do it all.'

He shook his head, his throat working. 'All of it?'

'All of it.'

His shoulders slumped a little. 'And then home?'

Home. This was actually happening. She shucked the nerves away. She was going to treat this as a fact-finding mission. She was going to do the sex without emotion. She was going to be the sex-savvy woman she wanted to be. 'If you're good.'

His slow, lazy smile transformed his face. 'And what do you mean by that? Bad good? Or good bad? Good good? Or, my current favourite, very, very bad?'

'Just good.' Then she slipped into step with him as they went to exchange their skates. She had no intention of making him do the rounds of the attractions. There was only one place she wanted to be with him, and it certainly wasn't outside. She just prayed that she could be good, but hoped, more, that she could be very bad indeed.

CHAPTER NINE

'ARE YOU SURE?' Isaac knew he needed to tread carefully. Poppy had put up a good show of enthusiasm—and God, she was hot. Too hot. So hot. But also so innocent. No, not innocent, because she certainly knew what a man wanted, how to turn a man on despite what she thought, but she was still…naive. So easy to be blasé outside, fully clothed. But now he had her in the flat, door closed. How they'd managed to get home without undressing each other he didn't know.

It was happening.

She stood in the centre of the lounge, her coat dropping from her shoulders into a thick woollen pool on the floor. Her smile was coquettish, but there was a nervousness to it. And hell, he didn't want to hurt her. But if she kept looking at him in that *I want you* way, well, he wouldn't ask again.

'Absolutely sure.' She nodded, slowly, keeping her dark heated gaze locked with his. Dark against light. Soft against hard. Pure against…well, he'd been round the block a few times. But never like this. Not with someone who stoked such a fevered response from him. He felt like she looked—a nervous teenager, the first time. And for a second he wavered.

'But, Poppy, you shouldn't learn these things from me, but from a man who…' Who what? The words stuck in his throat. A man who would love her, who would keep her safe, who could make promises and keep them. Not from someone who would walk away. Changed—yes, inevitably he'd change, he knew that much, but would walk, anyway.

She pulled her hair out of its tie, and let her curls fall loosely around her shoulders. Every man's fantasy. 'I said, absolutely, Isaac. Don't make me ask again.'

He took a few strands and ran them through his fingers, held them to his face. They smelled of citrus and her. His groin tightened again. Pure feral need ran through him. 'Any time you want me to stop, just say. Anything you don't—'

'I want everything, Isaac. Don't talk about it. Do it.' Her shaking fingers played with the buttons on her dark purple blouse. She flicked one open. Moved her hand lower—flicked the next, allowing glimpses of a pink lace bra underneath, creamy skin, perfect skin he ached to run his hands over. He was hard. So hard for her.

'Okay. So we're going to take this slow. Okay? No rushing.'

'Okay.' She swallowed, her throat working overtime. The little pulse at the base of her throat beat a ferocious tattoo. A frown settled across her forehead. Her fingers shook. 'Show me slow.'

And he almost gave up again. It was all kinds of wrong. Because he wanted to do it hard and fast. He wanted to be inside her. To take her. To make her his. And she could never be that.

But he could not imagine another second without kissing her again. Without feeling her skin against his. Her body against his. Her, around him.

When his mouth connected with hers any kind of hesitation evaporated. She tasted of everything he'd dreamt of. A zillion flavours of ice particles melting on his tongue. Magic. Wondrous.

As he kissed her his hands took over where hers had left

off. Undoing her bra made her moan, little throaty sounds that fired sensation after sensation through his body. He peeled the blouse from her and dropped it to the floor. Slid the bra straps down her shoulders and threw it somewhere. Who knew where? He didn't care. He stepped back a little and looked at her soft, perfect breasts, nipples pink and puckered. 'Oh, my God. You are so beautiful.'

'So are you.' Smiling, she reached for his T-shirt and pulled it over his head, her fingers lingering over his pecs. After a moment of just looking at him, eyes wide and bright, she kissed a hot trail across to his nipple and licked. Relentless need shimmered through him, white hot. Her arms circled his waist, hands exploring his back, his chest, his stomach. 'Oh, God, Isaac, why do you have to be so bloody magnificent?'

'And I thought you wanted me to teach you. You're doing just great as you are.' Pushing her hair back from her face, he cradled her cheeks and kissed her softly. Tried to be patient. Tried to show her slow, but the touch of her mouth set his veins on fire. He dragged his mouth to that pulse at her throat, slicked a kiss there, along her fine shoulder bone and down to her breast.

She arched her back as he sucked in a nipple, her eyes fluttering with pleasure as she relaxed and tensed at the same time. 'Oh, yes, that feels so good.'

'Then it's only fair I treat the other one the same.'

Her loud moan as he circled wet rings round those dark nipples spurred him further; she rocked against him and he wondered whether it would be he who pushed them to go too fast, who wouldn't last many moments longer. He ached to be in her, to feel her around him. To feel her complete him. This. This out-of-control fever that sent him perilously close to the edge.

With a swift move he unzipped her jeans, shucked them down her legs and left them on the floor, his gaze lingering over matching pink panties that skimmed her bottom as he picked her up and carried her to his room. 'Yours is too far. Stairs…' His breathing quickened—not with the exertion, but with anticipation of what was to come.

He laid her on his bed and straddled her, careful to hold his weight. Her hand went to his jeans' zip. 'Show me, Isaac. Show me how you like it. Tell me what you like. Tell me what turns you on.'

'Hey.' He touched her hand, regretting that by carrying her in here he'd broken the spell. 'You first. Then me.'

Dark sparkling eyes looked up at him. 'Why not together? Is that too difficult?'

'No. Not difficult at all—but I want you to relax and enjoy this.'

'Oh, I am. But we might as well do you, because I never—'

'"*Do you?*" What is this?' God knew why that street phrase bothered him. It wasn't as if this were meant to be more than sex. Emotion-free. That was what he'd told her he could do. That was what he always did. He didn't want to think further than that—didn't want to complicate something with thoughts and shoulds and maybes. 'Whatever happens we are both going to enjoy this. I have ways…'

Poppy saw the gentle teasing glint in his eye but it didn't help the new flush of nerves racing through her, mixing with the heat and the desire and making her thoughts jumbled. She'd never had a say in who got what before—and she'd always lost out. But that was too many years ago and this was now. She was about to have sex with Isaac Blair. *Good God.*

Relax? No chance. Wasn't it meant to flow better than this? Wasn't it meant to just happen without talking? 'I don't even know how to relax into this… Can we just concentrate on you?'

'Then that wouldn't be fair, would it?' He knelt up and shifted so he lay on his side facing her, propping himself up on an elbow. 'Are you feeling okay?'

'Physically fine. I think.' The bravado had well and truly evaporated. But she couldn't go on like this for the rest of her life, avoiding intimate contact. What the hell Isaac thought of her now she didn't know. But just a little respite, some space from the sensations that were threatening to overwhelm her, was helpful. 'Scared. A bit. To be honest.'

He gave her a small reassuring smile. 'Of what?'

'Of it all. Losing myself. Control. Doing something stupid. What if you're too big? If I can't do it? Everything.' It was too intense. All this focusing on her. Too real. Too much. She'd never had this—it had always been about Tony. Never about her. Sure, he'd pummelled her breasts a bit as he'd stabbed inside her. Quick. Hard. Hurt.

Isaac's voice brought her back to here. Now. His bed. His heat. His arms. His touch. He stroked her hair, which soothed her. 'You'll be fine, Poppy. I'm not all that—'

'Oh, no...' She shook her head, remembering. Hell, she didn't have to try hard—the man's boxer shorts had been at the forefront of her mind for weeks. 'I saw. Those black boxer shorts do not lie.'

His grin was kind. 'Optical illusion.'

'But black's supposed to be slimming. Which means you're even bigger up close.'

'Women and men are made to fit together. It'll work. It's been working for millennia.' He flipped the waistband of his boxers. 'You want to take a peek? See for yourself?'

'Oh...' Heat ran the length of her, turning her insides into molten liquid. An ache settled across her abdomen and then lower. A nice ache. Delicious—desperate. Wanting. Never enough. Never satisfied. Like a pulse, waxing and waning. Yes. She wanted to see him. Hold him. Feel him. *Focus on him. Focus on him.* 'I suppose I could.'

She reached for his shorts, eased them down his thighs and he kicked them away to the floor. And *oh, my God*— her breath stalled in her chest—he was amazing. She wrapped tentative fingers around his girth. He was hot and very hard. And the softening of his eyes as she gripped him sent waves of something shooting through her. If she focused on him, not on her, she could get through this. She might even enjoy watching his pleasure. 'Show me what to do.'

He wrapped his hand around hers and she felt him shiver as he moved her hand up and down—not too hard. Not too soft. Not too fast. Not too slow. His face was a mask of concentration. She leant down and covered his mouth with hers. Tasting him—a new taste now, fresh, elemental, hot, wet kisses that quickly slipped to a hungry pace. She started to move her hand more quickly, heard him groan. Heard herself groan as she rocked against his thigh. She wanted to feel him in her. On her.

He turned a little, parted her legs and his fingers sank into her core. With a splintering of vision she let go of him and sucked in air. 'Oh. My God.'

She hadn't known it could feel like this. That a man could give her such a feeling. That fingers could make her crave more and more. Before she could stop herself she was tearing her fingers down his back and asking for more. For him. Inside her.

He rubbed his erection against her inner thigh. The intensity of sensation at her core doubled. She moved away. Moved back. Wanted more. Wanted less. She shifted her bottom a little. He was pressing against her opening.

And then. At the touch of him against her shards of light exploded through her. It was a raw physical sensation. Greed. Hunger. More. Not enough. Not enough. She shifted again, felt him press against her, heard him groan. 'Condom. Poppy. We need a condom.'

'Isaac. Come back.' *Isaac.*

Isaac.

Barely believable. But real. He reached for his jeans. Too slow. Slipped on a condom. Too slow. And then he was back. 'You're so wet, Poppy. You're an angel. A bloody Christmas angel.'

'Now. Please. I can't wait.' She felt a sharp stretch. Then a push. Harder. A searing pain that made her catch her breath.

He paused. Kissed her neck, took his weight as he stretched out above her and murmured against her throat, 'Are you okay?'

'God, yes.' It hurt like hell, but the pain was receding and in its place was an ache that would not be sated until he was fully in her.

Then a gentle thrust. And another. Pure physical joy rushed from her abdomen to her toes, to her head. She squeezed against him. Tried to match his rhythm, moving beneath him, trying for faster.

'Hey. Slow down. If you do that it's going to be over way too quickly.'

His hand squeezed in between them, fingers finding a place that exploded her thoughts into tiny pieces. He rubbed as he thrust until she didn't know which she wanted more. His fingers. Him inside her. His kisses. She just knew she didn't want any of it to end.

Didn't want this to stop. To lose him. To lose herself. 'I want more. Can we do more? Another position?'

He grinned. 'You want to play, now? Are you sure?'

'Why not?' She shifted a little underneath him, felt bereft when he pulled out of her and the connection between them broke. 'I know there's heaps more. I just haven't ever done any. Can we try some? One?'

'You seriously want to talk at a time like this?'

'Show me.'

'Anything for you.' His smile was sexy and kind as he sat up on the bed. 'Okay, face me and sit on my lap. This one is great for maxed-out pleasure.'

She did as she was told, legs wrapped around his back, and he entered her again; this time he was so close she felt his full body the length of hers, skin on skin. He held her so tenderly, the intimacy was intense. She couldn't help but look into his eyes, watch as the sexual mist came over him. Kissed him deep and hard. Then the kissing became more powerful…more intimate somehow as she kept staring into his eyes. She was making him feel like this. Making him hard.

And then he began to move more quickly, more urgently and he moaned her name. Just hearing that voice, that word, made her heart contract. She wanted this, but she wanted him more. Wanted him in her today and tomorrow. And… 'Isaac. This is…this is…'

'I know. I know. This is… *You* are amazing. Oh, God, Poppy…' he growled as his gaze locked on to hers again as he stroked her cheek. His beautiful, intense blue eyes telling her that he felt this, too—whatever it was—this wondrous, unique sensation.

Then she couldn't think of anything. Only that the pleasure, the sensation, must never end. She heard a moan—it wasn't him. It must have been her. Heard herself cry out, beg for more. Beg for him to never stop. Her hand reached for his and their fingers tangled over her core as she clenched around him. Rubbing. Moving. Faster. Deeper. His body slick against hers, where he began and she ended she didn't know.

He arched his back and cried out. And then her body shook as wave after wave of delicious trembling took her over the edge into perfect, perfect bliss.

* * *

'Wow. Just…wow. That was fun, the best ever. Not that I have much to compare it to.' Poppy's head lolled against Isaac's shoulder. 'Thank you.'

'My pleasure.' He didn't want to think about her previous sexual experiences; this was not the time to be angry or jealous, even though his fists involuntarily tightened. He consciously tried to relax. Plus, he didn't like to compare. But in reality he'd never known any sex come close to that. Had never felt so connected to anyone before. Ever. 'First time lucky, eh?'

'I just didn't know…didn't expect it to be so all-consuming.' Her smile was satisfied and awestruck. 'A tick for the big O. Now I know what all the fuss is about. I liked it.'

'Good. Yeah, me, too. It is meant to be enjoyable.' But he wasn't so sure about the feelings rattling through him now. They weren't particularly enjoyable; they were…a mess. He watched as she came down from the high, the flutter of her eyelids as she finally let out a long, heavy sigh and curled into him. And he curled back into her, glancing out of the window, his curtains still open from the daytime. Outside, soft snowflakes swirled and fell silently. By morning London would be cosseted again by a pure white blanket. It was as if magic were being created by stealth—creeping slowly in, unnoticed—but tomorrow things would be changed.

He was aware, too, of the softening in his heart. The way he'd been unable to tear his gaze away from hers. How turned on he'd been to watch her come, to feel her around him—to smell her, touch her. How that naivety and wonder had chinked a piece of his heart. How *she* had chinked a piece.

Wow indeed.

Because that had never happened before.

And he sure as hell didn't know what to do about it.

But now, now that he'd taken the one thing she'd kept only for herself for the past eight years—her body, her sensuality, and a huge serving of trust that he'd treat it carefully—what the hell could he give her back?

Not what she needed. Not what she wanted or deserved.

Her curls grazed his nose as she snuggled deeper across his chest. She fitted just perfectly in the crook of his arm, long, lithe limbs entwined with his. Her heartbeat raged against his ribcage. He was still inside her. Didn't want to withdraw. Didn't want to let go. Didn't want to end this. But it was the only right thing to do—because if he didn't she'd get too involved. No one could do what they just had and not feel something.

Too much something. It felt weird, foreign. Comfortable and uncomfortable. Threatening the status quo that he'd worked so hard to establish. Man, he was okay on his own. He liked it. He didn't have to answer to anyone. Didn't have to care.

And he was starting to do just that with Poppy. Cared whether he hurt her. Cared who she had slept with—and what that had done to her. Cared. Period.

So he needed to get the hell out. Trouble was, it was his room. Their apartment. How could he leave?

Hell, he'd done it many times before—he didn't need geography to forge a distance.

He wriggled backwards, withdrawing, watching her sharp intake of breath as she curled her legs up. 'Sorry. Sore?'

She winced. 'Yes. But in a good way. Don't worry, I think I'll be ready again soon.'

'Whoa. Steady.' He smoothed her hair down because he needed to touch her, to keep some contact with her despite what he was going to say. 'Look, I think we need—'

'A moment? Yes. Just one moment. To catch our breath.'

Her smile was wicked and made him hard at the thought of her being ready for him again. Wanting him again. But it would hurt to do it again so soon. He didn't want to hurt her.

He'd thought he could do this. There was so much he could teach her: how to touch him, what turned him on, how to touch herself. How to tease, how to take the lead. How to submit to pure pleasure. What to say. How to prolong the ecstasy. Games they could play. Toys they could use.

Could. But wouldn't. The enormity of the mistake they'd just made shook through him. He should have known: Poppy was different. And now he was different, too.

'No. Poppy—'

'Then you can show me a few more things…because I don't feel as if my education is anywhere near complete. First, I want to taste you…'

He didn't think she meant his mouth. A groan escaped his throat. He was fighting. Losing, but fighting. Was there no end to the feelings she instilled in him?

Before he could answer she kissed him again. Gentle at first, but when she slipped her tongue into his mouth and writhed against him he was gone. Again. Lost in the experience of her. His brain was working overtime trying to find all the reasons why they shouldn't do this, but his body knew exactly what he wanted.

Her.

CHAPTER TEN

POPPY WOKE FROM her exhaustion-induced half-sleep to a noise. Somewhere out in the lounge. A scuffle or a scratching.

The mouse trap?

'Isaac,' she whispered, trying to squint at the green display on his digital clock. Everywhere and everything ached. Not just muscles. Parts of her that hadn't been stretched or even touched in such a long time. Her lips were sore from his kisses. Her chin raw from his stubble. A delicious raw. A *want more* raw. Although walking might well be a problem tomorrow. She stifled a smile. She felt well and truly spent. A wicked, wild woman.

The clock came into focus. Four-thirty-eight. 'Isaac.'

'Again already? Do you never sleep?' Isaac's voice was thick and deep and husky; his hand slid across her stomach as he nuzzled against her head.

Sleep? She'd managed what? Thirty-odd minutes. 'I'm a doctor—I get by on many hours without sleep. Whole weekends with not one moment of shut-eye. Think you've got the stamina for that?'

He grinned, eyes still closed. 'Hmm.'

'Listen…did you hear that? A scratching or something. A noise, in the lounge.'

'Maybe little Mickey has come back?' His mouth was on her nipple now; her gut clenched as heat shimmered through her. Glorious heat. A glorious night of lovemaking, of discovery. Most noticeably, that Isaac was a very attentive and patient lover who gave more pleasure than he received.

She didn't want to leave him, but just like the last time she'd responded to the mousetrap noise she couldn't help satisfy her curiosity. Make sure the darned thing had been caught and wasn't making merry with her Christmas baubles...the couch...her food.

And, yes, she had to admit she had fallen just a little bit in love with her four-legged flatmate and had been quite sad to release him into Holland Park's long grass after all. 'Maybe he's homesick. Maybe he's scurried all this way back home. Shall we go see?'

'Sure. Tomorrow. Later.'

'Now. Come on.' Reluctantly dragging herself away from Isaac's lips, she pulled back the covers and tugged at his hand. The curtainless window shed fingers of moonlight over his beautiful body. And for a second she was pinned to the spot just looking at him. The broad shoulders that had held his weight as he'd entered her, the hair she'd spiked her fingers through. The delicious dip where his back curved into his backside, the soft downy hair just there where she'd kissed, before she'd turned him over and taken him full into her mouth.

And suddenly she wanted to do it again. And again. To crawl back in beside him and let him enter her, to place her fingers on herself and have him watch. To watch him draw slow strokes up his erection. Watch him lose control. There was so much she wanted to do with him. To him.

She had, what? Twenty-nine days left, according to his record—if not less. A brief affair. A holiday fling—the kind of thing her friends had done once upon a time, while she'd spurned any male advances. Not any longer.

But twenty-nine days meant twenty-nine nights, too.

Her stomach tightened at the thought.

She blew out a slow breath. She'd known what she was getting into. Known he wasn't offering her any more than sex. And it had seemed enough last night. An hour ago even. Now, however, she wasn't so sure. And it wasn't as if she could share this delicious secret with anyone, talk things over, or have a girly chat... Her friends would have a fit if they knew what she was doing. Isaac came with a pretty bad reputation that even she'd been previously happy to broadcast. He broke hearts. Period.

Tori and Izzy wouldn't stand by and let her get hers shattered—not the first time she dipped her toe.

First time that they knew about, anyway.

Her brother's reaction would be worse. His best friend and his nun-like sister—she could see the fallout now, and she definitely didn't want to get in between Isaac and Alex's friendship. Hers were hard fought for and very precious; she had no doubt the guys felt the same. This was something they'd have to keep very secret indeed.

There was the noise again. 'Come on, Isaac. Come and see if Mickey's back.'

'Okay. Okay. I'm clearly not going to get any peace until I do.' He stood, butt-naked, sleepily scratching his head, and again the sight of him stripped the air from her lungs.

'Wait. Clothes.' She handed him a pair of black sweatpants from the back of a chair, ignoring his frown, trying to drag her eyes away from him. But failing, because he was an absolute joy to look at. 'Put these on. Much as I like to see you naked I'm not sure Mickey would cope. It might scar the poor thing for life.'

'Well, I'm sure he'd love seeing you naked as much as I do. But hell...I feel way too overdressed now.' He threw Poppy a dark grey T-shirt, which she put on; it skimmed her thighs. She tugged it down, inhaling his smell, suddenly feeling a little shy to be so casual and yet intimate with him out of bed—especially after everything they'd done.

Things had irrevocably changed between them—could never be the same. Especially once it ended. She'd be back to smiling politely at his plus-one dates. Wondering how it was for them in bed. Whether he'd given them the same attention, pleasure. And the jokey entente they'd shared would be gone for ever. Because how could it not? How could it find a new equilibrium after this?

He watched her and smiled. 'It looks a hell of a lot better on you than it does on me. I'll go first, just in case it's not a mouse.'

'Why? What else could it be?' Suddenly panicked, she clung to his bare chest.

He pressed a hard kiss on her mouth, his hands gripping her waist and dragging her to him. Teeth against teeth. Protective. Possessive. Reassuring. Feral.

He finally pulled away. 'I'm sure it's just a mouse. Let's get this over and done with, then we can catch some sleep before morning.' Fingers trailed along her bottom, squeezing a cheek. 'Or we could find something more interesting to do...'

'Here, take this.' She handed him the softball bat, grabbed his hand and followed him out of the bedroom. As they crept towards the lounge they heard a louder noise. Not a mouse at all. Whispered voices that sounded very human. At least one distinctly male.

Isaac's fist tightened around Poppy's; he pushed her behind him. 'Stay here.'

'Like hell I will.' She kept hold as he increased his pace.

'Hey. What the hell's going on?'

'Oh, my God. Oh, my God, Isaac. You made me jump.' The flick of a switch flooded the lounge with bright light, and in the middle of the room, suitcases at their feet, stood Tori and Matt. Suntanned, stupefied and staring. Tori's voice was incredulous as her eyes took in Isaac's naked torso, Poppy's scantily covered legs and the hand-holding that connected them. 'And...*Poppy*? Really?' Her voice rose an octave. 'Poppy?'

Busted. Isaac's gut tightened. This was not the plan. How the hell would they explain this?

And what did it matter? They had nothing to be guilty about. Just two people participating in advanced adult activities. Consenting. Fun. 'Hey, guys. Good trip?'

'Great.' Matt grinned. 'Sorry, are we interrupting?'

'Hi.' Poppy stepped out from behind Isaac's back, grabbed a cushion from the nearest chair and held it in front of the T-shirt that showed her legs off to their full glory. But her cheeks blazed and she barely made eye contact with her friends. 'Welcome home. We weren't expecting you until...er...' She frowned. 'When were you supposed to be coming home?'

'Last night, actually. I sent an email. As it was, we got delayed. Clearly you weren't expecting us—look at the place...' Tori wrestled some of the smile from her mouth and pointed to the debris left over from last night's pash session. Articles of clothing littered the floor, couch, and the bra had landed on the Christmas tree. 'Interesting choice of decoration. I thought we were being burgled and I'd caught you in the act.'

In one act, yes. Definitely not the act Tori was thinking about. Isaac dropped the bat onto the sofa. 'Likewise. I'll sort it out tomorrow. We got a little distracted...' He was not going to explain or apologise. 'So, if you don't mind we'll be going back to bed. See you in the morning.'

'Okay. No worries.' Matt gave a know-it-all, well-done-mate smile that Isaac wanted to wipe from his face.

But Tori glanced over to Poppy, her smile slipped and she didn't move.

Neither did Poppy.

Isaac looked at her and she looked back at him, her face still bright red and yet devoid of any discernible emotion. Her hand dropped away from his and he knew in that instant that she regretted it all. Maybe not the sex, but the fallout, the explaining. The reality. Knew she wouldn't be coming back to his bed. This exposition was too intense, the connection too fresh and fragile and new to sustain under the glare of others.

Because knowing the tight-knit friendship Poppy and Tori had there would be post-mortem ad infinitum and Poppy just wouldn't be able to explain what they'd got themselves into.

For that fact, neither could he.

Poppy shook her head minutely. 'I'll just have a quick word with Tori if you don't mind? I'll see you…er…later.'

'Poppy. It's okay.' He reached a hand to her waist and tried to pull her close. He didn't know what to say to make it better—it wasn't as if he were going to make any kind of declaration, or offer her a future. But it would be better for them all if they went back to bed and reconvened later. Preferably never. For once he was well out of his depth. Genial Isaac who always had the right drinks, the right answers, knew how to do the right thing, was stumped.

But she shrugged him off. 'So, Tori, how was South Africa? You look amazing, great tan. Shall I put the kettle on?'

And he should have been pleased she was letting him off the hook. And normally he would have been. Hell, he never thought twice about cooling things off when liaisons started to get uncomfortable. But…well, this thing with Poppy was beyond anything he'd ever known and he didn't know how to react. Except to take her lead and do what he usually did.

Walk away.

* * *

Poppy watched as Isaac slunk back to his room and then let out a deep rush of air from her lungs. She couldn't do the walk of shame and follow him. To do what? How could they sleep now? How could they do anything now? When Tori and Matt would hear. Would question—and she didn't have any answers. Not for them and certainly not for herself.

Tori kissed Matt goodnight and sent him to bed. 'Save a bit of space for me in that single bed, won't you? Oh, wait, Poppy did you ever get it fixed?'

Poppy grinned at the memory of an over-enthusiastic sex session between Tori and Matt that had resulted in a broken bed and the red-faced next-morning admission to their landlady. 'It was unfixable. But I bought a new one, so you owe me extra rent for that.'

Tori grinned back, eyes glinting. 'It was worth it. Every penny.' Then she turned to Matt. 'Tomorrow we'll go flat-hunting, hon. Finally.' She put a hand out to her friend, eyes wide, whispering, 'To be honest I could sleep any-where, that flight was so long. But you! Whoa. That was a surprise. What the hell is going on?'

'No, you first. Flat-hunting?' There went another friend flying the coop. She was going to suffer a bad case of empty-nest syndrome very soon when there'd only be her and Isaac left. *Oh, God*—how would that pan out? He'd have to go. That was all. Then she'd find herself a whole new set of flatmates.

Now that didn't appeal at all. She'd loved having this place with her friends around her. Loved her girly chats, her best friends who'd seen her through thick and—if only she'd been honest with them at the start—almost the very thin.

It was the end of an era.

No, she couldn't think like that. They'd still be friends,

just with extras, too—husbands, fiancés, maybe even kids some day. The group was just getting bigger, was all. It was still a group. Still her group. 'Tell me more. Tell me everything.'

'Oh, no. You can very definitely go first, Pops.' Tori pulled her through to the kitchen and closed the door, switched on the kettle and found two cups. 'You're sleeping with Isaac? Really? What's happening? Because this is so far from the Poppy I know, I'm very confused.'

You and me both. She felt so exposed. Not least because she hadn't a clue what was happening.

Desperately trying to keep out of the unwanted spotlight, Poppy shrugged as embarrassment shuddered through her. Not unlike the first time she'd been with a man. *Just a quickie before we go home? Atta girl. You know I'd choose you if I could but she needs me.* No— then she'd felt guilt and shame. Used. Dirty.

With Isaac she'd felt none of that. Just wanted, and close. Touching someone after being so independent for so long. So…lonely. Someone stroking her skin. Someone wanting to make her happy. She bit her lips together as unbidden emotions ran through her. She wanted it again. She wanted more. To feel normal, to give in to feelings and needs she'd locked away in disgust and refused to open for too long.

The embarrassment was just a reaction to being caught out.

Would it ever be normal for her? Would she ever feel happy about having sex?

She had. Ten minutes ago she had. She'd felt reborn. Alive. Vibrant.

Her jaw tightened. *Damn.* It was all so temporary. This feeling of absolute satisfaction was temporary. Isaac was temporary.

She hoped to goodness the embarrassment would be temporary, too, and not likely to last almost a decade.

Tori patted her arm. 'Pops, are you okay?'

'Oh, sorry. I'm fine. It was just tonight. I mean…we've been skirting around each other for a few days now, weeks even…'

'Try years? It was bloody obvious to all of us, but neither of you seemed to realise… Can't count the number of times we'd thought you would…you know. It was just a matter of time.'

'Really, you all thought—?' That this thing had been there all along? How come neither of them had ever noticed? How come no one had ever said anything? Had they? She'd been so determined to deny any vestige of sexual attraction to anyone she'd shut them all up with a stare. 'Things came to fruition a few hours ago.'

'Details, sweetie. Now. Everything.' Teabags were plopped into mugs. Milk taken out of the fridge. A packet of chocolate digestives opened and thrown onto a plate.

Her appetite had fled along with her dignity when she'd been caught wearing nothing but Isaac's shirt, and suddenly Poppy felt depleted, bone tired. Exhausted. 'I'm not going to tell you anything past we slept together.' *And it was epic.*

'But, Poppy. You don't sleep with anyone. Ever. Not in all the time I've known you. So why choose Isaac? Why now?'

Poppy shrugged. 'It was an itch and we needed to scratch it.'

Tori threw her an incredulous look that said, *as if.* 'So what's going to happen next? Are you two dating?'

'No.' Slumping down at the table, Poppy forced a quarter of a biscuit into her mouth. Crunched. Chewed. Swallowed, with little enthusiasm. 'Relationship status—complicated. Or very simple—there isn't one.'

'Do you want one?'

'It's not an option for either of us. We're both too busy, too—'

'You could make time.' Tori came over and put her hand on Poppy's arm. 'Or is it another one of Isaac's crazy ideas? Friends with benefits? Does he just want cheaper rent? Because I'd have slept with you, too, if you'd dropped it by fifty quid...' She winked just in the nick of time. 'Joke.'

'Yeah. Hilarious. No, we haven't discussed anything, really. It just happened.' They hadn't needed to go beyond *just do it*.

Tori poured hot water into their mugs, smiling gently through the steam. 'But you know what Isaac's like. He's never here, for a start. He's hardly a contender for husband of the year.'

'I don't want a husband.' And, yes, she knew all this already. Tori's reality check wasn't helping to put things into perspective.

'You didn't want sex, either, Poppy. For how many years? Which brings me back to my original question. Why now? Why him? I mean. He's gorgeous. But—' In response to Poppy's anxious face Tori threw her arms round her friend's neck and gave her a hug. 'Okay. No more questions. I don't want to push you into a corner. Just be careful. You have a sensitive heart, Poppy Spencer, and I don't want to see you get hurt. Hurting's what he does.'

'I know. I know exactly what he's like. And that's why I'm not going to let myself get involved.' Which was the first big fat lie she'd told Tori in quite a long time. Because she had a feeling that it was already too late. Sex without emotion hadn't happened. Emotion had been there between them, deep and fierce and raw, and neither of them could deny it.

Just thinking about the way he'd looked at her had a thick lump forming in her throat. The way he'd made her feel. And that made things even more complicated because he was bound to run a mile now. 'No one else knows about this. You must promise not to tell any of the others. I can't face any questions, not when we don't know what's happening ourselves. And swear Matt to secrecy, too.'

'I will, I will. But promise me you'll protect yourself. And I'm not just talking condoms. I'm here if you need me, Poppy, any time. For a chat. Anything. I'm still shocked. I've never known you to have sex before. You look different. In fact, it suits you.'

She leaned close and squinched her eyes, peering at Poppy's face. 'Okay...one teeny question...just one.' She lowered her voice. 'Was it good? Come on. This is Isaac we're talking about. *Isaac*. Of all the men we know you have to go and choose the best-looking—Matt excepted, of course—most edgy and streetwise of them all. He's like...the full Monty with a cherry on top!'

'It was bloody fabulous. Okay?' Poppy resisted a fist-pump. 'Now stop with the questions.'

Tori leaned back, took a bite of biscuit and frowned. 'Seriously, if he hurts you, I'll break his legs.'

'Thanks, but if he hurts me, I'll do the leg breaking. And I'll break anything else hanging below his waist. I'm a doctor, I know how to do these things.'

'Well, then you can teach me.'

'You won't ever need it with Matt. He's just perfect for you.'

'Just shows you what a good judge of character I am.' Which was a hell of a joke considering the loser boyfriends Tori had brought home in the past. The list started with cross-dressers and got a whole lot worse from there. She'd eventually, with the help of her friends, discovered that relationships were all about giving and not receiving. In other words, Tori had grown up.

'Finally you are, yes, after a few false starts and dodgy

partners. Matt is lovely.' For the first time in a while Poppy laughed. Thank God for her friends. 'I know it's beyond cruel and we always share everything, but truth is, I don't know where this thing with Isaac is going, if anywhere. Which I doubt. So I'm not saying any more, it's late and I'm tired.' And, like Tori, in shock. And still a little embarrassed.

But not regretful. She was proud that she'd followed through on taking what she wanted. Felt powerful that she'd taken Isaac again and again, that she could make him want her, too. And she'd already added a little of the *Kama Sutra* to her sexual repertoire. That had to count for something? 'But I do want to hear all about your trip.'

Tori's eyes widened. 'Oh, well…I was going to wait, rather, we were going to wait and announce it, but…I have to tell someone or I'll burst.'

'Announce what?' Poppy's heart sped up a little. Good news clearly, judging by her friend's ecstatic grin. Tori had already let the cat out of the bag about flat-hunting—so things were still very serious between the two of them.

Tori handed her tea mug over but when Poppy took it her friend kept her hand out and waved the fingers of her left hand. 'We have news…'

A stunning solitaire diamond set on a white-gold band sat on her ring finger. Poppy jumped up and hugged her gorgeous friend, the lump in her throat surprisingly raw. 'Oh, my God. You got engaged. I hadn't noticed, I'm so sorry. How could I have missed that? It's beautiful.'

'You are a little distracted…I don't blame you.'

'Bad friend. Very bad friend. That's amazing. Just amazing. I'm so happy for you. Tell me what happened.'

Tori eyed her suspiciously. 'But I thought you were tired?'

'Not for this. This is spectacular news.' Her heart swelled at the thought of another wedding, another happy couple amongst her friends. And Matt was just the perfect laid-back foil to Tori's go-get-'em personality. If ever there were opposites that attracted and worked this was a shining example. 'Details. Now. Did he propose? I thought you were going to take things slow?'

Tori's grin spread. 'Well…you know I don't like to waste time?'

'Yes?'

'I asked him! It just came out one day when we were walking along the beach. Everything was perfect. He was, is, perfect and I don't ever want it to end. So…ta-da! He said yes and we're getting married. I'm a little shocked actually—it happened pretty fast even by my standards.' She beamed and Poppy felt a rush of love for her friend. 'But very happy.'

'You are one hell of a woman, Victoria. Does Matt realise what he's taking on?'

The love shone from her eyes. 'Oh, yes. And he says he loves me all the more for it.'

'I wish I had half your balls. Go you for taking what you want.'

It was so much easier to share her friend's elation than to delve any deeper into her own confused personal life. Everyone around her was loved up and settling down. And she felt as if she were in the slow lane swimming through thick soup to catch up.

No, of course it didn't matter that she wasn't engaged or planning a wedding. Of course she didn't really mind that her friends were starting fresh new lives. Without her. Away from the flat.

Their lives were changing, moving on. The past few years the apartment had been a cocoon of friendship, they'd simply carried on where boarding school had left off.

But change was happening, people pairing off, moving

forward. It was wonderful, the natural way of things and she was pleased to be able to share their joy.

But part of her, just a small part, wished she could have some of what they had.

And she knew it was never going to happen with Isaac. He was a stepping stone to being a fully-fledged independent and sexually aware woman, really. Someone she could hone her skills with until The One turned up—at least that was what she'd thought. Now she wasn't so sure. Emotion had become embroiled and she didn't know how to handle that.

So the next time she saw him she'd spell it out. Explain that this had been a mistake and that nothing like last night could happen again. And if that didn't throw a large ice-cold bucket of reality over their temporary liaison then she would treble the rent and hope like hell he didn't have enough cash to pay.

CHAPTER ELEVEN

ISAAC WAS NOT going to have it all thrown back in his face. He was not going to skulk around the apartment trying to avoid Poppy any longer. He would not spend the next few weeks being in the same space as her and not be able to look at her because things had got awkward again. Being at a wedding and unable to chat. Being in the damned kitchen and not able to share a cup of tea—or even talking to her alone without the Tori/Izzy chaperone she seemed to have amassed. Talking about anything other than what needed to be said. Leaving frosty notes. Back to texting one-word messages again.

Not being able to touch her.

His mind wandered back to the free way their bodies had meshed, uninhibited. No awkwardness there. He just couldn't get rid of the images of her, head thrown back, moaning as she'd folded around him. Or the images of her red-faced in front of Matt and Tori, guilty of nothing except enjoying herself. So he was damned well going to talk to her. Make sure she understood that there was nothing to be ashamed about. But that his life was chaotic and he would be shuttling from here to Amsterdam and Paris, that he could not be there for her geographically or in any other way she wanted. Or expected.

Trouble was, she was damned difficult to get on her own now she was back at work and things for his bars had upscaled to Crazy Christmas Busy so somehow a week had flown by in a stiff kind of silence and the tension in the flat had escalated to a surging boiling point.

And now he'd got back from the boxing club—once again disproving that exercise helped clear the head—and the flat was quiet. She could be in. Or out. But she wasn't making her whereabouts known.

After downing a pint of water he finally bumped into her outside the bathroom. She was wearing a full-length blue fleece dressing gown, hair scraped back in a scruffy ponytail. She looked sleepy. Sexy. Uncertain.

He stepped back indicating that she could use the bathroom first. 'You go.'

'No.' She glanced around at anywhere other than at him. 'You can go.'

A silence wove round them. Hesitant. Painful.

One of them would have to say something soon or it would get plain weird staring at the tiles, a huge cloud of anxiety hanging over them.

Go big or go home. Taking a deep breath, he started, 'Poppy, we need to have a chat. About things.'

Not a flicker of movement. She was perfectly still. Finally, she raised her chin and her dark eyes bore into him. 'No, we don't. We both know where we stand.'

'Do we?' He didn't have a clue. Which was a novel experience.

She nodded, curls bobbing around her shoulders. 'I'm good with it.'

'With what?'

'With what we did.'

'Oh? Because I thought you looked embarrassed.' Still did in fact. 'And there's nothing to be embarrassed about. It happened. These things do. We can move forward, be grown-up.'

She leaned against the doorframe, arms crossed over

her chest, attempting casual. Relaxed. Although the stance did nothing to hide the crackling strain in her eyes. Eyes that wandered over his body, his running top and shorts, stopping momentarily at places she'd kissed. Purred over. Licked.

Was this really a moment to feel turned on? He doubted it—but he did. Even at her most petulant she stoked a feverish kind of want in him.

She cleared her throat and her voice was all emergency-room professional *don't mess with me*. 'Well, thanks for the validation, Isaac, but it's unwarranted. I had sex because I wanted to. Nothing wrong with that. I can do it again, too, if I like.'

Now she was talking. 'Really? And will you?'

'I haven't decided yet.' Her eyebrows rose a little. 'Now, are you going to use the shower? Because I have a long list of things to do before the hen party this afternoon.'

He nodded. 'Oh, yes, the hen party at the spa? Then the hen-stag party at the bar?'

'Yes. The girls are meeting up first. Girly chats and all that. Massages…mani-pedis, man talk. You know the drill. Or maybe you don't, being a guy. Whatever. Then we're all coming round to Blue for drinks, apparently. Exciting.' She flashed a look that told him the prospect of spending the evening in his company was anything but.

And that was another thing. Joint hen and stag parties. Who the hell did that?

Poppy's lot did. Joined at the hip. Dating her would be like dating a posse. Handling the needs of one woman was bad enough, but four? He shuddered.

Still, hosting it at Blue meant he would be too busy working to be distracted by her. 'Be my guest—the shower's all yours. But if you're already going to a spa to be prettified what other kinds of things do you need to do?'

'Prepping…for this afternoon. We're only getting a

manicure and massage at the spa. There are other things a lady needs to do before she goes out.'

'Oh...so, you have to shave your legs and that kind of stuff...?'

'Why? It doesn't affect you.'

Yeah? Seemed everything she did affected him these days. 'Then maybe I should use the bathroom first. I've got to get to work and prepping takes a lot of time, in my experience.'

'Well, you should get a decent electric razor, then.' She eyed his legs. 'And do it more often. You've got terrible re-growth. Try threading? IPL? Waxing? If you need anyone to rip hot wax off your hairs I'll be first in line.'

Why the hell was she so angry with him? 'You'd enjoy that, wouldn't you?'

'Every second.' She opened the bathroom door and he got the distinct feeling that she wasn't angry so much as frustrated. She wanted something she couldn't have. But she'd decided she couldn't have it when she'd dropped his hand and refused to go back to bed with him. Her mouth tipped into a smile just short of evil. 'Actually, I've de-cided that I am going first and I'll be as quick as I can. But please don't use any taps until I'm done. The water supply's gone weird again. The plumbing really does need sorting.'

Now this was one thing he could do to make things a little easier in the flat. 'It might be the cold; freezing pipes are not happy pipes. Although, face it, they've been shot for years. I could get one of my guys to have a look if you like? Pretty reliable. I could talk to him about mates' rates?'

'Would you? I never seem to have the time. Although having just had more than a week off I should have put it higher up the list.' The tautness in her shoulders relaxed a little now they were talking about something that wasn't contentious. The smile turned warm. That almost cut him in two. It certainly warmed him in places that had been very warm a week ago. In bed with her.

'Well, you were pretty busy. Other things on your mind?'

Her eyes widened as her gaze locked on to his and the anxious, angry tension was replaced by a very different kind of tension altogether. The air around them super-charged, a crackle of electricity that rebounded between them. At the memory of tangled sheets the pulse at her throat quickened. She licked her lips. They had been dry. Now they were wet. He imagined wetting them more with his tongue.

Her mouth opened just a little bit—just enough. 'Yes. I was…distracted.'

'Very.' Heat fizzed around them, shimmering. He inched closer, unable…unwilling…to have another second without touching her. He thought she might move away but she didn't. She just kept on looking at him, eyes not moving from his. A dare almost. *Just do it*.

Then she stepped closer, too, her hand reaching for his shirt, fabric bunching in her fist. Her take-no-crap voice softened, eyes sparking a zillion wicked promises. So startling, the change in her. Breathtaking. She bit the bottom of her lip and smiled up at him. 'This is happening again, isn't it?'

'Yes. It is.' Ignoring the shadow of doubt that had put down roots in a corner of his mind, he stepped her into the bathroom, smiling against that pouty mouth that made him hard. He clicked the lock, not willing to chance any inter-ruptions or being caught, which would doubtless send her scuttling away again. 'Just once more for good luck.' Just to straighten things out between them, to smooth the waters.

He pulled her hair tie and let her curls fall over her shoulders. Stroked her cheek with his thumb, relishing her soft skin, the heated flush. 'But you see…here's the thing about showers…you don't want to use up too much water. Bad for global warming.'

'Is it?' she whispered.

'I don't know. It's bad for something.' He shrugged, far too concerned about current issues right here than global ones. His fingers trailed along her throat. 'How about we double up? Save the earth and all that.'

Thumb running along his upper lip. 'Oh, well, if it's for a good cause I can hardly refuse. We have to do our bit for the environment.'

He sucked her finger into his mouth. Watched the rapid flicker of eyelids that told him she wanted him. Very much. He grabbed her hand, nipped her forefinger. 'Excellent.' Her middle finger. 'Shower first. You are very dirty.'

'You, too. Very sweaty.'

Ring finger. 'Then we'll talk.' At her frown he backtracked a little. 'Or we'll talk first?'

'I have no intention of talking.'

'That's a first.'

Her eyes darted to the shower. 'And so is this.'

He twisted on the tap and a shot of icy water fizzed out. While he waited for it to heat up he took the opportunity to kiss her again, cupping her face, his lips pressed against hers. She tasted sweet and fresh and new. Exciting yet familiar. His heart thrummed hard in his chest.

Like coming home. Like Christmas come early.

She nipped his bottom lip with her teeth and he laughed, yelped. Unbuttoned her dressing gown and let it fall to the floor. The outline of two tight nipples pressing against her pyjama fabric made his mouth water. He gently stroked one watching her writhe under his touch. She pulled his face up to hers and gave him an urgent open-mouthed kiss filled with the past few days' need. Hungry. Wet.

Dragging her under the shower head, he leaned her against the wall. Water sluiced down his neck, over his arms, soaking his clothes and slicking them to his body. 'I do love these pyjamas. But I love them more when they're over there, and we're over here.'

He peeled her wet top from her body and threw it on to the bathroom floor. Then wiggled her bottoms down and kicked them to the side. He sucked a puckered pink nipple into his mouth, relishing her moans, the hand fisting into his hair. Gripping and pulling. He knew exactly what she liked, where she liked to be touched. What made her ready for him.

Everything felt light, electric. She felt perfect underneath his fingertips. Water dripped over the soft mounds of her breasts, running in rivulets down her cleavage. Heat surged through him, to hell with any doubt. He needed this.

Needed her.

He'd never needed anyone. Made damned sure of it his whole life.

Emotion plus sex.

Alarm bells began to ring in his ears, echoed in his heartbeat.

But he didn't care. Couldn't stop. He needed to be in her. With her.

She pulled at his top, dragged it over his head, laughing. 'I hate this T-shirt. And these shorts.' Her fingers made him groan as she shucked his jogging shorts off. 'But I do love these boxers. Oh. Not black today?'

'Red. Black. Whatever. Change is a good thing. Embrace it.'

'I fully intend to. I'm definitely embracing these.' Her hand slid along the front of his waistband, making him inhale sharply. She'd grown so much in confidence, knowing, in a very short space of time, exactly how to touch him to give maximum turn-on effect.

His voice was a growl against her neck. 'That prepping you have to do—how long does it take?'

She shook her head. 'What prepping? Did I not say I have hours to spare?'

'Me, too. How convenient. New housemates' rule. No clothes at all.'

'Okay. It's a deal.' She started to laugh as her hand cupped his backside and squeezed her against him. 'A few weeks ago I'd never have imagined me doing this. Naked with you?'

'It's amazing what you can do if you let yourself go.'

'I'm pretty gone. I have to admit.' She tiptoed her fingers around the top of his thigh. 'But I must warn you, this wet and wild experience is purely for research purposes.'

'How so?' He nipped her throat and pulled her under the water again.

'A client asked me about orgasms the other day—she wasn't getting any with just penetration—and I was able to make a few suggestions to help her.' Her smile widened and she gave him a dirty grin.

The bellow that came from his throat was quick and loud. 'Anything to help modern science. Come here.'

He squirted shampoo into his hands and slowly massaged it into her hair while she soaped his chest, his waist. Gasping when she took his erection in her hands and squeezed, sending shock waves through him.

But rinsing off the bubbles she pulled her hair tight back—making her look eighteen again and he was reminded of her innocent heart. How inexperienced she was underneath the bravado. No relationships over the years to harden her to the inevitable hurt of break-up. Even after a fling the rejection often stung. Apparently. That was what he'd heard—never being the one to be rejected. Something else he made sure of. He wouldn't ever give a woman the chance to cash him in for an upgrade.

'Are you sure about this?' Geez—he was the one with

the questions when he'd been assuming it would be her all along.

'Of course. But Tori says that if you hurt me she'll break your legs.'

Trying not to smile too much, he took both her hands in his, reluctantly drawing the delicious attention away from his hard-on. 'It's not my intention to hurt you.'

'You won't.'

'But I can't promise—'

Her finger covered his lips. 'I know and I'm not asking. So stop talking…I'm a big girl now and can look after myself.' Then she reached out of the cubicle to the bathroom cabinet. Fiddled around for a couple of seconds, and pulled out a small foil packet. 'See? Voilà.'

'Handy place to keep condoms.'

'Be prepared, I say. What kind of gynaecological registrar would I be if I didn't always practise safe sex?'

'Top of the class, Poppy Spencer.' He nuzzled against her neck. 'Vying to be teacher's pet?'

She froze. Pulled away. Her smile wavered at a memory. Fleeting. She shook her head and he realised what a dumb-ass faux pas he'd made. 'Pops. I'm sorry.'

Of all the stupid…

Why the hell had he brought that up? Now? For a moment she looked at him, God knew what the hell was going on in that head of hers. He thought she might hit him, jump out of the shower. Cry.

But she did none of those things. Instead, she took his hand and placed it on her breast, took the other one and squeezed it between her legs, pressing against her core. Rubbing slowly. Slowly. Placed hard kisses along his jawline. Bit him playfully and smiled. 'Just shut the hell up, Isaac. You are so not him. And look at me. Look at me.'

And so he did. He drank in her adamant pout, the honeyed eyes, the mussed-up hair. The perfect breasts that turned him on and the long legs he loved having wrapped around him. 'I'm looking.'

'And do you see that sad, pathetic, mixed-up kid?'

'Not at all.'

'Good. What do you see?'

'A beautiful, amazing, accomplished, naked woman.'

'Who wants you. And right now, if you please. There is nothing left of that girl. She's a memory. So kiss me again.'

God forgive him, but it was better to believe her—to go along with her—than to argue and blow this perfect scenario to smithereens. He'd probably go to hell and endure a thousand deaths but she was too much, too amazing to resist. 'Okay, if you insist. You're the boss.'

'That's the plan.' Not inviting any more discussion, she raised one of her legs and wrapped it around his hip. Taking her lead, he positioned her against the wall, and slid deep, deep inside her, his breath hitching at the tightness of her around him. The immediate intense rush of sensation almost knocked him sideways. He wanted to fill her again and again. And never stop. He gripped her, held her tight. Pressed rough kisses on her mouth.

In response to his primal impulse she kissed him back hard, urging him to thrust deeper. Faster. Fingernails dug into his shoulder as she braced against him, breasts pressed against his chest. Even with a condom he could feel her heat, her wetness as she squeezed around him, matching his rhythm in perfect time.

She gasped. Tensed a little. Then rocked against him. 'Oh, my God, Isaac. I've missed this. Missed you.'

So much for not talking. But it was cute. He cupped her cheek and pressed kisses over her face, while sliding in to the hilt. Deeper. 'What? Since last week?'

She gasped again, her words coming in short breaths. 'Since for ever.'

For ever?

Then she smiled, head thrown back as he filled her over and over—a perfect fit, a perfect match. His heart felt as if it were bursting into a zillion pieces, because she was right: despite every attempt to deny it—this had been growing between them for ever. Whatever it was, whatever was happening he couldn't name, but he knew she would be the only one who could put his heart together again. He thrust again, slowly this time because any faster and he'd lose himself.

But she pushed him to go harder. 'Oh, my God, Isaac. Don't stop.'

'Yes. *Yes.* Yes.' He could feel her tightening around him. Feel her growing climax as she increased the rhythm again, heard the moan that turned into a cry and that spurred his orgasm, shaking through him, blowing reality into a thousand glittering shards. He held on to her. Tight. Tighter, never wanting to let her go. Wanting this to last…yes, for ever.

As she rocked against him her head lolled forward on his shoulder and she nuzzled the soft spot at his neck in the last slow throes, her scent making his head swim. He turned his head and saw her eyes misted in a haze of spent desire, and she caught him looking, held his gaze. Moments passed and he couldn't find words to describe what this feeling was in his chest. A pressure building. But he realised that a new truth glittered between them now, a new connection…deeper and stronger than the last.

But even as they clung to each other that doubt he'd fisted down earlier sprang back with full force. He'd said he wouldn't hurt her, but it would happen in the end. He couldn't give her what she wanted and already she was in too deep—the look in her eyes told him that.

She was right: he couldn't remember a time when she hadn't been in his life somehow. Always there in the background. At first annoying, then entertaining. Then offhand. Then accommodating. Then…everything. But always there, with a ready if somewhat hesitant smile. He'd watched her grow up into a decent professional doctor. A good friend. A loyal sister. Fun. Serious. Sexy. Wow—that still felt new and weird.

He'd spent years wondering what a perfect woman would be like.

She'd been here all along.

And if he wanted her to stay in his life somehow—and he did, but back on the peripheries of his hard-fought-for, chaotic and commitment-free existence—if she could somehow remain untainted by this, then he had to put a stop to all this and let her go.

'Okey-dokey.' She sounded breezy and carefree as she levered herself away from him, switched off the still-running shower and grabbed a towel. 'I really do have to get ready. Is it okay if I finish off doing my stuff here?'

He found her a smile—it wasn't hard. 'So that's it? You've had your way and now *it's on your way*?'

'For now? I'm going to be awfully late if I don't get a wriggle on. I've got to dash. Thanks for the…research.' Her choice of words was very different from the stifled catch in her throat. She was trying to be light and stress-free, and failing. Something irrevocable had happened and they both knew it. 'I'll see you tonight? At Blue? Then maybe later…? I imagine Tori will be staying over with Matt so that means this place is available for us to activate our new no-clothes policy…' She pulled him to her and kissed him full on the mouth.

With just a simple touch of her lips he was hard for her again.

Damn. His hands were on her shoulders, creating just a little space. He needed about five thousand times more than he actually got. 'Look, stop. Enough. Can we just get something straightened out here?'

She paused, frowning, fist over a bright purple razor. 'Sure. What?'

He exhaled a heavy breath, saw the wince in her eyes as she steadied herself. 'Poppy, what do you want from me? From this? Because I don't do this. And you definitely don't. I'm hardly ever here, at some point soon I've got to go back to Europe—who knows for how long?—to get the bars sorted… You're busy at work…'

'Will you stop trying to analyse it to death? Let's just have some fun.' She held his gaze, her dark eyes swimming with undeniable affection, but he was drawn to them, to her, like a moth to a flame. And the thought of leaving again and going to stay in some cold, dingy hotel under a grey Parisian sky didn't appeal, not one bit. Which was mighty strange considering he loved Paris. That was where he had fun. In his bars, at work. Choosing venues, building his brand. *Working.* Not in the arms of a woman—at least not when his heart ached to stay. That never happened. He made sure of it.

So why the hell it was so difficult to distance his heart from his head this time he didn't know.

She tapped his backside with an open palm. 'Now, go and leave me to make myself beautiful. Go. Please. You do not want to watch me shave my legs.'

Then she ushered him out of the bathroom. Wet. Bedraggled. And still searching for the kind of words that would give him some semblance of peace.

CHAPTER TWELVE

'WHY DO SPAS always play this strange, tinkling, hippy ocean music? I feel like I'm in a birthing centre ready to deliver a whale or something.' Tori tightened the ties on her white bathrobe and sat down on a pure white sofa in the spa's relaxation lounge. With her deep tan and long blond hair Poppy thought she looked like something from an advert, gorgeously svelte as ever as she poured pink champagne into three flutes, engagement ring twinkling in the low-lit mahogany-walled room. Definitely not about to deliver a whale.

The gentle smell of lavender and ylang-ylang filled the air and seemed to be imprinted on the towels and plumped-up cushions, emanating good karma along with the chubby golden Buddhas grinning at everyone, hands on fat tummies from various corners of the room.

The outward calm contrasted with Poppy's inner excitement. Actually, it was more like excitement tinged with turmoil. All very well to play the detached, carefree card—but the problem was *feeling* it.

Anyhow, she refused to think about Isaac while she was celebrating her friend's upcoming wedding. She was going to live in the, hopefully, many moments of today's alcoholic hilarity. Then, tomorrow, after her body had absorbed the soothing aromatherapy vibes she would be fully Zen about Isaac and their…affair. Detached. That was what she was going to be. As soon as she'd worked out how to unattach her feelings from the very mention of his name. 'The plink-plink is supposed to enlighten your chakras. Or something.'

Izzy nodded. 'It does. But it just makes me want to go to sleep. Which is not what I need for my impending joint hen and stag night.'

Tori shook her head and laughed. '*Hag* night. Funny!'

Both Poppy and Izzy sat up. 'What?'

'Hen and stag. Hag.'

Izzy chuckled. 'Not exactly the image I was aiming for. I prefer stag and hen. Sten. Sounds kind of...German.'

Poppy picked up the tray of booze; no longer on the wagon, she intended to have some fun. 'Sten means "services" in Dutch. Services rendered? What do we have in store for us tonight?' She doubted much could beat the way her day had started. Sex in a shower. It had taken a lot of will power not to blurt that out in the steam room when the conversation had taken a decidedly devious tone. 'Take a glass each, ladies. Let's get this party started. We need to propose a toast.'

Poppy took hers and nestled into a soft, sumptuous chair opposite her two oldest friends. What a day. What a month. Her friends getting married, engaged, moving on.

And sex.

Sex with Isaac. *Blimey.* Her cheeks blazed at the memory. She cast a quick glance over to Tori. So far she'd stuck to her word and kept Poppy's dirty little secret, although she had given her plenty of strange concerned looks under raised questioning eyebrows.

'To darling Izzy. The first one to become an old married woman. Well done. Good luck. And...' She fought down a lump that had slipped into her throat. Nothing that a bit of champagne wouldn't dislodge. 'Never forget that we love you, you old...hag.'

'I love you all, too.' Izzy chinked. 'Thanks. Thanks so much, hags in waiting.'

'So good to see you glowing.' Poppy took a long drink. 'But a bit nauseating, really. All that happiness.'

Tori agreed. 'Sickening, actually.'

'Jealousy will get you everywhere. Besides, Tori, look at that diamond on your finger. Who'd have thought we'd both be almost old married women by the end of the year?'

Before she caught her friends looking at her with their usual sweet 'there, there, darling' puppy pity, Poppy suddenly found something very interesting in the hem of her robe.

She was happy for them. She was. Truly. Ecstatic.

Izzy downed the champagne and grinned. 'Cheers.'

'Hey! Hi! What have I missed? So sorry I'm late.' With a blast of cool air from the main reception area, in swept a flushed and breathless Lara, looking oddly out of place dressed in a thick coat and winter boots when everyone else was naked under their fluffy robes. But Poppy was grateful her arrival had changed the emphasis of the conversation away from happy and settled coupledom, all bright and rosy long term, when she'd had a bright and rosy start to the day but had no bloody idea how it would end—with Isaac or not.

She pulled herself up by her fluffy robe straps. 'Lara! You made it!'

After the group hugs Lara grinned. 'Sorry. Our flights were rerouted because of the snow. I thought I was going to miss the whole day, and all the gossip. But Alex was determined to get us back here in time so he made a few calls and here I am.'

'Yay! Well, we've done the steam room, massages and mani-pedis, I'm afraid...' Poppy pulled round a chair for Lara to sit on. 'All that's left is an hour or so before we head out to meet the guys. But you haven't missed any dirt and we've only just started on the bubbly. Good time?'

'Fabulous. Oh, my God, the hotel was to die for. Alex really knows the best places. We didn't do much, just a lot of relaxing…' Lara's hand went to her belly in a sort of unconscious protective gesture that Poppy thought a little odd. Perhaps she had indigestion. 'But I'm so glad I made it here in time. I wouldn't have missed this for the world.'

'And we're chuffed you made it, too.' They were all back together again. With a huge warm fuzzy in her heart Poppy looked round at her friends. So good to know that even though they were all half of a couple they still prioritised time for each other. And even though Lara was new to the group she was definitely one of them now. Not just because she had fabulous taste, was a brilliant designer and made the most exquisite lingerie—which reminded Poppy, perhaps she needed to do a little investing of her own…or would that breach the new no-clothes policy? Isaac could hardly complain though…could he, if she was naked in satin and lace?

She resolved to stop thinking about him. Again. 'Everyone's got a killer tan. Should I get a spray before the bridesmaid duties?'

Izzy snorted. 'I haven't got one and I'm the bride. Don't you dare turn up orange at my wedding.'

'Anything's got to be better than sickly winter white. Surely? No? Okay, I won't. I promise.' Noticing Lara's empty hands, Poppy remembered her manners. 'Hey, sorry, do you want some champagne? I'll grab a glass from the cabinet for you.'

'No. It's fine, thanks, I'll just stick to water. Jet lag, you know.' Lara held up her robe. 'Where's the changing room?'

'Jet lag? Are you sure? Not a cheeky hangover from your holiday? Hair of the dog will help you feel better.

Come on, everyone has to drink on a sten night. Hag's rules.' Izzy pushed a bowl over to her. 'Nuts? Nibbles? We didn't order too much food because we're going to eat at that restaurant next to Blue later. Plus we need to save room for the cocktails.'

'Er…no.' Lara looked a little uncomfortable. In fact she seemed to visibly pale underneath her tan. Then, looking more than uncomfortable, she hot-footed it to the Ladies. 'Oh, God. Sorry.'

They all looked towards the door and pretended not to hear her throwing up.

'Jet lag?' Tori took another sip of the bubbles. 'It never does that to me. Strange.'

Poppy smiled as the penny dropped. It didn't take a junior gynaecologist to work this out. 'Not strange. Natural. Under the circumstances.'

Perfectly plucked and waxed eyebrows peaked. 'What? You don't think? She's not…? Could she be…?'

'Pregnant?' Lara stood in the doorway, running a glass of water across her forehead. For someone who'd just had her head down a toilet bowl she looked remarkably pleased with herself. 'Yes. Yes, I am! Sorry. I wasn't going to say anything until twelve weeks, but heck…how can I keep a secret from you lot?'

A zillion more group hugs and not a little squealing ensued. Poppy pulled away and looked at Lara—there were a few shadows under her eyes now she'd got closer, and her boobs had grown already. But she had a big nervous smile. 'Wow. That's fabulous news! Oh, my God. A baby!'

'I know. Weird, huh? A little surprised, but we're thrilled.'

'I can give you the lowdown on maternity services at the local hospital and I know some excellent midwives—remind me later. Oh, my God. Alex is going to be a dad. Now that's scary.' Poppy squeezed Lara into another hug.

'No, it's not. It's wonderful. He'll be a great dad—a whole lot better than the one we were saddled with. And you're right, there's no way you could keep that secret from us.' Inwardly Poppy squirmed; she was the one doing a lot of secret keeping from her friends.

They settled down, clucked around Lara a bit more, brought her another glass of iced water, then Izzy clapped her hands. 'Okay, now everyone's here it's game time. Truth or dare.'

'Oh, no-o-o.' Poppy groaned, hoping like hell it would never get to be her turn. It was one thing to lie by omission—after all, no one had ever outright asked if she'd slept with Isaac, or their school teacher, so she'd never volunteered the facts. But it was another thing altogether to openly lie to their faces. She knew she was living on borrowed time.

Lara grabbed the empty bubbles bottle. 'Let the bottle decide the victim.'

'No-o-o.' Still squirming, Poppy retreated further into her seat. It was no use, though; they played this game every time they got a chance—usually with hilarious results.

Tori laughed. 'Hey, last time we played you got me to dish the dirt on my ex, which was pretty embarrassing, so you can at least allow me a chance to get my own back.'

Poppy swallowed another mouthful of bubbly then said, 'He needed dumping ,though. He was so not right for you.'

'Amen to that.' Izzy clinked Tori's glass. 'Good riddance.'

Tori nodded. 'And I guess I did learn that I was going about relationships all the wrong way. You were right—although I didn't think it at the time. You have to give something, too, not just take. See, these games are good therapy and lots of fun. Now, let's do it.'

Poppy didn't need therapy. Isaac had spelt out exactly

what he was prepared to give—she just had to decide whether to keep taking it or not.

See? She was the one in control.

Lara put the bottle on the floor and spun it around. As it whirled past each one of them they, in turn, hauled their feet off the floor with squeals of, 'Not me. Please not me.'

Poppy held her breath as the bottle spun more slowly. Past Lara again. Past Izzy. Even more snail-like past Tori. Until…

Tori looked at her. 'Okay, Pops. Truth or dare?'

Oh, God. She hated this. She remembered a dare that had ended with her having to run naked through the dorm. Aged thirteen. All breast buds and puppy fat. Almost the most humiliating event of her life. The sneering laughter of the older girls rang in her ears even now. That was not happening again.

'Truth.' How bad could it be? Tori wouldn't make things difficult.

'Okay. Let me think. Let me think—'

'I know. I know,' Lara interjected. 'Here's one! Have you ever…ever had sex with someone you shouldn't?'

They all fell silent for a second. All eyes on Poppy while her heart rate tripped into arrhythmia. Izzy cleared her throat and said in a voice that intimated that Lara should surely know this, but they'd all excuse her because she was new. And had pregnancy brain. 'Poppy doesn't have sex. Full stop.'

Lara gasped. 'Really? I know that's what everyone says, but I thought they must be exaggerating. You must have. Surely?'

Everyone says. Poppy winced. Since when was her private life a subject of general debate?

Tori's eyes widened. 'Okay. That's enough, it's fine. Let's move on.'

Poppy looked round at her friends in turn and thought

about everything they'd been through together. How they were always open and honest—no secrets. No regrets.

Even Lara, who was new to them all, had embraced their openness and shared her most private news. And yet she, Poppy, had always carried this hard lump of darkness around with her and it had tainted everything. Had had such an effect on her life for the last ten years that only now was she starting to actually live a full life again.

But instead of feeling fresh and rejuvenated she was making Tori cover up one thing for her, just as she'd made Isaac carry another secret around for a decade.

She couldn't keep doing this. The lies were piling up and dragging her down. Soon everyone would know something about her, but not everything, and she'd be in such a muddle remembering who knew what. Worse—she'd keep on feeling damned sick about it all, too. 'Actually I do need to tell you something. If I don't confess now and get this whole thing out in the open I think I'll explode. It's been eating me up for a long, long time.'

Tori shook her head. 'No, Poppy, you don't have to. It's your own private business. You don't have to say a thing.' Clearly she meant the Isaac sex.

'Yes, she does. Gory deets. Now.' Izzy laughed. 'You bloody dark horse.'

'Okay.' She took a deep breath. It was a lot harder than she'd thought. Finding the words. 'You remember Mr Gantry. Chemistry teacher at school?'

Izzy frowned. 'Yes…'

Lara shook her head. 'No.'

Izzy filled her in. 'Tall. Thin, youngish, about thirty. Sexy in a geeky kind of way, most girls had a crush on him at one time or another; but then, any male teacher in our all-girls' school got a lot of attention. He had floppy hair that fell over his eyes. Jackets with elbow patches. *Married*.'

Poppy looked at the floor and felt the keenness of her shame ripple through her. Even after so long it blew any self-respect away. 'Sorry. This is a downer on a hen night.'

Izzy shook her head. 'Not at all. I'm all ears.'

'Well, we had a thing.'

'At school? A thing? What kind of a thing?'

Poppy felt as if she'd been punched in the gut. 'We had sex. I would say relationship, but it wasn't. Not in the end.'

'You had sex with a teacher?'

Cheeks blazing, Poppy nodded. 'And a lot of sleazy pashing in his car down creepy dark alleys. In the chemistry lab at school, too, when he was supposed to be coaching me in extra lessons so I could get to med school.'

Izzy's eyes were huge. 'What? I'm in shock. You? Sex? What about his wife? Kids?'

'He didn't have any children, although he does now.' She huffed out a deep breath—and she hoped he showered them and his wife with affection and love. Hoped that having children and that extra responsibility might have changed him. 'He told me that he and his wife were living separate lives, that they didn't have sex, that he was going to leave her. For me. And I guess I chose to believe him.' She paused and looked at their open-mouthed expressions. Yes. It was shocking. Dirty. Shameful. 'Then I saw her in the toilets at the Leavers' Ball, overheard her telling another teacher they were so thrilled about her pregnancy. That they'd had difficult times and he'd been a little distant, but things were so good for them now. How much she loved him. They were planning to renew their wedding vows. I'm hoping he did and that he stuck to them.'

Tori's hand covered hers. 'God, how awful. Poor you.'

No. Not any more. Not since that heart-sickening moment of absolute shining clarity had she let herself fall prey to any man's words or charms. If anything the experience had shaped her. Made her stronger in some ways. More determined. Never had she allowed herself to get swept away on another silly teenage hormone-fuelled fantasy. Never again. She shook her head. 'Poor her, more like. In hindsight I had a lucky escape. He was manipulative, creepy. A liar who pretty much damaged any faith I had in men or relationships. But I promised myself then I'd concentrate fully and absolutely on my studies.'

'And you didn't tell anyone about this at all? Even when you were hurting? You must have been hurting. Afterwards?'

Poppy shrugged, trying to be nonchalant when she knew this admission could possibly hurt her friends. She hadn't told them, but she'd told someone else. 'Isaac knows.'

'Isaac? Isaac Blair? What the hell has Isaac got to do with anything?'

Quite a lot in the end. It seemed everything pretty much started and ended with him right now. 'Alex bribed him to be my date for the ball, although for me he was just a smokescreen for the real deal, Gantry. After I showed little interest in Isaac he slunk outside and hung around talking to some guys. Meanwhile I hovered round the disco to catch alone time with Mr Chemistry, drinking surreptitiously from a vodka bottle in my bag, thinking I was so sophisticated. Isaac found out the whole story when he saw me running from the hall in floods of tears. He held my hair while I vomited into the bushes. Listened as I drunkenly blurted out how much I loved Mr bloody Gantry. How I'd been duped and groomed and led on while all the time he was obviously still in love with his wife.'

And again she realised she'd spent a good part of her life avoiding Isaac because he'd seen her at her weakest. He *knew* her like no one else. Knew what she'd done and every time she saw him she'd relived the shame, living in fear he'd tell everyone. But he hadn't and he had never

ever called her on it or cast any blame to anyone other than Gantry.

Score one to Isaac.

Actually, score a lot to Isaac—he'd saved her from mortifying humiliation and hovered in the background of her life quietly making sure she was okay. She owed him more than she could say.

Izzy's voice lowered and, as in all times of stress, her northern accent rippled through her words. 'Seems like Isaac's done you a massive honour by keeping quiet. God knows what Alex would have done if he'd found out. But I wish you'd felt like you could tell us. We would have backed you. You know that, right?'

Guilt ripped through her. 'Of course, of course. But I was so ashamed of myself I couldn't admit it to anyone else and I swore him to absolute secrecy. It's so sordid. I'm so ashamed even now.'

'Well, you don't need to be. Gantry was in the wrong. He was the teacher. The authority figure. You should have reported him.'

Poppy shuddered at the thought. 'And put myself under that kind of spotlight? Imagine how my mother and father would have reacted to that. It was hard enough to get them to give me any kind of love and affection as it was. Something like this would have alienated them completely.' Which, as it turned out, would have mattered little in the end. Her relationship with her parents had remained fractured and distant, anyway. Something she'd come to terms with now. 'I suppose that's part of why I was attracted to Gantry. He was interested in *me*. Wanted *me* out of all the girls there. Or so I thought. But the hard lesson I learnt was that he was only interested in himself all along. Like all men.' She looked at her three girlfriends, all involved with decent honourable guys, including her brother. 'Well, a lot of men. Okay, some men. A few. Maybe a couple.'

Izzy came in for a hug. 'One day you'll find a good one, too. In the meantime you've got us.'

'Thanks. Hag.'

Silence stretched as the girls took all this new information in. She'd expected a backlash of sorts. Blame like that she'd heaped upon herself over the years, more to fuel her shame, but she got none. Just concerned smiles and hugs. And a strange release of all the destructive pent-up guilt. If she'd known she was going to get this reaction she'd have told them years ago. But she'd been nursing her broken heart, not wanting to open herself up to fresh hurt. Reluctant, too, to face up to the fact she'd been *that girl*. The one who'd willingly stepped into the middle of someone else's marriage. Who'd wanted attention so badly she was willing to make herself and others pay any price.

God, what an admission.

But then—as her friends had rightly pointed out, and Isaac, too—she'd been so young and naive and Mr Gantry had groomed her, had showered her with attention when he should have known better.

Izzy poured everyone another glass of bubbles from a fresh bottle. 'Right, I think we all need this. And no more secrets, okay?'

'No more secrets.' Lara clinked her tumbler.

'No more secrets,' Poppy whispered, and took another large slug of wine. Whether it was the alcohol or purging her soul she didn't know, but suddenly everything seemed just a little bit brighter. Even the thought of Isaac.

The other secret she'd just promised not to have.

Tori was still staring at Poppy, mouth open. 'Wow, well, that certainly set the game off to a heady start. No one's going to beat that.' Leaning closer, she whispered, 'And telling them about the other night will be child's play after this.'

Izzy leaned in. 'The other night? What about it?'

Tori mouthed *sorry* and winced.

But Poppy shook her head. 'Oh, and yes…another thing, while we're at it…I have something else to tell you…' They all stared at her again. The Poppy Show was pretty popular tonight. She felt a swell of affection for them all. Couldn't help smiling. Purging your soul was apparently good for you, and having a fling was nothing to be ashamed of. Wasn't that what Isaac had been telling her? If he didn't mind people knowing, then why should she? She wasn't ashamed; she was invigorated. *In for a penny…* 'Isaac and I are having sex now, too.'

A collective *what?* reverberated around the room.

'Isaac?'

'Wow. Isaac? You…and Isaac? Sex? *You?*'

'About bloody time.'

Her friends' reaction to this news was even more startling than the schoolroom clinches she'd told them about. The squeals almost as loud as the reaction to Lara's baby news. 'Poppy? Are you okay? I mean…'

'A bit sore.' She winked at the staring shocked faces. If it hadn't been so embarrassing this could have been fun. It wasn't often she stupefied her friends. 'But I'm absolutely fine. Fine.'

Then she thought about how hard she'd had to try to be light and cheerful this morning. How much she'd ached to stay with Isaac in that tiny bathroom and never let go. Never walk away from him. Never again see him struggling to let her down gently. Because she'd known that was what he was doing—trying to find kind words to put an end to this crazy sexy fling. And she hadn't wanted it to end so she'd put on the bravest face she'd been able to muster. A tight fist of pain lodged under her ribcage. 'I think.'

Izzy put her glass down. 'But Isaac? Whoa. This is more surprising than old Gantry. Isaac is, well, he's…

unobtainable. Mysterious. Sexy as hell. You do mean our Isaac? Your brother's best friend?'

'Oh, yes. But it's nothing permanent for either of us. Just scratching an itch. And he's great, by the way. In the sack. And the shower…' Wasn't that how people talked about their sex lives? Casually and with no emotion. 'A big kahuna.'

Lara coughed into her water. 'Whoa. Okay. We get the picture. Wow. I'm so glad I didn't miss this, but I really wish I could drink something stronger. You girls certainly know how to rock a hens' night.'

CHAPTER THIRTEEN

'LADIES AND GENTLEMEN, we are gathered here today...'

Poppy dragged her eyes away from the magnificent view of the twilit London skyline, amid drifting swirls of snowflakes, from Harry's rooftop garden and focused on the wedding. *Oh, my God.* None of them would ever have imagined this only a few months ago. The snow made the scene so perfect. As did the mistletoe hanging from the rafters. The giant Christmas tree with no-expense-spared decoration in the corner. The scent of pinecones. The lilt of the bridal march played by a string quartet.

On her right Poppy had Alex and Lara. Alex proud with his staunch military stance and yet softened features of a man in love and expecting a child.

Next to Poppy on her left stood Isaac, hands clasped in front of him. Solemn and serious in the smart charcoal suit that made his eyes darker, deeper. Just looking at him knocked the air from her lungs. She'd managed to keep a civilised distance from him today—but that didn't mean she couldn't wait until they were alone again tonight.

It might be her last chance.

But she'd taken her chances over the past week. Spending every night in either his bed or hers, making love for hours. No questions asked. No complicated conversations. It was just enough to be with each other. Talk about the day. About work. About nothing. It was as if by confessing to her friends she'd given herself permission to let go and have fun. To enjoy him, working their way steadily through his version of the *Kama Sutra*.

Hell, it was fun.

And so for a week there'd been blissful harmony in the flat. Tori had moved out with Matt. Alex and Lara were busy flat-hunting and not asking any questions. Which was surprising—if Alex had an opinion on his best friend dating his sister he certainly hadn't voiced it to Poppy. Yet.

Work was going well. Poppy had never felt as if her life could be so complete and fulfilled in all aspects.

Apart from the little glimpses of nagging doubt that whispered to her in the dark as she stroked Isaac's back. As she hurriedly got ready for work, or on the journey home. Or between consultations when she had a moment to think. Which inevitably led to questions and more doubts.

That things would unravel. That time was running out. The clock ticked too quickly towards day thirty-one. She had no illusions that she could change him. That would never work. He would never change, and certainly not if he was boxed into a corner. He had to want to fall in love with her.

And Isaac had no intention of falling in love with anyone.

'Take this?' Izzy turned and passed over her exquisite posy of perfect tiny white tulips and chamomile. For a second she held her friend's gaze.

Poppy smiled, nodded, that dratted lump rising in her throat again. She blinked away tears. 'I'm so proud of you. Be happy.'

'I am.' Izzy smiled back; not one doubt flickered across her face. She looked serene and joyful in the simple yet perfect cowl-necked gown designed by Lara, her shoulders covered in a sweet pure white angora cardigan, and surrounded by her family.

Few of Harry's family had made the day, so there would be another wedding celebration in Australia. No doubt a full-on major media event befitting Harry's celebrity status over there. But a lot of his friends were here—and that somehow seemed enough for him. Actually, Poppy got the impression that Harry would have been perfectly happy if no one else had been there at all. Just him, and his beautiful bride.

As they were pronounced man and wife Poppy felt Isaac's warm hand grip hers. The stroke of his thumb along her palm. Heard his regular breathing, so close. She daredn't look at him. Because things had become so intense so quickly, her emotions entwined in the sex and in Isaac so thickly, that she knew her real feelings would be there in her eyes, on display not just to him, but to everyone else, too.

So she squeezed his hand and let it go. Marched towards the wedding party and dragged on her very best, very proud smile. 'Oh, congratulations, Izzy. Harry! Make an honest woman of her? Good luck with that!'

'Do you want to dance? Or go home? Your call.' It was late. The food had been eaten and the drink drunk. The toasts and speeches finished. Now the hangers-on were stepping back and forth to an old slow number in the small area of dance-floor they'd created in the über-fancy restaurant, Ecco. Isaac had spent the day giving Poppy some space to be with her friends, and to revel in the whole wedding marathon, but now he wanted to run his hands over her body. Preferably in bed, but anywhere would do. The sooner the better.

She gazed up at him through long black eyelashes that he knew weren't in any way real. And he didn't care one bit; they accentuated her eyes, made her look innocent and wise at the same time. Which, he supposed, she was.

She looked amazing with her rich dark curls swept up into some sort of loose bun thing, and the dark claret sheath bridesmaid dress enhancing every inch of the curves he knew so well. His heart jolted a little as he realised just how much she made him smile. How much he wanted that smile to keep on happening.

She took his outstretched hand and stood on dark red heels that could easily pierce skin but made her legs longer and leaner, and he fought an urge to run his hand up to her thigh. And beyond. 'One dance? Then we go?'

He pulled her into his arms. 'You look beautiful today.'

'Thank you. And you're not so bad yourself.' She pressed a quick kiss onto his lips. Clearly not embarrassed to be seen with him after all. 'I prefer you without the suit. Well, without clothes in general.'

He led her to the floor and wrapped his arms round her tiny waist, swaying to the soft music, inhaling her perfume, which sent his head into a spin. Would he ever have enough of that scent?

Izzy and Harry swirled by, waving, and Isaac inclined his head towards them. 'A teensy bit jealous of Mr and Mrs?'

Poppy smiled and pressed closer to him. If he didn't know any better he'd have thought she was purposefully rubbing her breasts against his shirt. And for a second he wished he'd whisked her home instead.

'Actually, no. Not at all. Izzy is deliriously happy, but she deserves it all. Every bit of it. They all do. And, wow, Lara and Alex. A baby.' Her eyes widened and he got a glimpse of honeyed caramel flecks in her warm pupils. He hadn't noticed them before. He was learning something new about her all the time. Noticing things. Small things. Things he liked. Things that would be hard to forget. 'I still can't get my head around that.'

'Yeah, well, let's hope he doesn't lose that in Vegas,

like he did his inheritance.' Isaac felt a strange stab of something in his chest. Alex was moving on now, too. Finally becoming the decent adult Isaac had pegged him to be from the start. And a baby. Maybe a son of his own. A wife. Isaac had a sense of being left behind—that there was something missing—yeah, that he was missing out. Which was a whole heap of ridiculous because he had everything he wanted in his business. Stability, security. Success. What more did a man need? He rested his cheek on Poppy's. 'Him, a father! Miracles do happen. It's yet another thing I can rib him about.'

'Don't you dare. It happens to us all in the end,' a voice whispered close to his ear. *Alex.* 'And I'm watching you, matey. You hurt my sister and I'll break your legs.' Then he slapped him on the back with a friendly grin and sailed off across the dance floor with Lara.

Isaac frowned. 'Why does everyone want to break my legs?'

'Because they love me.'

'And what about me?' He couldn't help the smile. He knew Alex was being good-humoured about this thing with Poppy. But there was truth in her brother's threats. Everyone adored her; she was the glue that held the group together and he would never be forgiven for breaking her heart. 'They've known me for just as long. I need my legs. I like them.'

'Me, too.' Her hand went to his thigh and she slowly rubbed it tantalisingly close to his groin. 'Oh, don't worry. They all love you, too. But you do have a reputation, Mr Blair.'

'Excellent. And it's all true. You want to take advantage?' Why was it that each and every time he thought about letting her go he said something to make her stay?

Her eyes sparked heat and excitement and a thick sexual smog enveloped them. Her fingers played with his shirt collar, her touch sending shocks of need through him. 'I think I just might. Tonight I want to pick your brains about whipped cream…'

'You have some?'

She licked her lips, eyes tantalisingly bright and teasing. 'Maybe…'

'Why didn't you say so? Let's go now.' He tried to shut out the thought of her covered in strategic blobs of cream, and of him licking them off. But was glad he failed in any way to stop the image coming into his head.

'Ah, but first Izzy has to throw the bouquet. I have to hang around for that.'

Oh-oh. 'They still do that? I thought it went out in the fifties?'

'It's only a bit of fun. We all promised we'd stay. Look, I think she's going to do it now.'

'Oh. God.' This was the corny part of the wedding ceremony that made him want to run and hide. But he couldn't move too far without his trousers revealing just how turned on she made him. He held her in front of him. And she rubbed her backside against it as the bride took her place in the centre of the dance floor.

He groaned into her hair. 'You don't seem in much of a hurry to catch the flowers.'

She looked ahead at the giggling, jostling huddle of women with their hands in the air, and laughed. 'Don't worry. You're safe. Besides, I'd rather stay right where I am.'

'Me, too. Don't even think about walking away.' He nuzzled her neck and was just about to pull her into a kiss when something sailed towards him and, instinctively, he ducked. Somehow, though, the bouquet landed in his hands.

The watching crowd fell into roars of laughter. Wolf

whistles reverberated off the restaurant walls. He gave them all a rueful grin.

Not knowing what to do, he stared at the posy for a second. What happened now? Should he give them to Poppy? She believed all that hokum about marriage and everlasting love. He didn't want to give her the wrong impression by offering her the flowers. What would she read into that?

But...would it be such a mad idea? Would it be so difficult to relax into something more long term? Like his mates.

He blinked. Whoa. Stupid fantasy. He was already a hypocrite by being here. He didn't believe in ever after. Hadn't seen much evidence of it happening.

And yet...so many people did believe. So many took that leap of faith. People he respected. People who, he knew, might just make it all work. Alex and Lara, Izzy and Harry, Tori and Matt—they all bought into the fairy tale. And, looking at their shining faces, listening to their words, knowing what they'd all overcome to get this far, he knew now they were all going to make it.

Why wouldn't he want a slice of that?

Why wouldn't he even want to try?

Because it was a risk he wasn't prepared to take. It was too much to ask. And these kinds of things did not happen in his world. Marriages didn't last. Promises were broken. Not just once, but over and over.

But, for the record, if he were going to risk his heart on anyone, it would be Poppy Spencer.

For a few long moments she held his gaze. He saw the teasing in her eyes, her relaxed demeanour as she bent forward and picked the bouquet out of his grasp. 'I'll be having these, then.' She laughed and raised them into the air to cheers from the onlookers. 'Don't look so frightened. I won't hold you to it.'

'I thought...perhaps.'

She winked. 'Too much thinking. Now, I have whipped-cream plans...so come on.'

Later when the whipped-cream can was empty and Poppy lay sleeping next to him in her bed, soft sounds coming from her throat, Isaac couldn't shake that commitment thought away. He'd been on the verge of doing something very stupid back there in the restaurant.

And things were getting more complicated as each day passed. He'd never given so much thought to a... relationship. Yep. That was what this was starting to become. No denying that seeing someone every day for breakfast and sleeping with them at night could be called anything other. And this was everything he'd tried to avoid. His whole life. His heart contracted as he saw his life shrinking. As if everything he knew were balancing on a knife's edge and he couldn't stop it from falling. That he was going to be blasted open, raw and vulnerable. Again.

A spike of fear wedged into his ribcage.

He couldn't have her getting the wrong idea, getting used to this set-up. It was temporary. A stopgap. He needed to tell her.

That spike of fear intensified and he didn't know whether it was due to the thought of it ending, or because of the chink in his heart that made him want to stay.

Tossing the covers aside, he decided to get some distance. Some space elsewhere in the dark where she wouldn't be so tempting with her lush hair and her cute mouth. With her funny quips and interesting conversation that held him captive for hours.

She stirred a little, her arm reaching across him. One leg creeping over his as she pressed against his back. 'Where are you going?'

Hell.

He settled back to cuddle her. Starting an early Christmas morning at seven o'clock sucked; she needed some decent sleep. Creating a scene now wouldn't help. Disappearing would be a coward's way out. 'Nowhere. Just a little hot.'

'Do you want to get hotter?' Her fingers stroked along his chest and just that mere feather touch had him wanting her again.

He wouldn't ruin her Christmas. He wouldn't snatch away the happiness. Not yet. He'd wait.

Or was that the coward's way? He should be up-front—make her know that things would be going right back to how they were before. Before…he could barely remember a time when she wasn't in his thoughts.

'Shh.' He stroked her hair, slicked a small kiss on her forehead. 'Later. You've got work tomorrow. We'll catch up after you've caught a dozen screaming babies. You need to sleep.'

'I need you. In me.' She wriggled against him, hand inching over his erection. Her mouth found his and before he knew what he was doing he was inside her again. So easy to want her. To need her right back.

He took a nipple between his fingers, rubbed gently and felt her contract around him. Then sucked the pink bud into his mouth. The nipple puckered and she groaned again, a visceral roar that fired him more. She stabbed her fingers into his hair and pushed against him, deeper. Deeper.

Deeper.

He loved this. Loved the feel of her soft skin against his. Loved the dips and curves of her body. Loved the way they were together, instinctively knowing what each other wanted.

He loved… He closed his eyes, refusing to admit the feeling he recognised but had never felt before. It was just the rush of the sex, the crazy day, her. It wasn't anything. Nothing. It wasn't...

No. His heart slammed faster and faster. It wasn't. It couldn't be.

He couldn't allow it. Wouldn't...

When he opened his eyes again she was staring at him, her gaze filled with soft emotion, not the intense spark of sex, but something warmer, deeper. Something more...

He rocked against her deeper still. It would never be deep enough. And yet...

Her arm gripped his shoulders and rocked against him, their rhythm slow, infused with an unhurried intensity as if they had all the time in the world. He tried to commit this feeling to memory. The joy on her face. The soft moan as his lips met hers. Because he couldn't do this again. Not feel these intense emotions for someone so wrong, so precious, so perfect, and know they would never last.

It was a kiss like none he'd ever had before. As if his deepest emotions were suffused in his touch, as if he could see deep inside her. To her heart, her soul. To that precious part of her that was pure and raw and his. If only for this moment.

And he gave himself in return. Lost in her. With her. Because of her.

CHAPTER FOURTEEN

'*WE WISH YOU a Merry Christmas!*' Poppy sang as she carried a tray laden with warm croissants and coffee to her bedroom. When she'd offered to work all day today she hadn't banked on the fact she'd have to leave Mr Sexy Legs here. One of the aforementioned stuck out from the sheets and her gaze followed it all the way from his toes to…the most entertaining part of his body. He was magnificent.

Happy Christmas indeed! They'd certainly seen the dawn through with a bang. The only thing to make it absolutely perfect would be snow. The last fall had melted leaving a sheen of sludge on the pavements that had quickly turned to ice overnight. She peered through the chink in the curtains; the early weak sun was masked by cloud that, in the distance, looked dark and black. Rain-laden. Not snow.

After putting the tray down she sat on the bed and ruffled Isaac's hair. 'I wouldn't have woken you, only I'm going in soon and I wanted to wish you a happy day.'

Jerking awake, he rubbed his eyes and sat up, pooling the duvet across his middle. He had an early-morning frown that made him look less like his laid-back self. 'Er… okay. Thanks. You, too.'

No *happy Christmas*? No suggestion of mistletoe. Nothing different or special. She was fast understanding that

Isaac didn't wear his emotions on his sleeve. But...well, it was Christmas. 'Plans?'

'None.'

Having poured the coffee, she handed him a cup. 'You are going to see your family, aren't you? Surely you don't intend to stay here on your own all day?'

'Maybe.' He paused and took a sip of coffee. 'Unless I can convince you to phone in sick and spend it with me?'

Yes, please. 'Tempting, but no. It's no good if the doctor phones in sick, is it? Who's going to help deliver all those lovely Christmas babies today?' And, in truth, part of her wanted to be in the thick of things at the hospital where she could see the joy on people's faces on this special day. Working took her attention off the numerous 'what ifs' that had taken root in her head. And that were being amplified right now by the frown and the distinct lack of any kind of festive spirit.

She tried to focus on the conversation and distract herself. 'You need to go see them.'

'I don't need to do anything. I'm sure they won't miss me.'

'Of course they will. It's Christmas. Give her a chance.'

He stroked a finger down her arm. 'And you'd know all about it, would you? Seeing as you're going to work right now instead of taking a trip back home yourself.'

He had a point. Mummy and Daddy had issued their usual last-minute emotionless invitation but she was busying herself through the day, and seeing Alex later—he was really all the family she truly cared about. And that was okay.

Isaac, on the other hand, was doing nothing and she hated to think of him lonely and miserable. Especially when she knew his mother had asked him to visit and he was conflicted. 'But everyone deserves another go. Surely?'

'I'm not so sure I share your optimism. Everyone? Even people like Tony Gantry? You think?'

Tension prickled through her—but it was noticeably less than whenever she'd thought about her old teacher before. 'I hope his family have a good Christmas, even if I don't want him to have a good one ever. By the way, I told the girls about him. It was quite a relief actually. I think I've finally made my peace with that phase of my life. It felt good.'

'You told them about Gantry. Why? After all this time?'

'I'm sick of hiding it away. I think the only way of moving forward is to acknowledge my mistakes and be open to making new ones. I've decided I want to live a full life, not a half one.' She sucked in air and as she threw him the next comment she watched for his reaction. 'I want to have relationships. I want to fall in love. Like everyone else.'

He shook his head and frowned again, this time more deeply. Not exactly the response she'd hoped for. 'You sound more like Izzy every day. What happened to practical, logical Poppy?'

She fell in love.

Wham.

The realisation was like a sledgehammer to her chest and she inhaled sharply at the thought, clutched the corner of the sheet tight between her fingers.

She loved him.

Even after she'd worked hard not to. When she'd thought she was in control and calling the shots. She cared for him. Wanted him. Wanted him to be happy. Couldn't bear the thought of another moment without him in her life. If that meant she loved him. Then yes.

But telling him? God, no.

And yet…she'd changed so much through these past few weeks. Because of him she now knew she wanted more. Something meaningful. Something sustainable. She wanted to be loved, too.

And right there. *There.* She imagined how wonderful it would be if this would continue. If they stopped pretending, and got real. She wanted to be surrounded by love like the new parents at work, and her friends—even to have a baby of her own one day. She wanted it all. More frightening still, she wanted it with Isaac.

So being naked in bed with a gloriously sexy man who didn't know commitment from his elbow was so not the time to acknowledge this. 'Logical Poppy's still there. She just thinks that it might be possible to want it all—and have it. Why not? Alex has it. Izzy. Tori.'

'Nah. You just bought into the fairy tale, got carried away by the dress and the bling and the bouquet.'

And he was the wrong man to fall in love with. 'You think? Am I really so shallow? It's not just because they're doing it—don't be ridiculous. That would be idiotic. But I do know that they're happy and fulfilled.' And she'd had a slice of the same these past few weeks and knew that if she'd experienced a fraction of the feelings they had, then it had been worth it. But she wanted it to last. A large chunk of sadness filled her gut. 'It makes everything worthwhile in the end, all the struggles and the hard work to get to the top. Why have a career if you can't share that success with someone? Don't you think?'

He shrugged and his eyes flashed both a dare and a threat. 'How would I know?'

'Have you given it a chance? Like ever? Instead of running away from every scrap of feelings why don't you try to live through it?' She reached for his hand. 'What happened to you?'

His eyes narrowed. 'Nothing. I'm just a natural-born cynic.'

'No, you're not. You choose to believe that some good

things can happen. Like your business. Like…fun times with your friends. Even with me. You choose to invest in half of life but shun the other half. The good bit where you get the chance to be deeply happy.'

He scraped a hand across his stubbled jaw. 'I would never rely on someone else to make me happy. I can manage that perfectly well on my own.'

The words stung like a slap. He could sit here and lie all he liked but she knew he was different when he was with her. She saw the smiles, couldn't deny the laughter. And the sex—that was way more than fun. It meant something. And he knew it. He was just hedging. Running scared.

Anger mixed with sadness in her gut. 'Well, good for you. But it doesn't have to be like that. You just have to take a risk.' Glancing at the clock, she realised she was going to be late if she didn't leave now. But she couldn't go. Not yet. 'You ever think that just maybe the poets, the writers, the film makers, and millions and millions of people who settle down and have families might be right? That you can have it all? I repeat…what happened to you?'

She hiked up from the bed and threw on some clothes, twisted her hair into a knot and clipped it in place at the back of her head. Slipped on her shoes and with them an irritated tone to her voice. 'Go ahead and talk, Isaac. I'm dressed and ready to leave but I'm not going anywhere yet. Because right now I think this is more important. And, well—putting something else before work—that's a huge thing for me.'

He straightened in the bed. Looked everywhere else but at Poppy. 'For God's sake, you know damned well what happened. She traded one husband for another, then another. Worse, she traded one family for another. Have you any idea how that feels? When your mum prefers another kid to you? Holds them up as paragons of bloody virtue, a fresh start, a clean slate, and treats you like you're the devil incarnate. Because you're an inconvenience. Because you've lost your way and got into a bit of trouble. Police trouble—but not enough for juvenile centre. Just enough to make her embarrassed. And suddenly you don't fit her standards or her expectations.'

'Actually I do know exactly how it feels not to fulfil parental expectations. Alex and I have been a huge inconvenience to our parents our whole lives. That's normal for us. But it isn't for you—you had a good relationship with her once. Didn't you?' At the nod of his head she continued, 'It might be hard but I suggest you try to get over those kinds of things.'

He pointed to her work clothes, his face incredulous. 'Yeah? Like you do? So you're working today instead of going home. And for eight years you've hidden away from relationships, haven't acted on any kind of whim. Have kept secrets from your family because you've been ashamed of something you did a decade ago. That kind of *get over it*?'

'We're talking about you, not me.'

'Thanks, but I don't need to spill my guts about my mother. It doesn't make me feel better. It's just enough for you to know that I learnt from a young age never to seek any affirmation from anyone else and to be absolutely self-reliant.'

'Well, you certainly perfected that.' She looked around, wondering what to do next. What to say. He'd made up his mind to be distant and single for the rest of his life, wouldn't even entertain any idea otherwise.

She thought about how difficult it would have been to be a teenager in the midst of all that pubertal angst of discovering who he was—and to be rejected by the one person who should love him unconditionally. At least, that was how he saw it. Poppy was convinced his mum must have a different view. Because wasn't she now a devoted mother of two boys? In a successful sustained marriage? Hadn't she invited him back for Christmas? There was hope there.

Poppy also thought about how much she owed him, over the years, for holding her dirty secret close to his chest. For watching out for her. For noticing.

Her heart contracted at the thought that he'd been there all the time and she'd refused to notice him. Had kept her distance from him. 'For the record, I'm proud of how you turned out. You are successful and kind and loyal. All qualities I admire. For some reason I was always wary of the fact you knew the worst thing about me. But thank you for keeping my secret, Isaac. It's the best thing anyone's ever done for me.'

'For all the good it did. I just colluded in a web of secrecy that stunted you emotionally. You should have reported him.' He held his finger up. 'No. I should have hit the bastard.'

'Thank God you didn't.'

'I would have enjoyed it.'

She gave him a smile. 'It would certainly have been another thing to annoy your mother with.'

'Like she needed an excuse.' He looked at the clock by the bed and let out a deep breath. The shadows in the crevasses of his cheeks made him look tired. Haunted. 'Look, Poppy, time's ticking on. This is going nowhere.'

'What is?' Panic gripped her throat; she swallowed it down. She'd always known there would be an end. She'd just hoped she'd make it to day thirty-one.

'You should go. You're going to be late.'

'I already am. And you should go home, Isaac. Talk to her. Learn about her, give her a chance. Is she happy? Does she love him? Will they make it in the long haul? Perhaps, long ago she was confused and chose the wrong men—but that doesn't mean she hasn't found the right man now. Who knows? Maybe they have an unshakeable understanding, maybe they're soul mates. Maybe she does love you but doesn't know what to do about it now?'

Like me. She pressed a kiss to his lips and hoped she showed him just a little bit of how much she felt for him. That there was at least one person who loved him. For whatever good it would do her.

Something in his dark withdrawn expression told her she would not get the chance to do this again. That this was the end. That she had got from Isaac the most he had ever given to anyone. But that was it—he could give no more.

A chill as cold as the outside air ran through her. She wanted to wrap herself around him. But she had to go. Suspecting he wouldn't be here when she got back cut through her like a scalpel blade. 'Let me know how you get on. Text me?'

He nodded. 'Don't hold your breath.'

'About what? The progress…or the text?' She wished she hadn't brought him this tray. Hadn't woken up on a day so laden with pressure that she'd thought she might find something to make her happy. Wished she hadn't fallen in love with Isaac Blair. Wished wholeheartedly now that she hadn't probed into a deep conversation that reminded him of how little faith he had in love and relationships.

'Look, Poppy…'

No. Don't say it.

He didn't need to. She could see what was coming, heard it, felt the heavy vibrations of rejection like an out-of-control juggernaut bearing down on her, and if she could have blocked her ears like an eight-year-old she would have. Tears pricked at the backs of her eyes. She blinked them away, because she sure as hell wasn't going to show him how much this was hurting. 'What?'

Isaac inhaled, trying to choose the right words; the pain in his heart twisted tightly as he watched her smiling face crumble. She'd been expecting this, probably all along—

waiting for the cards to fall. But even he hadn't expected it to cut so deep. Hadn't expected to fall so hard for her. To care so much. Such pain was a shock. And although last night, last week he'd decided to end it, waking up to her this morning was the finest Christmas present he'd ever had.

The best way to do this was to cut ties now before things got messy. To go away somewhere and leave her to get over him. Then, to keep at the far edge of her circle of friends, to lie low where he could watch over her, make sure she was okay but keep a distance. Moving on. Which she would—she'd grown so much. Poppy was a beautiful, strong and independent woman. He only wished he had half her fortitude. To try. To love. To open himself up to risk.

The pain twisted harder. He couldn't think about her moving on with another man, someone who would love and cherish her. But she deserved someone who could give her what he couldn't.

Isaac's hand was on her hair, stroking it. His fingers loosening the tight knot. But he wasn't seducing her. He was saying sorry. His mind made up. A plan formulated. And okay, some might say it was running away…he just needed a clean break. They both did. 'I have to go to Paris soon. Maybe tomorrow. There's stuff happening. Problems with the electrics that Jamie couldn't get to the bottom of. I need to fix them. I could be there a while. I don't know when I'll be back…'

Bile burnt the back of Poppy's throat. Of all the rotten, stinking times to ruin her day he'd chosen this one? 'Have to go, or want to go?'

Don't say it.

But he looked away and she had her answer.

Both.

Silence stretched between them. She wanted to press against his body and keep him here. Wanted him to want to stay. To want her enough—to want *this* enough—to take a risk. Wanted to hear him say it. But instead he said nothing. And she would never ever beg. Or even ask.

Eventually she found what was left of her self-respect and her voice and croaked out a response. 'Okay. So send me a postcard, if they even exist any more. And I'd appreciate the rent in advance…but if you want to just pack up and leave then that's fine, too. I'll put an advert on the hospital noticeboard—'

'Poppy—'

'Paris is lovely. Lucky you. Of course, work. Yes. Work comes first for us career people.' She waved her hand at him, more to stop herself stroking her fingers down that beautiful bare chest, or pressing her hand to his cheek, than anything else. She couldn't touch him again. Not now. It would make things so much worse. 'It's fine. Really. I'll just need to find some more flatmates. The mortgage won't pay itself. Of course, I'll reword the flatmate policy…wouldn't want the whole naked thing going on with strangers… Stupid, really, to think…hope. Anyway, I really should just go to work. I'm going to be very late. I wonder how many Hollys and Noels we get today…'

He took her hand. 'Pops, stop. I'm sorry.'

'No need. We both knew. An end, you know. That's okay. Got to go to work. Happy Christmas.' She shook her hand out of his grip. Couldn't bear the feel of his skin against hers when it was goodbye.

Oh, God. The words, the thoughts, the emotions pierced her to her core—a sharp, glittering hurt that stabbed hard in her ribcage.

She loved him and he didn't love her back.

Loved him.

Of all the foolhardy, stupid things to do. The worst kind of stupid because he'd always be around somewhere—with Alex, with her friends, smiling, maybe with a new girlfriend, reminding her of what she'd had and could never have again. Being there. Breaking her heart every single time.

Somehow she left him there, in her bed. Somehow she walked away, closed the front door and strode down the steps, head held high. Somehow she got to work, dragged on a brave face and delivered two Hollys, a Gabriel and a Star. Somehow she laughed at the wonder of birth and new life and cried happy tears with the parents.

But later, after a quick crying-off to Alex and Lara on the pretext of a migraine, she crawled under the covers and inhaled Isaac's smell. She wrapped herself in sheets that had barely covered them both. Nuzzled her face in his pillow.

She lay in the dark empty room in her lonely apartment and wondered why the hell she had let herself do something so heartbreakingly stupid, something so spectacularly un-Poppy-like? Something so catastrophically crazy as thinking that she could have sex without emotion over and over again with a man like Isaac Blair. How she could share fears and dreams. Develop a sensual self-confidence from his tutelage—feel a sense of contentment. A part of something. Important. Special. Precious. How just breathing the same air as one man could feel rarefied and unique. How his laughter could infect her. His touch. Smell.

Why had she allowed herself to experience every emotion with him? Especially when she knew from the start he was incapable of doing the same.

Isaac fell back against the pillow and groaned. *Stupid bastard.*

Stupid. Dumb. Goddamn stupid.

If he hadn't believed this was the totally right thing to do he could have been convinced it was the far side of madness.

He'd watched the only woman he'd ever allowed himself to care for slip away—holding back her tears, trying hard to convince him that this was the best decision he'd ever made. That she didn't care. That everything was fine.

It wasn't fine.

And he'd let her go. On Christmas Day. The magic… gone. That was something he could never make up to her. He'd ruined her day.

But the feelings she stoked in him left him adrift, clamouring for some kind of anchor. His world tipped sideways as letting her go seemed right but keeping her close felt righter. His heart raced. His gut churned. He was hot and cold. And, yes…panicked. And he'd seen the light in her eyes blink out.

It *would* be fine. She'd get over him in time. She had a forgiving heart and she'd understand that what he'd done was the right thing to do after all. For them both. It just might take him a whole lot longer. Maybe a lifetime.

Three hours later a different kind of irritation rattled up Isaac's spine. Today he was the king of bad ideas. Christmas dinner had been difficult, conversation stilted. The only saving grace had been the two boys, who'd loved the gifts he'd brought them. But then, you couldn't go wrong with remote-control helicopters.

He was standing at the large bow window overlooking the manicured lawn, watching Archie and Henry run around screaming and playing with the remote controls. The sky hung heavily with thick dark clouds, threatening to pour with rain. No snow yet. Poppy would be disappointed.

And yes, every thought came back to her.

His mother, smiling beatifically in a powder-blue couture dress, stood next to him. She gave him a smile. And he thought that for once it might be genuine. 'You're good with them. They like you.'

He nodded. 'I like them, too.'

'I remember when you were that age—'

'What do you remember, Mum? Because I was at boarding school most of the time, and you were pretty distracted most holidays.' He knew exactly what he remembered. An affair. Secrets. Hushed voices. Divorce.

Then being whisked away from the place he'd made his home and sent to the local college. And still she was distracted. Another marriage. Then another one. Drama. Always drama. Raised voices. Then Hugo, and a stepbrother. Then a baby. And it all seemed so removed from his reality and he didn't fit anywhere. He'd looked on from a distance in detached bemusement.

That was what he'd thought. But in reality he'd crushed the pain and sunk his head into other things. Getting into trouble. Bars. Drinking. Then a friendship that led to a business partnership. Making his first thousand dollars. Ten thousand. A million.

And still his mother's lack of interest. He'd reached the point where he didn't bother to contact her from one Christmas to the next. And then this year she'd reached out.

She stared out of the window, but she seemed to be fixed on nothing in particular. Just a spot somewhere on the horizon. 'I wasn't a good mother to you, Isaac. And for that I'm very sorry. I know I could have done better.'

He shrugged, shoving his hands in his pockets. 'I understand.'

'No, you don't. And I don't really, either. I was young when you were born and trapped in an unhappy marriage. I didn't want you to feel that, so I sent you away to school to shield you from it. I hoped you'd be happier. I tried to make things work. They didn't. Then I tried again. And failed. I'm used to being a failure. I guess Hugo and these boys have been my biggest success. This marriage.' *Man, that stung.* 'I'm sorry you weren't part of it. I am so very proud of you, though.'

Yeah? 'Now. Maybe.'

'Yes, now. Not always, but I just wasn't looking for things to be proud of back then.' She turned to face him, handed him a glass of brandy she'd poured from a decanter. 'Do you have a girlfriend?'

'No.'

'Shame. I always imagined you'd be the kind to settle. You like stability. I realise that now. I should have given you that. I hope you find it.'

'I have my work.' He took a sip, felt the sting of heat and the rush through his body. 'I'm good on my own. I don't need it.'

She patted his arm. First real contact he'd had from her in for ever. 'We all need someone, Isaac. Even you. What the hell do you think I was doing all those years? Finding someone I could truly love. Who I wanted to stay with regardless of age, or money, or…anything. Someone who I wanted to be with night and day. Who I couldn't bear to be without. Who I wanted to do things for, who I wanted to make happy. And who could love me back the same way.'

'And did you? Find him in the end?' He heard his step-father's voice from the kitchen, singing a Christmas carol Isaac had learnt at boarding school. The atmosphere in this home was so different from when he'd grown up. Archie and Henry were lucky. 'Or is Hugo likely to be yet another version of Mr Wrong?'

'He's—what do you call it these days?—a keeper. You just have to keep looking, Isaac, and realise, when you find them, that they're worth fighting for.'

Could he really believe her? He seriously doubted it was worth the effort. The drama. The heartache. Although, Poppy…

He glanced outside at the kids on the lawn, the smile on

his mother's face, the feeling of contentment in this place. He could have had that. He could have had what Alex had. He could have had Poppy. It was all within his grasp.

His gut tightened against more brandy. He didn't want to go there—to relive the biggest mistake of his life. Because Poppy *was* worth the drama and the effort. He just hadn't realised. And now he hadn't a clue how to fix it. And then there was that flight to Paris tomorrow and the open-ended ticket with no return date...

He shook his head, not knowing whether his mother was telling the truth; maybe you did just have to realise what was worth fighting for. It had taken her years of searching. Was that what he had in store for him? Years of wilderness? She looked happy now, content. She certainly looked as if she meant every word.

Either that or she was sozzled on the cooking sherry.

CHAPTER FIFTEEN

'BUT YOU ALWAYS have a New Year's Eve party, Poppy? Come on.' Tori resecured one earring, then the other, then turned to Poppy in the pub's bathroom where they were fixing their make-up. 'We can text everyone and get them to meet us back at yours. It just won't be the same in Trafalgar Square. It's heaving with crowds already.'

Poppy sighed. Yes. That was the plan. So she could lose herself in the masses. 'We've fought our way through endless queues of people to get this far. The square's just around the corner. New Year, new start. I'm wiping the slate clean. Besides, the fireworks will be awesome. I only ever see them on TV.'

Tori stopped mid-mascara touch-up. 'You know, I'm just a little bit scared by you right now. You've changed. You're selling the flat from under our feet. You've booked a holiday to Mexico—'

'First off, I am not selling it from under your feet—you don't even live there any more. No one does but me. And the occasional mouse. All my chicks have left the nest, and Alex needs somewhere for his family. It makes sense to sell it to him and move on. There are too many memories there. It's about time I freed myself up financially. I want to live more, experience things. Lots of things...' Apart from another broken heart. She could do without that. But Isaac had awakened a sense of adventure in her that she wanted to explore. It was her time now, no more hiding herself away…

Just as soon as she fixed back the shattered pieces of her heart.

Poppy snapped her lips together, setting her new red lipstick. Truth was, she didn't want a party in her apartment where she would be the only single loose part. She wanted to be surrounded by thousands of people counting down to midnight. When the weird Isaac spell would be broken and she would turn back into her usual sensible, professional self. Normal service would be resumed. And she would start anew. Selling the apartment was the first step in her plan.

'He's not worth it, Pops.' Tori's eyes misted. 'If he doesn't know a good thing when he's got it.'

'It was never meant to be long term. I knew that going in.' She had her friends, her job, a future and freedom on the horizon—what more could she need? Ignoring the voice that whispered in her head…*Isaac*, she pulled on her hat and fastened her scarf, tucked her arm into Tori's thick woollen-coated one. Fixed on a smile. 'Let's go. Come on, next year's just around the corner. It's going to be so exciting.' And who knew, if she said it enough she might start to actually believe it.

An icy blast of air hit them as they stepped outside. Swirls of tiny snowflakes drifted from the sky and she smiled.

Thousands, maybe hundreds of thousands, of people surged alongside them towards the square; everyone had pink cheeks and big grins. The noise of happy chatter filled the night. Busier than she'd ever seen it before, the place was so congested there were huge LED signs detailing up-to-date road closures, safety notices and, every few minutes, a countdown to midnight.

Twelve minutes.

Heart racing, she linked arms with Lara and Tori and headed towards the fun, leaving the complex heart-aching emotions of this year behind her.

Well, almost.

Eleven minutes.

Isaac glanced at the blasted electronic display and cursed. The plane had been delayed by a snowstorm, which appeared to have caught them up, judging by the cold wet drifting down his neck. The tube had been an almost impossible crush and he'd run the length of Haymarket to get here. Ridiculous. The chances of finding her were minuscule. Impossible. But he forged ahead. She was here, Alex's text had said. Trafalgar Square. She was here.

Ten minutes.

Trying to keep his heart rate in check, he climbed a bollard. Every woman with long dark hair could be her. Every lyrical laugh. Every group of people could be her and her friends. But they weren't. So many people with streamers and glow-in-the-dark wristbands and every type of celebratory paraphernalia for sale. But he just wanted one thing. Poppy.

Damn. This was ridiculous.

Eight minutes.

Another bloody sign. He fought back an urge to kick the damned thing. Annoying, useless piece of technology stating the damned obvious and blocking his view.

Where the hell was she?

* * *

'I think here's a great place.' Poppy stopped when they could get no closer to the centre of the square. Revellers were already dancing in the fountains, practising 'Auld Lang Syne' with varying amounts of success—did anyone ever know the right words? All around them there was a wall of noise, of music, of singing. Strangers shared food, drinks and smiles. The buzz and high-energy atmosphere were infectious.

'Not exactly intimate, but it'll do.' Alex nodded and wrapped his arms around Lara. She smiled up at him. Matt grabbed Tori in for a hug. Poppy looked on, wishing Izzy were here instead of in Australia. Then at least they'd all be together. But there would be other times, plenty of times, when they would all be together again.

Her heart squeezed. Maybe coming here had been one of her worst ideas. Because no matter where she was, she wasn't anywhere with Isaac.

Ahem, what about that new start?

Today was the beginning. She took a moment, like the others, to gaze around at a snow-filled sky that she knew would soon be lit up by a rainbow of fireworks. Beside her, silent and watching disdainfully, a dark stone lion sat at the feet of the immense Nelson's column. God knew what he made of it all. She ran her fingers down the cool stone. 'Bet you'd make a fine mouse-catcher, my man. Fancy a job?'

Six minutes, a screen close by told her. It flickered again. New words formed.

URGENT: DR SPENCER CHECK YOUR PHONE

Then it was gone just as quickly, replaced by another announcement about congestion.

What? Poppy blinked, a tight catch in her ribcage. 'Did you see that?'

Matt nodded. '*You* Dr Spencer? Did it mean you? Check your phone.'

She couldn't drag her gloves off quickly enough. Five missed calls.

Isaac.

The noise all around her had masked her ringtone.

A text. Lots of texts.

WHERE R U?

Oh, my God. She blinked again, her throat working but words getting lost en route to her mouth. He was here? Her heart had begun to hammer against her chest wall.

No. He was in Paris.

She texted back.

Trafalgar Square.

NO KIDDING? MORE SPECIFIC?

She really did need to tell him about his caps lock. It felt as if he were shouting. Or desperate. Was he desperate?

He was here.

He was here.

He was here and desperate and there were too many people. Why the hell hadn't she had a party at home? There would have been—what? Twenty people? Forty? Not the whole of the damned capital.

Why? So you can bah, humbug New Year's Eve, too?

I'M SORRY. REALLY. I NEED TO FIND YOU.

He needed… Tears pricked her eyes. Texting proved difficult with shaky hands.

We're next to a lion. Near the road. There's a lamppost, too. We're all here. Find us.

Please.

DO NOT MOVE

She couldn't have if she'd tried. Her legs had gone so wobbly she leaned against the lion and waited. Ignoring the countdown. Ignoring the people, as she desperately tried to see his face, the most beautiful face in this crowd.

And then he was there. In front of her. Matt and Tori and Alex and Lara faded into the ether along with the noise and the people, and the stone lion and the very, very tall Admiral Nelson. It was just Isaac. And her.

He leaned in close, his smile sheepish. 'Poppy. Thank God. I thought I'd never find you.'

She shrugged, because her shoulders were the only things she had any control over. Her heart had started its own little dance and her feet were glued to the concrete. 'Well, here I am.'

'Why the hell, for the first time in your whole damned life, did you decide to come here?' His arm slipped round her waist and even though she didn't think it was the most sensible thing to do she fell into his arms, breathing him in. Feeling his heat around her.

'I wanted to forget you.'

'And did you?'

'No. How can I forget you when you follow me and tell the whole damned crowd with that sign thingy? How did you do that, by the way?'

His gorgeous mouth turned up at the corners and she wanted, ached, longed, to kiss him. But she didn't. She listened to him instead. 'I have my ways. I told them it was an emergency.'

'Is it?'

'Absolutely.'

The noise around them pressed in, louder. 'Nearly midnight?'

He nodded. 'Two minutes.'

Then she remembered he was supposed to be in Paris, because he didn't want to take any risks. He'd ruined her Christmas. She'd left and he hadn't tried to stop her. He'd broken her heart. 'Why are you here?'

His thumb stroked gently across her cheek, his eyes blazing with affection. Deep, solid, strong affection. 'I wanted to tell you—man, I wish we were somewhere private.'

'Tell me what?'

'That I want to try.'

'What do you mean?' Because she didn't want to jump to conclusions. Didn't want to think…anything. Hope…

The man who had an answer for everything seemed to be finding them hard to find tonight. 'I want you, Poppy. I can't sleep. I can't eat. Paris was dull. Everything is dull. Nothing's the same. I miss you. You're…a keeper. I'm sorry I ruined your Christmas. I really am. I'm an idiot. But…' He closed his eyes and tested out the words. She just knew it was the first time he'd said them. Knew he was trying to feel the shape of them, the taste. 'I love you.'

It was a big step. He'd put aside everything and come here for her. Taken a risk. Found her. Declared his love.

'Whoa. That's…that's gobsmacking.' She didn't tell him back. Not say the words and break the spell. Put her heart at risk. She didn't know if she could survive him leaving her again. And if he didn't believe in the hearts and roses of it all, then he didn't believe in her either. Because that was what she wanted. 'To be honest, it was just a fling.'

He took a step back, eyes snapping open. 'A fling? Poppy, really?'

'We haven't even had a proper date. I don't really know you that well.'

'You've known me your whole life. I was there, Poppy. The whole time. I know you more than anyone else and I love you more, too. We've had a gazillion dates—all those years, then this last month, nights in bed. Mornings. In the shower. Ice-skating. Every day I've got to know you just a little bit more. And every day I've loved you more, too.' Now his hands were on her back, stroking her, lulling her back to him. 'Besides, we live together already.'

'No, we don't. I've sold the flat, to Alex and Lara.'

'Wow—I turn my back for two minutes and you sell the place from under my feet.' His mouth was on her neck now, and goddamn if she didn't want it all over her.

'Oh? You, too? From under your feet? What was I supposed to do? Wait? You all went off and left me. I'm loosening the ties. I'm living my life instead of watching everyone live theirs. First off, I'm going on holiday. To South America.'

'Where?'

'Mexico.'

His eyebrows rose. 'That's in North America.'

'I'm going on holiday to North America.'

The sound of Big Ben's bells began to pound sonorously into the night air and the buzz of anticipation grew almost electric around them.

Ten.

Now he was taking her hands in his, facing her. Serious. Beautiful, but serious. 'You want to make it a honeymoon?'

Nine.

'What?'

Eight.

'You want to make it a honeymoon? You and me. Mexico.'

'This is a proposal? Here on New Year's Eve?'

Seven.

'Will they all just be quiet? I… Well, yes.' He looked a little surprised, but determined. 'Yes. Yes, it is. I love you, Poppy. I want to spend the rest of my life with you. I want you.'

'You're not just getting carried away by the bouquets and the bling?'

'Never. I'm carried away by you. Everything starts and ends with you. I want to wake up with you every day. God, I've missed that. I want to come home to you every night. And I want to make you happy, to give you everything you want. If you want a wedding we'll have one. A future. Our future. I don't want to spend my life in the wilderness when I know this is what I want.' Then he pressed his mouth to hers. 'I love you.'

His eyes filled with such affection, such tangible, real love, that she knew with every tiny fragment of her heart that he did. 'Oh, my God, Isaac Blair. I love you, too.'

'So is that a yes?' First time ever she'd seen hesitation and anxiety in his eyes.

'Yes! Yes! Yes!'

She was pretty sure there was a lot of cheering then, and hugging and kissing; and mixing with the snowflakes there was confetti and fireworks lighting up the sky. Somewhere, everywhere, a whole world was singing about cups of kindness and not forgetting about people you've known your whole life.

And if the celebrations weren't all for them and their future she didn't mind at all because there was a lot of kissing going on for her, anyway. And a whole lot more to come.

When she eventually opened her eyes it was to the fanfare of her friends' clapping and cheering amid brushing the now fast-falling snow from their shoulders.

Alex was the first to shake Isaac's hand. 'No leg breaking needed? Shame. But well done, anyway. I suppose I should say, welcome to the family—if you hadn't been part of it your whole life already.'

Tori was next with her generous hugs for them both. 'Oh, that's so perfect. Just perfect. Wait until Izzy hears about this—she's going to be spitting she missed it. We just knew you two were made for each other. Didn't I say so, Lara?'

'Yes, you did. Congratulations, Mr Big Kahuna and lovely Poppy.' Lara pulled her in for a hug and Poppy hung on tight. Another friend, another member of their very special family.

And Matt was there, last but not least, wrapping his old friend into a fist-pump, man-hug thing. 'Good on you. What do you reckon? Best man material?'

Alex coughed. 'Ahem? Oldest friend prerogative?'

'Now, now, boys, don't fight over me.' Isaac grinned, but his smile wasn't for anyone but Poppy.

She couldn't believe how lucky she was. From a very rocky start to the month when she'd felt as if she'd lost everything, she now had it all. They all did. And more. So much more.

It was going to be a very Happy New Year indeed.

* * * * *

A WHITE WEDDING CHRISTMAS

ANDREA LAURENCE

To Diet Coke & Jelly Belly –

A lot of people have supported me throughout my career and over the course of my multiple releases, I've done my best to thank them all. Now that I have, it would be remiss if I failed to thank the two crucial elements of my daily word count: caffeine and sugar. My preferred delivery methods are Diet Coke and Jelly Belly jellybeans (strawberry margarita, pear and coconut, to be precise). They have helped me overcome plot challenges and allowed me to keep up with my insane deadline schedule.

Prologue

A lot had changed in the past fourteen years.

Fourteen years ago, Natalie and her best friend, Lily, were inseparable, and Lily's older brother Colin was the tasty treat Natalie had craved since she was fifteen. Now, Lily was about to get married and their engagement party was being held at the large, sprawling estate of her brother.

He'd come a long way since she saw him last. She'd watched, smitten, as he'd evolved into the cool college guy, and when Lily and Colin's parents died suddenly, Natalie had watched him turn into the responsible guardian of his younger sister and the head of his father's company. He'd been more untouchable then than ever before.

Lily and Natalie hadn't seen much of each other over the past few years. Natalie had gone to college at the

University of Tennessee and Lily had drifted aimlessly. They exchanged the occasional emails and Facebook likes, but they hadn't really talked in a long time. She'd been surprised when Lily called her at From This Moment, the wedding company Natalie co-owned, with a request.

A quickie wedding. Before Christmas, if possible. It had been early November at the time, and From This Moment usually had at least fourteen months of weddings scheduled in advance. But they closed at Christmas and for a friend, she and the other three ladies that owned and operated the wedding chapel agreed to squeeze one more wedding in before the holiday.

Natalie's invitation for the engagement party arrived the next day and now, here she was, in a cocktail dress, milling around Colin's huge house filled with people she didn't know.

That wasn't entirely true. She knew the bride. And when her gaze met the golden hazel eyes she'd fantasized about as a teenager, she remembered she knew a second person at the party, too.

"Natalie?" Colin said, crossing a room full of people to see her.

It took her a moment to even find the words to respond. This wasn't the boy she remembered from her youth. He'd grown into a man with broad shoulders that filled out his expensive suit coat, a tanned complexion with eyes that crinkled as he smiled and a five-o'clock shadow that any teenager would've been proud to grow.

"It is you," he said with a grin before he moved in for a hug.

Natalie steadied herself for the familiar embrace. Not everything had changed. Colin had always been a hugger. As a smitten teen, she'd both loved and hated those hugs. There was a thrill that ran down her spine from being so close; a tingle danced across her skin as it brushed his. Now, just as she did then, she closed her eyes and breathed in the scent of him. He smelled better than he did back when he wore cheap drugstore cologne, but even then, she'd loved it.

"How are you, Colin?" she asked as they parted. Natalie hoped her cheeks weren't flushing red. They felt hot, but that could just be the wine she'd been drinking steadily since she got to the party.

"I'm great. Busy with the landscaping business, as always."

"Right." Natalie nodded. "You're still running your dad's company, aren't you?"

He nodded, a hint of suppressed sadness lighting in his eyes for just a moment. *Good going, Natalie, remind him of his dead parents straight off.*

"I'm so glad you were able to fit Lily's wedding in at your facility. She was adamant that the wedding happen there."

"It's the best," Natalie said and it was true. There was no other place like their chapel in Nashville, Tennessee, or anywhere else she knew of. They were one of a kind, providing everything a couple needed for a wedding at one location.

"Good. I want the best for Lily's big day. You look amazing, by the way. Natalie is all grown up," Colin noted.

Natalie detected a hint of appreciation in his eyes as his gaze raked over the formfitting blue dress her business partner Amelia had forced her into wearing tonight. Now she was happy her fashion-conscious friend had dressed her up for the night. She glanced at Colin's left hand—no ring. At one point, she'd heard he was married, but it must not have worked out. Shocker. That left the possibilities open for a more interesting evening than she'd first anticipated tonight.

"I'm nearly thirty now, you know. I'm not a teenager."

Colin let out a ragged breath and forced his gaze back up to her face. "Thank goodness. I'd feel like a dirty old man right now if you were."

Natalie's eyebrow went up curiously. He *was* into her. The unobtainable fantasy might actually be within her grasp. Perhaps now was the time to make the leap she'd always been too chicken to make before. "You know, I have a confession to make." She leaned into him, resting a hand on his shoulder. "I was totally infatuated with you when we were kids."

Colin grinned wide. "Were you, now?"

"Oh yes." And she wouldn't mind letting those old fantasies run wild for a night. "You know, the party is starting to wind down. Would you be interested in getting out of here and finding someplace quiet where we could talk and catch up?"

Natalie said the words casually, but her body language read anything but. She watched as Colin swallowed hard, the muscles in his throat working up and down as he considered her offer. It was bold, and she knew it, but she might not have another chance to get a taste of Colin Russell.

"I'd love to catch up, Natalie, but unfortunately I can't."

Natalie took a big sip of her wine, finishing her glass, and nodded, trying to cover the painful flinch at his rejection. Suddenly she was sixteen again and felt just as unworthy of Colin's attentions as ever. Whatever.

"Well, that's a shame. I'll see you around then," she said, shrugging it off as though it was nothing but a casual offer. Turning on her heel with a sly smile, she made her way through the crowd and fled the party before she had to face any more embarrassment.

One

Putting together a decent wedding in a month was nearly impossible, even with someone as capable as Natalie handling things. Certain things took time, like printing invitations, ordering wedding dresses, coordinating with vendors... Fortunately at From This Moment wedding chapel, she and her co-owners and friends handled most of the work.

"Thank you for squeezing this last wedding in," Natalie said as they sat around the conference room table at their Monday morning staff meeting. "I know you all would much rather be starting your holiday celebrations."

"It's fine," Bree Harper, the photographer, insisted. "Ian and I aren't leaving for Aspen until the following week."

"It gives me something to do until Julian can fly back

from Hollywood," Gretchen McAlister added. "We're driving up to Louisville to spend the holidays with his family, and working another wedding will keep me from worrying about the trip."

"You've already met his family, Gretchen. Why are you nervous?"

"Because this time I'm his fiancée," Gretchen said, looking down in amazement at the ring he'd just given to her last week.

Natalie tried not to notice that all of her formerly single friends were now paired off. Gretchen and Bree were engaged. Amelia was married and pregnant. At one time, they had all been able to commiserate about their singleness, but now, it was just Natalie who went home alone each night. And she was okay with that. She anticipated a lifetime of going home alone. It's just that the status quo had changed so quickly for them all. The past year had been a whirlwind of romance for the ladies at From This Moment.

Despite the fact that she was a wedding planner, Natalie didn't actually believe in any of that stuff. She got into the industry with her friends because they'd asked her to, for one thing. For the other, it was an amazingly lucrative business. Despite the dismal marriage statistics, people seemed happy to take the leap, shelling out thousands of dollars, only to shell out more to their divorce attorneys at some point down the road.

As far as Natalie was concerned, every couple who walked through the door was doomed. The least she could do was give them a wedding to remember. She'd do her best to orchestrate a perfect day they could look back on. It was all downhill from there, anyway.

"I'll have the digital invitations ready by tomorrow.

Do you have the list of email addresses for me to send them out?" Gretchen asked.

Natalie snapped out of her thoughts and looked down at her tablet. "Yes, I have the list here." Normally, e-invites were out of the question for a formal wedding, but there just wasn't time to get paper ones designed, printed, addressed, mailed and gather RSVPs in a month's time.

"We're doing a winter wonderland theme, you said?" Amelia asked.

"That's what Lily mentioned. She was pretty vague about the whole thing. I've got an appointment with them on the calendar for this afternoon, so we'll start firming everything up then. Bree, you're doing engagement photos on Friday morning, right?"

"Yep," Bree said. "They wanted to take their shots at the groom's motorcycle shop downtown."

Natalie had known Lily a long time, but her choice in a future husband was a surprise even to her. Frankie owned a custom motorcycle shop. He was a flannel-wearing, bushy-bearded, tattooed hipster who looked more like a biker raised by lumberjacks than a successful businessman. Definitely not who Natalie would have picked for her best friend, and she was pretty sure he was not who Colin would've picked for Lily, either.

He seemed like a nice guy, though, and even Natalie could see that under the tattoos and hair, the guy was completely hormone pair-bonded to Lily. She wouldn't say they were in love because she didn't believe in love. But they were definitely pair-bonded. Biology was a powerful thing in its drive to continue the species. They could hardly keep their hands off each other at the engagement party.

"Okay. If that's all for this morning," Bree said, "I'm going to head to the lab and finish processing Saturday's wedding photos."

Natalie looked over her checklist. "Yep, that's it."

Bree and Amelia got up, filing out of the conference room, but Gretchen loitered by the table. She watched Natalie for a moment with a curious expression on her face. "What's going on with you? You seem distracted. Grumpier than usual."

That was sweet of her to point out. She knew she wasn't that pleasant this time of year, but she didn't need her friends reminding her of it. "Nothing is going on with me."

Gretchen crossed her arms over her chest and gave Natalie a look that told her she was going to stand there until she spilled.

"Christmas is coming." That pretty much said it all.

"What is this, *Game of Thrones*? Of course Christmas is coming. It's almost December, honey, and it's one of the more predictable holidays."

Natalie set down her tablet and frowned. Each year, the holidays were a challenge for her. Normally, she would try going on a trip to avoid all of it, but with the late wedding, she didn't have time. Staying home meant she'd have to resort to being a shut-in. She certainly wasn't interested in spending it with one of her parents and their latest spouses. The last time she did that, she'd called her mother's third husband by her second husband's name and that made for an awkward evening.

Natalie leaned back in the conference room chair and sighed. "It's bothering me more than usual this year." And it was. She didn't know why, but it was. Maybe it was the combination of all her friends being blissfully in love colliding with the holidays that was making it doubly painful.

"Are you taking a trip or staying home?" Gretchen asked.

"I'm staying home. I was considering a trip to Buenos Aires, but I don't have time. We squeezed Lily's last-minute wedding in on the Saturday before Christmas, so I'll be involved in that and not able to do the normal end-of-year paperwork until it's over."

"You're not planning to work over the shutdown, are you?" Gretchen planted her hands on her hips. "You don't have to celebrate, but by damn, you've got to take the time off, Natalie. You work seven days a week sometimes."

Natalie dismissed her concerns. Working didn't bother her as much as being idle. She didn't have a family to go home to each night or piles of laundry or housework that a man or child generated faster than she could clean. She liked her job. "I don't work the late hours you and Amelia do. I'm never here until midnight."

"It doesn't matter. You're still putting in too much time. You need to get away from all of this. Maybe go to a tropical island and have a fling with a sexy stranger."

At that, Natalie snorted. "I'm sorry, but a man is not the answer to my problems. That actually makes it worse."

"I'm not saying fall in love and marry the guy. I'm just saying to keep him locked in your hotel suite until the last New Year's firework explodes. What can a night or two of hot sex hurt?"

Natalie looked up at Gretchen and realized what was really bothering her. Colin's rejection from the night of the engagement party still stung. She hadn't told anyone about it, but if she didn't give Gretchen a good reason now, she'd ride her about it until the New Year. "It can hurt plenty when the guy you throw yourself at is your best friend's brother and he turns you down flat."

Gretchen's mouth dropped open and she sunk back down into her seat. "What? When did this happen?"

Natalie took a big sip of her soy chai latte before she answered. "I had too much chardonnay at Lily's engagement party and thought I'd take a chance on the big brother I'd lusted over since I'd hit puberty. To put it nicely, he declined. End of story. So no, I'm not really in the mood for a fling, either."

"Well that sucks," Gretchen noted.

"That's one way of putting it."

"On the plus side, you won't really have to see him again until the wedding day, right? Then you'll be too busy to care."

"Yep. I'll make sure I look extra good that day so he'll see what he missed."

"That's my girl. I'm going to go get these email invitations out."

Natalie nodded and watched Gretchen leave the room. She picked up her tablet and her drink, following her out the door to her office. Settling in at her desk, she pulled out a new file folder and wrote *Russell-Watson Wedding* on the tab. She needed to get everything prepared for their preliminary meeting this afternoon.

Staying busy would keep Christmas, and Colin, off her mind.

Colin pulled into the parking lot at From This Moment, his gaze instantly scanning over the lackluster shrubs out front. He knew it was winter, but they could certainly use a little more pizzazz for curb appeal.

He parked and went inside the facility. Stepping through the front doors, he knew instantly why Lily had insisted on marrying here. Their box holly hedges might have left something to be desired, but their focus was clearly on the interior. The inside was stunning with high ceilings, crystal chandeliers, tall fresh flower arrangements on the entryway table and arched entryways leading to various wings of the building. Mom would've loved it.

He looked down at his watch. It was a minute to one, so he was right on time for the appointment. Colin felt a little silly coming here today. Weddings weren't exactly his forte, but he was stepping up in his parents' place. When he'd married a year and a half ago, it had been a quick courthouse affair. If they'd opted for something more glamorous, he would've let Pam take the lead. Pam wasn't interested in that, though, and apparently, neither was his sister, Lily.

If she'd had her way, she and Frankie would've gone down to the courthouse, too. There was no reason to rush the nuptials, like Colin and Pam, but Lily just wanted to be done. She loved Frankie and she wanted to be Mrs. Watson as soon as possible. Colin had had to twist her arm into having an actual wedding, reminding her that their mother would be rolling over in her grave if she knew what Lily was planning.

She'd finally agreed under two circumstances: one, that the wedding be at Natalie's facility. Two, that he handle all the details. He insisted on the wedding, he'd offered to pay for it; he could make all the decisions.

Lily intended to show up in a white dress on the big day and that was about it.

Colin wasn't certain how he'd managed to be around so many women who weren't interested in big weddings. Pam hadn't wanted to marry at all. Hell, if it hadn't been for the baby and his insistence, she wouldn't have accepted the proposal. In retrospect, he realized why she was so hesitant, but with Lily, it just seemed to be a general disinterest in tradition.

He didn't understand it. Their parents had been very traditional people. Old-fashioned, you might even say. When they died in a car accident, Colin had tried to keep the traditions alive for Lily's sake. He'd never imagined he would end up raising his younger sister when he was only nineteen, but he was determined to do a good job and not disappoint his parents' memory.

Lily was just not that concerned. To her, the past was the past and she wasn't going to get hung up on things like that. Formal weddings fell into the bucket of silly traditions that didn't matter much to her. But it mattered to him, so she'd relented.

Colin heard a door open down one of the hallways and a moment later he found himself once again face-to-face with Natalie Sharpe. She stopped short in the archway of the foyer, clutching a tablet to her gray silk blouse. Even as a teenager, she'd had a classic beauty about her. Her creamy skin and high cheekbones had drawn his attention even when she was sporting braces. He'd suppressed any attraction he might have had for his little sister's friend, but he'd always thought she would grow up into a beautiful woman. At the party, his suspicions had been confirmed. And better yet, she'd looked at him with a seductive smile and an openness he hadn't expected. They weren't kids anymore, but there were other complications that had made it impossible to take her up on her offer, as much as he regretted it.

Today, the look on her face was a far cry from that night. Her pink lips were parted in concern, a frown lining her brow. Then she took a breath and shook it off. She tried to hide her emotions under a mask of professionalism, but he could tell she wasn't pleased to see him.

"Colin? I wasn't expecting to see you today. Is something going on with Lily?"

"Lots of things are going on with Lily," he replied, "but not what you're implying. She's fine. She's just not interested in the details."

Natalie swung her dark ponytail over her shoulder, her nose wrinkling. "What do you mean?"

"I mean, she told me this is my show and I'm to plan it however I see fit. So here I am," he added, holding out his arms.

He watched Natalie try to process the news. Apparently Lily hadn't given her a heads-up, but why would she? He doubted Lily knew about their encounter at the engagement party. She wasn't the kind of girl to give much thought to how her choices would affect other people.

"I know this is an unusual arrangement, but Lily is an unusual woman, as you know."

That seemed to snap Natalie out of her fog. She nodded curtly and extended her arm. "Of course. Come this way to my office and we can discuss the details."

Colin followed behind her, appreciating the snug fit of her pants over the curve of her hips and rear. She was wearing a pair of low heels that gave just enough lift to flatter her figure. It was a shame she walked in such a stiff, robotic way. He wouldn't mind seeing those hips sway a little bit, but he knew Natalie was too up-tight for that. She'd always been a sharp contrast to his free-spirited sister—no-nonsense, practical, serious. She walked like she was marching into battle, even if it was a simple trip down the hallway.

After their encounter at the engagement party, he'd started to wonder if there was a more relaxed, sensual side to her that he hadn't had the pleasure of knowing about. He could only imagine what she could be like if she took down that tight ponytail, had a glass of wine and relaxed for once.

He got the feeling he would know all about that if he'd accepted her offer at the party. Unfortunately, his rocky on-again, off-again relationship with Rachel had been *on* that night. As much as he might have wanted to spend private time with Natalie, he couldn't. Colin was not the kind of man who cheated, even on a rocky rela-tionship. Especially after what had happened with Pam.

After realizing how much more he was attracted to Natalie than the woman he was dating, he'd broken it off with Rachel for good. He was hopeful that now that he was a free man, he might get a second chance with Natalie. So far the reception was cold, but he hoped she'd thaw to his charms in time.

He followed her into her office and took a seat in the guest chair. Her office was pleasantly decorated, but ex-tremely tidy and organized. He could tell every knick-knack had its place, every file had a home.

"Can I get you something to drink? We have bottled water, some sparkling juices and ginger ale."

That was an unexpected option. "Why do you have ginger ale?"

"Sometimes the bride's father gets a little queasy when he sees the estimate."

Colin laughed. "Water would be great. I'm not that worried about the bill."

Natalie got up, pulling two bottles of water out of the small stainless steel refrigerator tucked into her built-in bookshelves. "On that topic, what number makes you comfortable in terms of budget for the wedding?" she asked as she handed him a bottle.

Colin's fingers brushed over hers as he took the bottle from her hand. There was a spark as they touched, making his skin prickle with pins and needles as he pulled away. He clutched the icy cold water in his hand to dull the sensation and tried to focus on the conversation, instead of his reaction to a simple touch. "Like I said, I'm not that worried about it. My landscaping company has become extremely successful, and I want this to be an event that my parents would've thrown for Lily if they were alive. I don't think we need ridiculous extras like ice bars with martini luges, but in terms of food and decor, I'm all in. A pretty room, pretty flowers, good food, cake, music. The basics."

Natalie had hovered near her chair after handing him the water, making him wonder if she'd been affected by their touch, too. After listening to him, she nodded curtly and sat down. She reached for her tablet and started making careful notes. "How many guests are you anticipating? Lily provided me a list of emails, but we weren't sure of the final total."

"Probably about a hundred and fifty people. We've

got a lot of family and friends of my parents that would attend, but Frankie doesn't have many people nearby."

He watched her tap rapidly at her screen. "When I spoke with Lily, I suggested a winter wonderland theme and she seemed to like that. Is that agreeable?"

"Whatever she wants." Colin had no clue what a winter wonderland wedding would even entail. White, he supposed. Maybe some fake snow like the kind that surrounded Santa at the mall?

"Okay. Any other requests? Would you prefer a DJ or a band for the reception?"

That was one thing he had an answer for. "I'd like a string quartet, actually. Our mother played the violin and I think that would be a nice nod to her. At least for the ceremony. For the reception, we probably need something more upbeat so that Lily and her friends can dance and have a good time."

"How about a swing band? There's a great one locally that we've used a couple times."

"That would work. I think she mentioned going swing dancing at some club a few weeks back."

Natalie nodded and finally set down her tablet. "I'm going to have Amelia put together a suggested menu and some cake designs. Gretchen will do a display of the tablescape for your approval. I'll speak with our floral vendor to see what she recommends for the winter wonderland theme. We'll come up with a whole wedding motif with some options and we'll bring you back to review and approve all the final choices. We should probably have something together by tomorrow afternoon."

She certainly knew what she was doing and had this whole thing down to a science. That was good because Colin wasn't entirely sure what a tablescape even was.

He was frankly expecting this process to be a lot more painful, but perhaps that was the benefit of an all-in-one facility. "That all sounds great. Why don't you firm up those details with the other ladies and maybe we can meet for dinner tomorrow night to discuss it?"

Natalie's dark gaze snapped up from her tablet to meet his. "Dinner won't be necessary. We can set up another appointment if your schedule allows."

Colin tried not to look disappointed at her quick dismissal of dinner. He supposed he deserved that after he'd done the same to her last week. Perhaps she was just angry with him over it. If he could convince her to meet with him, maybe she could relax and he could explain to her what had happened that night. He got the distinct impression she wouldn't discuss it here at work.

"If not dinner, how about I just stop by here tomorrow evening? Do you mind staying past your usual time?"

Natalie snorted delicately and eased up out of her chair. "There's no usual time in this business. We work pretty much around the clock. What time should I expect you?"

"About six."

"Great," she said, offering her hand to him over the desk.

Colin was anxious to touch her again and see if he had the same reaction to her this time. He took her hand, enveloping it in his own and trying not to think about how soft her skin felt against his. There was another sizzle of awareness and this time, it traveled up his arm as he held her hand, making him all the more sorry she'd turned down his dinner invitation. He'd never had that instant of a reaction just by touching someone. He had

this urge to lean into her and draw the scent of her perfume into his lungs even as the coil of desire in his gut
tightened with every second they touched. What would
it be like to actually kiss her?

He had been right before when he thought Natalie
was caught off guard by their connection. He was certain he wasn't the only one to feel it. Colin watched as
Natalie avoided his gaze, swallowed hard and gently
extracted her hand from his. "Six it is."

Two

Discuss it over dinner? *Dinner!* Natalie was still steaming about her meeting with Colin the next afternoon. As she pulled together the portfolio for his review, she couldn't help replaying the conversation in her mind.

That look in his eye. The way he'd held her hand. Dinner! He was hitting on her. What was that about? Natalie was sorry, but that ship had sailed. Who was he to reject her, then come back a week later and change his mind? He had his shot and he blew it.

As she added the suggested menu to the file, she felt her bravado deflate a little. Natalie would be lying if she said she didn't want to take him up on the offer. She really, really did. But a girl had to draw the line somewhere. Her pride was at stake and if she came running just because he'd changed his mind, she'd look needy. She was anything but needy.

He had passed up on a one-night stand and what was done, was done. Now that she knew they were working together on the wedding plans, it was just as well. She didn't like to mix business with pleasure.

Natalie looked at the clock on her computer. It was almost six. The rest of the facility was dark and quiet. It was Tuesday, so the others were all off today. Natalie was supposed to be off, too, but she usually came into the office anyway. When it was quiet, she could catch up on paperwork and filing, talk with their vendors and answer the phone in case a client called. Or stopped by, as the case was tonight.

She slid open the desk drawer where she kept all her toiletries. Pulling out a small hand mirror, she checked her teeth for lipstick, smoothed her hand over her hair and admired her overall look. She found her compact to apply powder to the shinier areas and reapplied her lipstick. She may have put a little extra effort into her appearance today. Not to impress Colin. Not really. She did it more to torture him. Her pride stung from his rebuffing and she wanted him to suffer just a little bit, too.

Satisfied, she slipped her things back into the drawer. A soft door chime sounded a moment later and she knew that he'd arrived. She stood, taking a deep breath and willing herself to ignore her attraction to him. This was about work. Work. And anytime she thought differently, she needed to remind herself how she'd felt when he rejected her.

Natalie walked quickly down the hallway to the lobby. She found Colin waiting for her there. At the party and at their meeting yesterday, he'd been wearing a suit, but tonight, he was wearing a tight T-shirt and khakis. She watched the muscles of his broad shoulders move beneath the fabric as he slipped out of his winter coat, hanging it on the rack by the door.

When he turned to face her, she was blindsided by his bright smile and defined forearms. When he wore his suit, it was easy to forget he wasn't just a CEO, he was also a landscaper. She'd wager he rarely got dirt under his nails these days, but he still had the muscular arms and chest of a man who could move the earth with brute strength.

Colin looked down, seemingly following her gaze. "Do you like the shirt? We just had them made up for all the staff to wear when they're out on job sites."

Honestly, she hadn't paid much attention to the shirt, but talking about that was certainly better than admitting she was lusting over his hard pecs. "It's very nice," she said with a polite smile. "I like the dark green color." And she did. It had the Russell Landscaping logo in white on the front. It looked nice on him. Especially the fact that it looked painted on.

"Me, too. You didn't call to say there was an issue, so I assume you have the wedding plans ready?"

"I do. Come on back to my office and I'll show you what we've pulled together."

They turned and walked down the hallway, side by side. She couldn't help but notice that Colin had gently rested a guiding hand at the small of her back as she slipped into the office ahead of him. It was a faint touch, and yet she could still feel the heat of it through her clothes. Goose bumps raised up across her forearms when he pulled away, leaving her cold. It was an unexpected touch and yet she had to admit she was a little disappointed it was so quick. Despite their years apart, her reaction to Colin had only grown along with his biceps. Unfortunately, those little thrills were all she'd allow herself to have. She was first and foremost a professional.

They settled into her office and Natalie pulled out the trifold portfolio she used for these meetings. She unfolded it, showing all the images and options for their wedding. Focusing on work was her best strategy for dealing with her attraction to Colin.

"Let's start with the menu," she began. "Amelia, our caterer, would normally do up to three entrees for a wedding this size, but with such short notice, we really don't have time for attendees to select their meals. Instead, she put together a surf and turf option that should make everyone happy. Option one pairs her very popular beef tenderloin with a crab cake. You also have the choice of doing a bourbon-glazed salmon, or a chicken option instead if you think fish might be a problem for your guests."

She watched Colin look over the options thoughtfully. She liked the way his brow drew together as he thought. Staring down at the portfolio, she could see how long and thick his eyelashes were. Most women would kill for lashes like those.

"What would you choose?" he asked, unaware of her intense study of his face.

"The crab cake," Natalie said without hesitation. "They're almost all crab, with a crisp outside and a spicy remoulade. They're amazing."

"Okay, that sounds great. Let's go with that."

Natalie checked off his selection. "For the cake, she put together three concept designs." She went into detail on each, explaining the decorations and how it fit with the theme.

When she was finally done, he asked again, "Which one of these cakes would you choose?"

Natalie wasn't used to this. Most brides knew exactly what they wanted. Looking down at the three concept sketches for the cake, she pointed out the second option. "I'd choose this one. It will be all white with an iridescent shimmer to the fondant. Amelia will make silver gum paste snowflakes and when they wrap around the cake it will be really enchanting."

"Let's go with that one. What about cake flavors?"

"You won't make that decision today. If you can come Thursday, Amelia will set up a tasting session. She's doing a couple other appointments that day, so that would work best. Do you think Lily would be interested in coming to that?"

"I can work that out. I doubt Lily will join me, but I'll ask. I'm sure cake is cake in her eyes."

Natalie just didn't understand her friend at all. Natalie had no interest in marriage, therefore no interest in a wedding. But Lily should at least have the party she wanted and enjoy it. It didn't make sense to hand that over to someone else. Her inner control freak couldn't imagine someone else planning her wedding. If by some twist of fate, she was lobotomized and agreed to marry someone, she would control every last detail.

"Okay." Natalie noted the appointment in her tablet so Amelia could follow up with him on a time for Thursday. From there, they looked at some floral concepts and bouquet options. With each of them, he asked Natalie's opinion and went with that. Sitting across from her was a sexy, intelligent, wealthy, thoughtful and agreeable man. If she *was* the kind to marry, she'd crawl into his lap right now. Whoever did land Colin would be very lucky. At least for a while.

Everything flowed easily from there. Without much debate, they'd settled on assorted tall and low arrangements with a mix of white flowers including rose, ranunculus, stephanotis and hydrangea. It was everything she would've chosen and probably as close as she'd get to having a wedding without having to get married.

"Now that we've handled all that, the last thing I want to do is to take you to the table setup Gretchen put together."

They left her office and walked down to the storage room. She kept waiting for him to touch her again, but she was disappointed this time. Opening the doors, she let him inside ahead of her and followed him in. In their storage room, amongst the shelves of glassware, plates, silver vases and cake stands, they had one round dinner table set up. There, Gretchen put together mock-ups of the reception tables for brides to better visualize them and make changes.

"Gretchen has selected a soft white tablecloth with a delicate silver overlay of tiny beaded snowflakes. We'd carry the white and silver into the dishes with the silver chargers, silver-rimmed white china, and then use silver-and-glass centerpieces in a variety of heights. We'll bring in tasteful touches of sparkle with some crystals on white manzanita branches and lots of candles."

Colin ran the tip of his finger over a silver snowflake and nodded. "It all looks great to me. Very pretty. Gretchen has done a very nice job with it."

Natalie made a note in her tablet and shook her head with amazement. "You're the easiest client I've ever had. I refuse to believe it's really that easy. What are you hiding from me?"

Colin looked at her with a confused expression. "I'm not hiding anything. I know it isn't what you're used to, but really, I'm putting this wedding in your capable hands."

He placed his hand on her shoulder as he spoke. She could feel the heat radiating through the thin fabric of her cashmere sweater, making her want to pull at the collar as her internal temperature started to climb.

"You knew my parents. You know Lily. You've got the experience and the eye for this kind of thing. Aside from the discussion about flowers, I've had no clue what you were talking about most of the time. I just trust you to do a great job and I'll write the check."

Natalie tried not to frown. Her heated blood wasn't enough for her to ignore his words. He was counting on her. That was a lot of pressure. She knew she could pull it off beautifully, but he had an awful lot of confidence in her for a girl he hadn't seen since she wore a retainer to bed. "So would you rather just skip the cake tasting?"

"Oh no," he said with a smile that made her knees soften beneath her. "I have a massive sweet tooth, so I'm doing that for sure."

Natalie wasn't sure how much her body could take of being in close proximity to Colin as friends. She wanted to run her hand up his tanned, muscular forearm and rub against him like a cat. While she enjoyed indulging her sexuality from time to time, she didn't have a reaction like this to just any guy. It was unnerving and *so* inappropriate. This wedding couldn't come fast enough.

* * *

"Thank you for all your help with this," Colin said as Natalie closed up and they walked toward the door.

"That's what I do," she said with the same polite smile that was starting to make him crazy. He missed her real one. He remembered her carefree smile from her younger days and her seductive smile from the engagement party. This polite, blank smile meant nothing to him.

"No, really. You and your business partners are going out of your way to make this wedding happen. I don't know how to thank you."

Natalie pressed the alarm code and they stepped outside where she locked the door. "You and Lily are like family to me. Of course we'd do everything we could. Anyway, it's not like we're doing it for free. You're paying us for our time, so no worries."

Their cars were the only two in the parking lot, so he walked her over to the cherry-red two-seat Miata convertible. Had there been another car in the lot, he never would've guessed this belonged to Natalie. It had a hint of wild abandon that didn't seem to align with the precise and businesslike Natalie he knew. It convinced him more than ever that there was another side to her that he desperately wanted to see.

"Let me take you to dinner tonight," he said, nearly surprising himself with the suddenness of it.

Natalie's dark brown eyes widened. "I really can't, Colin, but I appreciate the offer."

Two up at bats, two strikeouts. "Even just as friends?"

Her gaze flicked over his face and she shook her head. "You and I both know it wouldn't be as friends."

Turning away, Natalie unlocked her car and opened the door to toss her bag inside.

"I think that's unfair."

"Not really. Listen, Colin, I'm sorry about the other night at the party. I'd been hit by a big dose of nostalgia and too much wine and thought that indulging those old teenage fantasies was a good idea. But by the light of day, I know it was silly of me. So thank you for having some sense and keeping me from doing something that would've made this whole planning process that much more awkward."

"Don't thank me," Colin argued. "I've regretted that decision every night since it happened."

Natalie's mouth fell agape, her dark eyes searching his face for something. "Don't," she said at last. "It was the right choice."

"It was at the time, but only because it had to be. Natalie, I—"

"Don't," Natalie insisted. "There's no reason to explain yourself. You made the decision you needed to make and it was the right one. No big deal. I'd like to just put that whole exchange behind us. The truth is that I'm really not the right kind of woman for you."

Colin wasn't sure if she truly meant what she said or if she was just angry with him, but he was curious what she meant by that. He was bad enough at choosing women. Maybe she knew something he didn't. "What kind of woman is that?"

"The kind that's going to have any sort of future with you. At the party, I was just after a night of fun, nothing serious. You're a serious kind of guy. Since you were a teenager, you were on the express train to marriage and kids. I'm on a completely different track."

They hadn't really been around each other long enough for Colin to think much past the ache of desire she seemed to constantly rouse in him. But if what she said was true, she was right. He wanted all those things. If she didn't, there wasn't much point in pursuing her. His groin felt otherwise, but it would get on board eventually.

"Well, I appreciate you laying that out for me. Not all women are as forthcoming." Pam had been, but for some reason he'd refused to listen. This time he knew better than to try to twist a woman's will. It didn't work. "Just friends, then," he said.

Natalie smiled with more warmth than before, and she seemed to relax for the first time since he'd arrived. "Friends is great."

"All right," he said. "Good night." Colin leaned in to give Natalie a quick hug goodbye. At least that was the idea.

Once he had his arms wrapped around her and her cheek pressed to his, it was harder to let go than he expected. Finally, he forced himself back, dropping his hands at his sides and breaking the connection he'd quickly come to crave. And yet, he couldn't get himself to say good-night and go back to his truck. "Listen, before you go can I ask you about something?"

"Sure," she said, although there was a hesitation in her voice that made him think she'd much rather flee than continue talking to him in the cold. She must not think he'd taken the hint.

"I'm thinking about giving Lily and Frankie the old house as a wedding present."

"The house you and Lily grew up in?" she asked with raised brows.

"Yes. It's been sitting mostly empty the last few years. Lily has been living with Frankie in the little apartment over his motorcycle shop. They seem to think that's great, but they're going to need more space if they want to start a family."

"That's a pretty amazing wedding present. Not many people register for a house."

Colin shrugged. "I don't need it. I have my place. It's paid for, so all they'd have to worry about are taxes and insurance. The only problem is that it needs to be cleaned out. I never had the heart to go through all of Mom's and Dad's things. I want to clear all that out and get it ready for the newlyweds to make a fresh start there."

Natalie nodded as he explained. "That sounds like a good plan. What does it have to do with me?"

"Well," Colin said with an uncharacteristically sheepish smile, "I was wondering if you would be interested in helping me."

She flinched at first, covering her reaction by shuffling her feet in the cold. "I don't know that I'll be much help to you, Colin. For one thing, I'm a wedding planner, not an interior decorator. And for another thing, I work most of the weekends with weddings. I don't have a lot of free time."

"I know," he said, "and I'm not expecting any heavy lifting on your part. I was thinking more of your organizational skills and keen aesthetic eye. It seems to me like you could spot a quality piece of furniture or artwork that's worth keeping amongst the piles of eighties-style recliners."

There was a light of amusement in her eyes as she

listened to him speak. "You're completely in over your head with this one, aren't you?"

"You have no idea. My business is landscaping, and that's the one thing at the house that doesn't need any work. I overhauled it a few years ago and I've had it maintained, so the outside is fine. It's just the inside. I also thought it would be nice to decorate the house for Christmas since they get back from their honeymoon on Christmas Eve. That way it will be ready to go for the holidays."

The twinkle in her eye faded. "I'm no good with Christmas, Colin. I might be able to help you with some of the furniture and keepsakes, but you're on your own when it comes to the holidays."

That made Colin frown. Most people enjoyed decorating for Christmas. Why was she so opposed to it? In his eyes it wasn't much different from decorating for a wedding. He wasn't about to push that point, however. "Fair enough. I'm sure I can handle that part on my own. Do you have plans tonight?"

Natalie sighed and shook her head. "I'm *not* going out with you, Colin."

He held up his hands in surrender. "I didn't ask you out. I asked if you were busy. I thought if you weren't busy, I'd take you by the old house tonight. I know you don't have a lot of free time, so if you could just take a walk through with me this evening and give me some ideas, I could get started on it."

"Oh," she said, looking sheepish.

"I mean, I could just pay a crew to come and clean out the house and put everything in storage, but I hate to do that. Some things are more important than others, and I'll want to keep some of it. Putting everything in storage just delays the inevitable. I could use your help, even if for just tonight."

Natalie sighed and eventually nodded. "Sure. I have some time tonight."

"Great. We'll take my car and I'll bring you back when we're done," Colin said.

He got the distinct impression that if he let Natalie get in her car, she'd end up driving somewhere other than their old neighborhood, or make some excuse for a quick getaway. He supposed that most men agreed to just being friends, but secretly hoped for more. Colin meant what he'd said and since she'd agreed, there was no need to slink away with his tail between his legs.

Holding out his arm, he ushered her reluctantly over to his Russell Landscaping truck. The Platinum series F-250 wasn't a work truck, it was more for advertising, although he did get it dirty from time to time. It was dark green, like their shirts, with the company logo and information emblazoned on the side.

He held the passenger door open for her, a step automatically unfolding along the side of the truck. Colin held her hand as she climbed inside, then slammed the door shut.

"Do you mind if we listen to some music on the way?" she asked.

Colin figured that she wanted music to avoid idle conversation, but he didn't mind. "Sure." He turned on the radio, which started playing music from the holiday station he'd had on last.

"Can I change it to the country channel?"

"I don't care, although you don't strike me as a country girl," he noted.

"I was born and raised in Nashville, you know. When

I was a kid, my dad would take me to see performances at the Grand Ole Opry. It's always stuck with me." She changed the station and the new Blake Wright song came on. "Ooh. I love this song. He's going to be doing a show at the Opry in two weeks. It's sold out, though."

Colin noted that information and put it in his back pocket. From there, it wasn't a long drive to the old neighborhood, just a few miles on the highway. Blake had just finished singing when they arrived.

They had grown up in a nice area—big homes on big lots designed for middle-class families. His parents honestly couldn't really afford their house when they had first bought it, but his father had insisted that they get the home they wanted to have forever. His parents had wanted a place to both raise their children and entertain potential clients, and appearances counted. If that meant a few lean years while the landscaping business built up, so be it.

The neighborhood was still nice and the homes had retained an excellent property value. It wasn't as flashy or trendy with the Nashville wealthy like Colin's current neighborhood, but it was a home most people would be happy to have.

As they pulled into the driveway, Natalie leaned forward and eyed the house through the windshield with a soft smile. "I've always loved this house," she admitted. "I can't believe how big the magnolia trees have gotten."

Colin's father had planted crepe myrtles lining the front walkway and magnolia trees flanking the yard. When he was a kid they were barely big enough to provide enough shade to play beneath them. Now the magnolias were as tall as the two-story roofline. "I've maintained the yard over the years," he said proudly. "I knew how important that was for Dad."

It was too dark to really get a good look at the outside, even with the lights on, so he opened the garage door and opted to take her in through there. His father's tool bench and chest still sat along the rear wall. A shed in the back housed all the gardening supplies and equipment. He hadn't had the heart to move any of that stuff before, but like the rest of it, he knew it was time.

They entered into the kitchen from the garage. Natalie instantly moved over to the breakfast bar, settling onto one of the barstools where she and Lily used to sit and do their homework together.

He could almost envision her with the braces and the braids again, but he much preferred Natalie as she was now. She smiled as she looked around the house, obviously as fond of his childhood home as he was. He wanted to walk up behind her to look at it the same way she was. Maybe rub the tension from her tight shoulders.

But he wouldn't. It had taken convincing to get her here. He wasn't about to run her off so quickly by pushing the boundaries of their newly established friendship. Eventually, it would be easier to ignore the swell of her breasts as they pressed against her sweater or the luminous curve of her cheek. Until then, he smoothed his hands over the granite countertop and let the cold stone cool his ardor.

"How long has it been since you've lived here, Colin? It seems pretty tidy."

"It's been about three years since I lived here full-time. Lily used it as a home base on and off for a while, but no one has really lived here for a year at least. I have a service come clean and I stop in periodically to check on the place."

"So many memories." She slipped off the stool and went into the living room. He followed her there, watching her look around at the vaulted ceilings. Natalie pointed at the loft that overlooked the living room. "I used to love hanging out up there, listening to CDs and playing on the computer."

That made him smile. The girls had always been sprawled out on the rug or lying across the futon up there, messing around on the weekends. Natalie had spent a lot of time at the house when they were younger. Her own house was only the next block over, but things had been pretty volatile leading up to her parents' divorce. While he hated that her parents split up, it had been nice to have her around, especially after his own parents died. Colin had been too busy trying to take care of everything and suddenly be a grown-up. Natalie had been there for Lily in a way he hadn't.

"Lily is very lucky to have a brother like you," she said, conflicting with his own thoughts. "I'm sure she'll love the house. It's perfect for starting a family. Just one thing, though."

"What's that?"

Natalie looked at him and smiled. "The house is exactly the same as it was the last time I was here ten years ago, and things were dated then. You've got some work ahead of you, mister."

Three

After a few hours at the house, Colin insisted on ordering pizza and Natalie finally acquiesced. That wasn't a dinner date, technically, and she was starving. She wasn't sure that he had put the idea of them being more than friends to bed—honestly neither had she—but they'd get there. As with all attractions, the chemical reactions would fade, the hormones would quiet and things would be fine. With a wedding and the house to focus on, she was certain it would happen sooner rather than later.

While he dealt with ordering their food, she slipped out onto the back deck and sat down in one of the old patio chairs. The air was cold and still, but it felt good to breathe it in.

She was exhausted. They'd gone through every room, talking over pieces to keep, things to donate and what renovations were needed. It wasn't just that, though. It was the memories and emotions tied to the place that were getting to her. Nearly every room in the house held some kind of significance to her. Even though Lily and Colin's parents had been dead for nearly thirteen years now, Natalie understood why Colin had been so reluctant to change things. It was like messing with the past somehow.

Her parents' marriage had dissolved when she was fourteen. The year or so leading up to it had been even more rough on her than what followed. Lily's house had been her sanctuary from the yelling. After school, on the weekends, sleepovers…she was almost always here. Some of her happiest memories were in this place. Colin and Lily's parents didn't mind having her around. She suspected that they knew what was going on at her house and were happy to shelter her from the brunt of it.

Unfortunately, they couldn't protect her from everything. There was nothing they could do to keep Natalie's father from walking out on Christmas day. They weren't there to hold Natalie's hand as her parents fought it out in court for two years, then each remarried again and again, looking for something in another person they couldn't seem to find.

Her friends joked that Natalie was jaded about relationships, but she had a right to be. She rarely saw them succeed. Why would she put herself through that just because there was this societal pressure to do it? She could see the icy water and jagged rocks below; why would she jump off the bridge with everyone else?

She heard the doorbell and a moment later, Colin called her from the kitchen. "Soup's on!"

Reluctantly, Natalie got back up and went inside the

house to face Colin and the memories there. She found a piping hot pizza sitting on the kitchen island beside a bottle of white wine. "Did they deliver the wine, too?" she asked drily. The addition of wine to the pizza made this meal feel more suspiciously like the date she'd declined earlier. "If they do, I need their number. Wine delivery is an underserved market."

"No, it was in the wine chiller," he said as though it was just the most convenient beverage available. "I lived here for a few weeks after I broke up with Pam. It was left over."

Natalie had learned from Lily that Colin got a divorce earlier this year, but she didn't know much about the details. Their wedding had been a quiet affair and their divorce had been even quieter. All she did hear was that they had a son together. "I'm sorry to hear about your divorce. Do you still get to see your son pretty often?"

The pleasant smile slipped from his face. He jerked the cork out of the wine bottle and sighed heavily. "I don't have a son."

Natalie knew immediately that she had treaded into some unpleasant territory. She wasn't quite sure how to back out of it. "Oh. I guess I misheard."

"No. You heard right. Shane was born about six months after we got married." He poured them each a glass of chardonnay. "We divorced because I found out that Shane wasn't my son."

Sometimes Natalie hated being right about relationships. Bad things happened to really good people when the fantasy of love got in the way. She took a large sip of the wine to muffle her discomfort. "I'm sorry to hear that, Colin."

A smile quickly returned to his face, although it seemed a little more forced than before. "Don't be. I did it to myself. Pam had been adamant when we started dating that she didn't want to get married. When she told me she was pregnant, I thought she would change her mind, but she didn't. I think she finally gave in only because I wouldn't let it go. I should've known then that I'd made a mistake by forcing her into it."

Natalie stiffened with a piece of pizza dangling from her hand. She finally released it to the plate and cleared her throat. "Not everyone is meant for marriage," she said. "Too many people do it just because they think that's what they're supposed to do."

"If someone doesn't want to get married, they shouldn't. It's not fair to their partner."

She slid another slice of pizza onto his plate. Instead of opting for the perfectly good dining room table, Natalie returned to her perch at the breakfast bar. That's where she'd always eaten at Lily's house. "That's why I've made it a policy to be honest up front."

Colin followed suit, handing her a napkin and sliding onto the stool beside her. "And I appreciate that, especially after what happened with Pam. You're right though. I'm the kind of guy that is meant for marriage. I've just got to learn to make better choices in women," he said. Pam had been his most serious relationship, but he had a string of others that failed for different reasons. "My instincts always seem to be wrong."

Natalie took a bite of her pizza and chewed thoughtfully. She had dodged a bullet when Colin turned her down at the engagement party. She'd only been looking for a night of nostalgic indulgence, but he was the kind of guy who wanted more. More wasn't something she could give him. She was a bad choice, too. Not lie-about-the-paternity-of-your-child bad, but definitely not the traditional, marrying kind he needed.

"Your sister doesn't seem to want to get married," Natalie noted, sending the conversation in a different direction. She'd never seen a more reluctant bride. That kind of woman wouldn't normally bother with a place like From This Moment.

"Actually, she's very eager to marry. It's the wedding and the hoopla she can do without."

"That's an interesting reversal. A lot of women are more obsessed with the wedding day than the actual marriage."

"I think she'll appreciate it later, despite how much she squirms now. Eloping at the courthouse was very underwhelming. We said the same words, ended up just as legally joined in marriage, but it was missing a certain something. I want better for my little sister's big day."

"She'll get it," Natalie said with confidence. "We're the best."

They ate quietly for a few moments before Colin finished his slice and spoke up. "See," he said as he reached for another piece and grinned. "I told you that you'd have dinner with me eventually."

Natalie snorted softly, relieved to see the happier Colin return. "Oh, no," she argued with a smile. "This does not count, even if you add wine. Having dinner together implies a date. This is not a date."

Colin leaned his elbows on the counter and narrowed his eyes at her. "Since we're sharing tonight, do you mind telling me why you were so unhappy to see me yesterday at the chapel?"

"I wouldn't say unhappy. I would say surprised. I expected Lily. And considering what happened the last time I saw you, I was feeling a little embarrassed."

"Why?"

"Because I hit on you and failed miserably. It was stupid of me. It was a momentary weakness fueled by wine and abstinence. And since you passed up the chance, this is definitely not a date. We're on a nondate eating pizza at your childhood home."

A knowing grin spread across Colin's face, making Natalie curious, nervous and making her flush at the same time. "So that's what it's really about," he said with a finger pointed in her direction. "You were upset because I turned you down that night at the party."

Natalie's cheeks flamed at the accusation. "Not at all. I'm relieved, really." She took a large sip of her wine and hoped that sounded convincing enough.

"You can say that, but I know it isn't true. You couldn't get out of the house fast enough that night."

"I had an early day the next morning."

Colin raised his brow in question. He didn't believe a word she said. Neither did she.

"Okay, fine. So what?" she challenged. "So what if I'm holding it against you? I'm allowed to have feelings about your rejection."

"Of course you're allowed to have feelings. But I didn't reject you, Natalie."

"Oh really? What would you call it?"

Colin turned in his seat to face her, his palms resting on each knee. "I would call it being the good guy even when I didn't want to be. You may not have noticed, but I had a date at the party. She was in a corner sulking most of the night. It wasn't really serious and we broke it off the next day, but I couldn't very well ditch her and disappear with you."

Natalie's irritation started to deflate. She slumped in her seat, fingering absentmindedly at her pizza crust. "Oh."

"Oh," he repeated with a chuckle. "Now if you were the kind of woman that *would* date me, you'd be feeling pretty silly right now."

Natalie shook her head. "Even if I were that woman, this is still not a date. You can't just decide to be on a date halfway through an evening together. There's planning and preparation. You'd have to take me someplace nicer than this old kitchen, and I would wear a pretty dress instead of my clothes from work. A date is a whole experience."

"Fair enough," Colin agreed, taking another bite of his pizza. "This isn't a date."

Natalie turned to her food, ignoring the nervous butterflies that were fluttering in her stomach. It wasn't a date, but it certainly felt like one.

They cleaned up the kitchen together and opted to climb in the attic to take a look at what was up there before they called it a night. Colin's father had had the attic finished when they moved in, so the space was a little dusty, but it wasn't the treacherous, cobweb-filled space most attics were.

"Wow," Natalie said as she reached the top of the stairs. "There's a lot of stuff up here."

She was right. Colin looked around, feeling a little intimidated by the project he'd put on himself. He'd put all this off for too long, though. Giving the house to Lily and Frankie was the right thing to do and the motivation he needed to actually get it done.

He reached for a plastic tote and peeked inside. It was filled with old Christmas decorations. After further investigation, he realized that was what the majority of the items were. "My parents always went all out at Christmas," he said. "I think we've found their stash."

There were boxes of garland, lights, ornaments and lawn fixtures. A five-foot, light-up Santa stood in the corner beside a few white wooden reindeer that lit up and moved.

"This is what you were looking for, right?" Natalie asked. "You said you wanted to decorate the house for the holidays."

He nodded and picked up a copy of *A Visit From St. Nicholas* from one of the boxes. His father had read that to them every year on Christmas Eve, even when he and his sister were far too old for that sort of thing. In the years since they'd passed, Colin would've given anything to sit and listen to his father read that to him again.

"This is perfect," he said. "I have to go through all this to see what still works, but it's a great start. I'll just have to get a tree for the living room. What do you think?"

Natalie shrugged. "I told you before, I'm not much of an expert on Christmas."

He'd forgotten. "So, what's that about, Grinch?"

"Ha-ha," she mocked, heading toward the stairs.

Colin snatched an old Santa's hat out of a box and followed her down. He slipped it on. "Ho-ho-ho!" he shouted in his jolliest voice. "Little girl, tell Santa why you don't like Christmas. Did I forget the pony you asked for?"

Natalie stopped on the landing and turned around to look at him. She tried to hide her smirk with her hand, but the light in her eyes gave away her amusement. "You look like an idiot."

"Come on," he insisted. "We've already talked about my matrimonial betrayal. It can't be a bigger downer than that."

"Pretty close," Natalie said, crossing her arms defensively over her chest. "My dad left on Christmas day."

The smile faded from his face. He pulled off the Santa hat. "I didn't know about that."

"Why would you? I'm sure you were spared the messy details."

"What happened?"

"I'm not entirely sure. They'd been fighting a bunch leading up to Christmas, but I think they were trying to hold it together through the holidays. That morning, we opened presents and had breakfast, the same as usual. Then, as I sat in the living room playing with my new Nintendo, I heard some shouting and doors slamming. The next thing I know, my dad is standing in the living room with his suitcases. He just moved out right then. I haven't celebrated Christmas since that day."

"You haven't celebrated at all? In fifteen years?"

"Nope. I silently protested for a few holidays, passed between parents, but once I went to college, it was done. No decorations, no presents, no Christmas carols."

He was almost sorry he'd asked. So many of Colin's favorite memories had revolved around the holidays with his parents. Even after they died, Christmas couldn't be ruined. He just worked that much harder to make it special for Lily. He'd always dreamed of the day he'd celebrate the holidays with his own family. He'd gotten a taste of it when they celebrated Shane's first Christmas, but not long after that, he learned the truth about his son's real father.

"That's the saddest thing I've ever heard." And coming from a guy whose life had fallen apart in the past year, that was saying a lot.

"Divorce happens," Natalie said. A distant, almost ambivalent look settled on her face. She continued down the stairs to the ground floor. "It happens to hundreds of couples every day. It happened to you. Heck, it's happened to my mother three times. She's on her fourth husband. My sad story isn't that uncommon."

"I actually wasn't talking about the divorce." Colin stepped down onto the first-floor landing and reached out to grip the railing. "I mean, I'm sure it was awful for you to live through your parents' split. I just hate that it ruined Christmas for you. Christmas is such a special time. It's about family and friends, magic and togetherness. It's a good thing we've decided to just be friends because I could never be with someone who didn't like Christmas."

"Really? It's that important?"

"Yep. I look forward to it all year. I couldn't imagine not celebrating."

"It's easier than you think. I stay busy with work or I try to travel."

Colin could only shake his head. She wasn't interested in long-term relationships or holidays, both things most people seemed to want or enjoy. Her parents' divorce must've hit at a crucial age for her. He couldn't help reaching out to put a soothing arm around her shoulder. "You shouldn't let your parents' crap ruin your chances for having a happy holiday for the rest of your life."

"I don't miss it," she said, shying away from his touch, although she didn't meet his eyes when she said it.

He didn't fully believe her. Just like he didn't believe her when she said she wasn't interested in going on a date with him. She did want to, she was just stubborn and afraid of intimacy. As much as he might be drawn to Natalie, he wasn't going to put himself in that boat again. He was tired of butting his head against relationship brick walls. But even if they were just friends, he couldn't let the Christmas thing slide. It was a challenge unlike any he'd had in a while.

"I think I could make you like Christmas again."

Natalie turned on her heel to look at him. Her eyebrow was arched curiously. "No, you can't."

"You don't have much faith in me. I can do anything I put my mind to."

"Be serious, Colin."

"I am serious," he argued.

"You can't make me like Christmas. That would take a lobotomy. Or a bout of amnesia. It won't happen otherwise."

He took a step closer, moving into her space. "If you're so confident, why don't we wager on it?"

Her dark eyes widened at him and she stepped back. "What? No. That's silly."

"Hmm…" Colin said, leaning in. "Sounds to me like you're too chicken to let me try. You know you'll lose the bet."

Natalie took another step backward until her back

was pressed against the front door. "I'm not scared. I'm just not interested in playing your little game."

"Come on. If you're so confident, it won't hurt to take me up on it. Name your victor's prize. We're going to be spending a lot of time together the next two weeks. This will make it more…interesting."

Natalie crossed her arms over her chest. "Okay, fine. You're going to lose, so it really doesn't matter. You have until the wedding reception to turn me into a Christmas fan again. If I win the bet, you have to pay for me to spend Christmas next year in Buenos Aires."

"Wow. Steep stakes," Colin said.

Natalie just shrugged it off. "Are you confident or not?"

Nice. Now she'd turned it so he was the chicken. "Of course I'm confident. You've got it. I'll even fly you there first class."

"And what do you want if you win?"

A million different options could've popped into his mind in that moment, but there was only one idea that really stuck with him. "In return, if I win the bet, you owe me…a kiss."

Natalie's eyebrow went up. "That's it? A kiss? I asked for a trip to South America."

Colin smiled. "Yep, that's all I want." It would be a nice little bonus to satisfy his curiosity, but in the end, he was more interested in bringing the magic back to Christmas for her. Everyone needed that in their life. He held out his hand. "Shall we shake on it and make this official?"

Natalie took a cleansing breath and nodded before taking his hand. He enveloped it with his own, noting how cold she was to the touch. She gasped as he held her, her eyes widening. "You're so warm," she said.

"I was about to mention how cold you are. What's the matter? Afraid you're going to lose the bet?"

She gave a soft smile and pulled her hand from his. "Not at all. I'm always cold."

"It *is* Christmastime," Colin noted. "That just means you'll need to bundle up when we go out in search of some Christmas spirit."

She frowned, a crease forming between her brows. "We're both really busy, Colin. What if I just kiss you now? Will you let the whole thing drop?"

Colin propped his palm on the wall over her shoulder and leaned in until they were separated by mere inches. He brought his hand up to cup her cheek, running the pad of this thumb across her full bottom lip. Her lips parted softly, her breath quickening as he got closer. He had been right. She was attracted to him, but that just wasn't enough for her to want more.

"You can kiss me now if you want to," he said. "But there's no way I'm dropping this bet."

His hand fell to his side as a smirk of irritation replaced the expression on her face. This was going to be more fun than he'd expected.

"It's getting late. I'd better get you home."

He pulled away, noting the slight downturn of Natalie's lips as he did. Was she disappointed that he didn't kiss her? He'd never met a woman who sent such conflicting signals before. He got the feeling she didn't know what she wanted.

She didn't need to worry. They might just be friends, but he would kiss her, and soon. Colin had no intention of losing this bet.

Four

Natalie was on pins and needles all day Thursday knowing that Colin would be coming for the cake tasting that afternoon. She was filled with this confusing mix of emotions. First, there was the apprehension over their bet. Colin was determined to get her in the Christmas spirit. Wednesday morning when she'd stepped outside, she found a fresh pine wreath on her front door with a big red velvet bow.

She was tempted to take it down, but she wouldn't. She could withstand his attempts, but she knew the more she resisted, the more she would see of Colin. That filled her with an almost teenage giddiness—the way she used to feel whenever Colin would smile at her when they were kids. It made her feel ridiculous considering nothing was going to happen between the two of them, and frankly, it was distracting her from her work. Thank goodness this weekend's wedding was a smaller affair.

She was about to call the florist to follow up on the bride's last-minute request for a few additional boutonnieres when she noticed a figure lurking in her doorway. It was Gretchen.

Natalie pulled off her earpiece. "Yes?"

"So Tuesday night, I was meeting a friend for dinner on this side of town and I happened to pass by the chapel around nine that night. I noticed your car was still in the parking lot."

Natalie tried not to frown at her coworker. "You know I work late sometimes."

"Yeah, that's what I thought at first, too, but none of the lights were on. Then I noticed on your Outlook calendar that you had a late appointment to discuss the Russell-Watson wedding." A smug grin crossed Gretchen's face.

Natalie rolled her eyes. "It was nothing, so don't turn it into something. We finalized the plans for the wedding, that's all. Then he asked me for help with his wedding present for Lily. He's giving her a house."

"A house? Lord," Gretchen declared with wide eyes. "I mean, I know I'm engaged to a movie star and all, but I have a hard time wrapping my head around how rich people think."

"It's actually the home they grew up in. He asked me to help him fix it up for them."

Gretchen nodded thoughtfully. "Did you help him rearrange some of the bedroom furniture?"

"Ugh, no." Natalie searched around her desk for something to throw, but all she had was a crystal paperweight shaped like a heart. She didn't want to knock

Gretchen unconscious, despite how gratifying it might feel in the moment. "We just walked around and talked about what I'd keep or donate. Nothing scandalous. I'm sorry to disappoint you."

"Well, boo. I was hopeful that this guy would make it up to you for his cruel rebuffing at the engagement party."

"He didn't make it up to me, but he did explain why he'd turned me down. Apparently he had a date that night."

"And now?"

"And now they've broken up. But that doesn't change anything. We're just going to be friends. It's better this way. Things would've just been more...complicated if something had happened."

Gretchen narrowed her gaze at her. "And you helping him with the house now that he's single won't be complicated?"

Natalie swung her ponytail over her shoulder and avoided her coworker's gaze by glancing at her computer screen. There were no critical emails to distract her from the conversation.

"Natalie?"

"No, it won't," she said at last. "It's going to be fine. We've been family friends for years and that isn't going to change. I'm going to handle the wedding and help him with the house and everything will be fine. Great, really. I think it's just the distraction I need to get through the holidays this year."

Gretchen nodded as she talked, but Natalie could tell she wasn't convinced. Frankly, neither was Natalie. Even as she said the words, she was speaking to herself as much as to her friend. She certainly wasn't going to tell her that she was fighting her attraction to Colin like a fireman with a five-alarm inferno. Or that she'd gotten herself roped into a bet that could cost her not only a kiss, but a solid dose of the holidays she had just said she was avoiding.

"Okay, well, whatever helps you get through the holidays, hon."

"Thank you."

"Uh-oh. Speak of the devil," Gretchen said, peeking out Natalie's window.

"He's here?" Natalie said, perking up in her seat, eyes wide with panic. "He's early." She was automatically opening her desk drawer and reaching for her compact when she heard Gretchen's low, evil laugh.

"No, he's not. I lied. I just wanted to see how you'd react. I was right. You're so full of it, your eyeballs should be floating."

Natalie sat back in her chair, the panic quickly replaced by irritation. Her gaze fell on the drawer to the soft foam rose stress ball that the florist had given them. She picked it up and hurled it at Gretchen, who ducked just in time.

"Get out of my office!" she shouted, but Gretchen was already gone. Natalie could hear her cackling down the hallway. Thank goodness there weren't any customers in the facility this morning.

There would be several clients here after lunchtime, though. Amelia had three cake tastings on the schedule today, including with Colin.

Hopefully that would go better than just now. Gretchen had already called her on the ridiculous infatuation that had reignited. Amelia would likely be more tactful. She hoped. Natalie didn't think she'd been that obvious. In the end, nothing *had* happened. They'd finalized plans, she'd helped him with the house and they'd had pizza. They hadn't kissed. She had certainly wanted to.

It was hard to disguise the overwhelming sense of disappointment she felt when they had their near miss. Natalie had been certain he was about to kiss her. She thought maybe dangling that carrot would serve her on two levels: first that they could call off the silly bet, and second, that she'd finally fulfill her youthful fantasy of kissing the dashing and handsome Colin Russell.

Then…nothing. He knew what he was doing. He'd turned up the dial, gotten her primed, then left her hanging. He was not letting her out of the bet. It might be a painful two weeks until the wedding while he tried, but in the end, she'd get a nice trip to Argentina out of it.

Colin was well-intentioned, but he wasn't going to turn her into a jolly ol' elf anytime soon. It wasn't as though she wanted to be a Humbug. She'd tried on several occasions to get into the spirit, but it never worked. The moment the carols started playing in the stores, she felt her soul begin to shrivel inside her. Honey-glazed ham tasted like ash in her mouth.

With her parents' marriages in shambles and no desire to ever start a family of her own, there wasn't anything left to the season but cold weather and commercialism.

That said, she didn't expect Colin to lose this bet quietly. He would try his damnedest, and if last night was any indication, he was willing to play dirty. If that was the case, she needed to as well. It wouldn't be hard to deploy her own distracting countermeasures. The chemistry between them was powerful and could easily derail his focus. She wouldn't have to go too far—a seductive smile and a gentle touch would easily plant something other than visions of sugarplums in his head.

Natalie reached back into the drawer for the mirror she'd sought out earlier. She looked over her hair and re-applied her burgundy lipstick. She repowdered her nose, then slipped everything back into her desk. Glancing down at her outfit, she opted to slip out of her blazer, leaving just the sleeveless burgundy and hunter-green satin shell beneath it. It had a deep V-neck cut, and the necklace she was wearing today would no doubt draw the eye down to the depths of her cleavage.

Finally, she dabbed a bit of perfume behind her ears, on her wrists and just between her collarbones. It was her favorite scent, exotic and complex, bringing to mind perfumed silk tents in the deserts of Arabia. A guy she'd once dated had told her that perfume was like a hook, luring him closer with the promise of sex.

She took a deep breath of the fragrance and smiled. It was playing dirty, but she had a bet to win.

"I brought you a gift."

Colin watched Natalie look up at him from her desk with a startled expression. From the looks of it, she'd been deep into her work and lost track of time. She recovered quickly, sitting back in her chair and pulling off her headset. "Did you? What is it now? A light-up snowman? A three-foot candy cane?"

"Close." He whipped out a box from behind his back and placed it on her desk. "It's peppermint bark from a candy shop downtown."

Natalie smirked at the box, opening it to admire the

contents. "Are you planning to buy your way through this whole bet?"

"Maybe. Either way, it's cheaper than a first-class ticket to Buenos Aires."

"You added the first class part yourself, you know, when you were feeling cocky." She leaned her elbows on the desk and watched him pointedly.

His gaze was drawn to a gold-and-emerald pendant that dangled just at the dip of her neckline. The shadows hinted at the breasts just beyond the necklace. He caught a whiff of her perfume and felt the muscles in his body start to tense. What were they talking about? Cocky. Yes. That was certainly on point. "Do you like the wreath?" he asked, diverting the subject.

"It's lovely," she said, sitting back with a satisfied smile that made him think she was teasing him on purpose.

That was definitely a change from that night at the house. She'd been adamant about being the wrong kind of woman for him and that they should be friends. Now she was almost dangling herself in front of him. He couldn't complain about the view, but he had to question the motivation.

"It makes my entryway smell like a pine forest."

At least she hadn't said Pine-Sol. "You're supposed to say it smells like Christmas."

"I don't know what Christmas is supposed to smell like. When I was a kid, Christmas smelled like burned biscuits and the nasty floral air freshener my mom would spray to keep my grandmother from finding out she was smoking again."

Colin winced at her miserable holiday memories. It sounded as though her Christmas experiences sucked long before her dad left. His next purchase was going to be a mulling spice candle. "That is not what Christmas smells like. It smells like pine and peppermint, spiced cider and baking sugar cookies."

"Maybe in Hallmark stores," she said, pushing up from her chair and glancing at her watch. "But now we need to focus on cake, not sugar cookies."

Colin followed her into a sitting room near the kitchen. It had several comfortable wingback chairs and a loveseat surrounding a coffee table.

"Have a seat." Natalie gestured into the room.

"Are you joining me?" he asked as he passed near to her.

"Oh yes," she said with a coy smile. "I've just got to let Amelia know we're ready."

He stepped inside and Natalie disappeared down the hallway. He was happy to have a moment alone. The smell of her skin mingling with her perfume and that naughty smile was a combination he couldn't take much more of. At least not and keep his hands off her.

Something had definitely changed since Tuesday. Tuesday night, she'd been more open and friendly once he told her why he'd turned her down, but nothing like this. Not even when she'd leaned into him, thinking he was about to kiss her.

Perhaps she was trying to distract him. Did she think that keeping his mind occupied with thoughts of her would shift the focus away from bringing Christmas joy back into her life? This had all happened after the bet, so that had to be it. *Tricky little minx*. That was playing dirty after her big speech about how she wasn't the right kind of woman for him. Well, two could play at that game. If he was right, now that he knew her ploy he'd let her see how far she was willing to push it to win.

No matter what, he wouldn't let himself be ensnared by her feminine charms. They were oil and water that wouldn't mix. But that didn't mean he wouldn't enjoy letting her try. And it didn't mean he'd let himself lose sight of the bet in the process.

He heard a click of heels on wood and a moment later Natalie came back into the room. She settled onto the loveseat beside him. Before he could say anything, the caterer, Amelia, blew in behind her.

"Okay," Amelia said as she carried a silver platter into the room and placed it on the coffee table. "Time for some cake tasting. This is the best part of planning a wedding, I think. Here are five of our most popular cake flavors." She pointed her manicured finger at the different cubes of cake that were stacked into elegant pyramids. "There's a white almond sour cream cake, triple chocolate fudge, red velvet, pistachio and lemon pound cake. In the bowls, we've got an assortment of different fillings along with samples of both my buttercream and my marshmallow fondant. The cake design you selected will work with either finish, so it's really just a matter of what taste you prefer."

"It all looks wonderful, Amelia. Thanks for putting this together."

"Sure thing. On this card, it has all the flavors listed along with some popular combinations you might like to try. For a wedding of your size, I usually recommend two choices. I can do alternating tiers, so if a guest doesn't one like flavor, they can always try the other. The variety is nice. Plus, it makes it easier to choose if you have more than one you love."

"Great," Colin said, taking the card from her and setting it on the table. He watched as the caterer shot a pointed look at Natalie on the couch beside him.

"And if you don't mind, since Natalie is here with you, I'm going to go clean up in the kitchen. I've got another cake to finish piping tonight."

Colin nodded. He was fine being alone with Natalie. That left the door open for her little games anyway. "That's fine. I'm sure you've got plenty to do. Thanks for fitting me in on such short notice."

"Thanks, Amelia," Natalie said. "If we have any questions about the cake, I'll come get you."

Amelia nodded and slipped out of the room. Colin watched her go, then turned back to the platter in front of them. "Where should we start?"

Natalie picked up the card from the table. "I'd go with Amelia's suggestions. She knows her cake."

"Great. What's first?"

"White almond sour cream cake with lemon curd."

They both selected small squares of cake from the plate, smearing them with a touch of the filling using a small silver butter knife. Colin wasn't a big fan of lemon, but even he had to admit this was one of the best bites of cake he'd ever had.

And it was just the beginning. They tried them all, mixing chocolate cake with chocolate chip mousse, lemon pound cake with raspberry buttercream and red velvet with whipped cream cheese. There were a million different combinations to choose from. He was glad he'd eaten a light lunch because by the time they finished, all the cake was gone and his suit pants were a bit tighter than they'd been when he sat down.

"I don't know how we're going to choose," he said

at last. "It was all great. I don't think there was a single thing I didn't like."

"I told you she did great work."

Colin turned to look at Natalie, noticing she had a bit of buttercream icing in the corner of her mouth. "Uh-oh."

"What?" Natalie asked with concern lining her brow.

"You've got a little…" his voice trailed off as he reached out and wiped the icing away with the pad of his thumb. "…frosting. I got it," he said with a smile.

Natalie looked at the icing on the tip of his thumb. She surprised him by grasping his wrist to keep him from pulling away. With her eyes pinned on his, she leaned in and gently placed his thumb in her mouth. She sucked off the icing, gliding her tongue over his skin. Colin's groin tightened and blood started pumping hard through his veins.

She finally let go, a sweet smile on her face that didn't quite match her bold actions. "I didn't want any to go to waste."

For once in his life, Colin acted without thinking. He lunged for her, capturing her lips with his and clutching at her shoulders. He waited for Natalie to stiffen or struggle away from him, but she didn't. Instead, she brought up her hands to hold his face close to her, as though she was afraid he might pull away too soon.

Her lips were soft and tasted like sweet vanilla buttercream. He'd had plenty of cake today, but he couldn't get enough of her mouth. There was no hesitation in her touch, her tongue gliding along his just as she'd tortured him with his thumb a moment ago.

Finally, he pulled away. It took all his willpower to do it, but he knew he needed to. This was a wedding chapel, not a hotel room. He didn't move far, though. His hand was still resting on Natalie's upper arm, his face mere inches from hers. She was breathing hard, her cheeks flushed as her hands fell into her lap.

He could tell that he'd caught her off guard at first with that kiss, but he didn't care. She'd brought that on herself with her distracting games. If her body was any indicator, she hadn't minded. She'd clung to him, met him measure for measure. For someone who thought they were unsuitable for each other, she'd certainly participated in that kiss.

He just wished he knew that she wanted to, and she wasn't just doing it as a distraction to help her win the bet. There was one way to find out. She wasn't good at hiding her initial emotional responses, so he decided to push a few buttons. "So, what do you think?" he asked.

Natalie looked at him with glassy, wide eyes. "About what?"

"About the cake. I'm thinking definitely the white cake with the lemon, but I'm on the fence about the second choice."

Natalie stiffened, the hazy bliss vanishing in an instant. He could tell that cake was not what she'd had on her mind in that moment. She'd let her little game go too far. He was glad he wasn't the only one affected by it.

"Red velvet," she said. She sniffed delicately and sat back, pulling away from him. Instantly, she'd transformed back into the uptight, efficient wedding planner. "It's a universal flavor. I'm told it's a Christmas classic, so it suits the theme. It's also one of my favorites, so admittedly I'm partial."

"Okay. The choices are made. Thanks for being so... helpful."

Natalie looked at him with a narrowed gaze that softened as the coy smile from earlier returned. "My pleasure."

Five

Monday afternoon, Colin made a stop by Frankie's motorcycle store on his way home from his latest work site.

When he'd first found out that his sister was dating a guy who looked more like a biker than a businessman, he'd been hesitant. Meeting Frankie and visiting his custom bike shop downtown had changed things. Yes, he had more tattoos than Colin could count and several piercings, but he was a talented artisan of his craft. The motorcycles he designed and built were metal masterpieces that earned a high price. Over the past year, Frankie's business had really started to take off. It looked like he and Lily would have a promising future together.

Slipping into the shop, Colin walked past displays of parts, gear and accessories to the counter at the back. Lily was sitting at the counter. Frankie had hired her to run the register, making the business a family affair. Living upstairs from the shop had made it convenient, but he couldn't imagine they had enough space to raise a family there or even stretch their legs.

"Hey, brother of mine," Lily called from the counter. "Can I interest you in a chopper?"

"Very funny." Colin laughed.

Lily came out from behind the counter to give him a hug. "If not for a bike, to what do I owe this visit?"

"Well, I thought you might want to know about some of the wedding plans Natalie and I have put together." Colin had a copy of the design portfolio to show her. He hoped that by showing her the designs, she would start getting more excited about the wedding.

Lily shrugged and drifted back to her post behind the counter. "I'm sure whatever you've chosen will be great."

"At least look at it," Colin said, opening the folder on the counter. "Natalie and her partners have worked really hard on putting together a beautiful wedding for you. We went with the winter wonderland theme you and Natalie discussed. For the cake, we chose alternating tiers of white almond sour cream cake with lemon curd filling and red velvet with cream cheese. Natalie said those were two of their most popular flavors, and they were both really tasty."

"Sounds great," Lily said, sitting back onto her stool. "I have no doubt that it will come together beautifully. As long as I have someone to marry us, it's fine by me. The rest of this is just a bonus."

"Have you ordered a dress yet?"

His sister shook her head. "No."

Colin frowned. "Lily, you don't have a dress?"

"I was just going to pull something from my closet. I have that white dress from my sorority induction ceremony."

"Are you serious? You've got to go get a wedding dress, Lily."

His sister shrugged again, sending Colin's blood pressure higher. He couldn't fathom how she didn't care about any of this. Pam hadn't been very interested in planning their wedding either. Since they were in a hurry, they'd ended up with a courthouse visit without frills. It was a little anticlimactic. He didn't want that for Lily, but she seemed indifferent about the whole thing.

"I've got a job, Colin. Frankie and I work at the shop six days a week. I can't go running around trying on fluffy Cinderella dresses. If you are so concerned with what I'm wearing, you can pick it out. I wear a size six. Natalie and I used to be able to share clothes when we were teenagers. At the engagement party she looked like she might still wear the same size as I do. I'm sure you two can work it out without me."

Colin fought the urge to drop his face into his hands in dismay. "Will you at least go to a dress fitting?"

"Yeah, sure."

"Okay. So we'll get a dress." He pulled out his phone to call Natalie and let her know the bad news. He knew she had been busy over the weekend with a wedding, so he hadn't bothered her with wedding or holiday details. He couldn't wait any longer, though. He was certain this was an important detail and could be the very thing that pushed his cool, calm and collected wedding planner over the edge.

She didn't answer, so he left a quick message on her

phone. When he slipped his phone back into his pocket, he noticed Lily watching him. "What?"

"Your voice changed when you left her a message."

"I was trying to soften the blow," he insisted.

Lily shook her head. "I don't know. That voice sounded like the same voice I remember from when you would tie up the house phone talking to girls in high school. What's going on between you two?"

"Going on?" Colin tried to find the best way to word it. "I don't know. We've spent a lot of time together planning the wedding. Things have been…interesting."

"Are you dating?"

"No," Colin said more confidently. He was determined not to wade into that territory with Natalie. She was beautiful and smart and alluring, but she also had it in her to crush him. "Natalie and I have very different ideas on what constitutes a relationship."

Lily nodded. "Natalie has never been the princess waiting for her prince to save her. She always kept it casual with guys. I take it you're not interested in a booty call. You should consider it. Going from serious relationship to serious relationship isn't working for you either."

Colin did not want to have this conversation with his little sister. Instead, he ignored the kernel of truth in her words. "I am not going to discuss booty calls with you. I can't believe I even said that phrase out loud."

"Have you kissed her?"

He didn't answer right away.

"Colin?"

"Yes, I kissed her."

Lily made a thoughtful clicking sound with her tongue. "Interesting," she said slowly, her hands planted on her hips. "What exactly do you—?"

Colin's phone started to ring at his hip, interrupting her query. He'd never been so relieved to get a call. "I've got to take this," he said, answering the phone and moving to the front of the shop. "Hello?"

"There's no dress?" It was Natalie, her displeasure evident by the flat tone of her query.

"That is correct," he said with a heavy sigh. "And like everything else, she says to just pick something. Lily says she's a size six and that you used to share clothes, so fake it."

"Fake it?" Natalie shrieked into his ear.

"Yep." He didn't know what else to say.

Natalie sat silent on the other end of the line for a moment. "I need to make a few calls. Can you meet me at a bridal salon tonight?"

Colin looked down at his watch. It was already after five. Did they have enough time? "Sure."

"Okay. I'll call you back and let you know where to meet me."

Colin hung up, turning to see a smug look on his sister's face.

"I told you she could handle it."

"That well may be, but she wasn't happy about it." At this point, they'd probably be lucky if Lily didn't go down the aisle in a white trash bag. They had about two weeks to pick the dress, order it, have it come in and do any alterations. He wasn't much of a wedding expert, but he got the feeling it would be a rough road. "What about Frankie? Do I need to dress him, too?"

Lily shook her head and Colin felt a wave of relief wash over him. "He's good. He's got a white suit and picked out a silver bowtie and suspenders to go with the theme."

He should've known a bit of hipster style would make its way into this wedding. Whatever. It was one less person he had to dress.

Returning to the counter, he closed the wedding portfolio. He was anxious to get out of here before Lily started up the conversation about Natalie again. "Okay, well, I'm off to meet Natalie at some bridal salon. Any other surprises you're waiting to tell me until an inopportune time?"

The slight twist of Lily's lips was proof that there was. "Well..." she hesitated. "I kind of forgot about this before, but it should be fine."

Somehow, he doubted that. "What, Lily?"

"Next week, Frankie and I are flying to Las Vegas for a motorcycle convention."

"Next week? Lily, the wedding is next week."

"The wedding isn't until Saturday. We're flying back Friday. No problem."

Colin dropped his forehead into his hand and squeezed at his temples. "What time on Friday? You've got the rehearsal that afternoon and the rehearsal dinner after that."

"Hmm..." she said thoughtfully, reaching for her phone. She flipped through the screens to pull up her calendar. "Our flight is scheduled to arrive in Nashville at one. That should be plenty of time, right?"

"Right." He didn't bother to point out that it was winter and weather delays were a very real concern this time of year. With his luck, she was connecting in Chicago or Detroit. "When do you leave?"

"Monday."

Colin nodded. Well, at the very least, he knew he

could work on the house without worrying about her stopping by and ruining the surprise.

A chime on his phone announced a text. Natalie had sent him the name and address of the bridal shop where they were meeting.

"Anything else I need to know, Lil?"

She smiled innocently, reminding him of the sweet girl with pigtails he remembered growing up. "Nope. That's it."

"Okay," he said, slipping his phone back into his pocket. "I'm off to buy you a wedding dress."

"Good luck," she called to him as he slipped out of the store.

He'd need it.

Natalie swallowed her apprehension as she went into the bridal shop. Not because she had to get Lily a dress at the last minute—that didn't surprise her at all. They were close enough to sample size to buy something out of the shop and alter it.

Really, she was more concerned about trying on wedding dresses. It wasn't for her, she understood that, but it still felt odd. She'd never tried on a wedding dress before, not even for fun. Her mother had sold her wedding dress when her parents divorced.

She knew it was just a dress, but there was something transformative about it. She didn't want to feel that feeling. That was worse than Christmas spirit.

She'd avoided the bulk of Colin's holiday bet by staying busy with a wedding all weekend. But now it was the start of a new week and she had no doubt he would find some way to slip a little Christmas into each day.

In addition to the wreath and the peppermint bark,

she'd also received a Christmas card that played carols when she opened it. A local bakery had delivered a fruitcake to the office on Friday, and a florist had brought a poinsettia on Saturday morning.

What he didn't know was that she'd received plenty of well-meaning holiday gifts throughout the years. That wasn't going to crack her. It just gave her a plant to water every other day.

As she entered the waiting room of the salon, she found Colin and the storekeeper, Ruby, searching through the tall racks of gowns. Ruby looked up as she heard Natalie approach.

"Miss Sharpe! There you are. Mr. Russell and I were looking through a few gowns while we waited."

"Not a problem. Thanks for scheduling us with such late notice."

"This is the bridal business," Ruby said with a dismissive chuckle. "You never know what you'll get. For every girl that orders her gown a year in advance, I get one pregnant and in-a-hurry bride that needs a gown right away. After being in this industry for twenty years, I've learned to keep a good stock of dresses on hand for times like this."

Ruby was good at what she did. Natalie referred a lot of brides to her salon because of it. "Did Colin fill you in on what we need?"

"Yes. He said you need something in a street size six that will fit a winter wonderland theme. He also said the bride won't be here to try them on."

"That's correct. We wear the same size, so I'll try on the dresses in her place."

"Okay. I'd recommend something with a corset back. You don't have a lot of time for alterations and with a corset bodice, you can tighten or loosen it to account for any adjustments in your sizes."

Brilliant. She'd have to remember this in the future for quick-turnaround brides. "Perfect."

"Great. If you'd like to take a seat, Mr. Russell, I'll take Miss Sharpe to the dressing room to try on a few gowns to see what you like."

"Have fun," Colin said, waving casually at her as she was ushered into the back.

She was officially on the other side now. She'd passed the curtain where only brides went. It made her stomach ache.

"I've pulled these three dresses to start with. I think you're pretty close to the sample size, so this should be a decent fit. Which would you like to try first?"

Natalie looked over the gowns with apprehension. She needed to think like Lily. Everything else about the wedding had turned out to be Natalie's choice, but when it came to dresses, it seemed wrong to pick something she liked. "It doesn't matter," she said. "I'm going to let her brother choose."

"Then let's start with the ruched satin gown."

Natalie slipped out of her blouse and pencil skirt and let Ruby slip the gown over her head. She was fully aware how heavy bridal gowns could be, but for some reason, it seemed so much heavier on than she had expected it to.

She held the gown in place as Ruby tightened the corset laces in the back. Looking in the mirror, she admired the fit of the gown. The corset gave her a curvy, seductive shape she hadn't expected. She never felt much like a sex kitten. Her shape had always been a little lanky and boyish in her opinion, but the gown changed that.

The decorative crystals that lined the sweetheart neckline drew the eyes to her enhanced cleavage.

"Do you like the snowflake?"

Natalie narrowed her gaze at her reflection and noticed the crystal design at her hip that looked very much like a snowflake. Perfect for the theme. "It's nice. It's got a good shape and the crystals give it a little shine without being overpowering."

"Let's go show him."

There was more apprehension as Natalie left the dressing room. This wasn't about her, but she wanted to look the best she could when she stepped onto the riser to show him the gown. She focused on her posture and grace as she glided out into the salon.

Her gaze met his the minute she cleared the curtain. His golden hazel eyes raked up and down the length of the gown with the same heat of appreciation she'd seen that night at the engagement party. Natalie felt a flush of heat rise to her cheeks as she stepped onto the pedestal for his inspection.

"It's beautiful," he said. "It's very elegant and you look amazing in it. But I have to say that it's not right for Lily at all."

Natalie sighed and looked down. He was right. "Ruby, do we have one that's a little more whimsical and fun?"

Ruby nodded and helped her down. "I have a few that might work. How fun are we talking?" she asked as they stepped back into the dressing room. "Crazy tulle skirt? Blush- or pink-colored gowns?"

"If she was here, probably all that and more. But she should've shown up herself if she had that strong of an opinion. Let's go for something a little more whimsical, but still classically bridal."

The minute Ruby held up the gown, Natalie knew this dress was the one. It was like something out of a winter fantasy—the gown of the snow queen. It was a fitted, mermaid style with a sweetheart neckline and sheer, full-length sleeves. All across the gown and along the sleeves were delicate white-and-silver-stitched floral designs that looked almost like glittering snowflakes dancing across her skin.

She held her breath as she slipped into the gown and got laced up. Ruby fastened a few buttons at her shoulders and then it was done. It was the most beautiful dress she'd ever seen, and she'd seen hundreds of brides come through the chapel over the years.

"This gown has a matching veil with the same lace trim along the edges. Do you want to go out there with it on?"

"Yes," she said immediately. Natalie wanted to see the dress with the veil. She knew it would make all the difference.

Ruby swiftly pinned her hair up and set the veil's comb in. The veil flowed all the way to floor, longer than even the gown's chapel-length train.

It was perfect. Everything she'd ever wanted.

Natalie swallowed hard. Everything she'd ever wanted *for Lily*, she corrected herself. Planning a wedding in the bride's place was messing with her head.

She headed back out to the salon. This time, she avoided Colin's gaze, focusing on lifting the hem of the skirt to step up on the pedestal. She glanced at herself for only a moment in the three-sided mirror, but even that was enough for the prickle of tears to form in her eyes.

Quickly, she jerked away, turning to face Colin. She covered her tears by fidgeting with her gown and veil.

"What do you think of this one?" Ruby asked.

The long silence forced Natalie to finally meet Colin's gaze. Did he hate it?

Immediately, she knew that was not the case. He was just stunned speechless.

"Colin?"

"Wow," he finally managed. He stood up from the velour settee and walked closer.

Natalie felt her chest grow tighter with every step. He wasn't looking at the gown. Not really. He was looking at her. The intensity of his gaze made her insides turn molten. Her knees started trembling and she was thankful for the full skirt that covered them.

Just when she thought she couldn't bear his gaze any longer, his eyes dropped down to look over the details of the dress. "This is the one. No question."

Natalie took a breath and looked down to examine the dress. "Do you think Lily will like it?"

Colin hesitated a moment, swallowing hard before he spoke. "I do. It will look beautiful on her. I don't think we could find a dress better suited to the theme you've put together." He took a step back and nodded again from a distance. "Let's get this one."

"Wonderful!" Ruby exclaimed. "This one really is lovely."

The older woman went to the counter to write up the slip, completely oblivious to the energy in the room that hummed between Natalie and Colin. Natalie wasn't quite sure how she didn't notice it. It made it hard for

Natalie to breathe. It made the dress feel hot and itchy against her skin even though it was the softest, most delicate fabric ever made.

Colin slipped back down onto the couch with a deep sigh. When he looked up at her again, Natalie knew she wasn't mistaken about any of this. He wanted her. And she wanted him. It was a bad idea, they both knew it, but they couldn't fight it much longer.

She also wanted out of this dress. Right now. Playing bride was a confusing and scary experience. Before Colin or Ruby could say another word, she pulled the veil from her head, leaped down from the pedestal and disappeared behind the curtains into the dressing room as fast as she could.

Six

"I'd like to take you to dinner," Colin said as they walked out of the shop with the gown bagged over his arm. "I'm serious this time. You really bailed me out on this whole dress thing."

It was a lame excuse. It sounded lame to his own ears, but he couldn't do anything about it. There was no way he could look at Natalie, to see her in that dress looking like the most beautiful creature he'd ever set his eyes on, and then let her just get in her car and go home. It no longer mattered if they were incompatible or had no future. The taste of her already lingered on his lips, the heat of her hummed through his veins. He wanted her. End of story.

Natalie stopped and swung her purse strap up onto her shoulder. "Dinner? Not a date?"

This again. You'd think after their kiss, and after the intense moment they'd just shared in the salon, that she wouldn't be so picky about the details. "No, it's not a date, it's a thank-you. I believe that I have yet to meet your stringent qualifications for a date."

Natalie's lips curled into a smile of amusement. He expected her to make an excuse and go home, but instead she nodded. "Dinner sounds great."

Colin opened the door of his truck and hung the gown bag up inside. "How about the Italian place on the corner?"

"That's perfect."

He closed up the truck and they walked down the sidewalk together to the restaurant. Colin had eaten at Moretti's a couple of times and it had always been good. It was rustic Italian cuisine, with a Tuscan feel inside. The walls were a rusty brown with exposed brick, worn wood shelves and tables, warm gold lighting and an entire wall on the far end that was covered in hundreds of wine bottles. It wasn't the fanciest place, but it was a good restaurant for a casual dinner date, or a thank-you dinner as the case was here.

It was a pretty popular place to eat in this area. Typically, Moretti's was super busy, but coming later on a Monday night the restaurant was pretty quiet. There were about a dozen tables with customers when they arrived and no waiting list.

The hostess immediately escorted them to a booth for two near the roaring fireplace. Nashville didn't get very cold in the winter, but with the icy December wind, it was cold enough that the fire would feel amazing after their walk down the street. Colin helped Natalie out of her coat, hanging it on one of the brass hooks mounted to the side of the booth.

The waiter arrived just as they'd settled into their

seats, bringing water and warm bread with olive oil. He offered them the daily menus and left them alone to make their choices. After a bit of deliberation, Natalie chose the angel-hair primavera and Colin, the chicken parmesan. They selected a bottle of cabernet to share and the waiter returned with that immediately.

The first sip immediately warmed Colin's belly and cheeks, reminding him to go slow until he ate some bread. He'd had a quick sandwich around eleven, but he was starving now and wine on an empty stomach might make him say or do something he'd regret, like kissing Natalie again. Or maybe he'd do something he wouldn't regret, but shouldn't do. At the moment, Lily's suggestion that he indulge himself in something casual with Natalie was sounding pretty good. He took a bite of bread as a precaution.

"Well, this is certainly not how I envisioned this evening going," Natalie noted as she tore her own chunk of bread from the loaf.

"It's not bad, is it?"

"No," she admitted. "But when I woke up this morning, I didn't figure I'd be trying on wedding dresses and having dinner with you."

It hadn't been on his radar either, but he was happy with the turn of events. There was something about spending an evening with Natalie that relaxed him after a stressful day. "Did you have plans for tonight that I ruined?"

"Not real plans. I'd anticipated a frozen dinner and a couple chapters of a new book I downloaded."

"I was going to grab takeout and catch up on my DVR. We're an exciting pair. Are you off tomorrow?"

Natalie shrugged, confusing him with her response

to a simple question. "Technically," she clarified. "The chapel is closed on Tuesday and Wednesday, but I usually go in."

"That means you don't get any days off."

"I don't usually work a full day. And I only work half of Sunday to clean up."

Colin shook his head. "You sound as bad as I used to be when I took over Dad's business. I worked eighteen-hour days, seven days a week trying to keep afloat. Is that why you put in so many hours? How's the wedding business?"

If the bill he'd received for the upcoming wedding was any indication, they were doing very well. He'd told her money was no object and she'd believed him. It was well worth it for Lily, but he'd been surprised to see so many digits on the invoice.

"Business is great. That's why it's so hard not to come in. There's always something to do."

"Can't you hire someone to watch the place and answer the phones while you all take time off? Like a receptionist?"

Natalie bit her lip and took a large sip of wine as though she were delaying her response. "I guess we could. Anyways, I'm the only one without a backup, but I'm the only one of us without a life. It's kind of hard to swap out the wedding planner, though. I'm the one with the whole vision of the day and know all the pieces that have to fall into place just perfectly."

"Getting a receptionist isn't the same as getting a backup planner. It just frees you up so you're not answering the phones and filing paperwork all the time. You should look into it. Of course, that would require you not to be such a control freak."

Natalie perked up in her seat. "I am not a control freak."

At that, Colin laughed. "Oh, come on now. Your office is immaculate. You're always stomping around with that headset on, handling every emergency. I'm beginning to think you run a one-stop wedding company because you won't let anyone else do any of it."

She opened her mouth to argue, then stopped. "Maybe I should look into a receptionist," she admitted.

"If you had one, you could spend the next two days with me instead of sitting alone in that lonely office of yours."

Natalie's eyebrow raised in question. "Spend the next two days with you doing what?"

"Working on the house. Helping me decorate. What we discussed last week. I've turned over the reins of the company to my second-in-command to manage our remaining projects through the end of the year so I can focus on what I need to do before the holidays."

"Oh."

That wasn't the enthusiastic response he was hoping for. "Oh, huh? I guess I should sweeten the deal, then. Spending time with me to help your childhood best friend isn't enough incentive."

"Quit it," Natalie chided. "I told you I'd help you with the house. Since I work on weekends, it makes sense to come over tomorrow, you're right. And I will. I was just expecting something else."

"Like what?"

"I don't know…a trip to the Opryland Hotel to look at the Christmas decorations and visit Santa, maybe?"

Opryland! Colin silently cursed and sipped his wine to cover his aggravation. The hotel in central Nashville was practically its own city. They went all out every holiday with massive decorations. They usually built a giant ice village with slides kids could play on. They even hosted the Rockettes' Christmas show. That would've been perfect, but of course he couldn't do it now that she'd brought it up. He refused to be predictable.

There wasn't really time for that, either. When he'd made that impulsive bet, he hadn't given a lot of thought to how much they both worked and how incompatible their schedules were. Between their jobs, working on the house and the wedding, there wasn't much time left to reintroduce Natalie to the holiday magic. He'd find a way, though. He was certain of it.

"I figured it was something related to the bet, although I don't know why you'd bother after that kiss we shared at the cake tasting. I'm not sure the one you'll win will be better than that."

Colin smiled wide. "Are you serious?" he asked.

She looked at him blankly. "Well, yes. It was a pretty good kiss, as kisses go."

"It was an amazing kiss," Colin conceded. "But it won't hold a candle to the kiss I'll get when I win."

Natalie sucked in a ragged breath, her pale skin growing a more peachy-pink tone in the golden candlelight. "I guess as a teenager I never realized how arrogant you were."

"It's not arrogance when it's fact. I intend to make your pulse spike and cheeks flush. I want you to run your fingers through my hair and hold me like you never want to let me go. When I win this bet, I'll kiss you until you're breathless and can't imagine ever kissing anyone else."

He watched Natalie swallow hard and reach a shaky hand out for more wine. He hid away his smile and focused on her so she knew he meant every word.

"Y-you've still g-got to win the bet," she stammered. "I'm pretty sure you've run out of Christmas stuff to mail to the office."

"Don't underestimate me," Colin said. "Those holiday gifts were just to get you in the right mindset." There were a lot of sensory elements to Christmas—the smell of pine and mulling spice, the taste of peppermint and chocolate, the sight of bright lights and colorful poinsettias. "I wanted to…prime the pump, so to speak. When you're ready, that's when I'll move in for the kill."

The waiter arrived with their salads, but Colin had suddenly lost his appetite. He knew what he wanted to taste and it wasn't on the Moretti's menu. A part of him knew it was a mistake to let himself go any further with Natalie, but the other part already knew it was too late. He needed to have her. Knowing nothing would come of it going in, he would be able to compartmentalize it. Just because he rarely had sex for sex's sake didn't mean he couldn't. What they had was a raw, physical attraction, nothing more. Natalie was certainly an enticing incentive to try to start now.

Perhaps if he did, he could focus on something else for a change. He had plenty going on right now, but somehow, Natalie's full bottom lip seemed to occupy all his thoughts.

As they ate, Natalie shifted the conversation to the wedding and his sister, even asking about his business, but he knew neither of them was really interested in talking about that tonight. They just had to get through dinner.

It wasn't until they were halfway through their pasta that she returned to the previous discussion. "I've been thinking," she began. "I think you and I started off on the wrong foot at the engagement party. I'd like us to start over."

"Start over?" He wasn't entirely sure what that meant.

"Yes. When we get done eating, I'm going to once again ask if you'd like to go someplace quiet to talk and catch up. This time, since you're not dating anyone, I hope you'll give a better response."

Was she offering what he thought she was offering? He sincerely hoped so. He finished his wine and busied himself by paying the bill. When the final credit card slip was brought to him, he looked up at Natalie. She was watching him with the sly smile on her face that she'd greeted him with the first time.

"So, Colin," she said softly. "Would you be interested in getting out of here and finding someplace quiet where we could talk and catch up?"

Colin had replayed that moment in his mind several times since the engagement party and now he knew exactly what he wanted to say.

"Your place or mine?"

It turned out to be his place, which was closer. Natalie's heart was pounding as she followed Colin down the hallway and into his kitchen. She'd only been here once before, the night of the engagement party. The house looked quite different tonight. There were no huge catering platters, no skirted tables, no jazz trio. It was just the wide open, modern space he called home.

It actually looked a little plain without everything else. Spartan. Like a model home.

She couldn't help but notice the sharp contrast between it and the warm, welcoming feel of his parents' house. It was about as far as you could get between them. Natalie had no doubt that this was a million-dollar house, but it was far too contemporary in style to suit her.

"May I offer you more wine?" he asked.

"No, thank you," she said, putting her purse down on the white quartz countertop. "I had plenty at dinner." And she had. She was stuffed. Natalie had focused on her food to avoid Colin's heated appraisal and now she regretted it. If she'd fully realized that her fantasies would actually play out after dinner, she would've held back a touch. She didn't exactly feel sexy, full to the gills with pasta, bread and wine.

"May I offer you a tour, then? I'm not sure how much you got to see of the place the other night."

"Not much," Natalie admitted. Since she'd only known the bride and her brother, she hadn't done much socializing. She'd hovered near the bar, people watching most of the evening.

Colin led her out of the sleek kitchen and through the dining room to the two-story open living room with a dramatic marble fireplace that went up to the ceiling. She followed him up the stairs to his loft office, then his bedroom. "This is the best part," he said.

"I bet," Natalie replied with a grin.

"That's not what I meant." He walked past the large bed to a set of French doors. He opened them and stepped out onto a deck.

Natalie went out behind him and stopped short as

she caught a glimpse of the view. They'd driven up a fairly steep hill to get here, she remembered that, but she hadn't realized his house virtually clung to the side of the mountain. While precarious, it offered an amazing view of the city. The lights stretched out as far as the eye could see, competing with the stars that twinkled overhead.

She had a really nice townhouse she liked, but it couldn't hold a candle to this. She could sit out here all night just looking up at the stars and sipping her coffee. Natalie bet it was amazing at sunrise, too.

"So, what do you think?"

Natalie hesitated, trying to find the right words. She turned to Colin, who was leaning against the railing with his arms crossed over his chest. "The deck is amazing."

"What about the rest of the house?"

"It's very nice."

"Nice, huh? You don't like it at all."

Natalie avoided the question by stepping back into the bedroom with him on her heels. "It's a beautiful home, really. The view alone is worth the price you paid for it. The aesthetic is just a little modern for my taste."

Colin nodded. "Me, too. To be honest, Pam picked this place. If I hadn't been so mad about Shane, I probably would've let her keep it."

Natalie stiffened at the mention of his ex-wife and the son who'd turned out not to be his. She still wasn't sure exactly what had happened, but prying seemed rude. Since he brought it up... "Does she ever let you see Shane?"

Colin shook his head once, kind of curt. "No. I think it's better that way though since he's still a baby. If he'd been any older, it would've been harder to help him understand where his daddy was. He's probably forgotten who I am by now."

"I don't know about that," Natalie said, stepping toward him until they were nearly touching. "I know I've never been able to forget about you."

"Is that right?" Colin asked, wrapping his arms around her waist. The pain had faded from his face, replaced only with the light of attraction. "So, did you fantasize about what it would be like to kiss me?"

Natalie smiled. How many nights had she hugged her pillow to her chest and pretended it was Lily's handsome older brother? "An embarrassing number of times," she admitted.

"Did our first kiss live up to those expectations?"

"It did, and then some. Of course, when I was fifteen, I didn't know what was really possible like I do now."

"Oh really?"

"Yes. And now I want more."

Colin didn't hesitate to meet her demand. His mouth met hers, offering her everything she wanted. She ran her fingers through his hair, tugging him closer. Natalie wasn't letting him get away this time. He was all hers tonight. She arched her back, pressing her body against the hard wall of his chest.

He growled against her lips, his hand straying from her waist to glide along her back and hips. He cupped one cheek of her rear through the thin fabric of her skirt, pushing her hips against his until she could feel the firm heat of his desire.

Natalie gasped, pulling from his mouth. "Yeah," she said in a breathy voice. "There's no way I would've imagined a kiss like that."

Pulling back, she reached for the collar of his jacket. She pushed his blazer off his shoulders, letting it fall to the floor. Her palms moved greedily over his broad shoulders and down the front of his chest, touching every inch of the muscles she'd seen in that tight T-shirt. Starting at his collar, she unbuttoned his shirt, exposing the muscles and dark chest chair scattered across them.

Colin stood stiffly as she worked, his hands tightly curled into fists at his sides. When Natalie reached his belt, he sprang into action, grasping her wrists. "That's not really fair, is it?"

"Well," she reasoned, "I've been fantasizing about seeing you naked for years. I think it's only right I shouldn't have to wait any longer."

Colin gathered the hem of her blouse and lifted it slowly over her head. Natalie raised her arms to help him take it off. He cast her shirt onto a nearby chair. "I don't think a few more minutes will kill you."

He focused on her breasts, taking in the sight before covering the satin-clad globes with the palms of his hands. Natalie gasped when he touched her, her nipples hardening and pressing into the restraining fabric. He kneaded her flesh, dipping his head down to taste what spilled over the top of the cups. Colin nipped at her skin, soothing it with the glide of his tongue. Tugging down at her bra, he uncovered her nipples, drawing one, then the next into his mouth.

Natalie groaned, pulling his head closer. The warmth of his mouth on her sensitive flesh built a liquid heat in her core. She wasn't sure how much longer she could take this kind of torture.

"I need you," she gasped. "Please."

In response, Colin sought out the back of her skirt

with his fingers. He unzipped it, letting it slide down over her hips. She stepped out of the skirt and her heels, then let Colin guide her backward through the room until the backs of her legs met with the mattress. She reached behind her, crawling onto the bed.

While Colin watched, she unclasped her bra and tossed it aside, leaving nothing on but her panties. His eyes stayed glued to her as he unfastened his pants and slipped them off with his briefs. He pulled away long enough to retrieve a condom from the bedside stand before he climbed onto the bed.

The heat of his body skimmed over hers. He hovered there, kissing her as one hand roamed across her stomach. It brushed the edge of her panties, slipping beneath to dip his fingers between her thighs. Natalie arched off the bed, gasping before meeting his lips once more. He stroked her again and again, building a tension inside her that she was desperate to release.

Colin waited until she was on the very edge, then he retreated, leaving her panting and dissatisfied. "Just a few more minutes," he reassured her with a teasing grin.

He moved down her body, pulling the panties over her hips and along the length of her legs as he moved. Tossing them aside, he sheathed himself and pressed her thighs apart. He nestled between them and positioned himself perfectly to stroke her core as his hips moved forward and back. He rebuilt the fire in her belly, then, looking her in the eye, shifted his hips and thrust into her.

Natalie cried out, clawing at the blankets beneath her. He started slow, clenching his jaw with restraint, then began moving faster. She drew her legs up, wrapping them around his hips as they flexed, eliciting a low groan deep in Colin's throat.

"Yes," Natalie coaxed as he moved harder and faster inside her.

The release he'd teased at before quickly built up inside her again and this time, she knew she would get what she wanted. She gripped his back, feeling the knot tighten in her belly. "Please," she said.

"As you wish." He thrust hard, grinding his pelvis against her sensitive parts until she screamed out.

"Colin!" she shouted as the tiny fire bursts exploded inside her. Her release pulsated through her whole body, her muscles tightening around him as she shuddered and gasped.

Thrusting again, Colin buried his face in her neck and poured himself into her. "Oh, Natalie," he groaned into her ear.

The sound of her name on his lips sent a shiver down her spine. She wrapped her arms around him as he collapsed against her. She gave him a few minutes to rest and recover before she pushed at his shoulders. "Come on," she said.

"Come where?" He frowned.

"To the shower. You and I are just getting started. I've got fourteen years to make up for."

Seven

Colin was making coffee downstairs the next morning when he heard the heavy footsteps of a sleepy Natalie coming down the stairs. He peeked around the corner in time to see her stumble onto the landing. She'd pulled her messy hair into a ponytail and was wearing her professional office attire, but it was rumpled and definitely looked like a day-two ensemble for her.

He watched as she hesitated at the bottom of the stairs. She looked around nervously, almost like she was searching for an exit route. Was she really trying to sneak out without him seeing her? Yes, there wasn't anything serious between them, but she didn't need to flee the scene of the crime. She started slinking toward the front door, but he wasn't about to let her off so easily.

"Good morning, Natalie," he shouted.

She stiffened at the sound of his voice, and then reluctantly turned and followed the noise toward the kitchen. "Good morning," she said as she rounded the corner.

He loved seeing this unpolished version of her. With her wrinkled clothes, her mussed-up hair and day-old makeup, it was a far cry from the superprofessional and sleek wedding planner at the chapel. It reminded him of just how she'd gotten so messy and made him want to take her back upstairs to see what more damage he could do to her perfect appearance in the bedroom.

From the skittish expression on her face, he doubted he'd get the chance. Last night was likely a one-time event, so he'd have to be content with that. Instead, Colin returned to pouring the coffee he'd made into a mug for each of them. "How do you take your coffee? I have raw sugar, fake sugar, whole milk and hazelnut creamer. Oh, and getting it in a go-cup isn't an option, by the way."

She smiled sheepishly, clearly knowing she'd been caught trying to make a quick getaway. "I promise not to drink on the run. A splash of milk and a spoonful of raw sugar, please."

He nodded and worked on making her the perfect cup. "Would you like to have coffee downstairs or on the deck?"

She looked up at the staircase to the bedroom, which they'd have to pass through to get to the deck. "The kitchen nook is fine," she said, obviously unwilling to risk the pleasurable detour. "I'm sure we missed the best of the sunrise a long time ago."

Colin handed over her mug and followed her to the

table with a plate of toasted English muffins with strawberry jam and butter. He sat down and picked up one muffin, taking a bite with a loud crunch. He finished chewing and let Natalie sip her coffee before he pressed her about her great escape.

"You seem to be in a hurry this morning. What's the rush?"

Natalie swallowed her sip of coffee and set the mug on the kitchen table. "I was hoping you wouldn't notice. It's just that I'm, uh, not used to staying over. I'm sort of a master of the four a.m. vanishing act. I prefer to avoid the awkward morning-after thing."

"You mean coffee and conversation?"

"I suppose," she said with a smile.

"What kept you from leaving last night?" Colin wasn't quite sure what he would've done if he'd woken up and she was gone. He wasn't used to this kind of scenario with a woman. He was a relationship guy, and that usually meant enjoying a nice breakfast after a night together, not cold empty sheets beside him in bed.

"I think it was all the wine we had at dinner on top of the…exercise I got later. When I fell asleep, I slept hard. I didn't so much as move a muscle until I smelled the coffee brewing downstairs."

Colin considered her answer. He tried not to let it hurt his pride that she hadn't stayed because she felt compelled, or even wanted to. "You know, despite what happened last night, we're still friends. I don't want this to change that, so there's no need to run before you turn back into a pumpkin. Do you mind me asking why you feel the need to leave?"

Natalie bit at her lip before nodding. "Like I told you

before, I'm not much on the relationship thing. I like to keep things simple and sweet. Uncomplicated."

What was more complicated than this? Colin couldn't think of anything else. A normal relationship seemed a lot more straightforward. "What does that even mean, Natalie?"

"It means that what we shared last night is all I'm really wanting."

"I get that. And I'm on board with that or I wouldn't have let it go that far last night. I'm just curious as to why you feel this way about guys and relationships in general."

"There's nothing really in it for me after that first night or two because I don't believe in love. I think it's a chemical reaction that's been built up into more. I also don't believe in marriage. I enjoy the occasional companionship, but it's never going to come to any more than that with any man."

Colin listened to her talk, realizing this was worse than he'd thought. It could've just as easily been his ex-wife, Pam, sitting across the table talking to him. Yes, Natalie had said she wasn't the marrying kind, but this was more than just that. She didn't believe in the entire concept. He raised his hand to his head to shake off the déjà vu and the dull throb that had formed at his temple. It was a good thing he knew about her resistance going into this or it could've been a much bigger blow. "A wedding planner that doesn't believe in love or marriage?"

She shrugged. "Just because I don't believe in it doesn't mean that other people can't. I'm organized and I'm detail-oriented. I was made for this kind of work, so why not?"

The whole thing seemed a little preposterous. "So even though you spend all your days helping people get married, you never intend to marry or have a family of your own?"

"No," Natalie said, shaking her head. "You know what I grew up with, Colin. My mother is on the verge of dumping her fourth husband. I've seen too many relationships fall apart to set myself up for that. The heartache, the expense, the legal hassles... I mean, after everything that happened, don't you sometimes wish that you'd never married Pam?"

That wasn't a simple question to answer. He'd spent many nights asking himself the same thing and hadn't quite decided on what he'd choose if he had the power to bend time and do things differently. "Yes and no. Yes, never marrying or even never dating would've been easier on my heart. But more than not getting married, I just wish Shane had been mine. I don't know how long Pam and I would've been able to hold our marriage together, but even if we'd divorced in that case, I'd still have my son. I'd have a piece of the family I want. Now I have nothing but the lost dream of what I could've had. As they say, 'a taste of honey is worse than none at all,' but I wouldn't trade away my time with Shane. The day he was born was the happiest day of my life. And the day I found out he wasn't my son was the worst. I lost my son and I wasn't even allowed to grieve the loss because I never truly had him to begin with."

Natalie frowned into her coffee cup. "That's exactly the kind of heartache I want to stay away from. I can't understand how someone could go through that and be willing to dust themselves off and try again."

"It's called hope. And I can't understand how someone could go through their life alone. Having a family, having children and seeing them grow up is what life is all about."

"Exactly. It's survival of the species, our own biology tricking us into emotional attachments to ensure stability for raising the next generation. Then it fades away and we're left feeling unfulfilled because society has sold us on a romantic ideal that only really exists in movies and books."

Colin could only shake his head. "That's the worst attitude about love I've ever heard."

"I don't force anyone else to subscribe to my ideas. I didn't come up with this overnight, I assure you. I learned the hard way that love is just a biological impulse that people confuse with Hallmark card sentiment. Have you ever noticed that all the fairy tales end when the Prince and Princess get married? That's because the story wouldn't be that exciting if it showed their lives after that. The Prince works too much. The Princess resents that she's constantly picking up his dirty socks and wiping the snotty noses of his children, so she nags at the Prince when he comes home. The Prince has an affair with his secretary. The Princess throws the Prince out of the palace and takes him to court for child support. Not exactly happily ever after."

"Don't ever write children's books," Colin said drily.

"Someone needs to write that book. That way little girls won't grow up believing in something that isn't going to happen. It would save them all a lot of disappointment."

Colin had tasted every inch of Natalie last night and there hadn't been the slightest bitterness, but now, it seemed to seep from every pore. He was frankly stunned by her attitude about love. It was even more deep-seated and angry than Pam's negative ideas. Pam just didn't want the strings of marriage and monogamy. Natalie didn't believe in the entire construct.

"Hopefully you weren't disappointed with last night."

"Of course not. Last night was great, Colin. It was everything that I'd hoped it would be, and more. And by stopping right now, we get to preserve it as the amazing night that it was."

He knew she was right. He could feel it in his bones. But he also couldn't just let this be the end of it. He wouldn't be able to finish dealing with the wedding plans and the house, being so close to her, without being able to touch her again. "What if I wanted another night or two like last night?"

Natalie watched him with a suspicious narrowing of her eyes. "Are you suggesting we have a little holiday fling?"

He shrugged. Colin had never proposed such a thing, so he wasn't entirely sure. "I did bet you that I could put a little jingle in your step. I think the time we spend together would be a lot more fun for us both if we let this attraction between us be what it is. No promise of a future or anything else, and you don't have to dash from the bed like a thief in the night. What do you think?"

"It sounds tempting," she admitted. "I wouldn't mind getting a little more of those toe-curling kisses you promised me. But you have to agree that after the wedding, we part as we started—as old friends. No hard feelings when it's over."

"Okay, it's a deal. I promise not to fall in love with you, Natalie."

"Excellent," she said with a smile before leaning in to plant a soft kiss on his lips. "I don't plan on falling in love with you either."

"So, what do you think?"

Natalie hovered in the doorway of Colin's family home, her mouth agape in shock. It had only been a week since she was in the house, but it had been completely transformed. "Is this the same place?"

Colin smiled. "A lot has happened since you were here. While I have been busy planning Lily's wedding and seducing you, I couldn't just sit around doing nothing all weekend while you were working, you know."

He'd worked magic in Natalie's opinion. A lot of the old furniture and things they didn't want to keep were gone. In their place were new pieces that looked a million times better. There was new paint on the walls, updated light fixtures and window coverings...the place looked better than she ever remembered. "You've worked a miracle."

"I didn't do it alone, I assure you. The Catholic charity came and picked up all the old things we didn't want to keep. I've had contractors in and out all week. We didn't do any major renovations, so it's mostly cosmetic, but I think it turned out nicely."

"Well, what's left for me to do?"

Colin took her hand and led her into the formal dining room. There, in front of the bay window, was a giant Christmas tree. Apparently her plan to distract him with sexual escapades hadn't worked the way she'd thought.

"Colin," she complained, but he raised a hand to silence her.

"Nope. You agreed to go along with the bet. It's not fair if you stonewall my plans. If you're confident enough to win, you're confident enough to decorate a Christmas tree without being affected by the cloying sentimentality of it all."

Natalie sighed. "Okay, fine. We'll trim the tree."

Colin grinned wide. "Great! I got all the decorations down from the attic."

They approached the pile of boxes and plastic totes that were neatly stacked by the wall. He dug around until he found the one with Christmas lights.

"When did you have the time to get a live tree?"

"I went by a tree lot while you went back to your place to shower and change. It took some creative maneuvering to get it into the house, but I was successful. Would you like a drink before we get started?" he asked as he walked into the kitchen.

"Sure. Water would be fine."

"How about some cider?" he called.

Cider? Natalie followed him into the kitchen, where she was assaulted by the scent of warm apple, cinnamon, orange zest and cloves. It was almost exactly like the scented candle she still had sitting on her desk from one of his holiday deliveries. She could hardly believe it, but Colin actually had a small pot of mulled cider simmering on the stove. Sneaky.

She wasn't going to acknowledge it, though. "Some cider would be great," she said. "It's a cold day."

"All right. I'll be right out and we can get started on that tree."

Natalie wandered back into the dining room and stared down the Christmas tree. She hadn't actually been this close to one in a long time. The scent of pine was strong, like the wreath on her door. She'd never had a real tree before. Her mother had always insisted on an artificial tree for convenience and aesthetics. While perfectly shaped and easy to maintain, it was lacking something when compared to a real tree.

The soft melody of music started in another room, growing louder until she could hear Bing Crosby crooning. Before she could say anything, Colin came up to her with a mug of cider and a plate of iced sugar cookies.

"You're kidding, right? Did you seriously bake Christmas cookies?"

"Uh, no," he laughed. "I bought them at a bakery near the tree lot. I didn't have time to do everything."

"You did plenty," she said, trying to ignore Bing's pleas for a white Christmas. "Too much." She sipped gingerly at the hot cider. The taste was amazing, warming her from the inside out. She'd actually never had cider before. It seemed she'd missed out on a lot of the traditional aspects of the holiday by abstaining for so long.

While it was nice, it wasn't going to change how she felt about Christmas in general. Natalie reluctantly set her mug aside and opened the box of Christmas lights. The sooner they got the tree decorated, the sooner she could get out of here.

They fought to untangle multiple strands, wrapping the tree in several sets of multicolored twinkle lights. From there, Colin unpacked boxes of ornaments and handed them one at a time to Natalie to put them on the tree. They were all old and delicate: an assortment of glass balls and Hallmark figurines to mark various family milestones.

"Baby's First Christmas," Natalie read aloud. It was a silver rattle with the year engraved and a festive bow tied around it. "Is this yours?"

Colin nodded. "Yep. My mom always bought a few ornaments each year. This one," he said, holding up Santa in a boat with a fishing pole, "was from the year we went camping and I caught my first fish."

Natalie examined the ornament before adding it to the tree with the others. "That's a sweet tradition."

"There are a lot of memories in these boxes," Colin said. "Good and bad." He unwrapped another ornament with a picture of his parents set between a pair of pewter angel wings.

When he handed it to Natalie, she realized it was a memorial ornament and the picture was one taken right before their accident. It seemed an odd thing to put on the Christmas tree. Why would he decorate with bad memories?

"Put it near the front," Colin instructed. "I always want our parents to be a part of our Christmas celebration."

Natalie gave the ornament a place of honor, feeling herself get a little teary as she looked at the two of them smiling, with no idea what was ahead for them and their children. "I miss them," she said.

Colin nodded. "Me, too." He took a bite of one of the iced snowman cookies. "Mom's were better," he said.

That was true. Mrs. Russell had made excellent cookies. But as much as Natalie didn't like the holidays, she didn't want to bring down the evening Colin planned with sad thoughts. "Do we have many more ornaments?"

The sad look on Colin's face disappeared as he focused on the task of digging through the box. "Just one more." He handed over a crystal dove. "Now we just need some sparkle."

Together, they rolled out the red satin tree skirt with the gold-embroidered poinsettias on it, then they finished off the last decorating touches. Colin climbed onto a ladder to put the gold star on the top of the tree while Natalie wrapped some garland around the branches.

"Okay, I think that's it," Colin said as he climbed down from the ladder and stepped back to admire their handiwork. "Let's turn out the lights and see how it looks."

Natalie watched him walk to the wall and turn out the overhead chandelier for the room. She gasped at the sight of the tree as it glowed in front of the window. The red, green, blue and yellow lights shimmered against the walls and reflected off the glass and tinsel of the tree.

Colin came up behind her and wrapped his arms around her waist. She snuggled into him, feeling herself get sucked into the moment. The tree, the music, the scents of the holidays and Colin's strong embrace… it all came together to create a mood that stirred long-suppressed emotions inside her.

"I think we did a good job," Colin whispered near her ear.

"We did a great job," she countered, earning a kiss on the sensitive skin below her earlobe. It sent a shiver through her body with goose bumps rising up across her flesh.

"Are you cold?" he asked. "I can turn on the gas fireplace and we can drink our cider there. Soak in the ambience."

"Sure," Natalie said. She picked up her cider and the plate of cookies and followed Colin into the living room. Natalie noticed that above the fireplace were a pair of stockings with both Lily's and Frankie's names embroidered on them. There was pine garland with lights draped across the mantel with tall red pillar candles and silk poinsettias. It was perfect.

With the flip of a switch, the fireplace roared to life. Colin settled down on the love seat and Natalie snuggled up beside him. She kicked off her shoes and pulled her knees up to curl against him. It was soothing to lie there with his arm around her, his heartbeat and the Christmas carols combining to create a soundtrack for the evening.

It had been a long time since Natalie had a moment like this. She didn't limit herself to one-night stands, but her relationships had focused more on the physical even if they lasted a few weeks. She hadn't realized how much she missed the comfort of being held. How peaceful it felt to sit with someone and just be together, even without conversation.

Sitting still was a luxury for Natalie. Once they had opened the chapel there was always something to be done, and she liked it that way. Now she was starting to wonder if she liked it that way because it filled the holes and distracted her from what she was missing in her life. Companionship. Partnership. Colin hadn't convinced her to love Christmas again, but he had opened her eyes to what she'd been missing. She could use more time like this to just live life.

Unfortunately, time like this with a man like Colin came with strings. It had only been a few short hours since they'd agreed to a casual fling, but in her heart, Natalie still worried.

While the decisive and successful owner of Russell Landscaping was driven and in control of his large company, the Colin she'd always known was also sentimental and thoughtful on the inside. The business success and the money that came with it were nice, but she could tell that he'd done all that to honor his father's memory. And more than anything, he wanted his own family, and had since he lost his parents. No little fling would change that.

She liked Colin a lot, but even her teenage infatuation couldn't turn it into more than that. More than that didn't exist in her mind. She could feel her hormones raging and her thoughts kept circling back to Colin whether she was with him or not, but that wasn't love. That was biology ensuring they would continue to mate until she conceived. He might be attracted to her now, but she would never be the wife and mother he envisioned sitting around the Christmas tree with their children. She just wasn't built for that.

Natalie knew she had to enjoy her time with Colin, then make sure it came to a swift end before either of them got attached to the idea of the two of them. She was certain that their individual visions of "together" would be radically different.

"That wasn't so bad, was it?" Colin asked.

The question jerked Natalie from her thoughts and brought her back to the here and now, wrapped in Colin's arms. "It wasn't," she admitted. "I have to say that was the most pleasant tree decorating experience I've had in ten years."

"Natalie, have you even decorated a Christmas tree in ten years?"

Of course he'd ask that. "Nope. I appreciate all your efforts, but even if it had been a miserable night, it still would've been the best. So sorry, but you haven't won the bet yet."

Eight

Tomorrow night, Natalie's cell phone screen had read on Wednesday.

Colin followed it up with another text. You and I are going on a date. Per your requirements, you will wear a pretty dress and I will take you someplace nice. I will pick you up at seven.

She ignored the warning bells in her head that insisted a real date fell outside their casual agreement. While going on a date with Colin had the potential to move them forward in a relationship with nowhere to go, it also might do nothing other than provide them both with a nice evening together. She tried not to read too much into it.

Natalie made a point of not staying at work too late on Thursday so she could get home and get ready for their date. She ignored the pointed and curious glare of Gretchen when she announced that she was leaving early. She would deal with that later.

Back at her townhouse, she pored through her closet looking for just the right dress. She settled on a gray-and-silver lace cocktail dress. It was fitted with a low-plunging scalloped V-neckline that enhanced what small bit of cleavage she had. It also had shimmering silver bands that wrapped around the waist, making her boyish figure appear more seductively hourglass-shaped.

Once that was decided, she spent almost a half hour flatironing her hair. She wore it in a ponytail most every day. At work, she liked it off her face, but tonight, she wanted it down and perfect.

The doorbell rang exactly at seven and Natalie tried not to rush toward the door. She took her time, picking up her silver clutch on the way.

"Hello there," Natalie said as she opened the door.

Colin didn't respond immediately. His gaze raked over her body as he struggled to take it all in. Finally, he looked at her and smiled. "I like going on dates with you, pretty dress and all."

She preened a little, taking a spin to show off how good her butt looked in the dress before pulling her black wool dress coat from the closet. "I made a big deal of tonight's requirements so I wanted to hold up my end of the bargain."

Colin held out her jacket to help her into it. "You certainly have. You look amazing tonight."

"Thank you."

"Your chariot awaits," Colin said, gesturing toward a silver Lexus Coupe in the driveway.

"Where's the truck?" she asked.

"I didn't think you'd feel like climbing up into it when you're dressed up. Besides, this car matches your dress. It's fate."

He helped her into the car and they drove through town, bypassing some of the usual date spots and heading toward one of the high-end outdoor shopping plazas in Nashville. "Where are we going?" she asked as they pulled into the crowded parking lot. She made a point of avoiding any major shopping areas in December. She was guaranteed to run into Christmas music, decorations and grumpy people fighting their way through their chore lists.

"You'll see," Colin replied, ignoring her squirming in the seat beside him.

"Is this part of the Christmas bet? Telling me you're taking me on a date, letting me get all dressed up and then taking me to see Santa at the mall is cruel. I can assure you it won't fill me with Christmas spirit. More than likely, it will fill me with impatience and a hint of rage. These heels are pretty and expensive, but I'm not above throwing them at someone."

Colin just laughed at her and pulled up to the valet stand at the curb. "Keep your shoes on. I doubt you'll have need to use them as a weapon. I didn't bring you here for the holiday chaos. I brought you here for the best steak and seafood in Nashville."

"Oh," she said quietly. There *were* some nice restaurants here; it was just hard to think about going to them in mid-December. Natalie waited until Colin opened her door and helped her out of the car. "What's that under your arm?" she asked as they made their way through the maze of shops.

Colin looked down at the neatly wrapped package

beneath his arm and shrugged. "It's just a little some-thing."

Natalie wrinkled her nose in a touch of irritation. She hated surprises, hated not knowing every detail of what was going on in any given situation. Being a wedding planner allowed her to legitimately be a control freak. She wanted to press the issue with him but let the sub-ject go since they were approaching the heavy oak doors of the restaurant. A man opened one for them, welcom-ing them inside the dark and romantic steakhouse. They checked in and were taken back to a private booth away from the main foot traffic of the restaurant.

They ordered their food and a bottle of wine, settling in for a long, leisurely dining experience. "So, now will you tell me what's in the box?"

Colin picked up the shiny silver package. "You mean this box?" he taunted.

"Yes. That's the one."

"Not right now. I have something else to discuss."

Natalie's eyebrow went up. "You do, do you?"

"Yes. I was wondering what you're doing Sunday evening."

Natalie wished she had her tablet with her. "Sunday morning, we clean and break down from Saturday's wedding. I don't think I have plans that night, aside from kicking off my shoes and relaxing for the first time in three days."

"That doesn't sound like it's any fun. I think you should consider coming with me to a Christmas party."

"Oh no," Natalie said, shaking her hand dismissively. "That's okay. I'm not really comfortable at that kind of thing."

"What's there to be uncomfortable about? We'll eat,

drink and mingle. Aside from the reason for the party, you might even forget it's a holiday gathering."

"Yes, but I won't know anyone there. I'm awful at small talk."

"Actually, you'll know everyone. It's Amelia Dixon's party."

"Amelia?" Natalie frowned. "My friend Amelia invited *you* to a Christmas party?"

Colin took a sip of his wine and nodded. "She did. Why are you so surprised? Did she not invite you?"

Honestly, Natalie wasn't sure. She didn't really pay much attention to her mail this time of year if it didn't look like an important bill of some kind. A few folks, Amelia included, always seemed to send her a Christmas card despite her disinterest. If she'd gotten an invite, it was probably in her trash can.

"I typically don't attend Amelia's Christmas party. I'm more curious as to how you got invited. You don't even know her."

"I know her well enough for a little Christmas gathering when I'm dating her close friend."

"Are we dating?" Natalie asked.

"And more importantly," he continued, ignoring her question, "I think she understands you better than you'd like to think. I get the feeling she invited me to make sure you showed up this time."

"I wouldn't be surprised." Amelia had proved in the past that she was a scheming traitor when it came to men. She'd lured Bree to a bar to see Ian after they broke up. Natalie had no doubt she would stoop to similar levels to push her and Colin together *and* get her to come to her annual Christmas soirée. "Despite how much she pesters me, she knows I won't come."

"Well this year, I think you should make an exception and go. With me."

She could feel her defenses weakening. It all sounded nice, and she couldn't wait to see what kind of party Amelia could throw in their big new house with all that entertaining space. But she wished it didn't have to be a Christmas party. The last Christmas party she went to was for kids. Santa was there handing out little presents to all the children, they ate cupcakes and then they made reindeer out of clothespins. She was pretty certain that wasn't what they'd be doing at Amelia and Tyler's. What did adults even do at Christmas parties? "I don't know, Colin."

"It's settled, you're coming." Colin picked up his phone and RSVP'd to Amelia while they were sitting there. Natalie opened her mouth to argue, but it was too late. There was no getting out of it now. Amelia would insist and there would be no squirming.

"Why do you hate me?" Natalie asked as he put his phone away.

"I don't hate you. I like you. A lot. That's why I'm so determined to make the most of our short time together. It also doesn't hurt that it might help me win that kiss." His hazel eyes focused on her across the table, making her blood heat in her veins.

Natalie sighed, trying to dismiss her instant reaction to him. "I've kissed you twenty times. What's so important about *that* kiss?"

"It's The One. The most important kiss of all. Nothing can compare to it, I assure you. But I'll make you a deal," he offered.

"A deal? Does it allow me to skip the Christmas

party? I'll gladly spend that whole night naked in your bed if you'll let me skip the stupid party."

Colin's lips curled up in a smile that dashed her hopes of that negotiation. "While that sounds incredibly tempting, no. You're going to that party with me. But, if you promise to come and not give me grief about it the entire time, I'll let you open this box." He picked up the silver-wrapped box with the snowflake hologram bow and shook it tantalizingly at her.

Considering she was pretty much stuck going to the party anyway, she might as well agree and finally soothe her curiosity about that package. "Okay," Natalie conceded. "I will go with you to the party, and I will not bellyache about it."

"Excellent. Here you go."

Natalie took the box from Colin's hand, shaking it to listen for any telltale clues. No such luck. She'd just have to open it. Peeling away at a corner, she pulled back the wrapping to expose a white gift box. Lifting the lid, she found a Swarovski-crystal-covered case for her tablet.

This wasn't some cheap knockoff they sold at the flea markets. Natalie had done enough weddings to recognize real Swarovski crystal when she saw it. She'd seen covers like these in the hands of Paris Hilton and other celebrities. Out of curiosity, she'd looked it up online once and found far too many zeroes at the end to even consider it. It was impossibly sparkly, each crystal catching the flickering candlelight of the restaurant, and it twinkled like thousands of diamonds in her hands. It cast a reflection on the ceiling like stars overhead.

"Do you like it?" Colin asked.

"Yes, I love it. I've always wanted one, but I don't

think I ever told anyone that. What made you think to buy me something like this?"

"Well," Colin explained, "whenever I see you at the chapel, you've got your iPad in your hands. It's like a third arm you can't live without. It seemed a little boring though. I thought a girl that drove a little red sports car might like a little bling in her life. Besides, jewelry seemed…predictable."

Natalie shook her head. "I'm pretty certain that a fling doesn't call for gifts, much less jewelry. This is too much, really. What is this for?"

"It's your Christmas present. I thought you could make good use of it at your upcoming weddings so I wanted to give it to you early. Besides, we're not supposed to make it to Christmas, so I thought if I was going to give you something, the sooner the better."

"It's perfect," Natalie said. Even as she ran her fingertips over the shining stones, she felt guilty. Not just because he'd bought her a gift, but because Colin had given it to her early because she was too flaky to stick with a relationship for two more weeks. She shouldn't feel bad, though. They'd agreed to the arrangement. It had even been his suggestion, and yet she found herself already dreading this coming to an end. "But you shouldn't have done it. It's too much money."

Colin only shrugged at her complaints. "What is the point of earning all this money if I don't do anything with it? I wanted to buy you something and this is what I came up with. End of discussion."

"I haven't gotten you anything," she argued. And she hadn't. She hadn't bought a Christmas gift in years and she was adamant about not receiving one. Every year she had to remind people she was on the naughty list, so no gifts. It had worked so far. Then Colin came in and started busting down every wall she had, one at a time. Soon, if she wasn't careful, she'd be completely exposed.

Colin reached across the table and took her hand. "You've given me plenty without you even knowing it. The last year has been really hard for me with the divorce and everything else. For the first time since I found out about Shane, I'm excited for what each day holds. That's all because of you."

"That may have been the most amazing bread pudding I've ever had," Natalie said as they stepped out of the restaurant and back into the mingling flow of holiday shoppers.

"It was excellent, I have to admit." He wasn't entirely sure where he wanted to take Natalie next, but he knew he didn't want to rush home. Not because he didn't want to make love to her again, but because he wanted her to take in some of the holiday ambience. This was a shopping center in December, but it wasn't the day-after-Thanksgiving crush. There was rarely a riot over a sale at the Louis Vuitton.

He also wanted to simply spend time with Natalie. He'd meant what he said in the restaurant earlier. For the past year, he'd been going through the motions, trying to figure out what his life was supposed to be like now that he wasn't a husband or a father any longer. It had been easy to focus on work, to center all this attention on expanding Russell Landscaping into Chattanooga and Knoxville.

It wasn't until his sister announced her engagement that he'd snapped out of his fog. Pam may not have been the right woman for him, but there was someone out there who could make him happy. He'd started dating again, unsuccessfully, but he was out there. And then he'd spied Natalie at the engagement party and his heart had nearly stilled in his chest from the shock of how beautiful she'd become.

How had the quiet teenager with the dark braid, the braces and the always-serious expression grown up into such a beauty? The timing was terrible, but Colin had known that he would do whatever he had to do to have Natalie in his life again.

Of course, at the time, Colin hadn't known about her pessimistic stance on love and marriage. That had been like a dousing of ice water. It was cruel for the universe to bring him into contact with such a smart, beautiful, talented woman, then make it impossible for them to have any kind of chance of being together. She even hated Christmas. That was a smack in the face of everything he held dear.

Their night together after the bridal shop had just been a chance to release the unbearable pressure building up. He had been dismayed to wake the next morning and find he wanted Natalie more than ever. Continuing to see each other casually until the wedding was a good idea in theory, but it was prolonging the torture in practice. This date, this night together, would probably do more harm than good in the end. But he couldn't stop himself.

Colin knew he was playing with fire. He hadn't gone into this thinking any of it would happen the way it had, or that he could somehow change Natalie's mind. At least about love and marriage. His determination to help her find her Christmas spirit had made slow progress, but progress nonetheless. He could already see cracks in that facade after only a week of trying.

He could see a similar weakness when she was around him. Her mouth was saying one thing while her body was saying another. When she'd stepped out in that wedding gown, it was like nothing existed but her. As much as she built up her theories about biology interfering in relationships, he could tell she was comfortable around him. Happy. Passionate. If they could both be convinced to take whatever this was beyond the wedding, there would be more between them than just sex.

But would what she was willing to give him be enough to make him happy? Companionship and passion seemed nice, but without love in the mix, it would grow tired, or worse, she might stray, like Pam. Without the commitment of love and marriage, there was no glue to hold two people together. It didn't matter how alluring or wonderful Natalie seemed, she would never be the woman he wanted and needed. But for now, for tonight, none of that mattered. They'd had a nice dinner and he had a bet to win. Reaching out, he took her hand. "How about a stroll to walk some of that dinner off?" he asked.

"I probably need to."

They walked together through the outdoor mall, passing a trio of musicians playing Christmas carols. Farther up ahead, Colin could spy the giant Christmas tree that the mayor had lit the week before. The whole place was decorated. There were white twinkle lights in all the bushes and wrapped around each light post. Near the fountain was a fifteen-foot gold reindeer with a wreath of holly and a cluster of oversize ornaments around his neck.

"The lights are pretty," Natalie admitted as they neared the big tree. "It reminds me of the tree in Rockefeller Center."

"Now why would a Grinch go see the tree in New York?" he asked.

"I was there on business," she insisted. "I went down to see the ice skaters and there it was. It's pretty hard to miss."

They approached the black wrought iron railing that surrounded and protected the tree. It, too, was wrapped in lighted garland and big velvet bows. Colin rested his elbows on the railing and looked up at the big tree. "I think our tree is nicer."

Natalie cozied up beside him and studied the tree more closely. "I think you're right. This tree is kind of impersonal. Ours had a special something."

"Maybe we need hot cider," he suggested.

"No," Natalie groaned, pushing away from the railing. "There is no room left in me for anything, even hot cider."

She reached for his hand and he took hers as they started back to the other end of the shopping center where they'd left his car.

"Thank you for bringing me here tonight," she said. "I've never seen this place decorated for the holidays. It's pretty. And not as crowded and chaotic as I was expecting it to be."

"I'm glad you think so," Colin said with a chuckle. "If you'd have been miserable, it could've set me back days."

"No," Natalie said, coming to a stop. "It's perfect. A great first date, I have to say."

"It's not over yet." As they paused, Colin noticed a decorative sprig of mistletoe hanging from a wire overhead. He couldn't have planned this better if he'd tried. "Uh-oh," he said.

Natalie's eyes grew wide. "What? What's wrong?"

Colin pointed up and Natalie's gaze followed. He took a step closer to her, wrapping his arms around her waist. "That's mistletoe up there. I guess I'm going to have to kiss you."

"Sounds like a hardship," she said. "Christmas is such a burdensome holiday. Shop, eat, decorate, make out... I don't know how you people stand it every year with all these demands on your time."

"Am I wrong or does it sound like you're coming around to Team Christmas?"

Natalie wrapped her arms around his neck and entwined her fingers at his collar. "I wouldn't say I'm that far gone yet. A lot hinges on this kiss, though. I've never been kissed under the mistletoe, so I can't understate how critical this moment is to you potentially winning this bet."

"No pressure," Colin said with a smile. Dipping his head, he pressed his lips to hers. Her mouth was soft and yielding to him. She tasted like the buttery bourbon sauce from the bread pudding and the coffee they'd finished their meal with. He felt her melt into him, his fingertips pressing greedily into her supple curves.

Every time he kissed Natalie, it was like kissing her for the first time. There was a nervous excitement in his chest, tempered by a fierce need in his gut. Combined, it urged him to touch, taste and revel in every sweet inch of her.

As they pulled apart, Colin felt the cold kiss of ice against his skin. Opening his eyes, he saw a flurry of snowflakes falling around them. "It's snowing!" he said in surprise. Nashville did get cold weather, but snow was an unusual and exciting event. "How's that for your first kiss under the mistletoe? I kiss you and it starts to snow."

"Wow, it really is snowing." Natalie took a step back, tipping her face up to the sky. She held out her arms, letting the snowflakes blanket her dark hair and speckle her black coat. She spun around, grinning, until she fell, dizzy, back into Colin's arms. "I guess I haven't been paying enough attention to the weatherman," she admitted when she opened her eyes.

"I'm not sure snow was in the forecast. It must be a little Christmas magic at work." Colin looked around as the other shoppers quickly made their way back to their cars. Not everyone appreciated the shift in the weather. In the South, snow typically ended up turning icy and the roads would get bad pretty quickly. They all had to make an emergency run to the grocery store for milk, bread and toilet paper in case they lost power.

He wasn't worried about any of that. Colin just wanted to be right here, right now, with a flushed and carefree Natalie in his arms. She'd worn her hair down tonight for the first time and it looked like dark silk falling over her shoulders and down her back. The cold had made her cheeks and the tip of her nose pink, accentuating the pale porcelain of her complexion.

But most enticing of all was the light of happiness in her eyes. It was the authentic smile he'd been so desperate to lure out of her. The combination threatened to knock the wind out of him every time he looked at her.

"When I picked you up for our date tonight, I didn't think you could get more beautiful," he admitted. Colin brushed a snowflake from her cheek. "I was wrong. Right this moment, you are the most beautiful woman I've ever laid eyes on."

Natalie tried to avoid his gaze and ignore his compliment. He wasn't sure why she was so uncomfortable hearing the truth. She was beautiful and she needed to believe it.

Instead, with a dismissive shake of her head, she said, "Flattery won't help you win the bet, Colin."

"I'm not trying to win a bet," he said, surprising even himself. "I'm trying to win you."

Nine

"You're here!" Amelia nearly shrieked when she spied Natalie and Colin come through the front door of the sprawling mansion in Belle Meade she and Tyler had bought earlier that year. "I didn't believe it when he said you'd agreed to come."

"It's not a big deal," Natalie muttered as she slipped out of her jacket. "You just saw me this morning."

Amelia took both their coats to hang them in the hall closet. "It's not about seeing you, it's about seeing you at my Christmas party. That's a pretty big deal, considering you've never bothered to come before."

"You always held it at your cramped apartment before," Natalie argued, although Colin doubted that the setting had anything to do with it.

"Whatever," Amelia said dismissively. "The important thing is that both of you are here. Come in. Everyone is in the kitchen, of course. Thousands of square feet and everyone congregates there."

Colin took Natalie's hand and led her away from the nearest exit into the house. It was a massive home, large even by his standards, though it looked as if Amelia and her husband were still trying to accumulate enough furniture to fill it up. They had the place beautifully decorated for the holidays, though. A cluster of multiple-sized Christmas trees with lights sat by the front window like a small indoor forest. A decorated tree that had to be at least fourteen feet tall stood in the two-story family room. Any smaller and it would've been dwarfed by the grand size of the house. The banisters were wrapped with garland and ribbon. There was even holiday music playing in the background. Colin was pleased to drag Natalie to a proper holiday gathering.

"Everyone, this is another of my friends and coworkers, Natalie, and her date, Colin. He owns Russell Landscaping."

A few welcomes and hellos sounded from the crowd of about twenty-five people milling through the kitchen, dining room and keeping room area. He recognized a few of them—the wedding photographer, Bree, and Gretchen, the decorator. Bree was hanging on the arm of a dark-headed guy in a black cashmere sweater. Gretchen was alone despite the huge diamond on her finger. He wasn't sure what that was about.

"What would you like to drink?" Amelia asked, rattling off a long list of options.

"I also have a nice microbrew from a place downtown," Tyler offered, holding up a chilled bottle he pulled from the refrigerator.

"Perfect," Colin said, taking it from his hand. Natalie opted for a white wine that Amelia poured for her.

"Help yourself to something to eat. There's plenty, of course," Amelia said, gesturing to the grand buffet table along the wall.

Plenty was an understatement. The caterer in her had gone wild. He and Natalie perused the table, taking in all their options. There were chafing dishes with hot hors d'oeuvres like barbecued meatballs, chicken wings and fried vegetable eggrolls, platters of cold cheeses, finger sandwiches, crudités, dips and crackers, and more desserts than he could identify.

"She's gone overboard," Natalie said. "This is enough to feed a hundred wedding guests. She's just no good at cooking for small numbers. You'd think being pregnant would slow her down, but she's like a machine in the kitchen."

After surveying everything, they each made a plate and moved over to a sitting area with a low coffee table. They ate and chatted with folks as they milled around. Eventually Gretchen approached with her own plate and sat down with them.

"I'm sorry Julian couldn't be here with you tonight," Natalie said.

Gretchen just smiled and shrugged. "It's okay. He's almost done refilming some scenes the director wanted to change and then he'll be home. We'll have a great first Christmas together even though he missed this."

"Your fiancé is in the movie business?" Colin asked.

Gretchen nodded. "Yes, he's an actor. You've probably heard of him. Julian Cooper?"

Colin hesitated midbite. "Really?"

"I know, right?" Gretchen said. "Not who you'd expect me to be with."

"That's not what I meant," he countered. "I'm sure he's very lucky to have you. I've just never met anyone famous before. Feels odd to be one degree of separation from an action hero."

Gretchen smiled, obviously bolstered by his compliment. "You're also officially four degrees from Kevin Bacon."

Colin laughed and lifted his drink to take another sip.

"Excuse me, did I hear Amelia say you own Russell Landscaping?" the man beside him asked.

Colin turned his attention to his right. "Yes." He held out his hand to shake with the man, turning on his bright, businessman charm. "I'm Colin Russell."

"I'm in the construction business with Bree's father," he explained. "I'd love to talk to you about landscaping at our latest project. We're breaking ground on an apartment complex in the spring and looking for a company to handle that for us."

On cue, Colin pulled out his wallet and handed the man his business card. He lost himself in work discussions, realizing after about ten minutes that both Natalie and Gretchen had disappeared.

"Give me a call and we'll set something up," Colin concluded. "I'm going to hunt down my date."

Getting up, Colin carried his empty plate into the kitchen and got a fresh drink. Amelia was buzzing around with Bree helping her, but the others weren't in there. He wandered back into the living room toward the entry hall. Maybe they'd gone to the restroom as a pair, the way women tended to do.

He'd almost reached the entry when he heard Gretchen's voice. Still cloaked in the dark shadows of the room lit only with Christmas lights, he stopped and listened.

"All right, spill," Gretchen said.

Colin heard a hushing sound and some footsteps across the tile floor of the hallway. "Are you crazy?" Natalie asked in a harsh whisper. "Someone is going to hear you. What if Colin heard you?"

"Come on, Natalie. He's all tied up in talk about shrubs and mulch. It's perfectly safe. Tell me the truth. Bree and I have twenty bucks wagered on your answer."

"You're betting on my love life?"

Colin chuckled at Natalie's outrage. He liked her friends.

"Not exactly. We're betting on your emotional depth. That's probably worse. See, Bree thinks you're a shallow pool and believes your big talk when you go on about love not being real and blah, blah."

"And you?" Natalie asked.

"I think you've changed since you met Colin. You've bebopped around the office for the last week like you're on cloud nine. You've been texting him all the time. You haven't been as cranky. You were even humming a Christmas carol this morning."

"So, I'm in a good mood."

"Natalie, you even forgot about a bridal appointment on your calendar tomorrow morning. Your mind isn't on your work, and I think it's because you've realized you were wrong."

Colin held his breath. He was curious to hear what Natalie was going to say but worried he was going to get caught listening in. He leaned against the wall, casually sipping his beer as though he were just waiting for Natalie's return. Even then, he strained to catch the conversation over the holiday music.

"Wrong about what?"

"Wrong about love. You are in love with Colin. Admit it."

Colin's eyes widened. Would his skeptical Natalie really say such a thing? If she did, it could change everything.

"I am not," she insisted, but her voice wasn't very convincing.

Gretchen seemed to agree. "That's a load of crap. I get that you haven't been in love before, and until recently, neither had I. But when it hits you, you know it. And it's not biology or hormones or anything else. It's love. And you, sister, have fallen into it."

"I don't know, Gretchen. This is all new to me. I'm not sure I would call this love."

"Is he the first thing you think about in the morning and the last thing you think of at night? Is he the person you can't wait to share good news with? Does your busy workday suddenly drag on for hours when you know you'll get to see him that night?"

"Yes. Yes, yes and yes," Natalie said almost groaning. "What am I going to do?"

That wasn't exactly the reaction Colin was hoping for when a woman declared her love for him. Yes, she loved him, but she was miserable about it. Considering this was skeptical Natalie, he supposed that shouldn't surprise him. She'd go down kicking and screaming.

"Just go with it," Gretchen encouraged. "Love is awesome."

That was enough for him. Colin was about to cut it too close if he loitered here any longer. He scooted silently across the plush living room carpeting toward the kitchen to get something to nibble on and wait for Natalie's return. While he tried to look calm on the outside, he was anything but.

Could it be true? Was Natalie really in love with him? It had only been a few short weeks, but they'd technically known each other for years. Stranger things had happened. If he was honest with himself, he was having feelings for her as well. He could've answered yes to all of Gretchen's questions. Was that love? He was as clueless as Natalie there. He'd loved his parents, his son, but his attempts to fall in love with a woman had failed.

He felt more deeply for Natalie than he had for any other woman, even Pam. He was mature enough to admit that whole marriage had been about Shane, not about love.

Love. Was that what this was?

It could be. It felt different, somehow. Despite everything going on in his life, he was preoccupied with the brunette who had challenged him at every turn. She was like quicksand, drawing him in deeper the more he struggled against her. Colin had gone into this fling keeping his heart in check, or at least he'd tried to. Natalie wasn't the kind of woman he could settle down with and he knew that. But after spending time with her, he knew this couldn't be just a fling, either. He wanted more, and if Natalie was honest with herself, he was certain she wanted more, too. It was just a matter of convincing her not to run the moment her emotions got too serious or complicated. She might believe in love now, but he got the feeling that getting Natalie to believe in the beauty and power of a good marriage would be the challenge of a lifetime.

Colin popped a chocolate mint petit four into his mouth, looking up in time to see Natalie and Gretchen stroll back into the room. Natalie looked a little pale from their revealing discussion, her ashen color enhanced by her black dress.

No, Natalie might be in love with him, but she was anything but happy about it.

"You've been awfully quiet tonight," Colin said as they pulled into her driveway. "You've hardly said a thing since we left Amelia and Tyler's place."

Natalie shrugged it off, although she felt anything but cavalier about the thoughts racing through her head. "I'm just a little distracted tonight," she said. To soothe his concerns, she leaned in and kissed him. "I'm sorry. Would you like to come in?"

"I would," he said with a smile.

They got out of the car and went into her townhouse. Natalie didn't normally feel self-conscious about her place, but after being at Colin's and Amelia's, her little two-story home felt a bit shabby. Or maybe she was just an emotional live wire after everything that happened at the party.

"Nice place," Colin said as he pulled the door shut behind him.

"Thanks. It's nothing fancy, but it suits me." She led him through the ground floor, absentmindedly prattling on about different features. Mentally, she was freaking out, and had been since Gretchen cornered her at the party. Yes, she'd been quiet. She'd been analyzing every moment of the past two weeks. Was it possible that *she* was the one to break their casual arrangement and fall in love with Colin? Surely it hadn't been long enough for something like that to happen. They'd only been out a few times together.

Then again, Gretchen and Julian fell in love in a week. Bree and Ian fell in love again over a long weekend trapped in a cabin. Amelia had given Tyler thirty days to fall in love and they hadn't needed that long.

So it *was* possible. But was it smart?

Her brain told her no. Love equals heartache. But she couldn't stop herself from sinking further into the warm sensation of love. Colin made it so easy by being everything she never knew she always wanted. She wished he hadn't been so charming and thoughtful so it would be easier to fight.

But even if she *was* in love, it didn't change anything. It didn't mean she wanted to get married. Marriages seemed to ruin good relationships. Maybe it was marriage, not love, that was the real problem.

As Natalie turned to look at him, she realized he had an expectant expression on his face. "What?" she asked.

"I just complimented you on your large collection of classic country vinyl albums," he said, gesturing toward the shelf with her stereo and turntable.

Natalie glanced over at her albums and nodded. "My father bought a lot of them for me," she said. "We used to go to thrift stores looking for old records on Saturday afternoons."

"I mentioned it twice before you heard a word I said." Colin chuckled softly. "You're on another planet tonight, aren't you?"

"I am. I'm sorry." Natalie racked her brain for a way to distract him. She certainly wasn't going to tell him how she was feeling. Running her gaze over his sharply tailored suit, she decided to fall back on her earlier distraction tactic—seduction. She wrapped her arms around his waist and looked up at him. "Have I told you just how handsome you look tonight?"

He smiled, all traces of concern disappearing as he looked down at her adoringly. "Not in the last hour or so."

"Well, you do," she said, slipping her hands into his back pockets to grab two solid handfuls of him. "It's enough to make a girl want to throw the bet so she can experience that amazing kiss you've promised."

Colin shook his head. "There's no throwing the bet. You either shed your humbug ways or you don't. Either way, I'm not giving up until you've been converted. I don't care how long it takes."

"Even after I've won?" she asked.

"You bet. I think Christmas in Buenos Aires will be lovely, and I'll see to it that it is."

Natalie laughed. "You're inviting yourself to my vacation prize? I don't recall asking for company."

"I don't recall asking permission. I am paying for the trip, after all."

Natalie twisted her lips in thought. She was both thrilled and terrified by the idea of Colin still being in her life a year from now. She was so confused about all of this, she didn't know what to do. "So if I win the bet, will I ever get this infamous kiss? I don't want to miss out on it."

Colin narrowed his gaze at her. "How about this? How about I give you a little taste of how amazing it will be right now? That should be enough to tide you over until I've won."

She certainly couldn't turn down an offer like that, especially knowing that his talented mouth and hands would distract her from everything else she was worried about. "All right," she agreed. "Lay one on me."

Colin shook his head at her. "Before I do that, I think we'd better adjourn to the bedroom."

"Why is that?" Natalie asked. "It's just a kiss."

"You say that, but this won't be an ordinary kiss. You'll be glad we waited until we're in there, I promise."

"Okay." She wasn't sure if he could deliver on the hype, but she was looking forward to finding out. Taking his hand, she led him up the stairs and down the hallway to her master bedroom.

Her bedroom had been what sold her on the townhouse. The master was spacious with large windows that let in the morning light. Even filled with her furniture, there was plenty of room to move around. "All right," she said, standing beside the bed with her hands on her hips. "Let's get a sampling of this infamous kiss of yours."

Colin moved closer and Natalie couldn't help but tense up. She didn't know what to expect. This wasn't even *the* kiss and she was nervous with anticipation.

"You look like I'm about to eat you alive," he said with an amused smile.

"Sorry," she said, trying to shake the tension out of her arms.

"That's okay." He stopped in front of her, just shy of touching. Instead of leaning in to kiss her, he turned her around and undid the zipper of her dress. He eased it off her shoulders, letting it pool to the floor.

"What are you doing?" she asked, curiously. What kind of kiss required her to be naked?

Leaning in, Colin growled in her ear, "I'm about to eat you alive."

Natalie gasped at the harsh intensity of his words, even as a thrill of need ran through her body. Before she could respond, he unclasped her bra and pulled her panties to the floor. Completely naked, she turned around to complain about the unfairness, but found he was busily ridding himself of his clothing as well. In a few moments, it was all tossed aside and he pulled her close.

"When is the kissing going to start?" she asked.

"You ask too many questions. This isn't a wedding you're in charge of. There are no schedules, tablets and earpieces tonight. Go with it."

"Yes, sir," Natalie said with a sheepish smile. Admittedly, she had trouble letting go and not knowing every aspect of the plan. She didn't think she had anything to worry about here, so she tried to turn off her brain and just let Colin take the lead. That was the whole point tonight, anyway.

His fingers delved into her hair as he leaned in for the kiss. Natalie braced herself for the earth-shattering impact, but at first at least, it was just a kiss. He coaxed her mouth open, letting his tongue slide along hers. His fingers massaged the nape of her neck as he tasted and nibbled at her.

Then she felt him start to pull away. His lips left hers, but technically, they never lost contact with her skin. He planted kisses along the line of her jaw, the hollow of her ear and down her throat. He crouched lower, nipping at her collarbone and placing a searing kiss between her breasts. He tasted each nipple, then continued down her soft belly until he was on his knees in front of her.

He placed a searing kiss at her hipbone, then the soft skin just above the cropped dark curls of her sex. Natalie gripped Colin's shoulders for support as his fingers slid between her thighs. She gasped softly as he stroked the wet heat that ached for him.

With his mouth still trailing across her thigh, Colin gently parted her with his fingers. His tongue immediately sought out her sensitive core, wrenching a desperate cry from Natalie's throat. He braced her hips with his hands as her knees threatened to give out beneath her.

She wasn't sure how much of this she could take. Standing up added a level of tension she hadn't expected. "Colin," she gasped, amazed by how her cries were growing more desperate with every second that passed.

She was on the edge, and it was clear that he intended to push her over it. Gripping her hip with one hand, he used the other to dip a finger inside her. The combination was explosive and Natalie couldn't hold back any longer. She threw her head back and cried out, her body thrashing against him with the power of her orgasm.

When it was over, Natalie slid to her knees in front of him. She lay her head on his shoulder, gasping and clinging to his biceps with both hands. She was so out of it, it took her a moment to realize Colin had picked her up. He helped her stand, then carried her to the bed only a few feet away.

"That," she panted as reason came back to her, "was one hell of a kiss."

"And that wasn't even the winning kiss," Colin said as he covered her body with his own.

"I can't even imagine it, then. It seems odd that your prize would be more a reward for me than for you."

He slipped inside her, making her overstimulated nerves spark with new sensation. "I assure you I enjoyed every second of it now, and I'll enjoy every second of it when I've won."

For that, Natalie had no response. She could only lift her hips to meet his forward advance. Clinging to him, she buried her face in his neck. His movements were slow, but forceful, a slow burn that would eventually consume everything it touched. She didn't resist the fire; she gave in to it.

She was tired of fighting. She had spent her whole life trying to protect herself from the pain and disappointment of love. She'd fought her urges for companionship, suppressed her jealousy as each of her friends found a great love she was certain she would never have.

And yet, here she was. Despite all the fighting and worrying, she had simply been overpowered. Gretchen was right. Natalie was in love.

"Oh Natalie," Colin groaned in her ear.

She loved that sound. She wanted to hear it again and again. Her name on his lips was better than a symphony orchestra.

Placing her hand against his cheek, she guided his mouth back to hers. That connection seemed to light a fire in him. Their lips still touching, he moved harder and faster than before, sweeping them both up in a massive wave of pleasure. Natalie didn't fight the currents, she just held on to the man in her arms, knowing she was safe there.

She never wanted to let go. But could she dare to hold on?

Ten

"I can't believe we're almost done with the house," Natalie said. "You've worked wonders on it."

Colin smiled. "I'm pretty pleased with the results."

"Seems a shame you can't keep it after all the work you've put in. You don't appear to care much for your own house. This place suits you more."

That was probably true, but he didn't need this place. "I can always buy another house. I'd like to see Lily and Frankie raise their family here."

"What is left for us to do?" Natalie asked as she looked around.

"I have to clean out my parents' office. I left that for last because there's so much paperwork to go through. I need to figure out what should be kept. I'm hoping we can shred most of it, but I really have no idea what they had stored away in all those drawers."

"Let's do it, then."

They walked up the stairs together and Colin opened the door to the small, dusty room he'd avoided the longest. Turning on the overhead light illuminated the big old oak desk on the far wall. It had two large file drawers, one on each side, housing any number of documents and files they'd thought were important to keep. It took up most of the space like a large man in a small dressing room.

Colin had lots of memories of his dad going over invoices at this desk long before Russell Landscaping could afford their own offices, much less their own office building in the city. This was where his mother wrote checks to pay the bills and managed correspondence. She hadn't been a big fan of email, always penning handwritten letters to friends and family.

There was also a large bookshelf on one wall with all his father's books. His dad had always been a big reader. He loved to curl up in his chair by the fireplace and read in the evenings. Volumes of books lined the shelves, and Colin dreaded going through them. As much as he felt the urge, he didn't need to keep them all, just a couple of his father's favorites.

"I'll take the shelves if you want to start on the drawers," Colin suggested. "We can throw out all the office supplies."

They each started their tasks. Natalie filled a wastebin with dried-up pens, markers and old, brittle rubber bands. After that, she started sorting through the file drawers.

Colin easily found his father's favorite book—*Treasure Island*. His father had read, and reread, that book twenty times. It was his favorite, as evidenced by the worn binding and fraying edges. He set that book aside.

It would go on Colin's shelf until he passed it on to his children. Other volumes weren't quite as important.

Colin quickly built up a stack of books to keep, then another to donate. He scooped up a handful for charity and turned, noticing Natalie sitting stone still in the office chair. The expression on her face was one of utter devastation.

"Natalie?" he asked. "What is it?"

Looking up at him, she bit at her lip. "It's...um." She stopped, shuffling through the papers. "I started going through the filing drawers. It looks like your mother actually filed for divorce."

Colin's breath caught in his lungs. He set the books down on the desk before he dropped them. "What? You must be reading it wrong."

Natalie handed over the folder. "I don't think so. It looks like your mother filed two years before their accident."

Colin flipped through the paperwork, coming to the same conclusion despite how much it pained him. His parents didn't divorce. What was this about? Leaning back onto the desk, he tried to make sense of it all.

"It looks like she started the process, but they didn't go through with it." Somehow that still didn't make him feel much better.

"I'm sorry to hear they were in a bad place," Natalie said. "I never noticed anything wrong as a kid, but in my experience, there's no perfect marriage. Everyone has problems, despite how they might look from the outside."

Colin set down the pages and frowned. "Of course there's no perfect marriage. Just because I want to marry and have a family someday doesn't mean I think it's going to be a walk in the park. You have to work at it every day because love is a choice. But it's a choice worth making. And judging by this paperwork, it's worth fighting to keep it."

"How do you get that? I always thought your parents had a good relationship. If even they filed for divorce at one point, I don't see that as a positive sign."

"What's positive is the fact that they *didn't* get a divorce. Things got ugly, but they decided not to give up. That makes me hopeful, not disappointed. If my mother could go as far as filing for divorce and they managed to put the pieces back together, that means there's hope for any marriage."

Judging by the look on Natalie's face, he could tell she wasn't convinced. She was so jaded by other people's relationship failures that she couldn't fathom two people actually loving each other enough to fight through the tough times.

That worried him. Despite what he'd overheard at Amelia's Christmas party, he didn't feel that confident that Natalie would stay in his life. She might love him, but she was still a flight risk. When this wedding was over, the two of them might be over, too. That was the thought that kept his feelings in check when they were together.

"You know what?" he said. "Let's just put all these files in a box and I'll go through them later. I think clearing the room out is time better spent."

Natalie just nodded and started unloading files from the desk drawer into the file boxes he'd bought. They worked silently together until the room was empty of personal items, and then they hauled the boxes downstairs and into his truck.

The mood for the night had been spoiled and he hated that. His parents' near-divorce was hanging over his head, opening his eyes to things he'd never considered. It seemed strange to drink some wine and go on like he didn't know the truth.

And yet, it made him feel emboldened, too. He'd gone into this whole situation with Natalie consciously holding back. It was defensive, to keep himself from getting in too deep and getting hurt, but it also occurred to him that it might be a self-fulfilling prophecy. If he didn't give all of himself to Natalie, she wouldn't ever do the same.

If he wanted to keep Natalie in his life, he had to fight for her and be bold. His parents fought to stay together, and he was willing to do the same. But what would give her the confidence to believe in him and their relationship? She was so determined to think of marriage as a mistake that most people struggled to get out of. How could he convince her that he was in this for the long haul and she shouldn't be afraid to love him with all she had?

There was only one thing he could think of, and it was a major risk. But, as his father told him once, no risk, no reward. That philosophy had helped him build the family landscaping business into a multimillion-dollar operation across the Southeast. He had no doubt it would succeed. If he could pull it off, there was no way Natalie could turn her nose up at it.

Just like his Christmas bet, he intended to get everything that he wanted and make it into something Natalie wanted, too. He knew exactly what he needed to do. The timing couldn't be more perfect.

"What are you doing Wednesday night?" he asked.

* * *

Natalie looked out the window at the twinkling Christmas lights up ahead and knew exactly where they were. "Are you taking me to the Opryland Hotel?" Natalie asked.

"Actually, no, we're going someplace else."

Sitting back in her seat, she watched as Colin slowed and pulled into the parking area for the Grand Ole Opry. At that moment, she perked up, her mind spinning as she tried to figure out what day it was. It was the sixteenth. Blake Wright's concert was here tonight. But it was sold out...

"Colin?" she asked.

"Yes?"

"Did you...? Are we...?" She was so excited she couldn't even form the words. Why else would they be here if he hadn't managed to get tickets to the show?

"Yes, I did and yes, we are," he answered, pulling into a parking space.

She almost couldn't believe it. "There were no tickets left. They sold out in ten minutes. I know—I called."

Colin nodded as he turned off the car and faced her. "You're absolutely right. There were no seats left."

Natalie narrowed her gaze at him. "So, what? We're just going to lurk by the back door to see if we can get a glimpse of him?" She was willing to do that, of course, but it didn't seem like Colin's style.

"Something like that. Come on."

They got out of the car and he took her hand, leading her away from the crowd at the entrance and around the building toward the back. The door they were headed for said Private Entry in big red letters, and a very large man in a tight T-shirt stood watch. Colin didn't seem to care. He marched right up to him and pulled two tickets out of his jacket.

No, wait. Natalie looked closer. They weren't tickets. They were *backstage passes*. The security guard looked them over and checked the list on his clipboard.

"Welcome, Mr. Russell. So glad to have you joining us tonight." The mountain of a man stepped aside and let Natalie and Colin go into the sacred backstage of the famous concert hall.

She waited until the door shut before she lost her cool. "Are you kidding me? Backstage? We're going backstage at a Blake Wright concert? This is the Grand Ole Opry! Do you know how many amazing artists have walked where we are right now?"

Colin wasn't left with much time to answer her questions, so he just smiled and let her freak out. Passes in hand, they walked through the preconcert chaos until they located the stage manager.

"Looks like our special guests are here," the man said. "Welcome, folks. We've got two designated seats for you right over here." He indicated two chairs just off the curtained stage area. They were going to be watching the show from the wings, literally sitting unseen on the stage itself.

Natalie was so excited, she could barely sit down. Colin had to hold her hand to keep her from popping right up out of her seat. "Please tell me how you managed this," she said at last.

"Well, you know who does all the landscaping for Gaylord properties?"

She had no idea. "You?" she guessed.

"That is correct. Russell Landscaping has the contract to design and maintain all the outdoor spaces including the hotel and the concert venue. I called up a friend here and they set this up for me. Since there weren't any seats left, we had to get a little creative."

Natalie could hardly believe it. "This is amazing. I can't believe you did all this. I mean, you already gave me my Christmas present. What is this for?"

Colin shrugged. "Because I could. You told me how your dad used to take you and how much you liked Blake, so I thought it would be a nice gesture."

"Well, I'm glad I dressed appropriately," she said, looking over her off-the-shoulder red silk top and skinny jeans with cowboy boots. "You just said we were going someplace to listen to country music. I was thinking maybe a bar downtown."

"Well, I would've given away the surprise if I'd said anything else."

Natalie could only shake her head. As the opening act brushed past them to go out onstage, she muffled her squeal of delight in Colin's coat sleeve.

When Blake and his band finally took the stage, it took everything she had not to jump up and down. She tried to play it cool, since she was here because of Colin's business connections, but it was very hard. Natalie could hold her composure during any kind of wedding crisis, but this was too much.

It was not just a great concert, but there were so many memories centered around this place. Her parents had been house poor, putting everything they had into a nice home for their family at the expense of everything else. They didn't have the latest gadgets or the coolest clothes, but she went to a good school and had everything she truly needed.

But once a year, around her birthday, her dad always

took her out for what he called a Daddy-Daughter date. She'd grown up listening to his favorite country music, and starting on her fifth birthday, he took her to a show at the Opry. It didn't matter who it was or that they had the worst seats in the house. It was more about sharing something with her father.

That tradition had fallen to the wayside after the divorce, and it had broken Natalie's heart. She hadn't stepped foot back into this concert hall since the last time her daddy brought her here.

And now, here she was, backstage. She didn't talk to her father very often, but she couldn't wait to tell him about this. He'd be amazed. Maybe it would even inspire him to take another trip here with her for old times' sake.

Glancing over at Colin, she realized he looked a little anxious and not at all like he was having a good time. He was stiff, clutching his knees and not so much as tapping his toes to the music. "You don't like country music, do you?" she asked.

"Oh no," he argued. "It's fine. I'm just tired."

Natalie didn't worry too much about it, focusing on the amazing show. About halfway through, Blake started introducing the next song.

"The song I'm going to play next was one of my biggest hits," he said. "It was my first real love song, written about my wife. I want to dedicate this song tonight to a very special lady. Natalie Sharpe, please come out onto the stage."

Natalie's heart stopped in her chest. Colin tried to pull her up out of her seat, but it took a moment for her to connect everything. "Me?" she asked, but he gave her a little shove and suddenly, she was onstage where everyone could see her.

"There she is," Blake said. "Come on out here, sugar."

Natalie walked stiffly over to where Blake was standing. Under her feet were the very boards of the original stage. The lights were shining on her, the crowd cheering. She thought she might pass out.

"Are you enjoying the show?" he asked.

"Absolutely. You're awesome," she said.

Blake laughed. "Well, thank you. Do you know who else is awesome? Colin Russell. Colin, why don't you come on out here, too?"

Natalie turned and watched Colin walk out onstage. What the heck was going on? Her life had suddenly become very surreal. It was one thing for Colin to arrange for her to get to go out onstage with her idol. Both of them onstage changed everything.

Blake slapped Colin on the back. "Now, Colin tells me he has something he wants to ask you."

The whole crowed started cheering louder. The blood rushed into Natalie's ears, drowning out everything but her heart's rapid thump. She barely had time to react, her body moving like it was caught in molasses. She looked over at Colin just in time to see him slip down onto one knee. *Oh dear, sweet Jesus.* He wasn't. He couldn't be. This was not happening.

"Natalie," Colin began, "I've known you since we were teenagers. When you came back into my life, I knew you were someone special. The more time we spend together, the more I realize that I want to spend all my time with you, for the rest of my life. I love you, Natalie Sharpe. Will you marry me?"

Now Natalie was certain she was going to pass out.

She could feel the whole concert hall start to spin. Her chest grew tight, her cheeks burned. What was he thinking? All these people were watching. Blake was watching...

Colin held up the ring. It was beautiful—a large oval diamond set in platinum with a pear-shaped diamond flanking it on each side. The cut and clarity were amazing. The stone glittered with the lights on the stage, beckoning her to reach out and take it. All she had to do was say yes, and he would slip it on her finger.

And then what? They'd get married and last a few years at best? Then they'd get divorced and spend months squabbling in court? In the end, she'd become a bitter divorcée and sell this same beautiful ring in a ranting ad on Craigslist.

Yes, she loved him, but why did they have to get married? He was ruining everything they'd built together by changing their whole relationship dynamic. Love or no, she couldn't do it. She just couldn't get the words out. All she knew was that she had to get out of here. Avoiding his gaze, Natalie shook her head. "No. I'm sorry, I can't," she said, before turning and running off the stage.

As she ran, she was only aware of an eerie silence. The entire concert hall had quieted. The crew backstage all stood around in stunned confusion. Apparently no one had expected her to reject his proposal.

"Natalie!" she heard Colin yell, but she couldn't stop. She weaved in and out of people and equipment, desperately searching for the side door where they'd come in. Just as she found it, she heard the music start playing again. Life went on for everyone else, just as her life started to unravel.

Bursting through the doors, she took in a huge gulp of cool air that she desperately needed. The security guard watched her curiously as she bent over and planted her hands on her knees for support.

Marriage? He'd proposed marriage! He'd taken a perfectly wonderful evening and ruined it with those silly romantic notions. Why did he do that?

"Natalie?" Colin said as he came out the door behind her a moment later.

She turned around to face him, not sure what to say. She felt the prickle of tears start to sting her eyes. "What were you thinking?" she asked. "You know how I feel about marriage!"

"I was thinking that you loved me and wanted to be with me," he replied, his own face reddening with emotion.

"We had an agreement, Colin. We were not going to fall in love. This was supposed to be fun and easy."

"That's how it started, but it changed. For both of us. Tell me you love me, Natalie. Don't lie about it, not now."

She took a deep breath, trying to get the words out of her mouth for the first time. "I do love you," she said. "But that doesn't change my answer. I don't want to get married. That just ruins everything that we have going so perfectly right now. I've told you before I don't believe in marriage. Proposing out of the blue makes me think you don't listen to me at all. If you did, you never would've done something like...like..."

"Something so romantic and thoughtful?" he suggested. "Something so perfect and special to commemorate the moment so you'd never forget it? Something that a woman that truly loved me could never turn down?"

"Something so public!" she shouted instead. "Did you think that you could twist my arm into accepting your proposal by having four thousand witnesses? You proposed to me onstage in front of Blake Wright! All those people watching us." She shook her head, still in disbelief that the night had taken such a drastic turn. "That whole thing is probably going to end up on the internet and go viral."

Colin's hands curled into controlled fists at his sides. She could see the ring box still in one hand. "Is that what you think I was doing with all of this? I couldn't possibly have been trying to craft the perfect moment to start our lives together. Obviously, I was just *coercing you* into marrying me, because that worked out so well for me the first time."

It was perfect. It had been perfect. And if she was any other woman, it would've been the kind of story she would've told her grandchildren about. But she couldn't pull the trigger. This was too much, too soon. She'd just come to terms with loving him; she wasn't ready to sign her life away to this man. They might have known each other since they were kids, but how much did they really know about each other?

"You hardly know me, and yet you want to change me. If you really loved me, Colin, you wouldn't force me into something I don't want to do. You would understand that I need time for a step this big, and that I might never want to make that leap."

He ran his hand through his hair in incredulity. "Yes, I'm such a horrible person for inviting you to be a part of my family and to let me love you forever. What a bastard I am!"

Natalie stopped, his beautiful, yet rage-filled words

sending a tear spilling down her cheek. There was no stopping the tears now, and she hated that. She hated to cry more than anything else. How had this perfect night gone so wrong? "You can do all that without a marriage."

"But why would I want to? It doesn't make any sense, Natalie. Why can't you make that commitment to me? You know, I always thought you were such a strong woman. So in control, so self-assured. But in reality, you're a damn coward."

"What?" she asked through her tears.

"You heard me. You hide behind this big philosophical cover story about love and marriage being this forced social paradigm and whatever other crap you've recited because you're afraid of getting hurt. You're afraid to give in and let someone love you, then have it not work out."

Natalie didn't know what to say to that. It was true. She'd justified her own fears in her mind with all the statistics and academic findings she could spew. But the truth was that she used it all to keep men away. She'd done a hell of a job this time. She didn't want to lose Colin entirely, though. Couldn't they just go back to before he proposed? Pretend like tonight never happened?

"I might be scared to take the leap, but what if I'm right? What if I'd said yes and we had this big wedding and four kids and one day, we wake up and hate each other?"

"And what if we don't? What if we do all of that and we're actually happy together for the rest of our lives? Did you ever consider that option while you were wringing your hands?"

Did she dare consider it? Her mom considered it over

and over just to fail. Time had turned her into a bitter woman constantly searching for something to complete her. Natalie wouldn't let herself become like that. "I'm sorry, Colin. I just can't take that chance."

Colin stuffed his hands in his pockets, his posture stiff and unyielding. "Don't be sorry. If you don't want to marry me, that's fine. It doesn't matter what your reasoning is. But I'm done with the two of us. One marriage to a reluctant bride is enough for me. Come on, I'll drive you home."

"I think I should take a cab. That would be easier on us both."

She saw the shimmer of tears in his eyes for just a moment before he turned and walked away. Natalie could only stand and watch as he got into his car and drove away.

As his taillights disappeared into the distance, Natalie felt her heart start to crumble in her chest. She'd been so afraid to love and be loved that she had driven Colin away and made her fears a reality.

With one simple *no*, Natalie had ruined everything.

Eleven

Colin avoided going to the chapel for as long as he could. He didn't want to see Natalie. He didn't want to spend most of the evening with her, pretending everything was fine for the benefit of his sister and her fiancé. Like any injured animal, he wanted to stay in his den and lick his wounds alone.

The worst part was that he knew he'd done this to himself. Natalie had been very clear on the fact that she never wanted to get married and yet, he'd proposed to her anyway. He'd thought perhaps it was some sort of defense mechanism, insisting she didn't want it so people wouldn't pity her for not having it.

Overhearing her confession to Gretchen of being in love with him had given him a false hope. Somehow, he'd believed that offering her his heart and a lifetime commitment would not only show her he was serious, but that she had nothing to fear. That hadn't panned out at all.

What was wrong with him? Why was he so attracted to women who didn't want the same things he wanted? It was like he was subconsciously setting himself up for failure. Maybe *he* was the one who was really afraid of being hurt, so he chose women he could never really have. What a mess.

Pulling his truck into the parking lot of the chapel, he parked but didn't get out. The rehearsal was supposed to start in twenty minutes. No need to rush in just because there was no sense in going all the way home first.

Glancing out the window, he looked around at the other cars. He spotted Natalie's sports car, plus a handful of other vehicles he didn't recognize. There were no motorcycles, though. And no little hatchback. Where were Lily and Frankie?

Reaching for his phone, he dialed his sister's number. "Hello?" she shouted over a dull roar of noise around her.

"Lily, where are you?"

"We're stuck in the Vegas airport. Our flight got cancelled because of bad weather in Denver. We've been changed to a new flight, but it's not leaving until tomorrow morning."

"Tomorrow morning? You're going to miss the rehearsal and the dinner." Colin knew the weather wasn't Lily's fault, but things like this always seemed to happen when she was involved. Who booked a flight that connected through Denver in the winter, anyway?

"I know, Colin!" she snapped. "We're not going to make it in time for your choreographed circus. That's why I called Natalie first and told her. She said she'd handle things tonight and go over the details with us tomorrow afternoon before the service. We're doing what we can. It isn't the end of the world."

Nothing was ever a big deal to Lily. She said Colin was wrapped too tight and needed to loosen up, but he would counter that she needed to take some things— like her wedding day—more seriously.

"Just cancel the rehearsal dinner reservations," she continued. "It was only the wedding party and Frankie's parents, anyway."

That he could do. Thank goodness they hadn't opted for the big catered dinner with out-of-town guests. "Fine. You promise you'll be back tomorrow?"

"I can't control the weather, Colin. We'll get back as soon as we can."

Colin hung up the phone, a feeling of dread pooling in his gut. He was beginning to think this entire thing was a mistake. Lily didn't want this wedding, and he'd twisted her arm. If he hadn't done that, he wouldn't have made such a calculated error with Natalie. Lily would be happily courthouse married. He wouldn't have learned the truth about his parents' marriage yet. There also wouldn't be an extremely expensive diamond engagement ring in his coat pocket.

He needed to take it back to the jeweler, but he hadn't had the heart to do it. He'd return it on Monday when all of this was over. That would close the book on this whole misguided adventure and then, maybe, he could move on.

With a sigh, he opened the door and slipped out of the truck. After talking to Lily, he knew he needed to get inside and see what needed to be done to compensate for the absence of the engaged couple.

Inside the chapel, things were hopping. The doors to the reception hall were propped open for vendors to come in and out with decorations. He could see Gretchen and the photographer, Bree, putting out place settings on the tables. A produce truck was unloading crates of fruits and vegetables into the kitchen.

Natalie was in the center of the chaos, as always. She was setting out name cards shaped like snowflakes on a table in the crossroads of the chapel entrance. A large white tree was on the table in front of her, dripping with crystals, pearls and twinkle lights. She was stringing silver ribbon through each name card and then hanging it from a branch on the tree, creating a sparkling blizzard effect.

She reached for another, hesitating as she noticed Colin standing a few feet away. "Have you spoken with your sister?" she asked, very cold and professional once again.

"Yes. Will we still have a rehearsal?"

"Yes." Natalie set down a snowflake and turned toward him. "It's not just for the benefit of the bride and groom. It helps the pastor, the musicians and the rest of the wedding party. They only have a best man and maid of honor, so it might be a short rehearsal, but it's still needed to get everyone else comfortable with the flow."

"Are the others here?"

"We're just waiting on the maid of honor."

"What about the parts for the bride and groom in the ceremony?"

"We'll have to get someone to stand in for them both. I've had to do this before—it's not a big deal. I had a bride get food poisoning, and she missed everything leading up to the ceremony. It all turned out fine."

"Okay." Her confidence made him feel better despite the anxious tension in his shoulders. "I'll stand in for Frankie, if you need me to. I'm not in the wedding party, so I don't have anything else to do."

Natalie smiled politely and reached for her paper snowflake again. "Thanks for volunteering. You can go into the chapel and wait with the others if you like. We'll begin momentarily."

Even though he was angry with her, he couldn't stand to see the blank, detached expression on her face when she looked at him. He wanted to see those dark brown eyes filled with love, or even just the light of passion or laughter. He wanted to reach out and shake her until she showed any kind of emotion. Anger, fear, he didn't care. She had been so afraid to feel anything before they met. He worried that after their blowup, she'd completely retreat into herself. He might not be the one who got to love her for the rest of her life, but someone should.

Natalie would have to let someone, however, and he had no control over that.

He wanted to say something to her. Anything. But he didn't want to start another fight here. Instead, he nodded and disappeared into the chapel to wait with the others. That was the best thing to do if they were going to get through all this without more turmoil than they already had.

The maid of honor walked in a few minutes later with Natalie on her heels. She had her headset on and her stiff, purposeful walk had returned.

"Okay, everyone, I'm going to go over this once, quickly, then we will walk through the whole ceremony so everyone gets a feel for their roles and how it will all go."

Colin stood with his arms crossed over his chest as she handed out instructions to the string quartet in the corner, the ushers and the wedding party.

"Colin is our stand-in groom today. After you escort in your parents, you and the best man are going to follow the pastor in and wait at the front of the church for the ceremony to start. Everyone ready?"

All the people in the chapel, excepting the musicians, went out into the hall. Colin and the best man, Steve, followed Pastor Greene into the chapel, taking their places on the front platform. The string quartet played a soothing melody that sounded familiar, but he didn't know the name. At the back of the room, Natalie gave a cue to the pastor before slipping into the vestibule. He asked everyone to rise. The musicians transitioned to a different song, playing louder to announce the coming of the bridal party.

The doors opened and the maid of honor made her way down the aisle. She moved to the opposite side of the landing and waited for the doors to open a final time. The music built a sense of anticipation that made Colin anxious to see what was about to happen, even as a stand-in groom for a rehearsal.

The doors of the chapel swung open, and standing there holding a bouquet of silk flowers, was Natalie. His chest tightened as she walked down the aisle toward him. She was wearing a burgundy silk blouse and a black pencil skirt instead of a white gown, but it didn't matter. The moment was all too real to Colin.

But with every step she took, reality sunk in even more. This wasn't their rehearsal and they weren't getting married. She had turned him down, flat, in front of a couple thousand people and a country music star.

The sentimental feelings quickly dissipated, the muscles in his neck and shoulders tightening with irritation and anger.

Natalie avoided his gaze as she approached the platform. She looked only at the pastor. Her full lips were thin and pressed hard into a line of displeasure. Neither of them seemed very happy to have to go through all this so soon after their blowup.

This was going to be an interesting rehearsal.

Natalie wished there was someone else to fill in for Lily, but there just wasn't. Everyone else was preparing for tomorrow and Bree was capturing everything—including her awkward moments with Colin—on camera. All she could do was man up, grab the dummy bouquet and march down the aisle so they could get through this.

"Frankie will take Lily's hand and help her up onto the platform," the pastor explained. "Lily will pass her bouquet to the maid of honor to hold, then I will read the welcome passages about marriage."

Natalie took Colin's hand, ignoring the thrill that ran up her arm as they touched. She clenched her teeth as she handed off the bouquet and listened to the pastor go through his spiel. They had opted for the traditional, nondenominational Christian service, passing on any long biblical passages. Colin had insisted that Lily didn't want to stand up here for a drawn-out religious service. She wanted to get married and then cue the party.

"When I finish, Frankie and Lily will turn to face each other and hold hands while they recite the vows."

This was the part Natalie was dreading. Turning to Colin, she took the other hand he offered. It was awk-

ANDREA LAURENCE 161

ward to stare at his chest, so she forced her chin up to meet his eyes. The initial contact was like a punch to her stomach. There wasn't a hint of warmth in those golden eyes. He hated her, and she understood that. She had thrown his love in his face. She didn't know what else to do. Say yes? Dive headfirst into the fantasy of marriage like everyone else? She could see now how easy it was to get swept up into it. The current was strong.

Even now, as they stood on the altar together, she felt her body start to relax and her resistance fade. Colin repeated Frankie's vows, the words of love and trust making Natalie's chest ache. His expression softened as he spoke, slipping a pretend ring onto her finger.

When it was her turn to recite Lily's vows, the anxiety was gone. She felt a sense of peace standing here with Colin, as though that was where they were truly meant to be. She loved him. She was scared, but she loved him and had loved him since she was fifteen years old. She'd never felt this way for anyone else because of that. Her heart was already taken, so why would she have any desire to love or marry another man?

She wanted to marry Colin. There was no question of it now. Why did she have to have this revelation two days too late?

She felt her hands start to tremble in his as her voice began to shake as well. Colin narrowed his gaze at her, squeezing her hands tighter to calm the tremble. She was glad to have an imaginary ring, because she was certain she would've dropped any real jewelry trying to put it on his finger.

Natalie felt tears form in her eyes as the pastor talked about their holy vows. She wanted to interrupt the rehearsal, to blurt out right then and there that she was wrong. She was sorry for letting her fears get in the way. And most important, that she very desperately wanted to marry him.

"I'll pronounce them man and wife, then instruct Frankie to kiss the bride," the pastor explained. "They'll kiss, holding together long enough for the photographer to get a good shot. Then Lily will get her bouquet and the couple will turn out to face the congregation. I'll announce them as Mr. and Mrs. Frank Watson, and then you'll exit the chapel."

The musicians started playing the exit song. Colin offered his arm and she took it. They stepped down the stairs and along the aisle to the back of the chapel.

When they walked through the doorway, he immediately pulled away from her. She instantly missed the warmth and nearness of his touch, but she knew the moment had passed. The Colin standing beside her now hated her once again.

She recovered by returning to her professional duties. She waited until the maid of honor and best man came out of the chapel behind them, then she returned to the doorway, clapping. "Great job everyone. Now, at this point, the bridal party will be escorted away so the guests can move into the reception hall, then we'll bring you back into the chapel to take pictures. Does anyone have any questions?"

Everyone shook their heads. It was a small wedding and not particularly complicated aside from the absence of the bride and groom. "Great. Let's make sure everyone is here at the chapel by three tomorrow. We'll do some pictures with Bree before the ceremony. If anything happens, you all have my cell phone number."

People started scattering from the room, Colin

amongst them. "Colin?" she called out to him before she lost her nerve.

He stopped and turned back to face her. "Yes?"

"Can I talk to you for a minute?"

"About what?" She'd never seen him so stiff and unfriendly. It was even worse than it had been before the rehearsal. "Everything for the wedding is set, isn't it?"

"Yes, of course."

"Then we have nothing to talk about."

His abrupt shutdown rattled her. "I, I mean, could you please just give me two minutes to talk about what happened at the concert?"

He shook his head, his jaw so tight it was like stone. "I think you said all you needed to say on that stage, don't you?"

She had said a lot, but she had said all the wrong things. "No. Please, Colin. You don't understand how much I—"

He held up his hand to silence her. "Natalie, stop. You don't want to marry me. That's fine. I'm through with trying to convince unwilling women to be my wife. But like I said that night, I'm done. I don't want to discuss it ever again. Let's just forget it ever happened so we can get through this wedding without any more drama, okay?"

Before she could answer, Colin turned and disappeared from the chapel. Natalie heard the chime as he opened the front door and headed for his truck.

With every step he took, she felt her heart sink further into her stomach. Her knees threatened to give out from under her, forcing her to sit down in one of the rear pews. She held it together long enough for the musicians to leave, but once she was alone, she completely came undone.

It had been a long time since Natalie cried—good and cried. She got teary at the occasional commercial or news article. She'd shed a tear with Amelia when she lost her first baby in the spring and a few at the concert the other night. But nothing like this. Not since... she paused in her tears to think. Not since her father left Christmas day.

She dropped her face into her hands, trying not to ugly sob so loudly that it echoed through the chapel. There were a lot of people going in and out of the building today, but she didn't want anyone to see her in such a wretched state.

"Natalie?" a voice called from behind her, as if on cue.

She straightened to attention, wiping her eyes and cheeks without smearing her mascara. "Yes?" she replied without turning around to expose her red, puffy face. "What do you need?"

Natalie sensed the presence move closer until she noticed Gretchen standing at the entrance of the pew beside her. "I need you to scoot over and tell me what the hell is going on."

She complied, knowing there was no way out of this now. Gretchen settled into the seat, politely keeping her gaze trained on the front of the chapel. She didn't say a word, waiting for Natalie to spill her guts on her own time.

"I like Christmas," Natalie confessed. "I like the lights and the food and the music. My holiday humbug days are behind me."

"What? That's why you're crying?"

"Yes. No. Yes and no. I'm crying because I've finally found my Christmas spirit and it doesn't matter. None of it matters because Colin and I are over."

Gretchen groaned in disappointment. "What happened? You seemed pretty enamored with him a few days ago."

"He…proposed. Onstage at the Blake Wright concert. In front of everyone."

"Well, I could see how a lifetime promise of love and devotion in front of thousands of witnesses could ruin a relationship."

Natalie noted her friend's flat tone. "I panicked. And I said no. And I didn't do it well. I said some pretty ugly things to him."

Gretchen put her arm around Natalie's shoulder. "Why are you fighting this so hard? What are you afraid of, Natalie?"

"I'm afraid…" She took a deep breath. "I'm afraid that I'm going to let myself fall for the fantasy and he's going to leave."

"The fantasy?" Gretchen questioned.

"Love. Marriage."

"How can you still see it as a fantasy when you know you're in love with him?"

"Because I can't be certain it's real. This could just be a biological attachment to ensure the care of my nonexistent offspring. And even if it is real, I can't be sure it will last."

"You can't be certain of anything in life, Natalie. Maybe it's biology, maybe it's not. But by pushing Colin away, you're guaranteeing that you're going to lose him. It doesn't matter if your feelings will last now."

"I know," Natalie said with a sigh. "I realized that

today when we were standing on the altar during the rehearsal. Up there, holding his hands and looking into his eyes, I realized that I want to be with Colin. I want to marry him. He's worth the risk. But it's too late. I've ruined everything. He won't even speak to me about anything but Lily's wedding."

"I think he might just need a little time. You've both got a lot on your minds with the wedding. They're so stressful. But once that's done, I say reach out to him. Put your heart on the line the way he did. Take the risk. If he says no, you haven't lost anything. But if you can get him to listen to how you feel, you can gain everything."

Natalie nodded and dried the last of her tears. Gretchen was right. How had she become a relationship expert so quickly?

She knew what she had to do now. She had to hand her heart to Colin on a silver platter and pray he didn't crush it.

Twelve

Colin was trying to keep his mind occupied. Just a few more hours and all this would be over. He could give the keys to the house to his sister, pay the bill for the wedding and walk out of this place like he'd never fallen in love with Natalie Sharpe.

Sure, it would be that easy.

He was busying himself by greeting guests as they came into the chapel. He assisted the ushers in handing out programs, hugging and kissing friends and family as they came in. A lot of folks had shown up for Lily's big day and he was pleased. They had sent out a lot of email invitations, but in the rush, he wasn't sure who had accepted until they walked in the door.

He was very surprised to see Natalie's mother and father walk into the chapel. They had big smiles on their faces as they chatted and made their way over to him.

Perhaps time and distance had healed their wounds, even if Natalie's remained fresh.

"Mr. Sharpe," Colin said, shaking the man's hand.

"How are you, son?"

"Doing well," he lied. "So glad you could make it for Lily and Frankie's big day."

He hugged Natalie's mother and the usher escorted them all down the aisle to their seats. Casually, he glanced at his watch. It was getting close to time. He'd expected to see Frankie by now, but every bearded, tattooed guy that caught his eye was just a guest of the groom.

Glancing across the foyer, he spotted Natalie and instantly knew that something was wrong. She looked decidedly flustered and he didn't expect that of her, even after everything that happened last night. She looked very put-together, as usual, in a light gray linen suit with her headset on and her crystal-encrusted tablet clutched to her chest, but there was an anxiety lining her dark eyes.

As much as he didn't want to talk to her, he made his way through the crowd of arriving wedding guests to where she was standing. "What's the matter?"

Taking him by the elbow, she led him into the hallway near her office where they were out of the guests' earshot. "They're not here yet."

"They who?"

"Your sister and her fiancé. The flight they were supposed to be on landed four hours ago, I checked, but I haven't heard a word from either of them. I've got a hair and makeup crew twiddling their thumbs. The wedding starts in thirty minutes and I've got no couple to marry."

An icy-cold fear started rushing through his veins. He'd worried about this almost from the moment he'd insisted that Lily have a formal wedding. It didn't surprise him at all. She'd given in to his request far too easily. He should've known she'd do something like this when the opportunity arose. "I'm sure they're on their way," he said, trying to soothe her nerves even as his lit up with panic. "This has to happen all the time, right?"

"No. It's *never* happened. I have had grooms bail, brides bail, but never both of them together. You've got to track her down. Now. She's not answering my calls."

"Okay. I'll try calling her right now." He stepped away from her office and went down the hall to the far corner where the sounds of the crowd wouldn't interfere. As he was about to raise the phone to his ear, it vibrated and chimed in his hand. When he looked down, it was like someone had kicked him in the stomach. The air was completely knocked out of him.

It was a photo text from his sister. She and Frankie were standing under the Chapel of Love sign, sporting wedding rings. They were wearing jeans. She had a little veil on her head and a carnation bouquet in her hand. "Guess what? We decided to stay in Vegas and elope! Sorry about the plans."

Sorry about the plans. His chest started to tighten. Sorry about the plans? There were two hundred people in the chapel, a staff in the kitchen preparing the dinner. There were *ten thousand dollars'* worth of flowers decorating the ballroom. That was just the ballroom! But the bride and groom decided to elope in Vegas. So sorry.

When he was finally able to look up from his phone, he caught Natalie's eye from across the hall. She looked the way he felt, with a distraught expression on her face. She held up her own phone to display the same picture he was looking at.

They moved quickly toward each other, meeting in the middle. "What do we do?"

Natalie took a deep breath. "Well, obviously there isn't going to be a wedding, so we can send the preacher home. The food and band are already paid for, and there's no sense in it all going to waste. So if I were you, I'd lie and tell them that Lily and Frankie got stuck in Vegas because of bad weather and decided to elope. Invite them to celebrate at the reception, have dinner, eat the cake and send everyone home."

Colin dropped his face into his hands. How had this week turned into such a disaster? His proposal to Natalie couldn't have gone worse. His sister was a no-show for her own wedding. He was feeling like he wanted to just walk out the door and lock himself in his bedroom until the New Year.

He supposed her suggestion was sensible. There was no point in wasting all that food. "I guess that's what we'll have to do, then. What a mess. I'm going to kill her when she gets home. I mean it."

"There is one other option," she said in a voice so small he almost didn't hear it.

Colin looked up to see Natalie nervously chewing at her lip. "What other option?"

She looked at him for a moment, a determined tilt to her chin that hadn't been there before. "This is going to sound crazy, but hear me out, okay?"

"At this point, I'm open to anything."

"I'm sorry, Colin. I'm sorry about the way I reacted to your proposal. I know I hurt you and I didn't intend to. But you were right, I was just scared. My whole life I've seen relationships fall apart and I told myself I'd never put myself through that. And then I fell in love with you anyway. I didn't know what to do. When you proposed, the moment was so perfect and I just panicked. I ruined it all and I can never tell you just how sorry I am. I would go back in time and change it if I could, but I can't."

Colin had certainly not been expecting this right now. With everything else going on, he wasn't entirely sure he was emotionally capable of handling her apology. "Natalie, can we talk about this later? I understand you want to get this off your chest, but we're in the middle of a crisis here."

"And I'm trying to fix it," she countered. "Do you love me, Colin?"

He looked down at her heart-shaped face, her brow furrowed in worry. The headset lined her cheek, the microphone hovering right at the corner of her full, pink lips. Of course he loved her. That was what hurt the most. They loved each other, but for some reason, everything had gone wrong and he didn't understand why. Although he didn't want to admit it, he figured it couldn't hurt at this point.

"Yes, I love you, Natalie. That's why I proposed to you. I wanted to start a life with you and I thought you wanted the same thing."

"I didn't know what I wanted, but now I do. I do want to start a life with you."

Colin barely had a chance to process Natalie's words before she dropped down onto one knee in front of him. "Natalie, what are you doing?"

"I love you, Colin. There's nothing I want more than to marry you and build a life together. I'm sorry that I ruined your grand proposal, but I have another one for you. Will you marry me?"

Colin looked around, trying to see if anyone was watching the bizarre scene in front of him. "Are you proposing to me?"

Natalie took his hand and held it tightly in her own. "Yes. I want to marry you, Colin. Right now."

He stiffened, then dropped down on his own knee, so they could discuss this eye to eye. "You want to get married right now?"

She smiled wide. "Why not? We've got a chapel full of your family just a few feet away. My parents are even here. The wedding gown fits me. Not to mention that we've got a big, beautiful reception waiting that you and I planned together. It's exactly the wedding I would choose if we were going to get married any other day. It's going to go to waste if we don't use it, so why not today?"

Colin's heart started racing in his chest. Would they really go through with this? "Natalie, are you sure? I can't bear to have another wife change her mind and walk out of my life. If we get married today, we're getting married forever. Are you okay with that?"

She reached out and cupped his face, holding his cheeks in her hands. "I am very okay with that. You're not getting rid of me, mister."

"Okay, then yes, I will marry you," he said with a grin. He leaned forward to kiss her, the mouthpiece of her headset getting in the way.

"Oops," Natalie said, lifting it up. "Just as well," she noted as she leaned back. "I think we need to save our next kiss for the one at the altar, don't you?"

It was entirely possible that Natalie had lost her mind. She wasn't just getting married, she was getting married on a whim. It was crazy. It was so unlike her.

And she'd never been more excited in her life.

She wanted this more than anything, and getting married quickly was the only thing that would keep her from sabotaging herself.

Natalie rushed toward the bridal suite, reaching out to grab Gretchen's arm and drag her down the hallway with her.

"Where are we going?" she asked. "I'm supposed to be fetching something for Bree."

She kept going. "Don't worry about Bree. I need you to help me get ready."

"Help you get ready to do what?"

"To marry Colin."

A sudden resistant weight stopped her forward progress and jerked her back. "Would you like to repeat that, please?"

Natalie sighed and turned toward her. "The bride and groom aren't coming. Colin and I are getting married instead. I need you to help me get dressed."

Gretchen's jaw dropped, but she followed her willingly to the bridal suite in a state of shock. The hair and makeup crew were loitering there, waiting for the missing bride.

"Change of plans, ladies," Natalie announced, pulling off her headset and tugging the band from her ponytail. "I'm the bride now. I need the best, fastest work you can do."

She settled down in the chair and the team quickly went to work. A soft knock came a few minutes later and Bree slipped in with her camera. "Are we ready to take some pictures of the bride getting read—?" Bree stopped short when she saw Natalie in the chair. "What's going on?"

"Natalie is getting married." Gretchen held up the cell phone picture of their wayward couple. "You're taking pictures of her and Colin instead."

Bree took a deep breath and started nervously adjusting the lens on her camera. "Well, okay then. You might want to give Amelia a heads-up in the meantime. She'll have a fit if she's in the kitchen and misses the ceremony."

Gretchen nodded and slipped out. Within about twenty minutes, Natalie was completely transformed. Her ponytail was brushed out, straightened and wrapped into a French twist. She was painted with classic cat eyes, dark lashes and rosy cheeks. They opted for a nude lip with a touch of sparkle.

By the time Gretchen returned, Natalie was ready to slip into the dress. "Colin has spoken to the pastor, so he's on board. I brought your dad out of the chapel to walk you down the aisle. He's waiting outside."

Perfect. That was an important detail she hadn't considered in her rash proposal. Thank goodness her parents were both here. She'd never hear the end of it if either of them had missed her wedding.

"Let's get you in this gown," Gretchen said.

It took a few minutes to get Natalie laced and buttoned into her wedding dress. The hairdresser positioned the veil in her hair and turned her toward the full-length mirror to look at herself.

Her heart stuttered in her chest when she saw her reflection. She made for a beautiful bride. And this time, unlike at the bridal salon, she was really going to be the bride. This was suddenly her day, and her gown. She was so happy they'd chosen this dress. Any other one just wouldn't have suited her.

"Wow, honey," Gretchen said. "You look amazing. Do you have heels?"

Natalie looked down at her sensible black flats and shook her head. That was one thing she didn't have. "I guess I'll just go barefoot," she replied, kicking out of her shoes.

Gretchen picked up the bridal bouquet that was waiting in a vase on the side table. She handed it over to Natalie with a touch of glassy tears in her eyes. "I can't believe this is happening. I'm so happy for you and Colin."

Natalie took a deep breath and nodded. "I can't believe it either, really. But let's make it happen before reality sets in and I launch into a panic attack. Go tell everyone the bride is ready and cue the musicians."

Gretchen disappeared and Natalie waited a few moments until she knew the doors to the chapel were closed. She stepped out to find her father, looking dumbfounded, on the bench outside. "Hi, Daddy."

He shot up from his seat, freezing as he saw her in her dress. "You look amazing. I'm not sure what's going on, but you look more beautiful than any bride I've ever seen in my life."

Natalie leaned in to hug him. "It's a long story, but I'm glad you're here."

The music grew louder, cueing up the bride. Natalie nearly reached for her headset before she remembered she was the bride this time. "Let's go get married, Daddy."

They walked to the doors and waited for them to swing open. The chapel was filled with people, all of them standing at the bride's arrival. It was hard for her to focus on any of them, though. Her eyes instantly went to the front of the chapel.

Colin stood there in his tuxedo, looking as handsome as ever. There wasn't a touch of nervousness on his face as he watched her walk down the aisle. There was nothing but adoration and love on his face. Looking into his eyes, she felt her own anxiety slip away. It was just like at the rehearsal. Everything faded away but the two of them.

Before she knew it, they'd walked the long aisle and were standing at the front of the chapel. Her father gave her a hug and a kiss on the cheek before passing her hand off to the waiting Colin. "Take care of my girl," he warned his future son-in-law before taking his seat.

They stepped up onto the raised platform together and waited for the pastor to start the ceremony.

"Dearly beloved, we gather here today to celebrate the blessed union of Frank and Lily."

Colin cleared his throat, interrupting the pastor as a rumble of voices traveled through the chapel. "Colin and Natalie," he corrected in a whisper.

The pastor's eyes widened in panic when he realized his mistake. Natalie had worked with this pastor before and knew that he had the names typed into his text. "Oh yes, so sorry. To celebrate the blessed union of *Colin and Natalie*."

The pastor continued on, but all Natalie could hear was the beating of her own heart. All she could feel was Colin's warm hand enveloping hers. When the pastor prompted them to turn and face each other, they did, and Natalie felt a sense of peace in Colin's gaze. He smiled at her, brushing his thumbs across the backs of her hands in a soothing motion.

"Are you okay?" he whispered.

Natalie nodded. She had never been better.

"Do you, Colin Edward Russell, take Natalie Lynn Sharpe to be your lawfully wedded wife? Will you love and respect her? Will you be honest with her? Will you stand by her through whatever may come until your days on this Earth come to an end?"

"I will."

"And do you, Natalie Lynn Sharpe, take Colin Edward Russell to be your lawfully wedded husband? Will you love and respect him? Will you be honest with him? Will you stand by him through whatever may come until your days on this Earth come to an end?"

She took a deep breath, a momentary flash of panic lighting in Colin's eyes. "I will," she said with a grin.

"Fra-*Colin*," the pastor stuttered. "What token do you give of the vows you have made?"

"A ring," Colin replied, pulling the same ring box from his coat pocket that he'd presented her with on the stage Wednesday night.

"You had the ring with you?" Natalie whispered.

"I was mad, but I hadn't given up on you yet." Colin opened the box and settled the exquisite diamond ring over the tip of her finger.

"Repeat after me. I give you this ring as a token of my vow." He paused, allowing Colin to respond. "With all that I am and all that I have, I honor you, and with this ring, I thee wed."

"...and with this ring, I thee wed," Colin repeated, slipping the ring onto her finger and squeezing her hand reassuringly.

"Natalie," the pastor asked, "what token do you give of the vows you have made?"

In an instant, Natalie's blood ran cold. She'd planned every moment, every aspect of this wedding. Everything but the rings. She had no ring. "I don't have anything," she whispered to the pastor.

The pastor hesitated, looking around the room for an answer to the problem as though there would be rings dangling from the ceiling on threads. This was probably the most stressful ceremony he'd ever done.

Even though she was the bride, Natalie was still a problem solver. She turned to the pews and the faces looking up at them. "Does anyone have a man's ring we can borrow for the ceremony?"

"I have a ring," a man said, getting up from Frankie's side of the chapel.

He was obviously a friend of Frankie's. They both shared a common love of bushy beards, tattoos and bow ties with matching suspenders. He jogged up the aisle, slipping a ring off his finger and handing it to Natalie.

"Thank you," she said. "We'll give it back as soon as we get a replacement."

"That's okay, you can keep it."

He returned to his seat and Natalie looked down at the ring in her hand. It was a heavy silver band with a skull centered on it. There were glittering red stones in the eye sockets. Natalie bit her lip to keep from laughing. A ring was a ring and that was what she needed. There was no being picky right now. She placed it on the tip of Colin's finger and repeated after the pastor.

It wasn't until the ring was firmly seated on his finger that Colin looked down. He snorted in a short burst of laughter and shook his head. Skulls must not be his thing.

The pastor didn't notice. He was probably just happy

they had rings and it was time to wrap up the ceremony.
"Colin and Natalie, as you have both affirmed your love
for each other and have made a promise to each other to
live in this union, I challenge you both to remember to
cherish each other, to respect each other's thoughts and
ideas, and most important, to forgive each other. May
you live each day in love, always being there to give
love, comfort and refuge in the good times and the bad.

"As Colin and Natalie have now exchanged vows and
rings, and pledged their love and faith for each other, it
is my pleasure and honor to pronounce them Man and
Wife. You may kiss the bride."

"This is the part I've been waiting for," Colin said
with a wide smile. He took a step forward, cradling
her cheeks in his hands and lifting her lips to his own.

"Wait," Natalie whispered just before their lips
touched. "I need to tell you something."

Colin hesitated, his eyes wide with panic. She realized then that he thought she was changing her mind.
"You won," she said quickly.

"Won what?" he asked.

"You won the bet," she admitted with a smile. "Merry
Christmas, Mr. Russell. It's time to claim your prize."

"That I will. Merry Christmas, Mrs. Russell."

The kiss was soft and tender, holding the promise of
a lifetime together and a thousand more kisses to come.
It sent a thrill through her whole body, both from his
touch and from the knowledge that they were now husband and wife. He had promised her a life-changing kiss
and that's what he had delivered in more ways than one.

"I love you," he whispered as he pulled away, careful not to smear her lipstick before they took pictures.

She could barely hear him over the applause of the

crowd, but she would know the sound of those words coming from his lips anywhere. "I love you," she said.

"Please turn and face your family and friends," the pastor said, and they complied. "I am pleased to present for the first time, Mr. and Mrs. Colin Russell."

They stepped down the stairs together as man and wife while the crowd cheered. Hand in hand, they went down the aisle as their guests showered them with tiny bits of glittery white-and-silver confetti that looked like snow falling down on them.

They stepped through the doorway into the lobby. Waiting for them was Gretchen. She had picked up Natalie's headset, stepping in as wedding planner. "Congratulations." She held out a tray of champagne to them both and escorted them to the bridal suite to wait while the guests moved to the reception hall.

Alone in the suite, Colin wrapped one arm around her waist and pulled her tight against him. "You're all mine now," he growled into her ear.

"And you're all mine. For this Christmas and every one to follow."

Epilogue

One year later, Christmas Eve

Natalie slowly made her way through the renovated kitchen carrying the glazed Christmas ham. She intended to put it on the dining room table, but Colin was quick to intercept her and snatch the platter from her hands.

"What are you doing? You don't need to be carrying heavy things."

Natalie sighed and planted her hands on her hips. Being seven months pregnant was certainly a bigger challenge than she'd expected it to be, but she was making do. "I'm just pregnant. I'm perfectly capable of doing a lot of things."

Colin put the plate on the table and turned around. "I know you are. You're capable of amazing things, my wife." He kissed her on the lips. "I'd just much rather you enjoy yourself and your friends instead of being in the kitchen."

"Okay," she agreed, "but you come with me. All the food is out and we're ready to eat."

Hand in hand, they walked into the great room in what had once been the childhood home of Lily and Colin. When Frankie and Lily had returned from Vegas, Colin had still wanted to give them the house despite everything, but Lily hadn't wanted it. Just like the wedding, she was happy with the simple apartment and less hassle.

Instead, after they got married, Colin and Natalie took up residence there. She was all too happy to call the old house her home. He sold the supermodern mansion and she sold her townhouse. After a few renovations to update some things to their liking, they moved into the house. It was where she'd had her happiest childhood memories and once she found out she was pregnant, she wanted her child to have those kinds of memories in this home, too.

The rest of the From This Moment business partners and their spouses were loitering around the seating area, warming themselves by the fireplace. Newlyweds Bree and Ian were snuggling on the couch with glasses of wine. They'd finally tied the knot in October—oddly enough, the first of the group to get engaged and the last to wed.

Gretchen was feeding a chocolate *petit four* to Julian as they stood at the front window admiring the extensive Christmas lights display Colin had put together outside. They had married in the spring in a small chapel in Tuscany, fulfilling Gretchen's dream of seeing Italy at last.

"The food is ready," Natalie announced from the entryway.

Amelia was the first to get up from her seat by the fire. "I wish you would've let me help you with that. There's no need for you to manage the whole dinner by yourself. I know what it's like to cook at seven months pregnant."

"I'm fine. You're always doing the cooking. I wanted to do it. Besides, you've got baby Hope to worry about."

Amelia gestured over her shoulder to her husband Tyler. He was standing by the Christmas tree, letting their six-month-old look at the lights and shiny ornaments. "Not really. He's hardly put her down since the day she was born."

"Still. I'm fine. I might be out of practice when it comes to Christmas, but I can still manage cooking dinner."

"Okay, but we're doing the dishes," Amelia argued.

"Absolutely," Gretchen chimed in. "You're not lifting a single fork."

"I won't fight you on that. I hate doing the dishes."

The crowd all migrated into the dining room in a chaotic rumble of conversation and laughter. They took their places around the table, with Tyler slipping Hope into her high chair.

It was hard for Natalie to believe how much their lives had all changed in the past two years. They had all found amazing men and fallen madly in love. Each of them had married, and soon, there would be two babies playing in the new chapel nursery. It was enough to make her start tearing up at the dinner table.

Damn hormones.

"I'd like to thank everyone for joining us tonight for Christmas Eve dinner. The holidays are times to be spent with friends and family and I know how important all of you are to Natalie, and to me." Colin raised his glass to the group. "Merry Christmas, everyone."

The four couples sitting around the table each raised their glasses to toast a festive holiday season. "Merry Christmas," they all cheered.

* * * * *

OUT NOW!

Available at
millsandboon.co.uk

MILLS & BOON

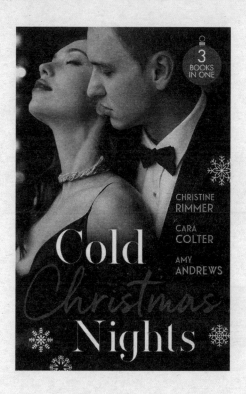

LET'S TALK
Romance

For exclusive extracts, competitions and special offers, find us online:

- MillsandBoon
- @MillsandBoon
- @MillsandBoonUK
- @MillsandBoonUK

Get in touch on 01413 063 232